THE WITCH OF
FLICKERWOOD

E.C. WATTS

Pumpkin Tea

Pumpkin Tea

The Witch of Flickerwood
Copyright © 2025 by Emily Rudacille

For questions, comments, or requests, visit www.pumpkintea.com

Cover Design and Art by Teague Rudacille

Publisher's Cataloging-in-Publication Data

Names: Watts, E. C., author.
Title: The witch of Flickerwood / E.C. Watts.
Description: York, PA: Pumpkin Tea, 2025.
Identifiers: ISBN: 979-8-9927811-9-9 (hardcover) | 979-8-9927811-8-2 (paperback) | 979-8-9927811-7-5 (ebook)
Subjects: LCSH Murder--Fiction. | Crime--Fiction. | Urban folklore--Fiction. | Mystery fiction. | Christian fiction. | BISAC FICTION / Christian / Suspense | FICTION / Mystery & Detective / Women Sleuths | FICTION / Women
Classification: LCC PS3623 .A88 W58 2025 | DDC 813.6--dc23

Contents

Acknowledgments

Thanks to all, named and unnamed, who have helped make this book possible.

First, I would like to thank my wonderful husband, Teague, for listening to me talk endlessly about this story for the last three years. Not only has he been a constant support through many drafts and revisions, but he's also patiently walked with me through many of my own trials of faith.

Many thanks are also owed to my mom and dad, who gave me a love of reading and always encouraged my imagination. And thanks to my friend Julia MacLeod, who was the second person to ever read the full manuscript and graciously lend her editing skills.

Above all, this book would not have been possible without the constant guidance and presence of the Holy Spirit. I pray that these words are not simply my own, but that they are what God intended me to share with the world. May He receive all glory and honor.

Thank you, dear reader, for picking up this book. I hope and pray that it finds you well, strengthens your soul, and inspires meditations of your heart that are pleasing and perfect to God.

"May these words of my mouth and this meditation of my heart
> be pleasing in your sight,
> Lord, my Rock and my Redeemer."

(Psalm 19:14 NIV)

Love you, Grandmom

Thanks for helping make my childhood
one of wonder and enchantment

April 1948 - April 2025

The Witch of Flickerwood

Chapter 1

Home

Flickerwood, Pennsylvania. My destination is printed in bold black letters on the train ticket in my hand. Outside my window, a blur of brown, barren trees rushes past as we hurtle across the countryside. A familiar outline of buildings soon appears on the horizon, and the train begins to slow. I gather up my things as the station approaches. The doors slide open, and I'm greeted with the chill of the January air.

I exit the train, dragging my suitcase behind me. I once believed that portals leading to other dimensions only existed in science fiction. It seemed impossible that a person could simply cross over a threshold and suddenly find themselves in another world. Yet, as I step onto the weathered platform, that's exactly what I do. In an instant, I leave behind the winter break I spent living at home with my parents. Though I was with them only a few hours ago, it already feels like a mere dream. Now, my reality is the hard tile beneath my feet at this little train station.

As I begin my journey across the platform, my attention is captured by the headline flashing on a nearby TV. A banner stretches the length of the screen on the local news channel: *Tragedy Strikes Close to Home—Beloved College Professor Found Dead in His Office*. I grind to a halt.

I scan the subtitles and learn that Professor Gregory Morrell, the dean of the School of Natural and Health Sciences

1

at my university, passed away three days ago. Police and doctors say he died of sudden cardiac arrest, and they're investigating the possibility of foul play.

Behind me, the doors shut, and the train cars lurch forward. I watch until the last one disappears down the track. *Death? Potentially foul play?! At my school?* What did I just watch? Fear creeps into a small corner of my mind, and I wonder if I made a mistake getting off that train.

I take a deep breath. What am I really gonna do? Drop out? Call my parents and tell them I'm coming home because an aging professor passed away? I shake my head. I'm sure there's nothing to worry about.

I pull my beanie over my ears and start down the sidewalk that runs through the town square of Flickerwood. Parked cars line the street, and light streams from storefront windows as people dine, shop, and mill about. The sound of tires driving over the road and distant conversation creates a buzzing background noise. After a short walk, I reach my destination: Wynhurst University.

The moment I turn onto campus, the noise from the road ceases. The hustle and bustle of town is immediately replaced by the almost artificial environment of the university. A fake village within a real one, housing many temporary residents yet not one permanent citizen.

The only sign of life is a sparse scattering of students in dark jackets moving quickly from building to building, none lingering in the cold for very long. Though I've journeyed many miles to get here, it's almost as if I never left. My arrival is largely inconsequential, and no one seems to notice my coming or going.

I approach my dorm building and scan my student ID to unlock the main lobby. A wave of heat flows out as I open the door, inviting me inside. The scent of coffee and citrus cleaner—a smell I've grown to like—reaches my nose as I cross the lobby and head up the stairs. Guided by muscle memory, I find the correct door and insert my key. The knob turns freely.

Marissa, my roommate, is standing amidst piles of clothing, working to organize them into the closet and drawers.

"Hey," I say as I enter.

"Hey," she returns. "How was your trip?"

"Uh, not bad. Train was a bit late, but that's to be expected."

"Huh. Maybe it's the weather? I hear we're supposed to get a snow storm at some point."

"Feels like it. It's pretty cold outside." I drop my backpack on the bed and pop open my suitcase.

"Did you check your school email?" she asks suddenly.

"Not in a few days. Why?"

"President Conley sent out a message to all staff and students. Apparently Dr. Morrell died on Thursday night."

My head snaps to look at her, and a sinking feeling returns to my stomach. "Did they say how it happened?" I reach for my phone and open my email.

Marissa shrugs. "They didn't say, only that it was from natural causes."

I look down at the screen and begin to read.

We are saddened to learn of the recent passing of beloved staff member, Dr. Gregory Morrell. Our thoughts and prayers go out to his family in this difficult time. While emotions may be running high, we would like to assure everyone that this tragedy was born of natural causes. There is no evidence to suggest that anyone else on campus is in danger, and our semester will continue as usual.

Dr. Morrell has been a staff member at Wynhurst for the better part of 30 years, and he leaves behind a space that will be hard to fill. He served our community in various capacities, as professor, advisor, and dean of the School of Natural and Health Sciences. His cheerful disposition and wisdom will be dearly missed by his students and coworkers. For students who would like to attend, a memorial service will be held on the Monday following winter break at Meyer Hall.

Sincerely,

President Conley and The Board of Trustees

"That's kind of...weird, don't you think? That they make a point to say no one is in danger," I say. "The local news was reporting on it at the train station, and they said the police were investigating potential foul play."

Her eyes widen. "Really? Well, maybe it was a rumor going around. I'm sure it's just standard practice for the police to rule out any crimes. The email is probably just setting the record straight."

"Yeah..." I say, my voice trailing off. She's probably right. Any inclination I had to voice doubt about his so-called "natural" death dissipates. "Do you think you'll go to the memorial?"

"I'm not sure," she answers. "I didn't really know him. He never taught any of my classes. Still, I might. You?"

I stare out the small window in our room, thinking back to freshman year. "I had him for one class my first semester, but I didn't know him well, either. We'll see."

I retreat to my side of the room and check my smartphone. 120 mg/dL—not a bad blood sugar. I check the time: 4:30 pm. The dining hall opens in half an hour. Marissa manages to tuck most of her clothes away before grabbing her bag and heading for the door.

"Hey, I'm gonna go meet some friends for dinner. Wanna come?"

"Uh, I might come down a little later. Thanks, though."

"Cool. See you then." She disappears into the hallway, closing the door behind her.

Left alone in our room, I'm struck again by the uncanny feeling of living in two realities at once. My brain struggles to comprehend the whiplash of apparent teleportation. Just this morning, I was in my childhood bedroom, but now I find myself back here. Didn't I just leave this place a few weeks ago? Yet tomorrow I have to be ready to start a whole new semester of classes.

I gaze around the room, taking in my surroundings. My first order of business is to create a more comfortable atmosphere. I turn off the glaring overhead light and switch on my bedside lamp, which has a softer glow, then put on some background music. With more friendly surroundings, I begin semi-neatly stacking my clothes inside my dresser

4

drawers. Once finished, I shove my empty suitcase under the bed and turn to my backpack.

I unzip the main compartment and reach inside, grasping my faded copy of the Bible. As I pull it into the light, I sigh, disappointed with myself. Despite lugging it home with me on every break, I never end up opening it.

For a moment, my hand hovers over the cover, poised to flip to the first page...but I pull back. I just don't think I can do it right now. I don't have the energy. Instead, I place the Bible neatly on my bookshelf before collapsing onto the bed. *Home at last.* Well, sort of. Second home.

Chapter 2

A Chill in the Air

I bundle up to walk to dinner in the cold. The first flakes of snow are starting to fall, and campus suddenly comes to life. Students flood from their dorms towards the dining hall, some avoiding the chill by piling into cars and driving the short distance. The meal line moves fairly fast, however.

Beep. I scan my student ID and filter through the various buffet stations with the rest of the crowd. I pile things onto my plate, a bit dazed as I try to reintegrate with the rhythm of college life. Once I have my meal, I survey the dining area, on the hunt for either someone I know or an empty table—

"Hey Addy!"

I turn to see who called my name. "Hey!" I answer. My friend Sidney pulls me back to reality. We first met during freshman orientation week and have gotten along well ever since. She's one of the few people in my major, ecology.

"You wanna sit together?" she asks.

"Sure!"

We find an empty table and set our trays down. Sid goes to get a drink, and I guesstimate the amount of carbs on my plate. Probably like 40? I adjust my insulin pen, pinch my stomach, and deliver the dose.

"How was your break?" she asks once she's seated.

"It was alright. I spent a lot of time with family. Nothing too crazy. How about you?"

"Let's see…my brother, the one in the Navy, got to come home for a few days, so it was nice to see him. Honestly, I'm a little worried for my mom, though, now that it's over. She was so happy to have us all back in the house, and now we've gone our separate ways again." She sighs, resting her head on her hand. "At least she still has my sister for the time being. She's in her junior year of high school."

I nod. "That must be hard, especially having a kid in the military. My mom had a hard time letting me go, too."

"Yeah," she says, turning her attention towards the chicken on her plate.

There's a momentary lull in the conversation, and my eyes are drawn to the TV hanging over the room. After a commercial about some special edition eggnog flavored soda, the local news channel comes on and reports the same headline as before: *Beloved College Professor Found Dead in His Office.* Sid turns her head to look.

"Did you hear about Dr. Morrell?" I ask. "I saw the headline at the train station this afternoon."

"I saw the email President Conley sent out. It's so crazy; I didn't think he was sick or anything."

"What do you think happened?"

"No idea. Probably had a heart attack or something. Maybe they'll say more at the memorial."

"Maybe."

Monday morning, on the official first day of the semester, I find myself walking into Meyer Hall for Dr. Morrell's memorial. As I pass by the stage, I notice the front two rows of chairs are filled with university staff members. Sitting dead center is the president, Dr. Conley. To his left is Dr. Morrell's recently bereaved wife, Edith Morrell, who's also a professor. Next to her is Dr. Gaines, the lead professor of the ecology department. Beyond that, I recognize a few more faculty members, but others are unfamiliar.

When the service starts, I'm surprised to see that the first person to appear behind the microphone is not part of Wynhurst at all, but the mayor of Flickerwood, Mr. Warren Sayer. I recognize him from the numerous flyers, campaign posters, and yard signs present around town. For the past year or so, he's been trying to raise support in his candidacy for state governor.

"Ladies. Gentlemen," Mayor Sayer begins. "We are gathered here today to honor a dear member of our community. I was so distraught to hear of Dr. Morrell's passing. He was a pillar in this university, a leader at his church, and a great supporter of our entire town. He was also a friend of mine. In the words of famous author Mary Shelley, 'Nothing is so painful to the human mind as a great and sudden change.' While I am thankful he was spared the pain of a gradual passing, the suddenness of this loss makes the sting a bit more sharp for those of us who were left behind." He pauses to recollect himself, wiping his eyes with a handkerchief. "I will now open the floor for anyone who would like to say a word about this beloved professor."

With that, Mayor Sayer descends the stairs and takes a seat beside a woman—presumably his wife—in the front row.

"He gave me a love for learning...he had a passion for teaching...was a true family man...thankful I got the chance to be his student..." Students shuffle to and from the microphone, showering the room with heartfelt stories. "He... h-h-he..." My heart goes out to the girl onstage as she struggles to keep from crying. Her face turns beet red and begins to contort. "I'm s-sorry," she manages to say before scampering down the stairs. I see her sit down beside the nurse, Ms. Bradshaw, at the edge of the room.

Despite only having Dr. Morrell for one class, I feel my own emotions swell. My eyes start to fill with tears, which I wipe away. I'm sure he was a good man, and it must be hard for his friends and family to cope with his loss.

After the last student finishes speaking, President Conley ascends the steps. He is younger than many of the professors at Wynhurst, with a reputation for being charismatic and a bit quirky, making him well-liked among the students. Today, however, his demeanor takes a somber tone. "Thank you all for coming to pay your respects to our dear professor, Dr. Gregory Morrell. Greg was a personal friend of mine, and his passing came as a shock. His absence will certainly be felt, and he will be dearly missed. Let us have a moment of silence in his memory." The room falls quiet. I whisper a prayer for his family and friends. In a minute or so, Dr. Conley ends the time of reflection and dismisses the crowd. With that, the memorial is over.

It's only when I'm halfway to my dorm that I realize they never did mention how Dr. Morrell died. I guess Sid was wrong. Is that suspicious? Or is that just normal? I mean, when someone dies, you generally focus on the life they lived, the family they left behind—it makes sense that a memorial service wouldn't go into disturbing detail about the exact mechanism which stopped his heart. Right?

I drop by my dorm, pick up my books, and head to my first class. In one way, it's nice to be back, to walk the sidewalks and greet friends in passing. But this feeling is coupled with something else. An overshadowing gloom hangs over the campus in the wake of Dr. Morrell's death. He was one of the most prominent professors at the university. Everyone either knew him or knew of him, but now…he's just gone.

I walk into class and scan the room to see if there's anyone I know. Students sit in clusters, making small talk about video games, Christmas concerts, and new movie releases. Among them, I finally locate Sidney, who's sitting between two other girls. I weave through the desks and take the seat behind her, though she's currently preoccupied with another conversation. Mostly for something to do, I pull out my schedule and search for the professor's name. According to the paper, Dr. Gaines is supposed to be teaching this class. However, the teacher who enters a few seconds later is not Professor Gaines.

"Good morning, everyone."

A female professor approaches the table at the front of the classroom and sets her bag on top of it. It looks vintage, like an old leather doctor's bag. She pulls off her long winter overcoat and drapes it on the back of a chair, then turns to face the class. Her posture is stick-straight and her expression unsmiling. "I'm Professor Leighton. There's been a last minute change to the schedule, and I will now be teaching in place of Dr. Gaines, who is filling in for some of Dr. Morrell's classes." There's a pause while the class takes in the news. "Let me start by taking attendance."

She pulls a piece of paper and a pen from her bag and starts calling out names. If I had to guess, I'd say she's probably in her late 20s or early 30s, which is young for a professor. She has on a patterned button-down shirt, dark pants, and black lace-up ankle boots. Her hair is somewhat short, falling just above her shoulders, and in the right lighting it's apparent she has dark blue highlights subtly mixed into her brown locks.

"Here!" I call when she gets to me.

"Alright, it looks like we have everyone. Is there anyone I didn't call?" Seeing as no one raises their hand, she continues, "Then I trust you're all here for Botany 240? Good. A little about myself. I have a background in the military, and I've spent a little over four years conducting medical and chemical research. I have a lot of experience in studying plant compounds and medicinal botany, so I plan to incorporate a considerable amount of chemistry into this course. This is my first semester teaching at Wynhurst, and I will only be taking on a few classes, but I'm excited to get to know you all moving forward.

"As for what to expect..." she pulls a stack of papers out of her bag and begins to pass them down the rows, "I am handing out copies of the revised syllabus. As you read over it, there are a few things I would like to highlight. As long as you respect me, respect each other, and do your work, we won't have a problem. I expect you all to be attentive and willing to learn. In my classroom, I do not allow laptops, as they are largely a distraction. I encourage you to bring paper and a writing utensil in order to take notes by hand. Secondly, very similar to the first rule, please have your phones on silent and put away—"

Beep! Beep! Beep! I nearly flinch out of my seat, startled by the blaring alarm. The minute I realize it's coming from my bag, I feel my face grow hot. Professor Leighton's eyes turn towards me, along with the entire class. I scramble for

10

the zipper, then realize it will take too long. I snatch up my backpack and bolt out of the classroom.

Great way to make a good first impression, Addy. In the hallway, I tug my phone out of my bag and check my blood sugar. 300 mg/dL with two arrows pointing up and a flashing "high alert." Not great. What did I eat?! I think back to breakfast...Shoot! With the memorial and everything going on, I forgot to bolus. I check the time, trying to deduce how long it's been and how many carbs I ate. I pull out my pen and uncap it, holding the cap between my teeth so I can screw on a needle. Just as I go to inject myself, I hear the classroom door open beside me.

I look up to see Professor Leighton step into the hallway, gently shutting the door behind her. In a frenzy, I pop the pen cap out of my mouth and speak before she has a chance to. "I'm so sorry for interrupting class," I sputter, gesturing towards all my gadgets. "I'm diabetic, just a high blood sugar..."

She nods, waving away my apology. "Please, don't let me interfere."

With my mind on the high, I finish my injection and cap the pen. She seems unfazed by the needle.

"I just came out to check on you. Is everything okay?" she asks, her voice softening.

I nod, caught off guard by her apparent concern.

"Don't worry about the glucose alerts. I understand. If you need to eat or inject or anything during class, don't hesitate. Let me know if there's ever something I can do to help."

I scan her face, searching for any hint of annoyance. "Thank you," I say earnestly.

She offers a small smile. "Come back in whenever you're ready," she says, then disappears back into the classroom.

When the door latches shut, I breathe a sigh of relief. That went better than I expected. After putting my supplies back in my bag—and setting my alerts to vibrate—I return to class.

"For today," Professor Leighton says after reviewing the syllabus, "I'm happy to answer any questions you may have about me, the class, the semester, or anything else that's on your mind."

When no one responds, she adds, "Of course, I would also

like to address the circumstances under which we are starting the semester. I understand that you have all lost a notable professor, Dr. Morrell, so I would like to give you an opportunity to process any thoughts or feelings you have surrounding his passing." She pulls her chair around to the front of the table and takes a seat facing us. "I'm sure it's been hard to hear such unsettling news just after Christmas break."

For a while, the classroom is silent. As this silence drags on, I grow skeptical that anyone will share anything, but then someone raises a hand.

"Yeah...I would say it's been a bit of a shock. I feel like I don't know what the 'right' response is."

"I can relate to that. It's sad what happened, but I'm also grateful we still get to be here."

"It's strange how his classes are just being picked up by other professors..."

During a break in the conversation, I tentatively raise my hand. Professor Leighton nods in my direction. "Well," I say, gathering my thoughts, "I first heard the news of what happened at the train station just as I was arriving. It was definitely a surprise and...I guess I've just been looking for answers. It almost seems like there's some secrecy surrounding the whole thing. Maybe it's just me, but—it feels like there's been a change in the air."

Chapter 3

Out of the Woodwork

I leave class feeling like some weight has been lifted. However, I'm still burdened by the thought that what we've been told isn't the whole story. That maybe Dr. Morrell didn't just die a natural death. Maybe...just maybe, something sinister was to blame. The fact that no one seems to share my concern only serves to deepen it.

As the weeks go by, the police tape disappears from Dr. Morrell's office, and the investigators withdraw their presence from campus. After a while, normalcy returns, and it's as if nothing ever happened. Sometimes I feel like I imagined it all, because I seem to be the only person who remembers. Any talk of potential murder is far out of the question.

Hey! Sid texts me one night. *You wanna come hang out in the game room? Micah and some other people are down here. We're gonna play pool.*

I take a look at my homework. Nothing is due tomorrow, and I'm not behind on anything. I contemplate my lonely college existence, then respond. *Sure! Be right there.*

I grab my coat and my bag, which is filled with snacks to treat potential low blood sugars, then head over to the building adjacent to my dorm. Sure enough, I find Sid, her boyfriend, Micah, and a small group of people in the game room. I don't know all of them well, but they seem nice. I'm handed a pool cue.

"Winners play each other?" Sid suggests.

"Sounds good to me."

Sid and I start a game beside Micah, who's playing another of her friends. I'm not the best at pool, but I must have some sort of luck on my side tonight. *Clack.* I sink two balls in one shot. Sid scratches. A genial conversation plays out between the two tables. "How are classes going…Any plans for the weekend?…Are you guys working this semester? …How is that going?…" Somehow, we get on the topic of Micah's job, which is working with campus security.

"Yeah," he says. "It's boring a lot of the time, honestly. Half my shifts are just spent watching the cameras." He sinks the eight ball, ending the game. "…Ya know, I was working the night Dr. Morrell died."

This catches my attention. I take my turn and join him as the winner.

"Nice," Sid says, impressed by my shot. "When did you get so good? Alright. Micah against Addy."

Micah shifts over to my table, and I reset the balls. One of the others checks her phone and announces she's heading out for the night.

"See you guys," she says. "We're meeting up with someone else for a movie."

"Have fun!" Sid replies, waving as the rest of our group clears out. She then leans against the vacant pool table, poised to watch Micah and I play.

"So…did you see anything interesting on those cameras?" I ask him.

Micah shrugs. "I really didn't think anything of it. Dr. Morrell was in his office late, which isn't unusual for a lot of professors. A little later, one of the janitors came through and mopped the hall, which they do every week. Dr. Morrell came out and microwaved some ramen in the faculty lounge, took it back to his office, then…well, he never came out again. They found him the next morning."

The gears in my head start to turn with this new information. Distracted, I take a shot and watch the cue ball roll into a pocket. Scratch.

"Oops," Micah says, retrieving the ball.

I'm on the edge of my seat, but not from the competition.

"Do you think that maybe…someone did something to Dr. Morrell?" I blurt suddenly.

In an instant, Micah and Sid both train their eyes on me. I get jittery with nerves.

"What do you mean?" Micah asks.

I swallow, hoping I don't sound too much like a conspiracy theorist. "You know…like, do you think another person might have had a hand in his death?"

He tilts his head, considering.

Beep. Beep. Whirr. Clank. A can of soda drops to the bottom of the vending machine behind the pool tables. A sweaty guy in a track jacket pops the tab and chugs out of the can.

"I can't help but overhear," he gasps, catching his breath from his apparent workout and the long drink. "Are you guys talking about Dr. Morrell?"

"It came up," Sid says, shrugging. "Why do you ask?"

"Cause you're onto something," he says, gesturing towards me. He lowers his voice. "Dr. Morrell didn't just die from some fluke medical issue."

"Oh?" I ask, my interest piqued.

He steps closer, and we all lean towards him, curious about what he has to say.

"Now, what I'm about to tell you may sound a little crazy, and I can understand if you don't believe me. But hear me out. Dr. Morrell's death was no accident. And it wasn't murder, either…at least not by any person." He pauses, his eyes traveling to each of us before continuing.

"If you know anything about the history of this town, you'll know there used to be big business in logging. The sawmill made this place a boomtown. However, as the years went on, more and more of the forest was demolished by the loggers. As they disrespected the land, a string of accidents started to happen. Ladders fell over for seemingly no reason, branches came down and crushed experienced lumberjacks, and the mill saw got out of control. Dozens of workers either died or disappeared, never to be found again. Still, they continued to harvest the trees, until one fateful day. Half the men fell mysteriously ill and dropped over dead. Those who remained quit their jobs, and the mill soon closed down.

"It's said that the attacks came from a witch who lived in the woods. The loggers were disturbing her domain, and she cast a spell to make them pay for the desecration of her forest. This university was built on the very land those loggers cleared away. Fortunately for us, the witch seems to tolerate her scholarly neighbors fairly well...unless, of course, they begin threatening her home."

Anthony nods in the direction of the woods on the outskirts of campus. "Dr. Morrell happened to be one of the main professors pushing for Wynhurst to expand into the wooded area and build more art studios. The next thing you know...well, he dropped dead just like the loggers so many years ago. And unless they leave those woods alone, he may not be the last." With that, he leans back and downs the rest of the soda.

Sid's laughter breaks the silence. "Dude, that's a nice ghost story."

The guy shrugs. "Hey, I'm telling you, it checks out."

"What do you think, Micah?" she asks, turning to him.

He cracks a sarcastic smile, "I dunno, Sid. Maybe there really is a forest-dwelling witch who cursed the school. That's probably why my socks keep disappearing when I do the laundry..." Sid playfully smacks his arm.

Undeterred, the stranger turns to me with a questioning look.

Rather than answer, I respond with a question of my own. "What's your name?"

"Ah, excuse me. My name's Anthony. I'm a history ed major and president of the Wynhurst Historical Society. It's my senior year here. And you all?"

"I'm Micah," Micah says, extending a hand. "I'm an economics major, and this is my junior year. This is my girlfriend, Sidney."

"Sophomore, ecology major," Sid says, then nods to me. "Same as her."

"Addy," I say with a small wave.

"Nice to meet you all. Junior, sophomores—I remember being in your shoes. Look, you guys still have a few years here. If I may, let me give you some advice. Not everything is as it seems around here. The president, the professors, the board...not to sound cynical, but really, don't believe everything you hear. Keep your eyes peeled." He crushes the soda can and tosses it into a nearby trash can. "Well, I should get going. Maybe I'll see you around."

"Maybe you will," Micah says. "Was nice talking to you. And hey, as an economics major, let me return the favor with some advice of my own—don't buy stuff from vending machines. The upcharge is outrageous."

Anthony snickers. "I know, I know. Poor planning, a weakness of mine." With that, he exits through the glass door and gradually disappears into the night.

I'm suddenly aware of the darkness outside the glass walls around us. A small shudder runs through me. "It is kinda late. I should probably be getting back, too."

"Yeah, sounds like a smart idea," Sid agrees. "Thanks for coming out."

"Thanks for inviting me."

"No problem. Hey, I'm gonna use the bathroom, but if you wait up, I'll walk with you." She ducks away, leaving me alone with Micah. I zip up my coat and lean against the pool table.

"Ya know, Addy," Micah says, breaking the silence. "I'm not sure about the whole Dr. Morrell thing. Personally, I don't see a reason to believe anything out of the ordinary happened. But, with that being said..." he shrugs a shoulder. "You're not the only one with some suspicions." He glances behind him, checking to see if anyone else is around. "My roommate, Matthew," he whispers. "He's pretty hung up on it, too. You might want to talk to him."

I'm taken by surprise. My curiosity is reignited. "Matthew who?"

"Matthew Bruner. He's an art major. He's got an exhibit up in the gallery now. But hey, he's pretty guarded about his theories, so don't tell anyone else. I can trust you to keep a secret, right?"

I hesitate, then nod. I don't foresee there being a reason to break his confidence. "Of course. Thanks, Micah."

"No problem."

Chapter 4

Local History

At breakfast the next morning, I take out a spiral-bound notebook and jot down what I can remember from last night's conversations. When I'm finished both my breakfast and my note-taking, I head to the library, intending to do some studying. Upon entering, one of the first things I notice is a large banner hanging above a bookshelf near the checkout counter.

Celebrating 150 Years of Wynhurst University. Below the banner, a variety of historical books are on display. Some are regional, dealing with the East Coast or Pennsylvania. Others are more local references, detailing the history of the town and the college itself. My hand stops on one book in particular: *Founders and Folklore: the Roots of Flickerwood, Pennsylvania.* The title is scrawled in an old-timey font, and a black and white photo of the town hall fills the cover.

I read the blurb and glance at the chapter titles, my mind drifting back to Anthony's story. I'm doubtful that a forest-dwelling witch's incantation was Dr. Morrell's true cause of death. Still, you never know—sometimes there's a morsel of truth to old legends.

I grab the book and step back, only now noticing a small poster taped to the bookshelf. It details the location, date, and time of a presentation the Wynhurst Historical Society will be giving in honor of the university's founding. I snap a picture of the poster with my phone, then check the book out at the counter.

With my newest prize in hand, I find a cozy spot to study. After several minutes of struggling through homework, I sit back in my chair. My eyes are drawn to the history book. After all, what's more important? Homework, or potentially solving a murder?

I close my laptop and open to the first page. *Chapter One: Native Inhabitants*. Time flies by as I read about the Native American tribes who originally lived in the area. They were eventually wiped out by disease and forced resettlement by European colonists. Hunters and trappers used the old trails the native people had made through the woods, and these eventually became some of the main routes through town.

Starting in the 1700s, German immigrants began to settle in the land, along with the Scotch-Irish, English, and Welsh. The town was eventually called Flickerwood, after the abundance of northern flicker birds. Among the loggers who worked there, stories began to surface about one woman who had built a cabin in the woods. Reports stated she cooked strange meat in a cauldron, wandered about at night, muttered incantations, and drew symbols. She was never brought to trial, but, as Anthony stated, Flickerwood suddenly ceased producing lumber, instead shipping in wood via the newly-constructed railway and investing in industries like furniture-making.

I check my phone and discover my sugar is starting to drop. You're not allowed to eat in the library, so I usually have to leave when this happens. Oh well. It's about lunch time anyhow. I collect my things and head towards the door. As I pass the historical society display, I turn my head for one last look. I bet I could come to that presentation.

At lunch, I spot Sid and Micah at a table. I sit down to eat just as they're prepared to leave.

"Sorry, Addy. I know you were just coming in. But we all have a class to get to," Sid explains, gesturing to herself, Micah, and a third guy near the trash bins.

"Oh, don't worry about it," I say, waving her away. "Who's the other guy?"

"You haven't met Micah's roommate? That's Matthew. Maybe I'll introduce you sometime."

"Sure," I say, smiling. "See ya later." I make a mental note of what Matthew looks like, as well as what he's wearing. I think I've seen him in passing, but now I can put a name to a face. Micah said he's a bit guarded about the whole Dr. Morrell thing. I might want to try and meet with him alone.

On Thursday, the night of the historical society presentation, I buzz into the library and climb the steps to the third floor. I pass glass cases full of Wynhurst paraphernalia, like old school colors, awards, yearbook photos, and autographed writings from past students. The faint buzz of fluorescent lighting escapes from a large room at the end of the hall. Inside, more glass cases hold antique books and other artifacts. Several people are already gathered around a large conference table, all facing a projector screen at the front of the room. Along the back are tables with light refreshments: coffee, tea, cookies, etc. Anthony stands casually behind the podium, waiting to start.

I scan the conference table for people I recognize. So far, all of the students are strangers to me. Only one face jumps out. Near the back of the room, I recognize a professor: Dr. Edith Morrell, the late Dr. Morrell's wife. I take a seat at the table, stealing glances at her. For some reason, I had envisioned her as a mourning, Victorian widow. In my conception, she was dressed in black lace and forever peering out the upstairs window of her stone colonial house while clutching a handkerchief to her chest.

In reality, she's not dressed all in black, but in the usual drab browns and grays professors seem to favor. Amidst her gray shawl, brown belt, and navy dress, the brightest pops of color come from a yellow flower encased in a resin necklace and the gold of her engagement and wedding rings still situated on her finger.

She is past middle age, with wavy gray hair falling just beyond her shoulders. I remembered her being a bit heavier-set, but she appears to have put on even more weight since

I saw her last, perhaps because of the grief. There is no handkerchief, but if you look closely, you can perceive an air of sadness in her eyes.

At five after, the lights are dimmed, and Anthony begins, "I'd like to thank you all for coming out, with thanks especially to my vice president and treasurer, as well as Dr. Edith, the faculty sponsor of the historical society." He gestures towards her, and light applause breaks out. "Now, I present to you, 150 years at Wynhurst University. As many of you may know, Wynhurst was founded in January of 18..."

I pull my spiral-bound notebook from my backpack and flip to a fresh page, just in case Anthony says anything noteworthy. As he talks, my attention is drawn repeatedly to the widowed professor. It's almost startling to have her sitting so close. For many on campus, the death of Dr. Morrell may already have faded from memory. For her, however, I am sure his passing is much more visceral.

I swallow my pity for a moment and try to think objectively. If Dr. Morrell was, in fact, murdered, her proximity alone would make her a potential suspect. You always have to investigate the wife. Was their marriage on the rocks? Did they have some sort of argument? While angling my paper towards myself, I jot down her initials in small letters and place a question mark behind them.

Almost immediately, a twinge of guilt hits my heart. Maybe this whole thing is ridiculous. I'm not a real detective. Dr. Morrell may very well have just died of natural causes. His wife is most likely innocent, and here I am treating this mourning woman with suspicion. This isn't some game; these are people's lives. I touch the tip of my pen to the paper, ready to scribble the writing out.

I stop myself. I'm not trying to disrespect the memory of the deceased. I'm trying to do right by him and his family, and the school as a whole. Even if I'm wrong, it's worth investigating, and investigating requires asking some hard questions. Besides, even if she's innocent, Dr. Edith Morrell will likely have some information that could be helpful. I tune back into Anthony's presentation.

"...the family of Johnathan Sayer, one of the original

businessmen in Flickerwood, is still prominent to this day. Many of you may draw the connection to our mayor, Mr. Warren Sayer, and his son, Michael Sayer, who is currently the chairman of the Wynhurst University Board of Trustees. The Sayer dorm building also bears the name of this family..."

I scribble down the names in my notebook. Funny, I never drew the connection.

"...Despite its small size, Wynhurst has maintained a dedication to attracting a variety of researchers to its campus. In my personal opinion, this area of Pennsylvania is an optimal place for historical study, considering its rich history of folklore, Native American legends, colonial beliefs in witchcraft and hexology, and significant contributions to the founding of America and the abolition of slavery. But I digress.

"Each year, the student body continues to grow, and Wynhurst is moving towards more expansion and building projects. In the past, there have been some setbacks, such as the fire which destroyed the music education building a mere decade ago. However, it was rebuilt with even larger dimensions, and the beautiful new building is what students use today. The most recent plans for expansion have to do with constructing a new, dedicated visual arts building, which would involve expanding the campus itself into what is now the southwestern woods, past the natural sciences building.

"Barring any sort of supernatural interference—" His statement is met with a few snickers from the audience. "— Wynhurst University is set up to have a bright future of growth as it continues to educate future generations. The last 150 years have included some major changes, yet the school has persevered through the challenges and continues to improve the quality of its educational experience, drawing more students to learn here. Here's hoping that the next 150 years will be just as productive and impactful. Thank you."

Anthony takes a small bow, and the room erupts into applause. I flip my notebook face down and join the clapping. As the applause dies down, I check my phone. 106 mg/dL. My eyes drift to the refreshment table. I could eat something small…I place my pen and paper safely back in my bag and slowly make my way to the snack table. After a brief assessment, I select a small brownie bite and head back to my seat. As I turn, I almost run into Anthony.

"Oh, I'm sorry—" His face breaks into a smile when he recognizes me. "Hey! Glad to see you stopped by. Remind me of your name?"

"Oh, you're fine. I'm Addy."

"Addy. Okay, I think I've got it."

I nod politely. "Great job with the presentation."

"Thank you, I appreciate that. I'm glad you enjoyed it!"

"I did. Very informative."

"Hey, if you're interested in this stuff, the historical society meets every Thursday, same time. It's usually up here, but next week it'll be in my dorm. Feel free to drop by."

"Maybe." I shrug. "We'll see."

"No worries."

"Great job, Anthony!" Dr. Edith approaches quickly and drapes an arm over his shoulders, pulling him into a brief side hug. "I was very impressed."

"Thank you, Professor. I was a bit nervous."

"Could've fooled me." Just as I'm awkwardly wondering if I should excuse myself, Dr. Edith draws me into the conversation. "Well hello. I don't believe we've been acquainted. What's your name?"

"Addy," I reply. "I'm a sophomore."

"Ah, nice to meet you. Is this your first time coming to a historical society meeting?"

"Yeah, it is. I didn't know it existed before this, honestly. Just saw the flyer in the library. Anthony was just inviting me to future meetings."

"Every Thursday," she chirps. "It's a lot of fun…Well, it's a lot of fun if you like history."

"Maybe," I repeat.

"Well, we'd love to have you. Anthony is a great president. Wonderfully knowledgeable, as you've seen tonight. Though he can't resist throwing in those ghost stories," she says, looking to him with a smile.

He bites his lip. "Hey, I tried to keep it toned down."

She snickers. "You did a good job. Very proud." With a

pat on the back, she heads towards the snack table and mingles with some of the other students.

"I take it most people here are part of the historical society club?" I ask Anthony, gazing around the room. We shuffle towards the table, moving out of the way. I finally take a bite of my brownie, strategizing how to avoid spilling crumbs on the floor.

"Uh, yeah, most of them," he answers. Like a revolving door, various students approach Anthony, congratulate him on the presentation, and make small talk. He introduces me to some of them, but his focus shifts towards other conversations.

With another bite, I finish my brownie and toss the napkin in the trash. I notice there are social media handles projected on the screen upfront and pull out my phone. I start following the historical society page, which lists the exact room number of Anthony's dorm for the next meeting. I screenshot the post, then look up from my phone. Many of the students have cleared out, and only a few still linger around Anthony.

"So, what's your major?" Dr. Edith asks, tossing her cup into the trash.

I slide my phone into my pocket. "Ecology."

"Ah, that's a fun one. Any idea what field you'd like to go into?"

"Uh, not really sure yet. But honestly, I haven't had a class I didn't like, so I think I'd be happy anywhere."

"Hey, that's great. You never know where life will take you. Always good to be flexible."

I nod.

"Where are you from?" she asks.

"About four hours northwest of here," I answer. I learned a while ago that no one recognizes the name of my town. "How about you?"

"Oh, I was born and raised here. Greg and I both went to Flickerwood High."

I pause, unsure of what to say at the casual mention of her husband. "I…I'm sorry for your loss."

Her face sports a tight-lipped smile, and she nods. "Thank you, my dear. So am I." She sighs, blinking away the tears forming in her eyes. "Take my advice; don't get old."

24

She nudges me with an elbow. "Eventually, your body just stops working. Greg, you know, he had a heart condition. Didn't like to talk about it, but we knew it was coming for some time...Ah, and somehow that doesn't make it any easier.

"In the first few days after he...you know, passed...I had some overzealous policemen in my house, investigating or whatever. I had to pull out his medical documents before they let it drop. Unfortunately, there are still some people out there who think something hinky happened. Wish they could just let the poor soul rest."

My head spins as I walk home. Is that really what happened? Am I chasing after the wind? Dr. Morrell just had a heart condition? In high school, I had a teacher who concealed the fact that she had a terminal illness so she could keep teaching. I'm sure if a professor is passionate enough about their work, they may wish to keep health issues private. The police already investigated; there was no murder. Just as I'm nearly convinced there's nothing more to discover, my eyes fall on the door to the art gallery. I stop.

The door is propped open, and a light is on inside. My mind returns to Matthew. I can't help but wonder what he thinks about the situation. Dr. Edith clearly believes her husband died from a longstanding medical problem, and she may be right. But then again, just because someone had a heart condition doesn't automatically mean that's what killed them. She could also be very wrong. I turn towards the door and head into the gallery.

Chapter 5

An Artist's Perspective

At first, I'm disappointed. Despite the open door and the lights, the gallery appears to be empty. I walk inside and examine some of the paintings hanging on the wall. According to the tags, they're made with ink and watercolor. Soft, muted colors are painted over dark outlines. Some have ink splattered over the page, almost like dark droplets of blood. A few depict scenes from around campus: a trail through the woods, as well as the gothic architecture of some of the dorms and academic buildings. Others are locations off campus, like the old sawmill and the train station. A few aren't locations at all. I am drawn to one for the colors alone.

At the top is the sun, a glowing orange orb. The light falls down in such a way that one half of the painting is tinted yellow, and the other red. In the center, a knight stands with his back to the viewer, facing the sun. He holds his helmet in his right hand, to the red side of the painting. A root system of black ink is visible underground, beneath his feet. In the center of the ink roots is a dark chalice. The ink appears to bubble up, flooding the knight to his knees. Splotches dot the whole canvas.

As I study the image, I hear someone come through the door. Behind me, Matthew walks in, carrying a stepladder. He notices me but continues what he's doing. I have a good opportunity to talk with him; I shouldn't miss it. "I like your paintings," I say, loud enough for him to hear across the gallery. "They're really good." He places the stepladder in the center of the room, then looks over at me with a smile.

"Thank you! That means a lot."

I smile back, and walk towards him. "Do you need help with that?"

"Uh, sure, actually." He climbs up a few steps. "Could you hold this? It fell down last night." To my surprise, he hands me a small wire sculpture of a bird. Only now do I notice the other wire birds spaced around the room. I watch as he fastens a small anchor into the ceiling, then motions for me to hand him the bird. He hangs it from a thin, nearly invisible string.

"Wow," I say as he steps down. "They're very pretty."

"Thank you." He turns to leave.

"Hey, Matthew, I don't think you know me, but my friend is dating your roommate, Micah."

"Ah, okay. You're friends with Sidney?"

"Yeah. My name's Addy."

"Nice to meet you. Thanks for stopping by the gallery. Most people just walk right past it."

"Kind of a shame. I should come by more; your stuff is really cool." I really should make some time to walk through the gallery. I forget how many talented students there are here. "But, I did actually drop by hoping to run into you."

"Oh?" he asks, looking confused.

"I...I heard you might have some thoughts on Dr. Morrell," I say, lowering my voice.

His expression changes. "Uh...why would you think that?" For a second, his eyes dart towards the painting of the knight with the chalice, then refocus on me.

"Well...Micah mentioned you had a theory..."

Matthew scratches his head. "Ya know, I really didn't mean for him to share that with anyone..."

I exhale. Here's hoping we can find some common ground. "Look, don't be mad at Micah or anything. He only told me because I've been wondering about it, too. I just...I have this gnawing feeling there's more to his death than they're telling us. And I was starting to feel a bit crazy."

He hesitates. "Have you ever been to Stone Creek Park?"

27

"Uh, no, I haven't."

"If you want to talk about this stuff, we should go off campus."

"Okay," I say, realizing the wisdom in his suggestion. I then add, "I don't have a car."

"No problem. If you're okay with it, I can pick you up and we can drive together."

I consider him for a moment, then answer. "Sure. When?"

"How's Saturday morning sound?"

"Works for me," I reply. "Do you want my phone number?" He adds my name and number to his contacts. So, I have a date, though not the romantic kind.

Come Saturday, Matthew picks me up outside the dining hall. I'm sure to bring my phone, snacks, and all my diabetes supplies. He seems tense but starts to relax as soon as we turn onto the road outside of campus. "How was breakfast?" he asks, making small talk.

"Pretty good. You didn't have any?"

"Nah. Little nervous, to be honest." He exhales. "Listen. I don't really know you all that well. Why don't you tell me a little about yourself and why you're so interested in the Dr. Morrell case?"

"Of course, sure," I say quickly. "Uh, my full name is Addy Warner. I'm from a small neighborhood about four hours northwest of here, and I'm a sophomore ecology major, like Sidney. I also have type one diabetes, so if I need to check my blood sugar or eat while we're out, that's why."

"Cool, cool," Matthew replies. "And you're interested because…?"

I watch the houses whizz by outside as we turn off campus. The side streets near the university are lined with large victorian-style mansions built in the town's glory days. I know several professors live back here, along with some underground frats.

"To be honest," I answer, "I'm not entirely sure. The first news story I heard about his death mentioned the possibility of foul play, so it seemed suspicious when everyone else just dismissed the idea. President Conley, the board, the police…

It's like a little whisper in the back of my mind that I just can't shake. A doubt. Plus, I don't know if you've noticed, too, but I think campus just feels...different. Like there's something off. It's colder, and less friendly, somehow."

Matthew nods. "I know what you mean. You're not alone. Campus hasn't been the same for me, either." He taps his fingers on the steering wheel, then adds, "Then again, Flickerwood as a whole isn't the same as when I started at Wynhurst."

"What do you mean?" I ask, intrigued. "How so?"

"Well, I'll show you, if you want."

He flips on his turn signal and we take a sudden detour down a narrow street running parallel to Main. As we pass the backs of businesses, Matthew starts to speak.

"I'm a senior now, but when I was a freshman, there were a few shops on Main Street where students would hang out. This building used to be a sub shop, this one was an ice cream place with an arcade setup inside, and that used to be a comic book store. They'd host game nights—nerd stuff. But now..." He turns onto the main road and we pass the storefronts. Most of the places he mentioned have been replaced with bars, shabby businesses, or are just sitting empty. A red and white awning still covers the old ice cream shop, but it's torn and faded from the sun. We reach the square and turn to the right.

"And that, on your right, used to be the crown jewel of Flickerwood. Sayer Furniture. A name known far and wide. Years ago, it was the main export, made this town what it was. But business dwindled over time. They finally closed down my sophomore year, after the older guy who was running it passed away. Or so I heard."

I stare at the beautiful stone building stretching towards the sky, with a grand golden sign sticking out of the side. The large windows are dark, however, and reveal only the emptiness and disrepair of the store that once was. Further down the road, Matthew takes another right and we head towards the train tracks. In the southern part of town, we pass some run-down apartment buildings bordering the forest.

"Not everyone is struggling, though," he says, though his tone is cynical. We change direction again and approach town hall. The car comes over the crest of a small hill, and I get a glimpse of the town skyline. Rows of rooftops neighbor a shining church steeple and the giant blue water tower. For a brief moment, the sun glints off the church's bell tower, and I'm struck by the quiet beauty of this place. Then the car dips back down to the bottom of the hill, leaving the view behind.

Past the gleaming town hall are wide streets leading to large houses clustered together. Some are ornate and historic, and others are newly constructed. They each have a patch of well-manicured grass and a small driveway. It's near here that we turn into Stone Creek Park.

I realize I never returned the question Matthew asked. "What about you?" I say. "What's your story?"

"Well, I grew up not far from here, about an hour away. I have two brothers, one older and one younger. I'm a fine arts major, and I'm set to graduate next fall. I've got an internship lined up this summer doing illustration and cover design for a small publishing company, which I'm excited for. In my free time, I enjoy doing landscape paintings. I'm also vice president of the Community Arts Club. Oh, and I grew up with two dogs. They're two of my most favorite things in the world."

I smile. "What kind?"

"A german shepherd named Chester and a beagle named Cookie." He seems more at ease now.

As we wind through the park drive, we pass a playground with some kids climbing over the equipment. Further down the road, I spot an older couple walking together on a trail. It's nice to see people out and about, even in January. The deeper we drive into the park, the less people there are dotting the landscape. Finally, Matthew pulls into a parking spot on the edge of the woods. At the start of a trail a few feet ahead, I can see a small white cross leaning against a tree. Faded flowers and toys lie at the base, and a sign beside it bears the picture and name of a boy who went missing.

"So, listen, Addy," Matthew starts. I turn my attention towards him. "I needed to get off campus to make sure we wouldn't be overheard. What I'm about to tell you...can I trust you not to tell anyone?" His tone becomes serious.

30

I laugh nervously. "So long as you don't tell me you killed him," I joke, partly to lighten the mood, and partly serious.

His expression brightens a bit. "No, I didn't. Seriously, though. Information is, well, dangerous."

"I wouldn't say anything that would get you into trouble," I assure him. "Honest. Your story is safe with me."

He takes a deep breath and stares ahead. We're over-looking a valley full of trees. It's quite beautiful; I can see why so many people talk about this park. From what I can see, no one else is around. It's a cold day, plus it's still fairly early in the morning.

"We might as well just stay here," he says, breaking the silence. "The car is probably the safest place to talk."

"Sounds good to me," I answer. The car is nice and warm. "It's a beautiful view."

He nods. "It is. I painted this view for one of my exhibition works." There is another moment of silence. "Alright. I'll tell you what you came to hear. I've mentioned it to Micah, but not the full story. He didn't seem that interested, but I feel like I need to get it off my chest. I…I'm torn. I don't know if I should go confess what I saw to the cops, or if I even saw anything at all…

"See, over break, I stayed in the dorms to finish the art for my show and work on campus. I'm a cashier at the cafe. One day, while I was working the register, I saw Dr. Morrell come in with another guy, both in suits. I didn't recognize the second man, but he was probably another staff member of some sort. They ate lunch and ordered coffees. At one point, Dr. Morrell got up to throw something away. When his back was turned, the other guy swiftly switched out his metal water bottle—you know, the kind Wynhurst gave out to all the staff—for an exact copy, placing Dr. Morrell's original one in his own bag. I thought it was weird, maybe a prank, but when I found out he died that same night…"

Matthew puts his head in his hands. "I should've told the police. I thought about it a million times but always talked myself out of it. I don't know who the man was. I've been terrified at the prospect of seeing him on campus again, but I'm also afraid of never knowing the truth." He drops his hands, hanging his head.

31

"I'm a coward. This thing—it's eating me up."

"Hey, don't be so hard on yourself," I say, startled by his self-deprecation. "That's a crazy thing to see! Anyone would wonder what to do."

He meets my eyes. "You think so?"

"Absolutely!"

He stares off into the distance.

"Uh...if you don't mind me asking...what did the guy look like?"

"No, no, you're fine. Gray hair cut short, with a trim beard. Typical professor/faculty look. He was thinner than Dr. Morrell, and a little taller."

"Do you think the cameras would have caught this?"

He shakes his head. "No. Thanks to Micah, I know the cameras in the cafe are broken. Half the ones around campus don't actually work."

"Dang."

"I...I should go to the police," he says finally. "Maybe I could draw a picture, or they could find some suspects... Maybe it's too late, but I can't take this to my grave."

I nod in support. "I think that would be a good idea."

"Thank you, Addy."

At night, I lie awake in my bed, turning over and over the story that Matthew told me. That's confirmation, isn't it? I'm not on a wild goose chase. There was foul play at hand, and we even have a suspect. Does this mean Dr. Morrell was poisoned? I shiver. Someone, maybe someone on this campus, is guilty.

Chapter 6

The Danger of Stories

On Monday, I walk into botany and take my seat behind Sid. She happens to see me and turns around. "Addy!" she says, raising her eyebrows. "How was your date?"

At first, I have no idea what she's talking about. "Date?"

"Yeah! I saw you and Matthew head off campus on Saturday."

"What? Oh, that wasn't a date, we were just—" I'm interrupted by Professor Leighton handing her a stack of papers.

"Take one, pass it down," she says. I grab the stack from Sid, take one copy of the quiz, then pass the rest to the person behind me.

"It wasn't a date," I whisper, leaning forward so she can hear. "He just had some stuff to tell me."

"Whatever you say…" she says, skeptical.

"No, honest, that's all it was," I say, flustered. I'm not hiding any feelings, but it seems like convincing her to believe me is an impossible task. "We're really just friends—"

"Just a reminder," Professor Leighton calls from the front of the room, "there is no talking during the quiz."

I clamp my mouth shut and sink back into my seat. As I stare down at the multiple choice questions, my mind drifts back to my conversation with Matthew. I remember the intensity with which he asked me not to tell anyone about what he saw. Maybe letting Sid assume we only went on a date isn't such a bad thing.

When botany ends, Sid heads off to her next class, and I exit the building alone. As I approach the street, a car slows to a stop. The driver, a local police officer, waves me on. I wave back as I cross to the other side, then watch as the cop car continues on its usual route through campus. It soon stops again, this time near the sparsely-populated parking lot just past the natural sciences building. I see a guy approach the car, then realize I recognize him; it's Matthew.

"Excuse me, officer. I...I may have some evidence to discuss," I hear him say from a distance. "Could we talk?" The officer converses with him a bit, then pops the passenger-side door open. Matthew slides into the front seat, and they drive off.

I smile, happy to see Matthew have the courage to share what he saw. Maybe his testimony will get this case moving again. As a precaution, I scan the surrounding area. Thankfully, there aren't many people around. Of the students who are present, I don't think any of them noticed. As I gaze across the road, my eyes land on only one person.

Professor Leighton's attention is directed towards the road, right where Matthew got in the car. For a split second, she looks my way, and our eyes meet. I look away as quickly as possible, hoping she didn't notice me. My mind starts to race. Did she see Matthew? Hear him admit to being an eyewitness? I can't help but steal another peek. The spot where she was standing just a minute ago is empty; she's gone.

I take a deep breath and try to bring my paranoia back to earth. If Professor Leighton was the only person watching, there's probably no reason to worry. The chances that she's somehow involved in a murder plot are very low. Most likely, she didn't even give it a second thought.

I see Matthew in passing the next few days, but I don't have the opportunity to ask him how the conversation with police went. On Thursday, I manage to sit with him at lunch, but Sid and Micah are also with us. I don't want to break my commitment to secrecy, so I have to wait until we're alone. As the three of them discuss a class they're taking together,

I briefly zone out of the conversation and gaze around the cafeteria. My eyes happen to fall on Professor Leighton, who is sitting with a group of other professors at a long table in the corner. To my embarrassment, she turns her head and we make awkward eye contact for a second time this week. I avert my eyes to my food. *Way to be subtle, Addy.*

"So, the historical society is having a meeting tonight. That guy we met playing pool, Anthony, he's hosting. Anyone interested in going?" I ask.

Sid and Micah look at each other. "Sure. I guess we could stay for a little bit."

"I think I'll pass," Matthew answers. "I have a lot of homework to do."

That evening, Micah, Sid, and I head over to Anthony's dorm, which is more of an apartment. A few people are already milling about by the time we get there. Glowy orange string lights hang from the wall, and bowls of chips and snack food cover a small folding table.

"Addy, welcome!" Anthony says, opening the door. "And— remind me again. I know we've met."

"Sidney, and this is Micah," Sid says.

"Sidney and Micah, come on in. So glad to have you." He closes the door behind us. "Please, help yourself to snacks. Tonight is a little different than what we normally do at the historical society meetings, more informal, but it's a great time to come."

Within half an hour, Anthony has us all take a seat. "I know that some of you are militant skeptics," he begins. "But tonight, I intend to change that—Just kidding. I'm sure you are all aware of my fascination with the myths of Flickerwood and Wynhurst University. So tonight..." He ominously flips a flashlight on and shines it at his chin, "...will be a night of ghost stories." A few people laugh, and most crack a smile. "Who has a story to tell?"

Some tales are predictable: a monster in the pond, a ghost in the bathroom, a cult in the forest. Others are ridiculous: the ghost of a squirrel, the lost sock goblin, the mayor vs. his evil twin. You can tell people are having fun with it. When the flashlight returns to Anthony, he seizes the opportunity to retell the story he told us about the witch of Flickerwood. This time, however, he adds a detail.

"This," he says, raising a yellowed scrap of newspaper in a plastic sleeve, "is an article about the fire that claimed the old music building ten years ago." He passes the newspaper around. "They were never able to pinpoint exactly what started it. All we know is that it destroyed the building from the ground up, burning clear through to the foundation. There is a recurring pattern in Wynhurst's history. Any time expansions into the forest are considered, tragedy strikes. At the time of the fire, the board had decided to add on to the music building by cutting into the northern woods. The fire occurred just a week before construction was to occur.

"They did rebuild it, of course, but expanded *away* from the trees, rather than towards them. Unfortunately, it seems we haven't learned from the past. Currently, the board and the president are talking about adding a visual arts building, expanding the campus southward by chopping down trees. Really, it was only a matter of time before these expansions would anger the witch. So long as they continue with their plans, we should be on the lookout for more bad things to come." Anthony wiggles his fingers spookily as he lowers the flashlight.

The room falls silent, all having been utterly captivated by his story.

Well, all except Sid and Micah, so it seems. Micah snickers. He raises a hand. "Alright, alright. You wanna hear a real scary story? I've got something to share."

With a smile, Anthony hands off the flashlight. Sid and I both turn to look at Micah. She looks just as surprised as me. What story could he have to tell?

"I probably shouldn't share this..." he starts, "but last semester, I got a call while I was working security one night. It wasn't very late in the evening, maybe seven or so, but it was dark outside when my phone went off. I answered it, and I heard a panicked young woman on the other end. She was breathing heavily, and the connection was cutting in and out.

"She explained that she was a student on the cross-

36

country team and had gone for a run on the new trail, the one further north, past the music building. *But*, she'd strayed off the path and gotten lost. And that wasn't all." He pauses for dramatic effect, scanning the room. "She said that she needed help. That she was being chased."

Sid skeptically raises her eyebrows. "Chased by what?"

"She said that she was being chased...by aliens!" Micah lurches forward, causing a few people to flinch. Scattered laughter ripples through the room. "She said they were hulking things with gray-green skin, razor-sharp teeth, and pitch black eyes."

"So what happened? What did you do?" I ask.

He shrugs. "I forwarded the call to my supervisor. Figured it was some sort of prank, and he agreed. We made sure she got back to her dorm okay, but she really wanted us to fall for the alien thing. We both looked, but there wasn't anything in those woods." He raises the flashlight again. "Unless of course, it just didn't want to be found. Consider yourselves warned...if you go walking at night and wander off the path, you may just be abducted by an alien. And, scarier still, subject to a disciplinary fine from campus services. Mwahaha."

The end of his story is met with more laughter. He's captured the hearts of the audience. I snicker as I gaze around the room. My eyes fall on one person, however, who isn't laughing. Anthony. His expression has grown serious, with his brows drawn in concern. A few more people tell stories, but his energy remains dampened.

When the party's over, people begin filtering out the door. As they do so, I choose to hang back and get a minute to talk with him. "Do you really believe this stuff, Anthony?" I ask.

He offers a one shoulder shrug, feigning a relaxed smile. "Hard to say," the smile fades. "What's for sure is that *something* weird is going on in this town. As of yet, no one has been able to offer a naturalistic explanation. So..." He shrugs. "Who knows."

It's a bit of a long walk from the senior dorms to our own. Sid, Micah, and I walk along the tree line, joking about the stories people told. All of a sudden, Micah stops dead in his tracks. Eyes wide, he stares into the dark trees.

"I don't mean to be paranoid or anything, but...did you guys hear that?" he asks.

Sid shoots him a look. "Are you messing with us? Hear wha—" Her sentence is cut short by the rustling of leaves. She stiffens, and we all stare into the darkness.

The sound of my pounding heart fills my head, along with all the stories we just heard about cults, witches, and monsters. Anyone could be in those trees. The leaves rustle again, louder this time. My eyes catch a slight movement, and I step backwards. The figure approaches. Just as I'm about to take off running, I recognize the outline of...a deer.

"Whew." We all sigh.

"Just a deer?!" Sid says, smiling.

Micah clutches his chest with a grin. "Those stories must have me on edge."

As I leave class on Friday, I happen to spot Matthew coming from the direction of the natural sciences building and heading towards the dorms. His expression looks troubled, but he relaxes a bit when he sees me.

"Hey Addy," he calls, quickening his pace.

"Matthew," I return, walking towards him. "You okay?"

He tilts his head from side to side. "Eh. Been better."

"I've been itching to hear from you. What happened on Monday?"

"Yeah, sorry I didn't reach out. It's just...well, I had a lot of homework and all..."

"Oh, don't worry about it," I assure him.

He pauses a moment and checks his phone, whispering the time under his breath. "Hey, do you want to come back to my dorm with me?" He raises his hands, "Not in a weird way. Just to talk. It's the middle of the day; most people should be out."

"Uh, sure," I reply, anxious to hear what he has to say.

We enter the building, and I follow him up the stairs to his floor. He buzzes in, and we walk down the hall to his room. After unlocking it with a key, the door swings open to reveal his and Micah's shared room. Light streams in from the window, filling the area with a bright glow. A blue rug lies in the middle of the floor, masking some of the cold white tile. It's cleaner than I would have expected a boys' dorm to be. The door latches shut behind us, and Matthew pulls out two desk chairs. I sit down across from him. As I'm about to ask about the police, he starts talking first.

"Do you have Professor Leighton for any classes?"

I'm a little thrown off by the question. Is he just making small talk again? "Yeah, for botany. Why?"

He moves his hand to his face. "I dunno. I just had a weird interaction with her."

"Oh? Weird how?"

"Well, I was walking out of class, which is near her office, and she happened to see me. She asked if I could meet with her for a minute, so I followed her into her office. I don't have any classes with her; I don't really know her, so it seemed odd. She asked me about collaborating with ecology majors on an art thing, though, so that was pretty cool. But then...it was like my worst fears came true."

I realize I'm literally sitting on the edge of my seat. "What happened?"

"She asked if I knew anything about Dr. Morrell's death."

"Really?!" I ask in disbelief. "What did you say?"

"I kind of just brushed the question off. But before I could leave, she gave me like a warning, saying if I told people...that there might be a target on my back."

"Whoa. Seriously?" I sit back in my seat, trying to comprehend how Professor Leighton could come out and say something like that. "Did it seem like a threat?"

He shrugs. "I'm not sure. Maybe? It was weird. How did she even know to ask me that?"

"I might be able to help answer that one," I say, remembering what I saw. "When you got in the cop car, I looked around to see if anyone noticed. The only person I saw was Professor Leighton. I hoped nothing would come of it."

"Weird," Matthew says.

"Weird," I agree. "Could you tell the police about that? They're supposed to like, protect witnesses and stuff, aren't they?"

He nods, looking out the window. "Maybe I should...I really shouldn't be talking to you about all this, though."

"What do you mean?" I ask, confused.

"Well, the cop told me I should keep what I saw to myself, at least while they investigate, or I could get in legal trouble. He wanted the names of anyone I already told, which is just you and Micah, but he said we're off the hook as long as we don't spread it to anyone else."

I consider his words. "I guess that makes sense?" My face grows hot. "Sorry if I pressured you into doing something illegal." So much for being an amateur detective.

"No, no, you're all good," he says, waving away my apology. "You helped me work up the courage to go to the police, and I feel better knowing they're going to look into it. If something did happen, at least I won't be the reason Dr. Morrell's killer walks free."

I nod. "Well, then I'm glad you feel better. They're going to reopen the case, then?"

He nods. "Yep."

I'm relieved to hear we're no longer the only ones out there who suspect something. It's not up to me. The police are aware of the evidence and they'll look into it. They'll figure out what happened.

I give him a thumbs up. "Good to hear...So, I guess we should stop talking about it, huh?"

He snickers. "Yeah, probably."

We chat about small stuff and play a round or two of cards. When I go to leave, I can tell he still feels unsettled about something.

"Everything alright?" I ask.

He nods. "Yeah, I'm okay. Just...can't stop thinking about that meeting with Professor Leighton."

"Can't blame you." I bite my lip. "If I were you, I'd try to avoid her for the time being."

He nods. "Hey, at least the police will have some sort of lead if something were to happen."

I pause. "Something were to happen? What do you mean?"

He opens his mouth, then closes it again and shakes his head. "Nothing, I'm sure. I'm probably just being paranoid."

I smile back. "I'm sure everything will be okay."

"Yeah."

I head back to my dorm, wrapping my scarf around my neck. Though it's not very late, the sun is already starting to set. I can hear the faint sound of music drifting from the right of campus. Someone must be having a party tonight.

Chapter 7

The Body on the Ground

I shuffle out of bed on Saturday morning and check my phone for my blood sugar. 98. Pretty good. I inject a dose of basal insulin, collect my clothes, then walk down the hall to the showers. As the water hits my face, I feel a sense of optimism for the day. I start making a mental to-do list, going over the homework assignments I think I could get done today. As it turns out, my plans are interrupted as soon as I return to my room. My phone buzzes, the screen alight with a name from my contacts. Sid is calling.

Casually, I answer her call, expecting some sort of invite for a weekend activity. Instead, I'm met with Sid's frantic voice. "Addy? Were you with Matthew yesterday?"

"Uh, yeah, in the afternoon. Why?" I answer, confused.

"I...I don't know how to say this," she says. "But... Matthew died last night."

My mouth suddenly feels like it's made of cotton. I force my tongue to move. "W-what do you mean? Why do you say that?"

"He went to a party last night, was found unresponsive... paramedics said they couldn't do anything." Her voice trembles. "I'm with Micah now, in his room. You wanna come meet us?"

"I'll be right there," I say instantly, then hang up the phone.

Feeling dazed, I float over to Matthew and Micah's dorm building. Sid comes to the door to let me in. As we ascend to the correct floor, my mind replays the talk I had with Matthew just yesterday.

"What happened?" I ask her.

She looks at me with a pained expression. In a low voice, she says, "They're saying it was alcohol poisoning. It's not uncommon for kids to get too drunk and...you know, not recover. He was just lying on the ground outside the house."

I nod, unsure of how to respond. A large part of me is still in denial. This can't really be happening. Matthew is still safe in his dorm with Micah...there must be some kind of mistake.

It's not until we reach his room that the truth really hits me. Save for the addition of Micah's bag, it looks unchanged from the day before. Light from the window illuminates the room, and the desk chairs we sat in are still on the blue carpet. This is all real. Matthew...something bad happened to him, and he's really gone.

Micah is sitting on the edge of the bed with an expression I've never seen him have. He holds a pillow close to his chest, and a box of tissues sits beside him. His eyes are red and watery, unfocused on anything in the room. Sid sits down beside him, wrapping one arm around his shoulders for support. He barely acknowledges her presence. I take a seat in my desk chair from yesterday, and we sit in silence.

After about twenty minutes, I start to feel my blood sugar drop. I glance at my phone to see a downward arrow. I guess I haven't had breakfast yet. The social awkwardness of eating at such a somber time kicks in. I can't imagine unwrapping a Quaker Oats bar in the room of a dead person while his mourning roommate sits in front of me. Instead, I excuse myself to the hallway. I slide to the ground and unwrap my granola bar.

In the quiet, my brain wraps around the events that transpired in the past few hours. Matthew, the boy I was just getting to know, the nice guy I talked with yesterday...He dropped dead last night. He is no more. He'll never walk these halls again. He'll never graduate. He'll never take that internship at the publishing company. A lump forms in my throat. Did I really even see him as a person while he was here? I am suddenly overwhelmed by the guilt of not going to see his art exhibit in its own right. I put my head to my knees and weep.

In a few minutes, I press my palms to the floor in an effort to anchor my body in reality. Breathe in...breathe out...I root around in my bag until I find a tissue. After blowing my nose and wiping my eyes, I regain my composure. The past few weeks have felt surreal, like I've merely been floating through life.

All of a sudden, I feel pulled out of my daze, as if waking up from a dream. I'm aware of my heart beating in my chest, this fragile organ keeping me alive. I run my fingers over the scarred injection sites on my abdomen. Death is a scary thing. Life is short. The reality washes over me like a wave. Chronic illness or not, all bodies decay over time, and mine is no different. Unless I'm caught up to Heaven like Enoch, death is something I'll have to face, too.

Dr. Morrell...he's *dead*. And so is Matthew. The boy I talked with yesterday. *Dead*. I shudder as the reality sinks in. I recall Matthew's words from yesterday. "*If something were to happen...*" I knew he was afraid, but I really never imagined...Well, something happened. Was it really alcohol poisoning, like they said? I mean, I'm sure the medical professionals know what they're talking about. Still, it does seem to be a strange coincidence that he died just after revealing what he witnessed.

A twinge of guilt strikes my conscience. Is this my fault? Did I encourage him to say something that got him killed? *God, please forgive me.* I try to remind myself that it was the right thing to do, and I'm not the one to blame. After all, whether this was a direct attack against Matthew or if the stress of knowing what he knew pushed him to drink too much, it is Dr. Morrell's killer who's responsible.

My sadness is displaced by a different feeling, a burning in my chest. Anger. All at once, I'm filled with an over-whelming desire for justice. Despite lacking any real power, I feel a sense of resolve. If I have anything to say about it, the identity of this killer will be brought to light. They won't just get away with it.

44

Having long since finished my snack, I stand up and open the door to the dorm. It's nice to see Sid and Micah, even though they're so distraught. I'm grateful for their company. Micah's phone rings on the bedside table. Sid answers for him. "Oh, hello Mrs. Bruner. Yeah, we're in the room now. I'll be right down." She hangs up the phone. "Matthew's parents are downstairs. I'm going to go let them in."

Micah nods, his eyes following her across the room. I shift my weight from foot to foot, unsure of whether to stay with him or go with Sid. I take too long to decide, and the door shuts behind her. I guess I'm staying here.

"I'm sorry for your loss." It's the only thing I can think to say. There is silence. Just when I think he's not going to answer, he turns towards me.

"It's just...hard to grasp, ya know?" I nod. "I'm not sure I fully believe it yet. Like...everything feels normal, but then I remember what happened, and it's the normalcy that kind of makes it even harder." He takes a deep breath, running his fingers through his hair.

The door opens, and Sid returns with Mr. and Mrs. Bruner. If Micah is distraught, Matthew's parents look like hollow shells of people. Dark circles line their eyes, and the weight of losing a child hangs heavy on their shoulders.

"...and this is my friend, Addy," Sid says, introducing me. I wave in their direction, but I'm not sure they see me. They scan the room. Mr. Bruner sighs. He pulls out a chair and collapses into it. Mrs. Bruner purses her lips. The sadness in her eyes mixes with something else. Wordlessly, she heads to Matthew's side of the room. I step out of her way; she's on a mission. She examines his desk, the bedside table, his bed, and the posters hanging above it. Finally, she turns towards Micah. The look in her eyes is wild.

"Micah," she says firmly. He flinches from his daze.

"Yes, Mrs. Bruner?"

"I'm going to ask you a question, and I need you to be 100% honest with me."

"Of course, ma'am," he replies, straightening his shoulders.

"Did Matthew drink?"

It's clear the question catches him off guard. She repeats it.

"Uh...no, no I don't remember him ever drinking,"

Micah says, stumbling over the words. "Sometimes I'd have friends over and we would have a few beers, but I remember Matthew always turning them down."

"Now, this isn't the time to spare his mother's feelings," she drills. "Was he a partier?"

Micah shakes his head. "No, he wasn't. I can only tell you what I know, but that's the truth. Actually, I thought it was weird he even went to the party with me last night. It was the first time he ever agreed to go. I thought maybe he wanted the college experience before graduation or something. He seemed stressed. I'm not sure."

"Was he drinking at that party last night?"

Micah spreads his hands. "I...I don't know. We drifted apart. I didn't see him for most of the night."

Mrs. Bruner takes a step back. She thinks for a moment. "Thank you."

Her husband locks eyes with her. "You don't believe that police report one bit, do you?" he asks.

She shakes her head. "I'm not stupid, but I know my son, and there's no way he drank himself to death. They must have made a mistake." She chews on her fingernails. "I'm going to call that investigator." Her husband rises and follows her out the door. "Kids, try not to touch anything. Could be—" she stops herself before alluding to the room being a crime scene. "Well, it could be important." A swell of hope rises in my chest. The truth will come out.

Chapter 8

Above and Below

Waking up is always harder the day after something terrible happens. In sleep, you can escape the pain of reality, but in the morning, it all comes flooding back. So I'm surprised to see Micah in the dining hall bright and early. He piles eggs, bacon, pancakes, and fruit onto his plate, then sits at a booth and stares into space. Even more perplexing is his attire, which consists of a gray suit and blue tie. Few people ever come to breakfast, and even fewer do so on the weekend, so the dining area is all but empty. I head towards him with my plate of waffles.

"Can I join you?"

He looks over at me, rubbing his eyes. "Sure, sure. Feel free."

I study him as I pull out my insulin pen, screw on a needle, and dial it to the correct dose. "I, uh, I thought the funeral wouldn't be for a little while."

He looks down at his suit. "Oh, no, I...I was actually thinking of going to church this morning."

It suddenly clicks in my head. "Ah, so that's why you're up early." I slice into my waffles. "I didn't know you were Christian."

Perhaps my food reminds him to eat, because he picks up his fork and stabs at his eggs. "Yeah, well, I went to a Catholic high school, actually. But I kind of got jaded after a while. The group prayers and ceremonies we used to do started to seem a bit weird, maybe a little cultish." He shrugs. "Been kind of distant from God for a while. But this whole thing...it's just got me thinking." He turns his eyes back to his eggs. "I dunno. You?"

Immediately, I feel the pressure which comes with any conversation about religion. Like the eternal fate of the other person's soul is resting on me. "I grew up Protestant," I answer. "Our church was nondenominational."

"Ah. I visited my friend's church once. He was Protestant. I don't remember what denomination it was, but it wasn't bad. Do you have a church you go to around here?"

In response to the question, my first instinct is panic and embarrassment. I've been such a lousy Christian, lately. I'm in no position to have an apologetic debate about the differences between Protestantism and Catholicism. For fear of making the gospel look bad, I'm inclined to try and portray my faith as stronger than it is.

However, this desire fades when I realize Micah and I may not be so different. Maybe he can relate. "I...I don't actually. To be honest, I've kind of been drifting from my faith, too. I mean, I would still call myself a Christian. It's just been hard, ya know. With college and everything."

He nods. "I get it. I think most people re-evaluate their beliefs as young adults, right? It's just a normal stage."

His response shakes me a little. Normal? Objectively, I suppose it does make sense, given all the changes of college life, that a re-examination of religious convictions would be among the growing pains. Thus far, I suppose I assumed there was just something deeply wrong with me. Maybe I'm not as terrible as I thought.

"Would you want to go to church with me this morning?" he asks. "There's one within walking distance."

I wasn't planning on going to church today, but it's been a long time since I've altered my plans for something I think is God's will. This could be good. Really good. I nod. "Yeah, absolutely. I'll go with you." I look down at my sweatpants and t-shirt. "Do you know what time the service starts?"

"It said 9 am on the website."

48

I check the time. "I'm gonna run and change. Where should I meet you?"

"Outside the rec center? I was going to see if Sid wants to come, too; she's at the gym. I'm not sure she'll be interested, though."

After changing, I head towards our meeting spot. I soon see both Micah and Sid standing outside. I guess Sid decided to come after all. She grabs his hand, lacing her fingers between his. "Hey, Addy," she calls.

"Hey!"

"Do you have any idea where we're going?"

"Nope." I nod towards Micah. "He suggested it."

"It's right over there," he says, pointing towards town. We start walking off campus, winding our way through the quiet streets and large houses.

"Have you ever been to church before?" Micah asks, directing the question towards Sid.

"Maybe when visiting my grandparents during the holidays." She turns back to look at me. "I wasn't raised Christian. I think I'd consider myself to be atheist or agnostic." There's a pause before she adds, "I don't have a problem with people who are religious, though."

I nod, unsure of what to say. The pressure to evangelize creeps back into my brain, but I remain silent, adding a layer of guilt to the burden on my shoulders. Though curious, I'm afraid to ask why she's ruled out Christianity. Afraid her answer may be the very same reason it's eating at me. If I don't even have a satisfactory answer for myself, how on earth would I respond to her questions? I push the thoughts away. Maybe the pastor will say something to make her reconsider. Bringing her to church is a good first step, right?

As we walk on, the steeple comes into view. It's a large spike stretching into the sky, topped with a cross. The building is made of gray stone and looks very old. The large wooden front doors are open wide, but the amount of people trickling in is thin. I check my phone. 9:00. The church bell starts to ring, so we pick up the pace.

We're greeted by a man handing out programs. "First time here?" he asks in a hushed tone. We nod. "Welcome."

We linger in the foyer outside the sanctuary, waiting so as not to disturb the opening prayer. Inside, there are many rows of pews, but most of them are empty. The church appears to be made up of mostly older people, along with several young families. Everyone is still, sitting with heads bowed. For a minute or two, the only sound is that of the pastor praying. I glance at Micah, whose head is also bowed. I think of doing the same, but then hear the word "Amen." Like a sudden spell being lifted, the whole congregation stirs. I nudge Micah forward, and we find a seat near the back.

In some ways, the routine of church is familiar. Stand up, sing, sit down, bow your head, pray, open your eyes. But rather than being comforting, I find it a little off-putting. The songs are different, the people are strangers, and the building is uncanny. A pang of homesickness strikes my stomach like a knife. I never had much trouble adjusting to life away from my parents, but this—never before have I missed home so much. All believers are supposed to be part of one family, yet this doesn't feel like my family. This is not my home.

As the pastor begins the sermon, I try to dissect my aching heart. Maybe this feeling would improve once I got used to a new church. It's just different, that's all. It's a good experience, anyway, to try different churches. I glance toward Sid. Her attention shifts back and forth between the pulpit and Micah, who's next to her. I don't know what I was expecting, but a part of me is disappointed it doesn't seem to be affecting her in any type of deep way.

In an effort to refocus, I pull out the pew Bible in front of me. I missed what Scripture we're on, so I randomly flip through the pages, happening to stop on a confusing, violent passage in the Old Testament. Defeatedly, I close it. I'm not going to be able to find the right verse. And just like everything else here, the translation is unfamiliar.

I start to feel a little funny and decide it's a good idea to check my blood sugar. A woman glances in my direction when I pull out my phone. Oh well. I cringe when I see the number. 80 mg/dL, with two downward facing arrows.

"I'll be right back," I whisper to Sid. I snatch up my bag

and my water bottle and head out of the sanctuary. I wander over to the restrooms and stand just outside the doors. Rooting through my stuff, I pull out some fruit snacks. Eating five at a time, I finish the pack and wait. I'd be mortified to have my low alarm go off during a quiet church service. I wince at the thought. Just as the arrows start heading back up, a woman walks out of the sanctuary holding a crying baby.

"Shhh," she coos, bouncing him up and down. The small infant continues to whine. A man, presumably her husband, follows behind her. He has dark hair, a short beard, and thick-framed glasses.

"Hey," he says sternly, looking the baby in the eyes. He cups its cheek with one hand. "Stop that." With the other hand, he slaps the side of the baby's face.

Involuntarily, I jolt. Did I just see that? The man turns in my direction, and I quickly direct my gaze out the window. He storms past and goes into the bathroom. I breathe a sigh of relief. The baby is still wriggling and crying, and the mom takes him outside. He wasn't slapped hard, only a light tap. I don't think he was hurt. But my stomach turns. Spanking is one thing, but across the face? Besides, that child seems too young even for a spanking. He's just a baby; he probably can't yet comprehend punishment.

I find myself in a prayer. *God...what is going on here? Is that supposed to happen?* I throw my empty pack of fruit snacks into the trash and head back into the sanctuary. I realize my perspective has changed. Before, I had some thoughts of getting past this feeling of weirdness. Like, maybe if I started coming here regularly I could find some community, and it wouldn't be so weird. But that thought disappears. It's too strange. The service, the people, that...whatever that was I just witnessed. I'm not coming back here.

"Everything okay?" Sid whispers.

My mind races, wondering if my emotions show on my face. Then I realize she just wants to know why I left. I tap my CGM and give a thumbs up. She nods. I bite my lip. It would be nice to have someone to talk to about what just happened, but if this is basically Sid's first interaction with church, I don't want to give her a bad first impression. I'm glad she didn't see it.

Following the closing prayer, we all filter out of the sanctuary. I'm left with mixed feelings. A part of me is glad no one really takes notice of us, and another part of me feels a bit lonely. I'm used to church being a warm place, but this... just seems a bit cold. I step outside into the frigid air, but Micah and Sid are no longer behind me. Peering inside, I see Micah walking towards the bathrooms and Sid standing in line for coffee. We make eye contact, and I wave to her. At least she'll know where to find me.

I angle myself to the side and forge a path out of the stream of people flowing from the doors. I see the man who slapped the baby walking out with his family. His expression is stern, and he takes long strides as he charges towards the parking lot. He has a little girl by the hand, and she struggles to keep up with his pace.

"Daddyyyyyyyy" she says. Trailing behind him is his wife, still holding the baby.

I turn around to face the graveyard behind me. It's beautiful, in an eerie kind of way. Old, gray tombstones stick out of the grass, almost like the teeth of a monster. A leafless, gnarled tree stretches towards the sky. My attention is drawn to the most recent plot. The tombstone is bright and new, and flowers lie at the base. In contrast to the drab green grass, a mound of freshly dug brown dirt sits in front of it. I follow the cracked concrete path through the rusty cast-iron gate. I hear Sid and Micah come up behind me. Standing over the grave, we read the name on the stone.

"Gregory Cecil Morrell."

Chapter 9

What Meets the Eye

The walk back to campus is unusually quiet. The only things I can think to talk about are things I should probably not bring up—the man at church, Matthew, Dr. Morrell...

Sid finally breaks the silence. "So, what do you guys plan to do for the rest of the day?"

"I dunno," I answer. "Probably homework."

"Yeah, I should probably do that, too," Micah adds. There is more silence.

"It's so sad, everything that's happened lately. It's been a rough semester so far," Sid says.

Micah and I nod in agreement.

"So...what did you guys think of church?" I ask.

Sid shrugs. "I mean, I'm not really qualified to say. What did you guys think?" I feel my insides twist, scrambling to formulate something to say that would make Sid think more about God.

"It felt nice to go back to church," Micah says. "I think I might go again next week. How about you, Addy?"

Any evangelistic strategies I was thinking of employing suddenly vanish like water down a drain. How can I talk about God with Sid when I have no intentions of returning to that church?

"I...I'm not sure. We'll see," I say noncommittally. "It was different than what I'm used to back home, ya know?

Felt kind of weird," I offer, trying to give a reason that's not about losing faith in God. They both seem satisfied by this answer.

I turn my attention to the shops we're passing by. There are still several spots in town that Wynhurst students frequent: a couple pizza shops, a coffee house, a thrift store, that kind of thing. However, like Matthew said, there are fewer now than there used to be. Not much seems to last here.

We pass by a mattress store. Even on a Sunday, the glowing sign says "open," yet I see no sign of a cashier or any employee, much less a customer. In fact, I don't think I've ever seen anyone enter that store at all. From the outside, the building seems to be falling apart piece by piece, with paint peeling off the side and chunks missing from the cinder block walls. It's strange, really, which shops close their doors and which ones manage to stay open. The thought makes me wonder what this place will look like in another hundred years.

On Monday, they call another memorial service—this time, for Matthew. By the time I get there, the auditorium is already full of students, and I can't find Sid and Micah. Thankfully, I spot an empty seat beside Anthony. He waves me over, and I sit down just as the service begins.

"Hey, Addy, how are you doing?" Anthony whispers.

"Eh," I reply, "could be better, could be worse."

He nods. "Did you know Matthew? I heard he and Micah were roommates."

I tilt my head side to side. "A little. We talked a few times. I was just getting to know him when…all this happened."

"Well, I'm sorry for your loss."

"Thanks."

Following President Conley, Dr. Gaines is introduced as the new dean of the School of Natural and Health Sciences, a position formerly belonging to Dr. Morrell. Well, that would explain why his teaching schedule has changed so much. He approaches the microphone, coming into view of the audience.

He is slimmer than many professors, likely due to spending

54

much of his time outdoors as head of the small ecology department. In the time that I've known him, his hair has
transitioned from being somewhat brown to decidedly gray,
a condition I'm sure will only be worsened by taking charge
of nearly half the departments at the university. He adjusts
the microphone, raising it to speak comfortably.

"I would like to thank you all for coming to honor the
memory of one of our own—Matthew Bruner. I was distraught
to hear the news that a student had passed away. It is always
a tragedy when someone so young is taken in their prime,
with so much life left to live. Regrettably, I did not have
the pleasure of meeting Matthew, but in talking with his
professors, I have learned that he was a very bright, talented,
compassionate, and thoughtful young man. I encourage you
all to visit the art gallery and take some time to appreciate
the work of this gifted student. I offer my deepest condolences
to his family and friends."

He steps back from the podium, and other professors,
students, and family members take turns sharing things
about his life. Micah, though struggling to hold back tears,
even gets on stage and talks about the fond memories he has
of his roommate. I spend the entire first half of the service
with a lump in the back of my throat.

The second half, however, turns into a public service
announcement. Clad in scrubs, Nurse Bradshaw ascends the
stage. The room quiets as we all wonder what she has to say.

"In light of this tragedy, we would be remiss not to discuss
a very serious problem, both nationally and locally. As many
of you know, drug abuse and alcoholism are on the rise. Our
town has seen more arrests for drug possession and related
crimes in the past five to ten years, and that number continues
to grow. The amount of deaths from overdoses has more than
tripled, and we're seeing new drugs appear which are even
more dangerous than fentanyl and traditional opioids.

"I know that parties, though discouraged by administration,
are an inevitable part of college life. With that, I urge you to
use good judgement. Don't drink and drive, know when
you've had too much, and please avoid these types of illegal
substances. Even prescription drugs can be a gateway. Addiction
is not an easy thing to escape, and it takes very little to

become dependent. It's just not worth the risk. Overdoses are avoidable deaths, and I ask you all to stay safe. Thank you, Wynhurst."

Anthony leans towards me and whispers, "I don't mean to be insensitive, but it's almost as if we weren't just here a few weeks ago."

I wrinkle my brow. "What do you mean?"

"Well, no one has mentioned how this is the second death already this semester. They're just treating it like it's an entirely separate event, ya know?" I stare blankly at him. He shrinks back beneath my gaze. "Sorry, I'm not trying to be rude."

"No, no, you're fine. Yeah, I guess they haven't."

"...Do you think they're connected?" Anthony asks. "I mean, do you really believe Matthew's death was just from substances at a party, completely unrelated?"

Nervously, I tap my foot on the ground, remembering the warning Matthew got from the police. I probably shouldn't be discussing an ongoing investigation, but I can't resist talking with someone who shares my suspicions.

"If I'm being honest, I do think the explanation has a few holes in it. There's...well, a lot of things seem fishy to me. I think it's a real possibility they're related." As it leaves my lips, I'm suddenly very aware of where I'm sitting. Anyone could overhear us. If someone on campus really is guilty, they're probably in this room. And they've shown they'll kill those who know too much.

"I agree," Anthony says.

"Hey, maybe we shouldn't talk about this now," I say, lowering my voice even more.

His eyes flit back and forth, examining the room. He appears to have the same realization I just did. "Sorry — would you want to meet up later?"

Unsure of how I could even back out, I agree. "I have class after this. Maybe around lunch?"

He responds with a thumbs-up. "See you then."

As I leave Meyer Hall, I try to reassure my conscience. The police warned Matthew not to talk about something he witnessed. Real evidence. Anthony and I are just discussing what's common knowledge. It's not like I know anything important that hasn't been shared with the police...right?

The minute I walk into botany and see Professor Leighton standing at the front of the classroom, I feel sick to my stomach. At first, I wonder if the grief of Matthew's death is finally hitting me. However, I soon realize it's something else. Something he told me mere hours before he died.

She strolls to the blackboard and begins writing the day's topic. The white chalk grinds against the hard surface, creating an excess trail of dust. I know two things about Professor Leighton that no one else does.

One: She saw Matthew talk to the police.

Two: Shortly after seeing this, she tried to get information out of him. When he didn't oblige, she told him he might be harmed.

Like she did with Dr. Morrell's passing, she starts class by addressing the events of this weekend. This time, I am silent. If she were guilty, would she really bring up the topic? It's a ridiculous thought, isn't it? That my professor could be a murderer?

"In light of this weekend, I will be postponing our unit test until our next class. I want to remind you all that our first lab assignment will still be due the following Wednesday," she says after everyone has shared. "Now, then." She holds up a resin block containing a preserved specimen. "Who can tell me what species of mushroom this is?" Her eyes fall on me. "Addy?" She walks forward and sets the mushroom down for me to examine.

Reluctantly, I pick up the block and study the fungus. It's a small white mushroom. Beside it is a cross section of the same type, with light brown gills running through it.

I look up at her and answer honestly. "I...I don't know." Mushrooms were never my strong suit.

She doesn't let me hand it back. "Do you have a guess?"

I think of the only white, wild mushroom I know of. "Puffball?" I answer.

"A common mistake," she replies. Leaning down, she points at the gills. "This is actually an immature *Amanita virosa*: a destroying angel."

Eagerly, I return the poison mushroom. As Professor Leighton launches into her lesson, I'm left wondering if I really should go talk to the police. After all, even if she's innocent, it's up to them to find out, isn't it?

Chapter 10

The Witch of Flickerwood

A bit shaken from botany, I almost forget about meeting with Anthony at lunch. Thankfully, one good thing about diabetes is it ensures I never absentmindedly skip meals. I find him standing outside the dining hall waiting for me.

"How's your day going?" he asks when I'm within earshot.

I shake my head. "It's been a long one."

"Oh?"

"Yeah, there's just a lot going on."

"I feel that. You mean, like, homework or...?"

We head inside the dining area, scanning our IDs as we pass through. He grabs two plates and hands me one.

"Thanks. No, I haven't even started my homework for today."

We temporarily part ways to get food. I float around the kitchen, surveying my options, while Anthony heads straight for the salad bar. I wait in line for the main entree, get some fries, and some salad on the side. We meet back up at the silverware, then find a booth in the back corner of the room.

Only slightly self-conscious, I set my heaping plate on the table beside his salad topped with tuna, then head towards the drinks. It still throws me for a loop whenever college guys are conscious about eating healthy. It certainly goes against the stereotypical image of ravenous young men who live on a steady diet of hot pockets, ramen, and Mountain Dew. Well—my brain jumps to the garden of

Eden—I suppose women were the first to eat something unhealthy—

"Sorry!" I say as I almost collide with a girl carrying a tray full of food. She smiles sheepishly and apologizes back, then heads to her table. The surprise pulls me from my thoughts and back to the present. I reach the soda fountain and grab a cup. While waiting for my turn at the machine, I scan the dining area. I'm glad we got here when we did; it's prime time, and students are quickly filling every available seat. The good news is, considering the noise level and our placement in the back, we shouldn't be overheard.

As I head back to the booth with my drink, my eyes snap towards the staff tables, which are also filling up. Professor Leighton is in the same seat as before, though if I'm not mistaken, her end of the table seems less densely populated than it was a few days ago. There are a number of empty chairs surrounding her, while the opposite end of the table contains almost no gaps. I don't let my eyes linger long, however, for fear of her seeing me again.

After weaving through the tables, chairs, and people filling them, I take my coat off and collapse back into the booth. I find Anthony with his head bowed, praying over his food. Like the salad, it surprises me. At a secular school, I expect the people around me to be mainly nonreligious. I bow my head and do the same.

"Amen." Anthony lifts his head and begins cutting his salad. "So, if you don't mind me asking, what's that thing on your arm?"

Once again, my assumptions fail me. I was bracing for a question about my religion, but he's curious about my CGM. "Oh, this?" I roll my sleeve up further so he can see the plastic transmitter on my upper arm. "It's a continuous glucose monitor. It connects to my phone so I can know what my blood sugar is." I unlock the screen and show him the app. A giant spike is present in the graph from a 300 earlier today, but currently I'm at 98 mg/dL. "I have type one diabetes." I pull out my insulin pen and dial the dose according to what I got for lunch. "And this is insulin. I hope you don't mind needles."

"Eh. They're not my favorite, but you do what you gotta

do." He looks away as I inject myself in the arm.

"All done."

His gaze returns. "Does it hurt?"

"Not usually. The needle is pretty small." Growing comfortable, I slide my own plate in front of me. "So, what was it you wanted to talk about?"

"Alright," Anthony says, lowering his voice. "I know you wanted to meet where there were less people, but I don't think anyone will hear us. I'll try not to say anything too incriminating. I also understand if you'd rather go somewhere else."

I give a thumbs up before slicing into my chicken. "Nope, this is good."

"You asked me, before, whether I actually believe in the ghost stories I like to tell...Do you believe in ghosts and witches and curses, Addy?"

I consider. "Well, I believe witchcraft is a real thing but not a good thing..." *The Bible commands against witchcraft.* "Curses exist, but I'm not sure exactly who can declare one or how they work..." *The Old Testament contains several of them.* "...and ghosts, maybe exist if witchcraft is involved." *Like the ghost of Samuel.* "...Judging from the Bible," I add.

"And—how about aliens?" he continues.

"Aliens? You mean, like, what Micah was talking about?"

He nods. "Something like that."

I struggle to answer. "I dunno. I mean, maybe they're out there somewhere, but I'm skeptical. I feel like the Bible would talk about them if they existed, but it doesn't really say."

"Astute," Anthony says, stroking his chin. "Wise answers. I take it you're also a Christian? I noticed you praying."

"I...uh...yeah," I say with a nod. That's the short answer, anyway.

"That's awesome. When did you get saved?"

"Um, well I grew up going to church. I kind of just reached an age where I started taking it more seriously and really developed my own relationship with God. What about you?"

"Nice, nice. It's great that your parents are believers. Mine never really came to faith. We didn't go to church as kids. My older brother was the first in our family to get saved, and he brought me to church with him. I gave my life to Christ my freshman year of high school."

"Praise the Lord," I respond, wishing I could be in a different headspace. There was a time in high school when I would have been over the moon to have a conversation like this. But now...my head is so full of doubts, I always feel like I'm hiding something. Putting on some sort of show. But I do mean it. I am happy for Anthony.

"Indeed. Where do you go to church?"

Here we go again. "I...well, college has been kind of weird. I definitely go when I'm home, but I don't have a car, and things have been busy, and...I haven't really found the right fit, ya know?"

I see a flash of emotion on his face, here and then gone. Hard to say exactly what it was. Disappointment? Judgement? "I've heard a lot of people say stuff like that. You're always welcome to ride with me if you need a church. I go to the small baptist one near the elementary school."

I'm sure some expression flashes across my own face.

"Uh, maybe," I say, suddenly aware of the difference between my pale complexion and his dark skin tone. I scramble to formulate a polite way to ask what I want to know. "...would I stick out too much?"

"Why?" he responds. "Cause you're white?"

My face grows hot.

He breaks into a smile. "Probably. About as much as I stick out here."

I follow his gaze and again scan the dining hall, though this time with a different lens. It strikes me, possibly for the first time, how large the percentage of white students is. I grimace when I realize the only other black person in the room is part of the kitchen staff. It never occurred to me how being a racial minority most of the time might affect a person. I just...didn't think about it.

"Still, like I said, you're more than welcome."

"Okay," I answer, feeling braver. The thought of attending a black church is...well, outside of my comfort zone. But I can try new things. Especially if I have someone to go with. This could be a good thing. "Sure, I'll come. Could I text you closer to Sunday?"

We exchange phone numbers. "Now then. I believe you were asking me about the supernatural?" I say, refocusing the conversation. He nods. "The truth is, I believe those things exist like I believe in the miracles of the Old Testament. I know on some level that they're real, but I struggle to reconcile that with the reality I live every day. Does that make any sense?"

"Plenty. Obviously, you can't go around attributing every strange occurrence to the supernatural. That'd be crazy."

"Right," I agree. "So you don't actually think there's a curse at Wynhurst?"

"Well…" he says slowly, "hear me out. Most of the time, the most logical explanation is something mundane and scientific. But sometimes…if those explanations are ruled out, and all evidence is taken into account…sometimes the most logical thing to believe is the seemingly impossible."

He leans back in his seat. "I used to feel the same way you do. Like, I believe there are spiritual forces in the world, but I've never seen them, ya know? My freshman year, some upperclassmen told me about the legend of the witch in the forest and the deaths and disappearances she caused. I thought it was crazy, too, didn't believe a word. Every college has spooky stories. That is, until they took me to see the cabin." He pauses, giving an eerie effect to his words. "One guy found some old maps of the town, and we were able to find it. Not only that, but we were dumb enough to spend the night inside."

"Wait, there's actually a cabin in the woods?"

"Oh yeah. Of course, it's been abandoned for who knows how long. It was all overgrown, and the roof was leaking when we found it. Really fit the image of a witch's house."

"And you *spent the night*!?"

"Hey, I didn't say it was a smart decision," he says, spreading his hands in surrender. "Please, don't follow my example. Freshman me was…a lot different." He shudders. "Anyway. Being the dumb college kids we were, we set up sleeping bags and told ghost stories. The usual. That night, I don't remember anything weird happening. It was just a dilapidated old cabin. But in the morning…one of the guys with us was gone.

"Eli, the guy who went missing, he'd left behind his sleeping bag and most of his stuff. At first, we assumed he just chickened out and went back to campus early. We went back to look for him, but he wasn't anywhere we checked. Not in any classrooms, not in his dorm, not at the gym or the dining hall. They tried to call his phone, but it wouldn't even ring. His car was still parked in the lot. It was as if he'd just vanished." Anthony gestures with a wave at the word "vanished."

I find myself captivated by his story, and also concerned. "Did you guys check the woods?"

"Eventually we realized that's what we should do. Armed with the old maps, we scoured what we could of the woods. As night started to fall, we realized we were in way over our heads. This wasn't just a prank. We went to campus security and explained what had happened, and they helped us file a missing persons report with the police. A giant search party showed up to comb the forest. It was in the news and everything. My friends and I were part of the search efforts. We all felt responsible." He hangs his head.

I hesitate, afraid to ask my next question. "Did they ever find him?"

He lifts his head. "Thankfully, they did. They found him a few miles north of the cabin, in the section of woods a short ways from the music building. He was alive but unconscious. But that...that's when the weird stuff happened."

"Weird stuff?"

"Yeah. First of all, I swear we had already looked in the place he was found. He wasn't there the day before. Then there was the fact that the clothes they found him in weren't the same as the ones he went missing in. We know he didn't pack a change or anything. But the main thing was...well, he just acted off. They looked him over at the hospital and tested him for substances, but everything came back negative. He told them he just got lost wandering around at night. That was kind of the end of it. We all went over to his and his roommate's dorm when he was released, and he told us a very different story.

"Before, Eli had always been very laid-back. After they found him in that ditch, though, he had this manic look in his eyes. He proceeded to tell us that he'd been abducted by aliens."

"Wait, so Micah's story about that girl wasn't the first time someone claimed to have seen aliens in those woods? I thought it was just a weird one-off..."

Anthony shakes his head. "Makes you wonder, doesn't it? He claimed they held him hostage that day and ran all sorts of experiments on him. Then, they knocked him out, and he only woke up when the search party found him."

"Weird," I say, struggling to make sense of it all. "Was there a chance he was messing with you guys?"

His eyes darken. "I might have thought that, too, were it not for what happened later that night. Shortly after we left his dorm, his roommate called us back in a panic. I will never forget the things that I saw. His eyes rolled back in his head, and he ran around the room on all fours, screeching and making animal noises. Then he flung himself on the ground and started screaming, as if he were in pain. He clawed at himself and ran into walls. It was...it was like he was possessed.

"We were all scared out of our minds. We got the RD and security involved, and they took him back to the hospital. He dropped out of classes and was never really heard from again. I have no idea if his psyche ever recovered."

I swallow.

"If I'm honest," he continues, "maybe that's why I'm so stuck on these legends and stuff. I'm still just trying to understand what the heck happened that night."

I shudder. For a moment, my doubts and questions about the Bible seem small. Anthony's story brings the truth of spiritual warfare to the forefront. I'm reminded that there are very real demonic forces which exist in the world...then again, my brain quickly begins to dismiss any supernatural component in favor of a material explanation. His friend probably had some sort of psychotic break. I've heard schizophrenia tends to develop in this age range. Who knows?

"I just want you to know I'm not trying to disrespect the memory of Dr. Morrell or Matthew with all this stuff," Anthony says. "I know it sounds crazy, but...there might be something to it."

"After hearing that, I can understand why you think so," I reply.

By this time, we've both finished eating. The dining hall is still buzzing, though not as much as before. Anthony moves his plate and cup to the side, then pulls out a stack of photocopies from his backpack.

"I...I know I could be wrong, but I think all of these things that have happened, or even just some of them, I think they're connected." He flips through the stack with his thumb like a deck of cards. "These are all news stories from the past ten years of anyone who has died suddenly or gone missing in Flickerwood." He hands the papers to me. "Dr. Morrell and Matthew aren't isolated incidents. They're part of a larger chain."

"Where did you find all these?" I ask, astonished.

"The library has access to the digital archives of local newspapers," he explains. "As a history major, I use them a lot."

I skim over the first page, feeling a bit overwhelmed. Just as Anthony said, dated three years ago, the article tells of Elijah Martin, a Wynhurst University student who was found in the woods after being lost for over twenty-four hours. Dated nine years ago, the next proclaims that a local youth disappeared while riding his bike in Stone Creek Park. I suddenly remember the little white cross I saw propped against the tree when I was there with Matthew. A shiver runs down my spine.

The story after it tells of a girl who lived in the apartment buildings on the southeastern part of town; she disappeared seven years ago. Following that, another article details how, a day after walking through the woods on their way home from work, two men were found dead in their homes. They died of sudden cardiac arrest—similar to Dr. Morrell.

Sheepishly, Anthony pulls a rolled up piece of paper from his bag. "So...I know it's a bit of a conspiracy theorist thing to do, but I simplified it a little. I made a map." He unfurls the paper on the table. I glance around at the other students in the dining hall, hoping we don't look too conspicuous. He could just be showing me a school project, after all.

"These red dots are all the people who have unexpectedly dropped dead, usually from some sort of cardiac incident. I know a good portion are probably just from natural causes, but some are particularly…intriguing. They're usually related to the woods, too. Like this one." He points to a dot. "This woman's dog got off its leash. She had to run after it into the forest near campus. They found her body two days later, and they said she dropped dead from some heart issue. But she was only in her 30s." He shrugs.

"Now the stars," he explains, "are the disappearances. There were only four of them that I saw. Most recently, of course, was my friend three years ago, but he was the only person to be recovered. Before that, there was a college student who went missing from the train station, the girl from the apartments near the forest, and the boy from the park."

I take in the map, overwhelmed by the information sitting in front of me. If there is even a modicum of truth to Anthony's theories, we're in way over our heads. "H-have you thought about bringing this to the police?" I stutter.

He shrinks back, his air of confidence dissipating. "I…I dunno. What police officer is going to take all of this seriously?"

"I mean, you've done a lot of research…" I start to argue, but stop when I remember what happened after Matthew talked with the police. If Anthony wants to keep quiet, I'm not going to be the one to pressure him into doing otherwise. "Well, if you're not going to the cops, why choose to tell me?"

He gazes at me with earnest brown eyes. "Believe it or not, for as much as I talk about the legends of Flickerwood, I don't often talk about my personal experience with them. You…I figured you wouldn't judge me. Like me, you think something suspicious is going on, even though everyone else seems to just brush it under the rug. I thought you'd be one of the few people to believe me. I had to tell someone."

It strikes me that I've missed a blessing; it is nice to have someone else who doesn't just dismiss the idea that Dr. Morrell and Matthew could be murder victims. My mind drifts to some of the things I might like to get off my own chest.

We share a brief smile, but worry returns to my mind.

"Aren't you scared of getting in trouble for talking about this stuff?"

He tilts his head.

"What do you mean? Like, by being overheard?"

"Well, that, but also...I was told it's illegal to discuss an ongoing investigation with anyone but the police."

He frowns. "Who told you that?" I'm grateful he doesn't wait for an answer. "I mean, lawyers often advise against it, I think, but it's far from illegal. Maybe if you're a juror, but if you were robbed or saw a crime or something, wouldn't you talk it over with your friends? My uncle's a lawyer."

I'm puzzled by this new information. His reasoning makes a lot more sense...maybe Matthew misunderstood? I should look it up later.

"There is another reason I wanted to share all that with you," Anthony says while rolling up the map. "I've been thinking. It's not that talking to the authorities is out of the question. But I think I'd have a better chance of them listening if I had some more concrete evidence. And, as much as I hate to say it, if there is anywhere that might hold some clues to this mystery...Well, I plan to hike back out to the cabin."

"You're serious?" I ask in disbelief. "After all you just told me?"

He nods. "I mean, I figure I'll go during the day. Things don't get really creepy until nightfall..." he rubs the back of his neck, then adds, "and, well, I was wondering if you'd want to come with me."

I blink. He wants me to go with him to this remote, abandoned cabin deep in the woods where his friend disappeared a few years ago and which is rumored to harbor a witch, a curse, an alien, or some combination of the three. What could go wrong? "When were you planning to go?" I ask simply.

He speaks slowly, watching my reaction. "...now?"

This is what I've been wanting these past several weeks, isn't it? Clues. Leads. An uncovering of the truth. If I want to know what really happened to Dr. Morrell and Matthew, this cabin may be the best shot. Besides. If you look at it the right way, we're just visiting a historic site. In broad daylight. We shouldn't witness anything too scary.

"You know what, I can't believe I'm saying this, but sure. I'll come with you. You remember where it's at?"

68

He pulls out two final sheets of paper and hands one to me. It's a map of the woods bordering Wynhurst, with the trails and cabin clearly marked. "I'm confident I can get us there."

Upon leaving the dining hall, Anthony leads me back towards the natural sciences building. We find the start to one of the nature trails and head into the woods. I make a mental note of where we entered. In the past, Dr. Gaines has led ecology classes back here. We identified trees and woodland creatures along the path and searched the creek for flatworms and tadpoles. His passion and care for all types of flora and fauna is contagious. Currently, most of the trees are missing their leaves, making them harder for me to classify at a glance. They all blend together as tall, brown spires stretching into the sky.

We take a wooden bridge over the water and make small talk as we follow the path. In the warmer months, the trails get a fair amount of use, but thanks to the winter chill, we seem to be the only ones out here. Regardless, I feel in my element. It's not until Anthony veers off onto a deer trail that I start having second thoughts.

"You sure it's that way?" I ask. He points out the path marked on the printed map we each have.

"Positive."

Tentatively, I step off the trail with him. We walk single-file, with Anthony in front and me following behind. "This isn't considered, like, trespassing, is it?"

He gives a light shrug. "Technically, we're still on school property. The cabin doesn't come with a lot of acreage, so we can get pretty close before it turns into private land." He jumps up on a fallen tree and walks along it like a balance-beam. "Actually, I heard Wynhurst was trying to purchase it from the bank. This is around where Dr. Morrell wanted to build the art building."

"Really? How do you know that?"

"One of my friends got a job in the fundraising department after he graduated. But also, their projected blueprints are on the website."

We turn deeper into the woods. I notice the peeling white bark of a sycamore tree, its branches almost beckoning us onward. "They would have to tear down a lot of these trees for that, wouldn't they?"

"Yep. I think the plan was to bulldoze the cabin and clear a sizable section for expansions."

Every time our class would take the trails, Dr. Gaines would stress the importance of conservation and native plant life. A prick of sadness jabs at my heart. "It'd be a shame to destroy more of this."

"Well, things are likely on hold for now. The board might decide to head in a different direction."

"I hope they do," I reply. "So what kind of clues do you think we might find at the cabin?"

"I'm not sure, but it could be anything. UFOs, sigils, fingerprints, a confession—who knows." He sighs. "A part of me hopes we find something of use, and a part of me is afraid of what we'll uncover."

Though he can't see, I nod in agreement.

"We're coming up on it soon," Anthony says. "I remember it being very run down and spooky-looking. There were vines growing up the sides, and the roof was nearing collapse. The inside was just as bad. We even explored the basement but didn't find anything besides furniture and books that were too damaged to read. It'll probably be in even worse shape by now—" he freezes in his tracks, mouth agape.

I freeze too, afraid of what he's seen. Moved by curiosity, I peer around his shoulder, and suddenly a cabin comes into view. "Wow. That doesn't look very run down at all."

"Exactly," he responds in a whisper. "What the heck?"

"Are you sure this is the same one?"

"Absolutely. It's definitely the same one, but..."

I creep forward to get a better view. Before us is a small clearing of trees. A quaint log cabin stands in the center. A section of creeping plants still climb the wall but in a tame, decorative fashion. To the right of the cabin is a small greenhouse, padlocked shut with a heavy chain. To the left is a patch of dirt for a driveway, on which sits a classic Dodge Monaco, like the cop cars in old movies. As far as I can see, no light shines from any of the windows, and the chimney produces no smoke.

"Someone else must have bought it. Do you think they're home?" Just as I take another step forward, the front door swings open. Instinctively, Anthony and I crouch down to avoid being seen. A woman in black boots, jeans, and a thick flannel jacket emerges from the doorway. In her right hand, she holds an axe. I turn to look at Anthony, but his eyes are fixed straight ahead. As she gets closer, my muscles tense up. Did she see us? Thankfully, she stops a few yards away at a large stump in the ground. Pulling from a pile of logs, she positions one on the stump, then raises the axe.

Smack. The metal blade splits through the wood with a satisfying clap. Methodically, she removes the split pieces and lines up another log. Once enough pieces are gathered at her feet, she brushes back her flannel, revealing a large knife strapped to her side. She pulls it from its sleeve and slices off a length of twine, then binds the split pieces of wood together. In such close proximity, her identity is unmistakable.

Professor Leighton.

Chapter 11

All in My Head

When I make it back to my dorm, I find Marissa on the phone with her boyfriend, relaying the events of the day. She waves when I walk in.

"Yeah, well we had the assembly this morning…He died after going to a party…They said it was alcohol, I think…" She looks sheepishly in my direction before continuing. "…It reminds me of that other student who overdosed at the diner a few years ago…Yeah, the RA told me the story…It's really getting out of hand…Wow, really? That many at your school? …mhm…The nurse was talking about that new drug, too. Deadlier than fentanyl…"

I sit down at my desk, knowing I need to get some homework done. Just as I'm about to put headphones on and tune out the world, I hear Marissa hang up the phone.

"Hi Addy, how are you doing?" she asks. I twist in my chair to face her.

"Um, I'm alright," I answer, following with the catch-all college response. "Tired."

In line with the social custom, Marissa nods. "Same." She opens her laptop and puts on her own set of headphones. I turn back to my desk. The library book on the history of Flickerwood is still sitting on the corner. I should probably return that. I open my backpack, and my hand touches a notebook—the same one I used earlier to record the various theories about Dr. Morrell. I pause, soberly realizing that the last time I wrote in here, Matthew was still alive. I place the notebook on my desk, then lay the map to the cabin beside it.

I look over my shoulder. Marissa isn't paying any attention. The glow from her laptop illuminates her face, and she laughs quietly at whatever video she's watching. She seems to have moved on from the topic of Matthew.

Solemnly, I bow my head and pray for his family, as well as for the family of Dr. Morrell. I wonder if his parents learned anything new. Hopefully the police are making some progress, even if behind the scenes. Matthew said they were going to reopen the investigation on Morrell. Now that Matthew himself has been found dead...well, they should be even more interested in getting to the bottom of things.

Once again, a guilty feeling gnaws at me. Should I be contributing what I know? It's not much, but what if it's important?

Thump! I nearly jump out of my seat, startled by the noise behind me. I snap my head to look at Marissa, visions of a crazed roommate scratching at the walls swirling in my head. She looks at me blankly.

"Sorry. My foot accidentally hit the wall."

I exhale, my heart rate returning to normal. "It's all good. Just scared me." I chuckle, then turn back around. Of all people to live in that cabin, the fact that it turned out to be Professor Leighton...I'm not sure if that makes her more suspicious, or if *I* should be the one warning *her* of its dark history.

Anthony's talk of spiritual forces has got me on edge. For the first time in a long while, I reach for my Bible. I open to the Gospel of Mark.

Lord, I do believe. Help my unbelief.

That night, I don't sleep well, and I wake up quite a few times. I can't seem to escape the conviction that I'm hiding some important piece of evidence. Some part of me knows I'm overreacting, but my mind fixates on it, convincing me I'm a terrible person.

Exhausted by the torture of my own psyche, I spring out of bed before the sun is up on Tuesday and grab my phone.

I look up the tip line for the local police force and—driven by the desire to escape the overwhelming guilt and the crushing weight of God's disapproval—I press call.

"Hello, you've reached the Flickerwood Borough Police Department. This is Chief Eric Boyer speaking. Please state your full name and reason for calling."

Though I was hoping to remain anonymous, the social pressure leads me to comply. "A-Addy Warner," I stutter. "I'm calling to share some information about the death of Matthew Bruner."

There is silence for a beat, followed by a heavy sigh into the phone. The speaker crackles with the breath. "There isn't a case for Matthew Bruner. We determined his death was not a homicide. There's nothing to investigate. Have a nice day."

Click.

I stand frozen in shock, my mouth agape. He just hung up on me. I didn't even get a chance to say anything! Well. At least I can say I tried. Maybe he's right. Maybe there isn't a killer after all.

At the end of the day, I manage to catch Sid and Micah at dinner. After a brief internal debate about being a third wheel, I join them at their table.

"Hey guys. Mind if I sit with you?"

"Not at all!" Sid assures me, moving her bag out of the way. Micah gets up to refill his drink.

"How are you doing?" I ask.

She shakes her head, watching Micah in the distance. "I just can't believe some people are trying to fear monger by connecting Dr. Morrell's passing with—you know—what happened with Matthew."

"Oh?" I say, dropping my eyes to my tray. Is that what I'm doing?

"Yeah," she continues. "One of my professors gave us this whole safety talk about not being out late at night and never leaving your drink unattended, as if there could be a serial killer or something on the loose." Seeing my blank expression, she explains further. "I mean, I guess there's nothing wrong with safety advice, but it just seems like she was sensationalizing the deaths." She crosses her arms. "I dunno. It just rubbed me the wrong way. The whole foul play thing is nonsense."

To my right, Micah stands over the table. "Foul play thing?"

"I was just telling Addy I had a professor today who drummed up the idea that there could be some sort of murderer around campus. It's a little ridiculous, don't you think?"

Micah slides back into his seat, looking a little pale. He forces a laugh. "Well, who knows? None of us can really say."

There is a marked change from his usual casual demeanor regarding Dr. Morrell. Sid notices too.

Her voice softens. "Is everything okay?"

"Yeah, everything's fine," he says quickly.

She reaches forward. "I'm sorry about Matthew."

He smiles sadly and squeezes her hand. "Thanks."

As I return to my room for the night, my phone vibrates. I look at the screen, expecting a spam call. My heart seizes when I see who it is. *Flickerwood Police*. Though nervous, I pick up the call.

"Hello?"

"Yes, this is Chief Boyer calling from the station. Is this Addy Warner?"

"Yes, it is," I answer.

"Hi Addy. Since we spoke this morning, there have been some...new developments regarding Matthew Bruner. You didn't happen to be calling about a Bryn Leighton, did you?"

This time, the officer listens to my account of what happened between Matthew and Professor Leighton. When the exchange is finished, he once again abruptly hangs up. I breathe a sigh of relief. I'm free.

Chapter 12

The Witness

Despite the studying I did manage to do, all thoughts of plant taxonomy leave my brain when I enter class on Wednesday. I abandon my usual seat in favor of one near the back, trying to put as much distance between me and Professor Leighton as possible. Though I'm glad I released myself of the burden of information by talking to the police, I can't help but wonder what their investigation has uncovered. What happened that made them suddenly take my observations seriously? Soon, Professor Leighton begins to pass out the tests.

"You may start as soon as you receive your packet. Please don't forget to put your name at the top of the answer sheet." She sets a test packet and bubble sheet in front of me. "Addy," she greets.

I nod weakly. For what seems like an eternity, I squirm in the silence, trying to focus on the test but struggling to put Matthew out of my mind.

Rap, rap, rap. The whole class turns to look at the door. Someone stands outside, knocking furiously. "Police!"

Professor Leighton swiftly crosses the room to meet the two uniformed policemen entering through the door. "Hello, officers," she says in a hushed tone. "Can I help you? My class is actually working on a test right now, so I'd appreciate it if—"

She's interrupted by a gruff voice. "Are you Mrs. Bryn Leighton?"

"Well, it's Ms." she responds.

"Ms.?"

"Yes. Ms. Bryn Leighton."

There's a heavy sigh. "Well, *Ms.* Bryn Leighton, we're here to conduct a search of your belongings." The officers push past her into the room, closing the door behind them. Their name tags gleam in the light of the classroom.

"This can't wait until after class?"

"'fraid not," one says, charging towards her desk at the front of the room. His tag identifies him as Chief Boyer. The other officer stands near the door, resting his hand on his gun. Any student still working on the test drops their pencil.

Professor Leighton calmly steps aside. I try to study her body language. Does she seem concerned? "Well, then be my guest. It's all school property," she says, gesturing towards her desk. Boyer starts aggressively pulling out drawers and rifling through the contents.

The officer near the door—Hopewell—addresses the class. "Alright, you're all dismissed for today. Everyone out." He stands aside. Some people grab their stuff and light out as fast as possible. Others, like Sid and I, stall as long as we can, desperate to see what will happen. After a few minutes, we know we can't stay any longer. Officer Hopewell is waving us out the door. Sid prods me forward, and we exit into the hallway. He watches us walk away, ensuring no one sticks around to observe.

"Daaaang," Sid says, turning to me. "What was that about?"

"Well, I might have some idea..."

"Wish we could see more. They never tell us anything."

"Yeah—" A thought pops into my head. "Ya know, I wonder if they'll search her office next."

Sid stops. "Are you thinking what I'm thinking?"

We continue past the exit everyone is currently taking to the outside, then turn into the girls' bathroom just outside Professor Leighton's office. We don't have to wait long before we hear the officers coming our way. With our ears pressed against the door, we listen for their conversation.

"Ms. Leighton, would you kindly let us in to search your office?" one of the policemen asks.

I hear the metallic zip of a key being inserted into a door. "Of course," she says. "Like I said before, it's school property. You're welcome to it." The knob turns, and I hear the door swing open. A few seconds later, however, it slams shut again. Their voices become too muffled to make out. Sid and I sit in silence.

"How long should we wait?" Sid asks. "Eventually I'll have to go to my next class."

I check my blood sugar and glance at the time. "Hopefully not too long. I'd like to be here when they come out."

"Me too," Sid admits. We start pacing in a square in front of the door, trying to pass the time.

"Do you think she's doing drugs or something?" Sid asks. "I've heard of a few professors getting busted for that at other schools."

"No," I answer. "I think it's about Matthew, and maybe Dr. Morrell."

"Wait, really?" she asks, eyes wide. "I thought everyone was just making stuff up…"

At the sound of the office door opening, we fall silent and race to listen. The voices once again become audible.

"Alright, now we're going to search your vehicle and your residence—"

For the first time, Professor Leighton protests. "Actually, I don't consent to a search of my private property," she states firmly. Sid and I exchange a look.

"Did you just hear that?" I mouth.

"What?" Sid whispers back.

I wave the question away, trying to focus on what's happening in the hallway.

Chief Boyer raises his voice. "Excuse me? Ma'am, are you refusing to cooperate with law enforcement? I'm telling you now, we need to search your vehicle and your home. Is that clear?"

Professor Leighton doesn't waver. "I know my rights, sir. I believe I've been perfectly cooperative today. But if you would like to search my property, you'll need a warrant. That's the end of it."

78

"Okay, ma'am," he huffs. "If it's a warrant you want, it's a warrant you'll get."

"Am I free to leave?" she asks.

Officer Hopewell speaks up, "Actually, we'd like for you to come to the station and answer a few questions."

There's a pause in the conversation. I realize I'm holding my breath.

"Okay," she answers finally. "I'll go with you."

When they seem to have walked far enough down the hallway, Sid and I exit the bathroom. Walking slowly to put distance between us and them, we exit the building out the same door. They continue along the sidewalk, heading towards the parking lot. College students, though trying to look inconspicuous, flock to the pathway when they see a professor is being led away by two police officers. Several snap pictures on their phones. The biggest group is gathered around the police car.

One of the officers opens the back door of the patrol car, and Professor Leighton gets inside. So much for the facade of normalcy. I spot my roommate standing nearby. When the cops drive away, she turns around and, after seeing me, starts walking in my direction.

"Addy!" she exclaims. "I heard that a whole class was disrupted by the police today. Were you there?" she asks.

"We both were," I answer, pointing to Sid and myself. "It was crazy."

"Yeah," Sid agrees. "We were taking a test, and then these two police officers started banging on the door. They searched through her desk and her office."

"Who was the professor?" Marissa asks.

"She was new this semester," Sid says. "Professor Leighton."

As Marissa floats away from us, Micah approaches and slides his hand into Sid's. She smiles at the touch. Before he has a chance to say anything, Anthony comes running towards us.

"Did you guys see that, too?!" he asks, nodding towards the cop car now pulling out of the parking space. "Did your professor just get arrested?"

Sid shrugs, turning her palms upwards. She recounts our experience again. "I have no idea what they were looking for or what she did to become a suspect."

Micah stares intently at the police car until it disappears from view. "Actually," he says quietly. "There's been something I've wanted to tell you guys."

We all look to him intently.

He swallows. "Not here. Wanna meet up in my dorm?"

Later, we all gather in Micah's room. He and Sid sit on the bed, and Anthony and I take the chairs. "So...there's something I didn't tell you about Friday night." He wrings his hands together. "But I should probably start by explaining something else.

"Addy, you already know this, but Matthew had a strong belief that Dr. Morrell was murdered. He hinted about having witnessed something which led to this belief, but he didn't tell me any details beyond that. Honestly, I didn't think much of it. A few days before he died, he said he'd gone to the police to share whatever it was he saw. He seemed on edge, like he was worried someone might be after him." Micah rises from the bed and begins pacing back and forth.

"Friday night, I told him I was going to this party. I asked if he wanted to come, like always, even though he always says no. That night, however, he said he wanted to go with me. When we got to the house, I started talking to some friends, and we got split up. I don't think it was for very long, but eventually someone asked where he was.

"I figured I should go check on him, and I started looking around. He wasn't upstairs or anywhere in the house, so I wandered over to the sliding glass door leading to the patio..." His lip quivers, but he quickly regains his composure. "He was lying motionless on the concrete. But he wasn't alone. Someone else was crouched beside him. As I got closer to the window, I glimpsed something in their hand—a syringe."

Anthony clamps a hand over his mouth.

"I didn't tell you before because it was an ongoing investigation and all, but I figured it would be safe now." He stops pacing and steps towards us. "At the sight, I opened the sliding glass door, and the figure turned to look at me. I recognized the face—it was Professor Leighton."

Sid audibly gasps. "Micah, are you sure?!"

He nods. "I'm sure. I've thought it over and second-guessed myself, but that's what I saw. When she realized she'd been spotted, she turned and ran into the woods. By the time the other students realized what was happening and emergency personnel arrived, she was long gone."

My blood runs cold, and I realize I'm holding my breath. I exhale.

Micah sits back down on the bed. "As soon as they got there, I told the cops what I'd seen. They seemed to take me seriously, but I was a little worried when everyone kept saying he died of alcohol poisoning." He shakes his head. "Like I said, Matthew didn't really drink. And for the amount of time we were there—he would have had to down an insane amount of shots or something to become that intoxicated…it just doesn't add up." He exhales. "So I'm glad to see that the cops came and did something about it, finally."

Sid turns to me with an expression of disbelief. "That's— I can't—I never—" she stumbles over her words. "I never would have guessed Professor Leighton was guilty of—of *murder*! We were just in her class this morning!" She gazes into space, focused on nothing in particular, likely trying to comprehend this new revelation.

My eyes drop to the floor, then fall on Micah. I nod towards him. "To be honest, I thought she was a bit suspicious, but I never thought she would have done something so bold. Actually, I talked to the police about her, too. When Matthew got in the cop car to go share his story, I noticed Leighton watching him. A few days later, he told me she drew him into her office and gave him a vague threat. Something along the lines of 'there's a target on your back.'"

Micah flinches.

Anthony shakes his head, incredulous. "So she's in jail now, right? I mean, they can't possibly let her walk free."

Micah looks to Sid and me.

"I would hope so," Sid replies. "I mean, they took her away in a cop car. And an eyewitness account like that should be more than sufficient evidence for an arrest."

"Yeah," I agree. Her logic checks out. "I didn't see them put her in handcuffs, but that doesn't mean they didn't arrest her at the station. I don't know how you wouldn't get arrested for that."

Anthony's index finger flies through the air, as if pointing to imaginary digits in a math problem only he can see. "If I'm understanding correctly, it sounds like Matthew became a target because he knew something about Dr. Morrell's killer. Which, for starters, means Dr. Morrell really was murdered. And secondly, if it's true that Professor Leighton is the one who killed Matthew, it stands to reason that she might also be the one who killed Dr. Morrell."

Micah runs his fingers through his hair, slouching his shoulders.

Sid draws her eyebrows together. "Why would Leighton kill Dr. Morrell? I mean, she's brand new, as far as we can tell..."

Anthony taps his chin and exchanges a glance with me. "Maybe she didn't like Dr. Morrell's plans to expand into the woods..."

Micah, who up until this point has been listening intently, scoffs, "The woods? Again? Like the witch?"

"No," I breathe, recognizing his train of thought. "On Monday, Anthony took me into the woods to find the creepy cabin from the story. He said it had been abandoned forever, but when we got there...it wasn't run down at all. It was clearly inhabited, and the person who came outside was none other than Professor Leighton. Morrell's expansion plans would likely have leveled her house."

There is silence from Micah and Sid, as if they're not quite sure what to do with this information.

"A part of me really wishes I would have asked Matthew what he'd seen," Micah says sadly. "I wonder if he saw Leighton kill Morrell."

I hesitate, thinking back to the promise I made Matthew. I sigh. I guess it doesn't matter much now if I share. The worst has already happened.

I speak up. "Do you...do you actually want to know what it was that Matthew saw? The information he was killed for knowing?"

Before saying it out loud, I hadn't really considered the danger *I* might be in. That day, when Matthew got into the cop car, Professor Leighton saw me, too.

"He told you?" Micah asks.

I nod.

"Well, of course I want to know!" he exclaims.

Sid agrees. "Please!"

Anthony leans towards me, listening intently.

"Just...be careful," I start, suddenly concerned about safety. "If the culprit ever knows we know this...well, it's not a stretch to say we could end up like Matthew. Can I trust you guys?"

"It'll be between us," Sid assures.

Micah nods.

"Of course," Anthony says.

With a fair amount of anxiety, I relay the story Matthew told me at Stone Creek Park, about the man and the water bottle swap.

"Gray-haired man?" Sid says. "Well that definitely wasn't Professor Leighton."

"Do you think Matthew got it wrong? Maybe that wasn't actually what killed him?" Micah asks.

"Or, if it was," Sid says, "it sounds like there's more than one killer at work here."

"It's starting to seem that way," Anthony says. "Maybe Professor Leighton is working with someone."

"Addy, did Matthew have any idea who this guy might have been?" Micah's voice is strained, desperate.

I shake my head, sorry to give him the bad news. "He didn't recognize him."

Sid places a hand on his knee. "I'm sure the police will find out whoever it was. It's only a matter of time, now."

I nod along, hoping she's right.

As we prepare to leave, Anthony stops in the doorframe. He turns to face Micah. "Hey, man...I'm sorry about all this. I...it's hard to lose a friend like that."

Micah's expression softens, and a silent understanding passes between them. He nods. "Yeah. It is."

Mere seconds after closing the door, Micah suddenly yanks it back open, phone in hand. "Guys, wait," he calls.

The three of us stop in our tracks.

Micah walks towards us, holding his phone forward.

"I just got this news alert."

With a puzzled expression, Sid takes the phone from him. We all peer over her shoulder to read the article.

Though previously thought to be an alcohol-related incident, police have uncovered new information related to the death of Wynhurst University student Matthew Bruner. At the insistence of his parents, a more thorough toxicology screen was conducted, which found a significant level of cyanide poison. What appeared to be a tragic accident has now become a murder investigation. Based on an eyewitness testimony of her presence and involvement at the scene, the primary suspect is a professor at Wynhurst who has been taken in for questioning by police...

"Cyanide," Sid breathes.

"Well, there you have it," Anthony says with wide eyes.

There on the page is the confirmation of my suspicions. Matthew didn't die from alcohol or partying. He was killed. And now that fact isn't a hunch bouncing around in my head, but public knowledge.

I gaze at the doors lining either side of the hallway, knowing that behind each one lies another dorm room. I wonder how many other students are also reading the article, and how long it will take for the truth to spread.

Chapter 13

Insufficient Evidence

Thursday morning is somehow less weird and more weird than I was expecting. There is no mass riot of panic like I half imagined, but a strange feeling starts to creep over me as I walk around campus. I pass a few acquaintances on my way, but none of them acknowledge my attempt at a polite greeting. Their focus is trained downward, and they avoid any eye contact. Another student enters a building ahead of me. Rather than hold the door, she lets it slam shut in my face. Maybe she just didn't see me?

When I grip the metal handle and tug it open myself, I'm met with a fairly empty study area. Usually there are groups of people sitting in chairs outside of classrooms, but almost no one is around now.

I scan my ID before entering the dining area for lunch. There's no line, so I walk right in. Behind me, however, I hear someone else enter and scan their card as well. Curious if it's someone I know, I look over my shoulder. At the sight, I nearly drop my plate.

Professor Leighton.

She spots me and nods politely. I snap my head away from her direction and try to focus on getting food.

What is she doing here?!

This proves somewhat difficult, as she slides in line directly behind me while I'm filling my plate. I hold my breath until—finally—I reach the end of the counter. Leighton curves around me, snatches some silverware, and heads towards the faculty seating area.

I'm grateful when I find Sid sitting alone. I take a seat opposite her.

"Uh—have you seen that Leighton is here?" I ask urgently.

She glances in the direction I'm nodding. "Yeah, apparently the cops let her go," she says quietly. "Micah's having a real hard time with it. He's a nervous wreck. Worried she'll recognize him as the witness from the party and come after him."

I ponder this as I inject myself. "He...he should be alright, don't you think?"

She bites her lip. "I sure hope so. Honestly, he's not the only one who's scared. I heard a lot of people debating whether they should drop their classes and call it quits for the semester. My morning class was half empty."

"I don't blame them. I can't believe she's still teaching," I say. Discreetly, we both look towards the faculty tables. One looks far more crowded than normal, with chairs pulled up far beyond its usual capacity. The other has only one occupant: Professor Leighton. She doesn't seem bothered by the isolation, however, and sits alone reading her book.

"I can't believe it, either," Sid agrees. "I mean, the police are trying to get a search warrant for her house! Even the other staff members feel unsafe. It's ridiculous."

I shake my head. "It is kind of weird. You'd think they would have at least suspended her or something."

"Right? I mean, I do love Dr. Gaines, but I feel like he needs to do something about this."

I nod along before realizing how right she is. "Yeah. He should. Maybe we should talk to him about it."

Late in the afternoon, during Dr. Gaines' open office hours, Sid and I head towards the natural sciences building. On autopilot, my feet take me to his old office, and I'm confused to find it empty. The plaque near the door no longer reads his name, and all of the shelves are bare.

Sid motions for me to walk further down the hall, and I suddenly remember his change in title. Sure enough, Dr.

86

Gaines now holds the end office reserved for the dean of the school—formerly belonging to Dr. Morrell.

A chill runs down my spine when I realize this is where Dr. Morrell was found dead. Sid knocks on the door.

"Come in!" Dr. Gaines calls from inside. She turns the handle and enters. "Sidney!" he says, turning towards us. "And Addy! Please, have a seat."

I'm immediately put at ease by his friendly demeanor. There are few professors I feel comfortable talking to about anything other than class, but Dr. Gaines is one of them. He smiles warmly and looks up from his computer.

I lower myself into a chair opposite his desk, propping my backpack against the side, as Sid sits down beside me. This office is certainly bigger than his old one. The books that used to be overflowing from his previous shelves barely fill half the available space. Even with his pictures and posters hanging on the wall, much of the room is left empty.

"Give me one second, let me see if I can find your files..." he says quickly. He begins rooting through the stacks of paper scattered around the room. "Sorry for the mess. If you can't tell, I'm not fully moved in yet."

"Actually, you probably don't need—" Sid's protest is cut short by a sound of victory.

"Ah-ha, Sidney. Now for Addy..." He opens two paper boxes full of files on the shelf behind him, but clicks his tongue and closes them again. "Wrong department..." He shuffles around some stacks on his desk, then opens a drawer and begins flipping through more files. So far unsuccessful, he yanks all the files from the drawer and plops them on the desk. As he does so, a loose piece of paper falls out and drifts to the floor. "No...no...Warner?" He sets a hand on his chin, his fingertips stroking the newly-emerging stubble. "You might be in the other filing cabinet. Give me one moment. I'll be right with you." He rises from his seat and walks out of the room, seemingly unaware of the paper he dropped.

Sid reaches down to pick it up, but as she goes to lay it on his desk, her eyes widen.

"Addy!" she hisses, shoving it towards me.

"What?" I ask, glancing at the paper.

Printed on university letterhead, there's a phrase at the

top in big red letters: *Warning of Termination*. I scan the first few sentences. It's dated November of last year—almost three months ago, and reads:

Dr. Neil Gaines: This letter serves as a formal warning of an impending termination of employment at Wynhurst University. You are hereby placed under a state of probation, in which you must meet the following conditions...

At the bottom, it is signed by none other than the former dean of the school, Dr. Gregory Morrell.

Before I can read any more, I hear footsteps approaching from the hallway. Panicked, I jump to my feet and tuck the paper face down in the stack of files on Dr. Gaines' desk. It disappears amidst the rest of the paperwork. I flop back down in my seat just before he opens the door.

"Found it," he says, waving a piece of paper in the air. He returns to his desk chair. "Now, how can I help you both?"

It takes all my energy to keep from glancing back towards the stack of papers.

"Um, we actually came because we wanted to talk about the new ecology professor," Sid says.

"Professor Leighton," I clarify.

"Oh?" he says, pushing his reading glasses up on his head to rest among his gray hair. "Is something wrong? I thought she did great in her interview. Had an impressive resume, too. But sometimes you don't know how a professor will do until you hear from the students. What's up?"

"Well, it's not necessarily about her teaching," Sid says. "I don't know if you heard, but there was a news article that came out yesterday. Matthew Bruner—the student who just passed away—was found to have been poisoned by cyanide."

He eyes us both.

"And Professor Leighton is the primary suspect," I say. "The police came and searched her things during class yesterday."

"To be honest, we're concerned for our safety," Sid says.

I nod in agreement. "People don't feel safe coming to class or being on campus."

"A ton of people skipped in my morning classes," Sid adds.

We both watch him intently, waiting for a response.

He spreads his hands. "Listen. There's no need to panic,

here. Midterms are coming up in a few weeks—it's not unusual for students to start using their skips to catch up on assignments. I am aware of the situation with Professor Leighton. Believe me, it's my job to stay on top of things. But as of yet, no one has been arrested or charged with a crime. She has been nothing but cooperative with the police, and I see no reason to punish her. People are innocent until proven guilty."

My mouth falls open. I can barely believe what I'm hearing. "But it's also possible she really is guilty of murder. Shouldn't she be put on leave or something while the police investigate?" I protest.

"I hear your concern, I do. But trust me, if I believed Professor Leighton was truly a danger to students I wouldn't allow her to still be teaching. Right now, there is no reason to take any further action against her."

"So, you want us to just continue going to class? As if nothing happened?" Sid asks.

He wobbles his head back and forth, then nods. "Yes. Preferably. And if you have any more concerns, please don't hesitate to tell me. But that's how things will go for the time being." He taps his fingers on his desk. "Besides—and I probably shouldn't say this—but the ecology program can't really afford to lose a professor right now, with all the responsibilities I've had to take on."

Dr. Gaines unscrews the cap of a water bottle and takes a drink. It's a metal cylinder with a decal of the university logo on the side, the same kind issued to all staff members. Only a handful of professors actually use them, however. At the sight, my will to argue leaves.

"I do take the safety of my students very seriously. If the situation changes, I'll let you know."

"Thank you for meeting with us," I say, reaching for the strap on my backpack.

He nods. "Anytime."

I rise. Thankfully, Sid follows suit. I can't get out fast enough.

I open the door and let Anthony into the private study room

we booked in the library. Sid and Micah are already sitting around the table.

Micah's leg bounces beneath the table, causing the whole thing to shake. He furiously chews on a piece of gum. Nervously, he glances between Sid and me.

"So. How did it go?"

Sid rests her chin on her palm. Slowly, she breaks the news. "Not as well as we'd hoped. Dr. Gaines has no intention of suspending or firing her. He said nothing's been proven, and he doesn't think she poses any danger to students."

He shakes his head. "Seriously?! They'll fire a professor for a slight disagreement with the board, but a murder suspect? No, please, carry on teaching..." Fear brings out an edge in his words. "I guess the fact that I *saw* her on the scene *holding the murder weapon* just wasn't evidence enough."

Sid sets a hand on his back. "Hey. It's gonna be okay."

He puts his head in his hands, and his voice grows softer. "I'm next. Not only can I not do anything to get justice for Matthew or his family, but it's only a matter of time before she comes for me, too." He straightens. "Should I drop out? I'm really thinking about it."

"Before you make any decisions, we have more to share," I interject.

Sid nods. "I didn't want to consider the possibility, but Addy and I have been talking. When we were in Dr. Gaines' office, we found a warning letter. As it turns out, Dr. Morrell was trying to fire Dr. Gaines. Because Dr. Morrell died, Gaines got a promotion, but if Morrell had lived, he would've lost his job."

"Really?" Anthony says, perking up. "Potential motive?"

"It's possible," I answer. "He also had the staff water bottle Matthew mentioned, and his physical features are similar to the description...it led us to believe his defense of Professor Leighton may not be entirely impartial."

"You think they may be working together?" Anthony asks.

"I'd like to think not," Sid says, "but why else would he so adamantly insist on her innocence?"

"Two deaths. Two killers," Micah says somberly.

"It's only circumstantial evidence, of course," Sid adds. "We don't know for sure. But we felt wary enough not to share any more with him."

"Is that it, then?" Micah asks. "She's here to stay? I mean, if Gaines is the dean, there's not much we can do, is there?"

"Not much," Anthony says. "Unless you want to talk to President Conley."

The three of us stare at him.

"We could do that?" I ask.

"Sure. If you want, I can email him tomorrow morning and set up a time. His TA is usually quick about getting back to people."

"That'd be great," Sid says.

"Might be the best shot we have," Micah says.

"And in the meantime," Sid says, looking particularly at Micah, "we'll all be extra careful. The more we investigate, the more reason they have to come after us. But now that we know the weapon is cyanide, we also know what to watch out for. We'll just be careful about food and drink..."

"And syringes?" I add.

"Those too."

"Well, I've gotta head upstairs," Anthony says, rising to his feet. "Historical society meeting tonight. Anyone is welcome to join. And I'll email President Conley bright and early."

Chapter 14

Feeling Sick

On Friday, I hit snooze on my alarm twice before finally rolling out of bed. I quickly put on clothes and head out the door. Why am I so tired? My tongue sticks to the roof of my mouth. Ugh. And thirsty.

At the end of my first class, I check my phone and find that Anthony has sent a group text.

Meeting with president 2:30?

I respond with a "thumbs-up."

The four of us meet outside the admin building, then walk in together. The president's office lies at the end of a long, narrow corridor. The desk where his TA usually sits is empty, so, after a brief deliberation, we all head straight to his office. The door is cracked, and his voice can be heard as he converses with someone.

Anthony knocks.

"Come on in!" he calls.

Slowly, Anthony opens the door, and we all spill into the room. President Conley is seated at his desk. His glasses are perched halfway down his nose, and his salmon-colored shirt is paired with a brightly-patterned Dr. Seuss tie. He smiles.

"Quite the gang you've got here."

The man sitting across from him turns to face us. I'm startled to realize it's the mayor. He is dressed in a formal black suit, absent even the trace of a wrinkle. The buttons of his white dress shirt strain against the slightly round form of his belly. I can't help but be reminded of a penguin, or a clean-shaven Mr. Monopoly.

"Hello," he says with a wave, also smiling.

Only now do I notice a third man reclining against the wall in the corner of the room. His suit is a silvery gray color, which matches his thinning hair and full beard. With his hands in his pockets, he greets us with a silent nod.

"Am I in trouble?" President Conley asks jokingly. He chuckles to himself. "Nah, what can I do ya for?"

"Well," Anthony starts, eyeing the mayor and the other man, "we came here to talk about a certain professor."

Evidently noticing Anthony's unease, Conley waves a hand. "Don't mind these two gentlemen. This is Dr. Boyer," he says, motioning to the man in the corner. "He's one of Wynhurst's long-standing board members. It's a shame really, that students aren't more familiar with the people on the board—but anyhow. We were just finishing up a meeting, and Mayor Sayer dropped by."

The mayor quickly jumps from his seat and offers us his chair. "Please, don't let me get in the way. We're all done." He gazes at us expectantly. After an awkward moment, Sid is brave enough to sit down. Anthony takes the chair next to her.

"A professor? Which one?" President Conley asks.

The mayor steps away from the desk and stops near the door. He begins to pull on his coat, dressing to leave. Dr. Boyer peels himself from the wall and heads towards a small side table housing a Keurig. He presses a button, initiating the familiar hum of water coming up to temperature.

Reluctantly, Anthony answers. "Professor Leighton. The new ecology professor. You know—" he says, waving his hand in a circle. "The same professor who was just questioned by the police."

"Ah," he says, nodding. His demeanor turns serious. "Yes, I know what you're referring to."

"Well," Micah says forcefully, "is she going to be suspended or fired or arrested or…?"

Dr. Conley glances towards Mayor Sayer, who has since paused in putting his scarf on.

"Now," he says carefully, "you all know I can't speak to

things like that. That's all confidential."

"I understand, sir," Anthony says, "but student safety comes first. We have some right to know what's going on."

I nod. "We're here because Sid and I are in her class. We're not sure if it's even safe to go."

Dr. Conley scans our faces, considering. "What I can tell you is this. An investigation is still underway, and we are following the advice of the police. They assured us there is no current danger to students."

From my periphery, I see Mayor Sayer nod, then tie his scarf around his neck.

"No current danger?" Micah asks. "How can you be so sure? I mean, two people have died on campus in less than two months!"

Dr. Conley spreads his hands. "Like I said, that's all I can tell you. But rest assured. We have things under control."

I see the panic in Micah's face. The truth, I'm sure, is hitting us all at the same time. We took a swing and missed. Looks like, for the time being, Leighton is here to stay. If she decides to kill again, there's nothing we can do about it.

Sssssss. A stream of steaming hot coffee pours into a styrofoam cup. Dr. Boyer adds in some cream and sugar packets, then presses the lid on top.

In defeat, we gather ourselves and return to the hallway. We walk single-file, and I end up at the back of the line. Suddenly, I feel a tap on the shoulder.

I flinch, jerking my head around. Dr. Boyer stands, coffee in hand. "I couldn't help but overhear," he begins, "that you're all a bit concerned about Ms. Leighton." By this time, Micah, Sid, and Anthony have noticed the visitor and come to a stop. I stare at him intently.

"What about it?" I ask.

"Well," he says, gazing ahead anxiously. "You're not the only ones. Personally, I share your feelings. Wynhurst is not doing nearly enough to protect the student body." He lowers his voice even further. "My son is the chief of police—"

Of course! Chief Eric Boyer, the cop I talked to. That's where I've heard the name before.

"—And they've been trying to get a search warrant for this woman. Old Judge Ritner is half-senile, though," he grumbles. "Denied. My son and his fellow officers are convinced she's guilty, but without the warrant, there's not much more investigating they can do. That's why everything's stopped in its tracks." He sighs. "I just wanted to say I agree with you. Leighton should absolutely be suspended. I'm working to convince the board, but I'm only one vote."

"Thank you, sir," Micah says. "We appreciate that. I was starting to feel like we were the only ones."

Dr. Boyer nods and offers a small, tight-lipped smile. "Just be careful out there, kids. Don't get yourselves into trouble. But—" he holds up a finger, "if you find anything that could help us out, be sure to tell me or Eric down at the station. You can always look me up in the staff directory."

He pats me lightly on the shoulder and takes a drink of his coffee. "Well, I'd better go. See you all around." With a wave, he heads down a stairwell to the left, heading to the exit.

With a glum mood among us, we all sit at a booth for dinner.

"At least we tried," Anthony says, ever the optimist. "Maybe that Boyer guy will actually get the board to do something."

"Maybe," Micah mutters. "I just can't believe the cops were denied a search warrant."

"She definitely didn't want them in her house, or her car," Sid says. "Maybe she really is hiding evidence that could put her away."

I suck down my glass of water. The dry air must be making me thirsty. "What happens if they were to go in and search anyway?" I ask.

Anthony shakes his head. "Cops aren't allowed to do that. It'd be illegal search and seizure, and any evidence recovered wouldn't be admissible in court." He snickers to himself. "You know, it's ironic. If some random person happened to rob her and accidentally found evidence, that would count. I just read about a case like that."

"What are the chances of that, though?" Sid asks sadly.

"Are there any other ways we could find evidence?" I ask, trying to brainstorm. "Could we interview anyone else who was at the party? Or maybe look more into Dr. Morrell's cause of death?"

"Maybe," Anthony says weakly. Even he seems tired.

"Addy, do you think you'll go to class on Monday?" Sid asks.

I bite my lip. "I—I'm not sure yet."

Chapter 15

Hindsight

By Sunday, it's clear I have a cold. After spending Saturday suffering from diabetic-related thirst and checking my ketone levels, I wake up the next morning with a sore throat, a runny nose, and a slight fever. I grab my phone and text Anthony to let him know I won't be coming to church with him. Truth be told, I'm kind of relieved. I still want to go eventually, but…maybe next week.

He responds with: *No problem. Feel better!*

I smile and fall back onto my bed. I'm almost happy the symptoms have progressed; at least my mouth no longer feels like it's coated in salt. The doorknob jiggles, and Marissa re-enters our room holding her curling iron. I launch into a coughing fit.

"Are you feeling okay, Addy?" she asks.

"I think I've got a cold."

"Want me to bring you back some breakfast?" she offers.

Probably best not to contaminate the whole dining hall. "That'd be great, actually. Would you?"

"Sure thing."

When she returns, she hands me a to-go container full of eggs, toast, and some fruit, then heads out to start her day. I'm left alone with my breakfast and my thoughts. I bolus for the food, remembering I'll have to watch my numbers more closely. As the day goes on, more people clear out of the dorms. I drag myself into the hallway and refill my water bottle at the fountain. A girl walks past me carrying a large sack of clothes. I groan. Yeah, I should probably do my own laundry at some point. I should also call my parents. Maybe after they're done with church.

A hot shower opens up my sinuses. Though I have a mountain of homework I could be doing, I don't think I can muster the motivation to start any of it. Besides, it's Sunday. I always feel a little guilty for doing schoolwork on Sundays. It's supposed to be a day of rest, right? I slog my way back to my room and sit down at my desk.

To make myself feel better, I open my Bible. What's something nice I could read? I flip through the Old Testament and land on a classic story: Daniel and the Lion's Den. It's nice to read a familiar narrative. I remember learning this one in Sunday school. Still, I can't help but find questions creeping in as I read. Daniel was thrown to the lions because he didn't stop praying to God for one day? Couldn't he have prayed silently? The authorities never would have known... My shoulders slump as I sigh. I surely wouldn't live up to the standard of Daniel. How many days do I go without praying even absent the threat of persecution?

I shut the Bible, bow my head, and pray my usual prayer of forgiveness. While I think of what else to say, my phone goes off. It's my mom. I snatch it up and swipe to answer.

"Addy? Hello?"

"Hey, mom, I'm here," I respond.

"Hi! Is this a bad time?"

"No, I'm free," I assure her, reaching for a tissue.

"Can I switch to video?"

"Sure. Here, I'll do it." I press the video call button, and soon my mom and dad become visible on my phone screen. I wave.

"Hi! It's good to see you," my mom says.

"How are things going?" my dad asks. "Anything new happening?"

A knot of anxiety immediately forms in my stomach. How are things going? Well, the main thing on my mind as of late has been Dr. Morrell and Matthew's murders, and how my professor is the primary suspect...but I don't think

I can share all that with my parents. My mom will just worry, and my dad will tell me I should be more careful, and maybe they'll want me to come home. Outside of that, there's all the questions I'm having about God and my faith...

"Um, well," I start to answer, "I have a bit of a cold."

"Oh, are you doing okay?" my mom asks.

"Yeah, I'm fine. Just taking it easy."

"Best thing you can do," my dad chimes in. "How are classes going?"

"Classes are good." I give what I think is a truthful answer. Aside from the police coming into one last week, they're all going well.

There's an awkward silence. "How about you guys?" I ask, directing attention away from myself.

"Well, remind me, but we'll need to get you a new house key," my mom says. "We've been doing some DIY projects, and last week we replaced all the doors, got some new locks. The house is looking like new."

I feel for my keychain, then hold up my childhood house key. "So this one no longer works?"

"Nope," she answers.

I set the key down on my desk, but find myself fixated on the little bead pendant it's paired with. The day my mom first gave it to me, back in elementary school, the beads were shiny and new. Now, after so many years of use, they've grown scratched and dirty. My whole life, every time I got home and unlocked the back door, this was the key I used. But just like that...it's suddenly obsolete.

When I was preparing for college, I was so focused on the changes I would face at school, I never stopped to think about how my hometown would change while I was gone. Each time I visit, it seems like a new business has closed, a new restaurant has opened, or a new construction project has been started. Little by little, the landscape of my childhood morphs into something unfamiliar. Part of me is afraid of what it will look like by the time I graduate.

My parents share more of what they've been up to, and my brother walks through and says hi. After a half an hour or so, they hang up, and I breathe a sigh of relief. I love my parents, and it's nice to talk to them, but for some reason they also bring stress.

When I wake up the next morning, I try to evaluate how I'm feeling. Better than yesterday but not 100%. I'll take the excuse to skip class. I grab my phone and text Sid.

Hey, are you still going to botany?

It doesn't take her long to respond.

I thought I would try. Should be safe enough in a large group. You?

No, I type back. *Still have a bit of a cold. Be careful...*

I will, she messages. *I'll let you know what happens.*

With the time I save by taking the day off, I plow through a considerable amount of my homework. In the late afternoon, I get a call from Sid. She recounts how class went. A little less than half the students showed up, and many were trying to drop the class. Professor Leighton said we didn't have to worry about Wednesday's test; the grade was dropped. However, we still have our laboratory assignment due this week.

As the last rays of light are disappearing, I check my email and realize my library book is due back. Wanting to avoid a fine, I jump to my feet and grab it off the shelf. I should only be gone for a few minutes, but I still shove a snack in my coat pocket, just in case. Juice box this time.

All bundled up, I head out the door and start down the pathway to the library. My first semester, I never felt unsafe walking alone on campus at night. People were always very friendly, security was out and patrolling. There was a cozy feel. Now, it's like a chill hangs thick in the air, and not just because of the winter weather. I feel more on edge.

As it comes into view, the glowing lights from the library provide a welcoming atmosphere. I'm happy when I make it inside. Immediately, I'm greeted by a gust of heated air and the comforting presence of other people. The library, at least, seems about the same as it always has. People are studying, reading, typing. I approach the front desk and hand over my book.

"Returning," I explain.

With a beep of the scanner, the girl behind the desk smiles. "You're all good."

As I turn to leave, Micah enters through the double doors, dressed in his security uniform.

"Hey," I say, waving. He waves back, but his expression remains stony. It's clear the worry is getting to him. He charges upstairs, committed to his routine inspection.

Reluctantly, I head back out into the cold. As I get further away from the building, the lamps lighting the way grow further apart, leaving considerable stretches of shadows. It's amidst this darkness that I notice a sound running parallel to my own footsteps. A sound like someone else walking.

I jerk my head around to see over my shoulder, but the path behind me is empty. The dark, well-trimmed grass on either side of the concrete also appears deserted. Probably just my imagination. I continue on, but only manage to walk a few steps before hearing the sound again. I turn around, this time glimpsing a faint blur moving in the shadows. My body freezes, and I stare hard into the black, my heart beating a million times a minute. My eyes, however, detect nothing.

With a growing feeling of anxiety, I turn back around and quicken my pace. Paranoia starts to take over my brain. Every shadow could be hiding a person. I strain my eyes to see, yet I fear what I might witness. I want to know, and I don't.

When I'm only a few yards from my dorm building, I break into a run. Desperately, I scan my key card and book it to my floor. Only when I make it to my room do I feel like I can relax. Who was that? What did they want? Or was my mind just playing tricks on me?

Chapter 16

The Key

On Tuesday, I power through a full day of classes. I finish an essay, stop to talk with friends, and linger at dinner. As I prepare to leave the dining hall, I close the book I was reading, feeling ready for the quiz I have on it tomorrow. Once my feet touch down on the sidewalk, however, it hits me. The one assignment I forgot to do—the lab assignment for botany. And it's due tomorrow. *Shoot.*

I'm still not convinced it's a good idea to go to Leighton's class, but considering how much of my overall grade this assignment is worth, my only real choice is to go or drop it altogether. I shake off my exhaustion and cut across campus to the laboratories, motivated by the panic of an imminent deadline.

When I get to the lab, I scan my ID. The motion-sensor lights turn on as I walk through the doorway. I'm the only one here. It's eerie, in a way, but also nice. I can do my work in peace. This shouldn't take too long. I just have to identify some specimens and do a few small experiments. To start, I take the sample ecology slides off the shelf and begin studying them beneath the microscope. Leaves, pollen, twigs, etc... Carefully, I record a description of each.

A few questions in, while I'm hunched over and peering into the microscope, I hear the beep of the door scanner, followed by the sound of someone entering the room. I look up, expecting to greet another student who also procrastinated. Instead, my heart skips a beat. Professor Leighton just walked in.

"Hi Addy," she greets. Her polite demeanor does nothing to calm my anxiety.

I'm too stunned to reply with words. I nod back. My eyes follow her as she briskly crosses the room. Maybe she just needs to grab something quick. Maybe she won't stay long. She opens the fridge and pulls out a tray of samples, then heads towards one of the big automated analyzer machines. To start it, she sticks her key in and begins loading samples.

I watch her plug in the desired settings and step back as the machine begins to work. I hold my breath, hoping she'll leave and just let it run. Unfortunately, she seems to settle in, setting her doctor's bag down and leaning against one of the lab tables.

I will myself to keep my eyes on my assignment. My pencil hovers over an equation, but my mind is fixated on Professor Leighton and the evidence surrounding the murders. I hear her boots tap against the tile floor as she paces back and forth. How much does she know I know? There are no cameras inside the rooms. Is it just a coincidence that we're in here at the same time, or something more?

I steal another glance in her direction, my eyes falling to the spot on her hip where I saw her wearing the knife. It's covered by her overcoat, but there is a slight wrinkle in the fabric. Is it hiding the outline of a weapon? My eyes flit back to my paper. As long as she stays over there...

Dread mounts in my body as the sound of her footsteps suddenly grows louder. Before I can react, she stops a few feet away.

"Have you solved it yet?"

I flinch so hard I nearly fall off my stool. I turn to look at her. "W-what?"

Her face is calm as ever. She points to the assignment in front of me. "The math equation. Sorry if I startled you."

I laugh lightly, relieved that I was simply being paranoid. She wasn't asking about the murder cases. Just homework. Of course. "Oh, uh, no. Just a little stumped on this one."

"Ah, you want any help?"

"No," I say, perhaps a bit too quickly. "Thanks. I think I can figure it out."

She nods and backs away. "Let me know if you need anything. I'm killing time until my night class."

Something in her demeanor is likable, and it almost puts me at ease. "You're taking a night class?" I venture.

"Teaching," she clarifies. "I guess it's the kind of thing they give to new professors, right? Three hours every Tuesday night."

I can't help but mirror her smile. "Yikes. What class is it?"

"Biology," she answers. "Part of the nursing program." Suddenly, a phone starts to ring. It sounds like an older ringtone. Professor Leighton reaches into her bag and pulls out a flip phone. She answers.

"Hello?...Oh, no problem, I have time. I'll be right there." She hangs up. "Dr. Gaines wants to meet with me," she explains. "Best not to keep the boss waiting." With a light-hearted smile, she slings her bag over her shoulder and heads towards the door. As she passes, she glances at my paper. "Looks like you're doing good work—keep it up." With that, she exits the lab.

I exhale, relieved to be alone. In the wake of her easy-going presence, I can almost understand why the police let her go free. Almost. Then thoughts of Matthew return to my head, and I'm disturbed at how easily a person can be deceived.

I go back to working on the equation, but something shimmers in the corner of my eye. I look to the side and quickly identify the shiny culprit: Professor Leighton's keys are still dangling from the analyzer machine. A sudden impulse overtakes me. I glance over my shoulder, then rise and walk towards them. Aside from the staff key, which needs to be inserted for the machine to operate, there are four keys attached to the ring. Two of them are rather small; they couldn't possibly go to a door. The third has the emblem of a car key. The fourth, however, is larger and actually looks very familiar.

I run my fingers over my own keychain. My old house key is of the same make as Professor Leighton's. It's different than the style used by the school, meaning it's not likely to go to anything on campus. If my assumption is correct, it's probably another house key. *Her* house key. My heart starts to race as I realize I'm staring at the key to the cabin.

My mind starts to turn. The police were denied a search warrant, meaning they can't go into her home. However, if a private citizen were to go poke around...well, according to Anthony, that could still count as evidence in court. Evidence enough, perhaps, to convict a murderer.

I hesitate, suddenly comprehending the gravity of what I'm considering. Would I actually break into someone's house?! I could go to prison for *years*! I wonder what kind of treatment they give diabetics behind bars...I shake my head. If Professor Leighton really is guilty, my *life* could be in danger, as well as Micah's and anyone else's in this town. Dr. Boyer basically said it himself. This case won't get anywhere unless someone can find more evidence against the killer. If not, Matthew and Dr. Morrell will never have justice. Their families will never have closure. At least not in this world. I bite my lip. If there's something in that house that could reveal the truth, maybe prison is a price worth paying.

Besides. I think I could get in and out without her even knowing. I check the door to the lab again. The hallway is empty. It's now or never.

With a rush of adrenaline, I pry apart the metal ring of my keys and slide off my house key. Before touching Leighton's keyring, I remember that fingerprints are a thing. I grab a pair of latex gloves from the wall, then carefully work the cabin key off the metal band.

Every stray noise makes me check over my shoulder. I have no idea what I would do if she walked in at the wrong time, so I just pray that she won't. It's a relief when I get her key off the ring, but it proves difficult to replace with my own. My hands are sweaty in the gloves, and the extra material dampens my fine motor skills. The key glances off the metal for the third time.

Suddenly, I hear footsteps in the hallway. My heart pounds against my ribcage; I don't have much time. By nothing short of a miracle, the key finally slides on. I grab the whole ring to keep it from swinging unnaturally, then charge back towards my table. I stuff the gloves, cabin key, and my own keys in my backpack just as Professor Leighton comes through the door.

I stare at my lab paper, hoping nothing on my face betrays what happened. Leighton sighs and walks over to the analyzer machine, which has since stopped. It's too late to turn back now. She records some data, takes the samples out, runs a few tests, then puts them back in the fridge. I grip my pencil as she goes to pull her keys out of the machine. She shouldn't notice any difference, right?

She holds them in her hand and looks them over. For a brief moment, the world seems to come to a stop. Evidently, she finds nothing amiss, as she tosses them in her bag.

"Well, I'm off to class. See you tomorrow?"

"Yep," I choke out.

After she leaves, I watch the door slowly close behind her, then latch shut. I frown at my lab assignment. If I'm committing a crime, missing a homework assignment is the least of my worries. I stuff it back in my folder and pull out the map Anthony gave me when we walked to the cabin. I think I can find my way back.

I unlock my phone and set a timer to go off in about three hours—right when Professor Leighton should be ending class. It's comforting to see how much time I have. I take out my keys and string the cabin key onto my own ring. If I didn't know any better, I'd say nothing had changed. I pack up my stuff and head to the door. I know if I falter, I'll lose my nerve.

Seeing no one in the hallway, I charge out the door and head outside. I march towards the back parking lot. Right now, to an outside observer, I could just be another student crossing campus. That ship sails, however, when I step foot into the woods. The barren tree branches distort the moonlight and cast shadows on the trail. It's much darker than the lamp-lit paths on the rest of campus. I shiver. I turn my phone flashlight on and try to keep it low.

This is crazy. This is crazy. This is crazy. What are you doing, Addy? My internal voice screams in protest, but I keep putting one foot in front of the other. For the greater good, right? To keep my mind off what I'm about to do, I try to identify the various sounds around me. A great horned owl hoots somewhere nearby. Less comfortingly, some coyotes howl in the distance. Out of nowhere, something furry shoots across the path and almost touches my foot. I gasp and jump back, waving my flashlight around. I glimpse the tail end of a possum as it disappears back into the trees.

I stand still for a moment, suddenly aware of how alone I am. I didn't tell anyone where I was going. How would I even explain this? I peer into the darkness, growing paranoid. Professor Leighton likely isn't working alone. Who else could be lurking in these woods, perhaps watching me? I start to pray as I walk. Is breaking into a murder suspect's house a sin? Before my conscience can tie itself into a knot, I push the question away. It's too late now. We can sort that out later.

As I get closer, it occurs to me that the cabin might be home to more than just Leighton. What if she has a husband or children or something? It seems unlikely, but I should keep an eye out. After what feels like an eternity, the cabin finally comes into view. All the lights are dark inside, and the car that was parked in the driveway is gone. It sure looks empty to me. As spooky as it is, I'm eager to escape the outside nightlife.

I pull my hood up, then creep onto the wooden porch. Only now do I have the presence of mind to think I should have grabbed another pair of gloves. I pull out the same latex ones and tug them back on. Then, hoping the key fits, I slide it into the front door. At first, I'm afraid it doesn't work, but with a little force the knob turns. Slowly, the door opens.

Chapter 17

Weapons and Tools

I wince as the hinges creak loudly. If there *is* anyone inside the house, they definitely would have heard that. I wait a few seconds. When no lights come on and no one comes to confront me, I step inside, closing and locking the door behind me.

Small beams of moonlight leak in from the windows, as well as from two large skylights in the ceiling above. I shine my phone flashlight around, illuminating the shadows cast by the trees outside. The house before me is not falling apart, as Anthony described, but actually looks quite well-kept. The first thing I notice is the sheer amount of plants. In the windowsills, on tables, on bookshelves and cabinets, even hanging from the ceiling—no corner is untouched by the vast array of potted plant-life. No less than four plants crowd around each window, though they're artfully arranged. Towers of herbs sprout familiar spices, and a well-trimmed tree sits in a pot beside the door.

To my left is the kitchen, and to the right is the living room. I first head to the right, finding a small sitting area beside a wood stove with nearby bookshelves overflowing with volumes. In the back right corner of the house is a small bathroom. Continuing along the back wall, past a spiral staircase, I enter what appears to be an exercise room. It contains a bench press and some weights, as well as some medals hanging on the wall that look like they're from the military. There's also a small closet housing a few tools, including the axe I saw earlier.

In the kitchen, an L-shaped countertop runs along two of the walls. Wooden cabinets hang above the counter, and dried herbs are strung from the ceiling. The vintage fridge and stove look like they're from the fifties. In the center of the room sits a wooden table with chairs, and in the far left corner is a walk-in pantry. The shelves are brimming with mason jars full of canned goods.

Having thoroughly explored the first floor, I return to the spiral staircase and ascend to the second floor. It's not as large as the floor below. There are only three rooms in a small corridor. One is a bedroom that is clearly lived in. The other contains a bed and furniture but appears unused. The third is a smaller room with a desk, a sewing machine, and several wooden chests. Of course, there are also more plants.

Save for the greenery, I really am alone in the house. I check my phone. Looks like I have a little over two hours before Professor Leighton comes back. I start going through the wooden chests but find only clothes and quilts. Among them are some Navy uniforms. I remember her telling the class she had a military background, and I shiver. I would like to think well of all veterans, but, unfortunately, I know it's not only good people who sign up to go to war. And then there are some who start out good but who become broken sometime during their service. Is that what drove her to kill? Some PTSD-induced insanity?

Moving on, I try the desk drawers, but they're mostly empty. In her bedroom, I search the bedside table. I mainly find books. There are a few old documents, but nothing incriminating.

I head back downstairs. What am I even looking for? Everything seems pretty normal. Was this all for nothing? I mean, it's not like she's going to have a confession written out and lying on the kitchen table.

As I stand in the darkened living room, a gust of wind blows against the outside wall, causing the wood to creak. Anthony's stories about this place start coming to mind. I try to ignore the parts about supernatural forces, lest I freak myself out, but I do remember he said there was a basement to the cabin. Where would that be? The spiral staircase doesn't go down any further. I re-examine the rooms on the first floor. Where would it make sense?

My instincts tell me to go to the kitchen. Once there, my focus falls on the pantry and its many jars of food. For someone who seems so into plants and DIY food preservation…I wonder if this cabin has a root cellar. I sprint inside the pantry and scour the floor. Sure enough, after moving a sack of flour, I find a wooden hatch embedded in the floorboards, held shut with an iron padlock. Now *that* is what I'm looking for.

With undue optimism, I try the key to the front door on the padlock. Unsurprisingly, it's too big to fit. Reasoning that there are no windows in the pantry, nor any neighbors around to see it, I pull the chain on the lightbulb above me and give my phone flashlight a break. I run my fingers over the hatch, formulating how to access what lies below.

I could try to pick the lock, though I've never successfully done so. I tug on the giant iron ring serving as a handle, just to see. The door gives a little but is held fast by the lock. The boards are fastened together with thick iron bands. It's doubtful I could pry them apart. I think of the axe resting in the closet. I could just…go at it. Try and hack it apart. I know it's not the best plan; the wood looks thick and there's no guarantee I could break through. Plus, I'd rather be *somewhat* subtle. So far I haven't looked at anything I haven't been able to put back.

Still, I stand up and return to the tool closet. There is, of course, the axe, as well as a couple saws. I could try and cut the lock out of the hatch. Before reaching for a saw, I scan the other tools. I pull out a plastic case and open it, revealing a power drill. Almost afraid to hope, I carry it back to the hatch. I know the screws near the padlock are hidden, but…

"Aha!" I exclaim out loud. There are visible screws which attach the hinges on the other side. I find a drill bit that matches and begin to unscrew them. It makes me nervous to start a construction project in the pantry, but I tell myself I'll have enough time to put the screws back. It'll be like nothing ever happened. She'll never know. As each screw comes loose,

110

I carefully place them in the smallest pocket of my backpack.

Once all the screws have been removed, I put the drill back in its case and return it to the shelf where I found it. Among the rest of the tools in the closet, I find a hammer. Time for the moment of truth. I return to the hatch and wedge the claw of the hammer in the gap between the wooden door and the floor. With a few tries, I pry it up. Holding the door at a ninety degree angle, I take a moment to admire my handiwork. I'm shocked I got it open. If Leighton really is hiding something, it's bound to be in this basement.

I tuck the hammer beneath one of the pantry shelves, switch my phone flashlight back on, and descend the newly revealed stairs. I try to close the hatch gently, but it still falls shut with a bang. I'm left below ground in the dark unknown.

A sudden fear grips me. What if I *do* find something down here? What if there's a dead body?! Or several? Or live prisoners who have been down here for who knows how long…my imagination starts to reel. I take a deep breath and shine my flashlight in front of me.

With each step, the room below slowly comes into view. At first, it seems like a normal root cellar. More shelves housing canned goods and bundles of vegetables line the wall closest to the stairs. As I turn and survey the rest of the space, however, it becomes clear this place is anything but normal.

Glass cabinets line the walls to the left and right, stocked with beakers, vials, tubes, gauze, gloves, and various scientific instruments. In the center of the room are several stainless steel tables, all lined with drawers. It appears to be a laboratory.

A wooden desk sits only a few yards away from me, and it's piled with journals and papers. I step forward to investigate. I flip through the pages of one of the journals, landing on a sketch of a flower I recognize. Bearing a similarity to Queen Ann's lace, my identification is confirmed by the hand-scrawled label. *Conium maculatum*: poison hemlock. In fact, the rest of the journal is full of nothing but scientific illustrations and notes on toxic plants. They all are. I set the books down and continue forward. What kind of professor has a hidden lab dedicated to poison research in their basement?

I pass by a taller desk housing a computer, heading for the lab tables. I'm eager to go through the drawers and supply shelves, but something along the far wall pulls me onward. I check the time; I'm still good. In fact, I turn the alarm volume off. Wouldn't want my phone to start ringing at the wrong time and give me away. Along the back wall, towards the left, I find that there's an alcove hiding another door. Though it's the size of a small room, the door looks like it belongs to a safe. There's a valve handle and a large combination lock in the center.

Trying my luck, I test the handle. Of course, the lock isn't set to open. I examine the outside, but I know I can't get into this one simply by undoing a few screws. I sigh and start taking pictures of the safe and the poison research I found. At least I have some evidence. Eventually, I wander back towards the combination lock. Maybe I could crack the code? From what I know, you have to listen and see if the pins click into place—or is that a different type of lock? I put my ear to the door and gently spin the dial.

After a few minutes, I realize this is useless. There's no way I'm going to crack it, especially not in the time I have left. I stare at the numbers. Guessing is an impossible task. There are too many possibilities to try them all. In the movies, they always find something special about the character and guess the password or code based on their personality—but that's not realistic. It could be anything! Her birthday, a date she likes, a random string of numbers.

I look back at the desk and get a stroke of inspiration. If she's anything like me, well, maybe she just wrote it down somewhere. I root through the drawers and flip through the various journals. Among everything, I don't see any type of password book. I sink back into a cynical mindset, though I continue looking. I flip through the edges of the books, keeping an eye out for pen marks or handwriting in the margins. Then, in one of the journals, I notice something.

Each of the hand-drawn illustrations is labeled with a number, as is typical in field guides. In the corner of one of the pages, I find a small plus sign in red ink. *No. 14, foxglove.* Though it might be nothing, I continue flipping through the book. Sure enough, another red sign appears.

No. 36, rose periwinkle. There's no way this could actually mean anything…right? Holding my breath, I slowly go through the rest of the pages. There are no more red marks.

I slump my shoulders, defeated. For a few seconds, I stare at the front of the journal, then the obvious answer hits me. I should start again with the first page. I almost drop the book when I see a red plus on number 9, *nightshade*.

Still skeptical, I walk back over to the safe. In order, I twist the dial to the numbers. 9…14…36…To my surprise, when I tug on the valve handle, it actually turns beneath my hands. Involuntarily, I hop with excitement.

"Yes!"

I set the book on a nearby table and pull open the door. A skull and crossbones symbol is spray-painted on the inside panel, along with the words *DANGER, KEEP OUT.* I swallow. In a way, this is what I expected to find. However, that doesn't make the truth of it any less unsettling. I snap a picture of the door with my phone, then step inside the small room.

I shine my flashlight around me. There are wooden shelves running along the walls, all stocked with dozens and dozens of glass vials. I pick up one of the vials and read the label: *ricin*. I quickly put it down, realizing the gravity of what I'm holding. This one vial full of poison could kill an untold number of people…I scan some of the other labels. Nightshade, oleandrin, digitoxin, poison hemlock, *cyanide*. I stop and stare. On the shelf in front of me sits not just one, but five vials of the deadly poison.

I quickly take pictures of the vials and the room. Surely this will get a conviction in court. As I document my surroundings, it dawns on me that this room is one of death. How many lives have been claimed with these substances? A chill creeps over me, striking to the bone. I knew at least one of the victims. And there are probably many more.

I suddenly feel a great need to escape this cursed place. I want to get as far away from this crime scene and the murderer who inhabits it as humanly possible. As I turn to leave, my ears perceive something that makes every hair stand on end.

Creeeeeeak. The wooden hatch leading to the basement swings open.

Chapter 18

Face to Face

My heart beating faster than a jackrabbit, I take the split second before she comes down the stairs to turn off my phone flashlight and dive away from the safe. My survival instincts kick in; I need to avoid being cornered. However, right now I need to avoid being seen. I crouch behind one of the lab tables, thankful the drawers reach to the floor and provide cover.

Tap, tap, tap. With each step she takes, the wooden stairs creak under the weight of her boots. I cover my mouth with my hand, trying desperately to muffle my breathing. Suddenly, the room falls silent. Panic surges in my veins, and I strain my ears to hear.

A startling white light fills the room as the overhead lights switch on. I blink rapidly as my vision adjusts. In an instant, the claustrophobic environment of a dark basement is replaced by the unsettling feeling of a bright, sterile lab. Though I haven't moved from my hiding spot, the light makes me feel more exposed.

"Hello?" she calls. "Who's in here?" Her tone is frigid, more severe than anything I've heard her say in class. "Show yourself!"

I flinch, clamping my hand even tighter over my face. As her footsteps draw closer, I try to hold perfectly still. *God, please help me. Please protect me. Please help me…* A wheeled cart clatters across the floor as she slides it to the side, searching for me.

As she approaches, I quietly creep to the other side of the lab table to remain out of view. For a moment, from this angle, I catch sight of her. It's all I can do not to cry out. Her knife is drawn and ready, the fluorescent lighting reflecting off the shiny gray surface. My stomach turns at the thought of the sharp edge piercing my skin.

Her attention turns to the safe, and she zeroes in on the open door. Purposefully, she steps towards it. If she's focused on the safe, this might just be my chance to escape. I set my eyes on the stairs, preparing to run.

I spring forward, but yank myself back mid-step. Leighton suddenly turns on her heel and walks briskly towards the stairs. I duck behind the long end of the table once more, praying she didn't see me. By some miracle, I think I've escaped her notice.

As the distance between us grows, hope rises within me. I might actually make it out of this. If she goes back upstairs, I just have to wait until she's asleep, or leaves the cabin, and I can sneak out unseen...

Beep! Beep! Beep! My low blood sugar alert screams, piercing the silence. I scramble to unlock my phone, but it's no use. She knows where I am. I need to run. In a panic, I bolt to my left, heading full speed towards the stairs.

Swiftly, Leighton blocks my path, knife in hand. "Addy?!"

My sneakers squeak as I turn in the opposite direction. I grab the edge of a nearby cabinet to propel myself forward. It rocks beneath my hand, and as I sprint away, I hear the sound of glass beakers shattering on the concrete floor as the whole thing crashes to the ground. I don't stop to look back.

As I turn the corner of the room, the only thing standing between us is the lab table I was hiding under moments ago. For a split second, we lock eyes. Then Leighton lunges forward, clearing the table with one jump. Seeing no other option, I turn and run back towards the fallen shelf.

She reaches towards me, and her fingers close around my backpack. A scream escapes my throat. I wriggle out of the straps and stumble forward, leaving it behind. The momentum throws me off-balance, and my hands fly out to break my fall. Shards of glass prick my skin, cutting through the gloves, and my phone goes skidding across the floor.

Beep! Beep! Beep! I reach for it, starting to feel the effects of low blood sugar. My hand is shaky, and my muscles feel weak. Ignoring my body's cues, I force myself to move. All my evidence, all my proof is on that phone. Before I can reach it, however, her boot lands beside it, and she plucks it off the ground.

Though it feels like I'm moving through molasses, I pick myself up and desperately charge towards the stairs. My heart echoes loudly in my ears, as if to let me know I'm running on empty. I have no more fuel to burn. My insides feel hollow, as if I will collapse in on myself at any moment. Still, I keep going. I step over the fallen cabinet and race forward.

One minute my eyes are trained on the escape hatch, which I'm desperately running towards, and the next I feel a hand on my shoulder. Before I can react, my legs are swept out from under me, and I fall backwards. Suddenly, I find myself sitting on a lab stool with my back pressed against the side of the table. Leighton stands over me.

"Sit," she commands firmly, pressing my shoulder down.

There's a tremor in my hands, whether from fear or hypoglycemia, I'm not sure. Reflexively, I put my arms up to protect myself and look away, bracing for the pain of being stabbed. *I'm gonna die. I'm gonna die. I'm gonna die.* The thought rings through my head as I desperately pray. Am I ready to meet God?

Through my squinted eyes, I notice that my phone is sitting face up on the same table, along with my backpack. Both are just out of reach. How can I make it out of this alive? A thought comes to mind.

"I...I already called the cops, so you know!" I lie. "They'll be here any minute."

Having not yet been stabbed, I tentatively venture a glance at Leighton through my spread fingers. Rather than being poised to attack, her arms hang loose at her sides. Slowly, I lower my hands away from my face. I'm relieved to find she's no longer holding the knife. I push away the question of what other murder methods she may prefer.

"Oh?" she snaps, her eyes boring through my skull. "So

you can tell them all about how you stole my key, broke into my house, and destroyed hundreds of dollars worth of lab equipment?!" She motions to the overturned shelf. I shrink back against the table.

She clenches and unclenches her fists, then swipes my still-beeping phone off the table. "Besides," she says after tapping the screen a few times. It must be unlocked from when I tried to turn off my alarm. "Based on your call history, I'm going to say that isn't true."

My heart sinks. She's seen my hand.

She lowers the phone. "Addy, what is going on here? Did someone put you up to this?" She scans my face. "The police? A professor? What are you doing in my house?!"

Her feigned ignorance ignites something in me. This, coupled with poor impulse control from low blood sugar and the knowledge that I have no way out, causes words to pour from my mouth. "*Me?!*" I sputter, indignant. "You have a vault full of poison in your basement!" I gesture to the room behind me. "You're a serial killer! *You* killed Dr. Morrell. And then Ma—" Hot tears rush to my eyes. "You killed Matthew because he knew too much." I aggressively rub the tears away and continue. "And you've fooled everyone. Dr. Conley, the mayor, the judge…The police can't do anything. So I came here to get proof, to bring you to justice," I jab my index finger into my chest. "And even if you kill me, too, you can't escape forever. One day the truth will come out."

Shaking with emotion and the low, I wait for a response. For Leighton to stab me or yell back at me. But she is quiet.

With wide eyes, she looks from me to the back corner of the room. I follow her gaze to the field guide still sitting on the far lab table. She meets my eyes.

"It's just you, isn't it?"

I'm silent.

"Addy…" she says gently, spreading her hands. "I'm sorry for everything that's happened. I am. And I know this is all confusing. But you've got it wrong; I'm not the one who killed your friend."

My mind is reeling. "How can you say that?!" I demand. "Mi—someone saw you do it!"

"I can explain, and I'm happy to tell you everything. I'm

a toxicologist; I'm not a murderer. You've seen my field guides and my research. I wouldn't hurt you." She tilts my phone so I can see the screen. "But your blood sugar is 62. Let me give you something to eat—"

"No! Th—that's okay. I have snacks, if I could just have my bag," I say, slowly reaching for it. To my surprise, Leighton slides it towards me. In a frenzy, I start going through the pockets. The cuts on my hands start to burn, but I ignore them for the time being.

As I search, Leighton crosses the room and heads towards the shelves at the bottom of the stairs. If I could just find something to bring my sugar up—juice box, granola bar, year-old candy, *anything*—but so far I'm coming up empty-handed. Where are all my snacks? Of course, I have plenty of insulin.

She returns, pops the lid off a glass jar of dark liquid, and sets it on the table next to me. "Black raspberry juice," she explains. "Homemade. Just in case." She pulls up another stool and sits beside me, setting my phone down. For a second, we both watch the number plunge. Two red arrows accompany the horrendous beeping. 54 mg/dL.

Growing more panicked, I dump the contents of my bag onto the table. Amidst all the papers and junk I've accumulated, I find nothing. Nothing! How is that even possible?!

Then it hits me. Before I left my room this morning, I cleaned out my bag. I meant to put the snacks back in, but I must have forgotten. Which means, currently, they're all sitting in a pile on my desk. Too far to be of any help now. My eyes fall on the glass jar of juice as a sinking realization sets in.

"Addy...you're making me nervous..." Leighton says, eyeing the number on my phone. *I'm* making *her* nervous?! "Please," she says, pushing the jar towards me.

"No, I'm sure I have something, thank you," I insist, hoping beyond reason. *Stupid. Stupid. Stupid.* I can't believe I failed diabetes 101 so drastically! I thought it wouldn't be hard to keep from drinking poison. If I'd only been more careful...After one final search, I set the bag down and make eye contact with Professor Leighton.

She knows I don't have another option. My choices, it seems, are either to die from severe hypoglycemia or agree to drink unmarked juice offered by someone with a stockpile of cyanide.

She taps her fingers on the metal table. "I promise you, it's just juice. Why would I hurt you if you're already suffering a medical emergency?"

"I dunno," I answer. "More certainty? For fun?"

"Listen. I didn't kill Matthew. Whatever that person saw—I was trying to help." She pulls out an oddly shaped vial of liquid and hands it to me. "Vitamin B12. The cure for cyanide poisoning."

I study the container, feeling weak. "If you had the cure, why didn't he live, then? Why did you run away?"

"Addy, you're at 47," Leighton says, growing flustered. The tapping of her fingers grows faster. At once, she pulls open one of the drawers beneath the lab table and takes out a syringe. "Drink it or I'll inject you with glucagon."

Suddenly panicked, my hands fly towards the jar. "Wait, wait, I'll drink it, please!" I plead. The gamble has changed.

Reluctantly, I grasp the container and lift it from the table. I stare into the mouth of the glass, studying the inky concoction.

Seeing my hesitation, Leighton suddenly grabs the jar from my hand.

"I'll prove it." She takes a big swig of juice from the bottle, swallows, and hands it back to me with a nod. My mouth falls open in shock. Well, if it *is* poisoned, at least we'll go down together. With a prayer, I take a drink.

Chapter 19

Clearing Away

The juice has a pleasant, sweet flavor. I take a few big gulps, then set it back down, keeping my eyes on my phone. I take note of my internal state, trying to assess if I'll need more sugar, or if I feel like I've just been poisoned. I watch Leighton, too.

Still feeling low, I take a few more sips. After several minutes, the downward facing arrow on the monitor turns upward, and my number becomes more stable. 50...55...64...

It doesn't take long for the feeling of rising blood sugar to kick in. Sometimes the sudden fluctuations in number feel worse than just being low. I almost feel sick. Somehow, my limbs feel even weaker than before; it's as if my body is made of lead. I lean against the table, feeling my heart pound in my chest. I have no more fight in me, at least not until the feeling passes.

Seeing the number rise, Leighton pats my shoulder and stands. "Take it easy." She looks down at my hands, still wrapped in thin latex gloves. "Your hands are bleeding."

Along with the awful feeling from my number climbing, I start to notice the sharp pain in my hands. I haven't even looked at how bad the cuts are, or how much glass is in them.

"Mind if I take a look?" she asks. In no condition to argue, I let her roll both of my hands over, so my palms are facing up. There are a few shreds in the gloves where glass poked through, as well as a fair amount of blood. I'm usually not very squeamish, but the sight of so much red is alarming. Leighton must see my horrified expression. "Ah, don't worry. Looks worse than it is. Glass will make you bleed like crazy."

She heads towards a sink in the back corner of the room. I hear the water run briefly, followed by the sound of her rifling through various shelves and drawers. She returns with a small tray of instruments, which she sets beside me on the lab table. I watch as she pulls on a pair of blue exam gloves.

"I thought you said you would explain," I say, feeling frustrated and confused. Twenty minutes ago I was 100% convinced she was guilty of murder, and now she's treating my low and tending my wounds? What is happening?!

"And I will," she says. "Just thought I'd give you a minute. We have time." Gingerly, she guides my hands onto the lab table and trains a small lamp on my palms. "I have nothing to hide." She selects a pair of scissors from the tray. When I flinch, she raises a hand. "For the gloves."

The cold metal scissors zap my skin as she slices through the thin latex. Swiftly, she removes and discards both gloves, revealing my bleeding hands.

She sets them in a shallow basin. "I'll answer any questions you have. *But*," she pauses as she lifts a beaker of water and begins to rinse the blood away, "before I do so, there's something I need from you."

"You need something from me?" I ask, watching a small stream of blood and water run off my hand and into the basin.

She nods. "I know you don't trust me. You wouldn't be here unless you thought I was guilty. And I can understand why; I know there are a lot of things that don't look good." She lifts her head, meeting my eyes. "But I'm going to ask you to keep an open mind. I have an explanation, and I'm happy to give it, but nothing I say will mean a thing if you've already decided what you believe about me. Can you do that?"

I consider her question. Can I actually, sincerely hear what she has to say? I respond with the most honest answer I can give. "I can try."

"Okay," she responds, "I can work with that." Her gaze returns to my hands. "See. Like I said, it's not so bad."

Now that the mess of blood has been cleaned away, it's clear I only have a few thin cuts near my palms. I only see one large piece of glass still present. Leighton retrieves a pair of tweezers and rotates a magnifying lens under the light to examine the cuts more closely. Holding my palm steady, she extracts the shard of glass and drops it in a tray, then continues searching for more.

"You—uh, seem like you've done this before," I say, commenting on her apparent skill with the tweezers.

"A good bit, yes." She drops another small shard of glass in the tray. "I was a corpsman in the Navy. Lot of experience with emergency medicine."

"Is that like a medic?"

She nods. "Yes. I was in search and rescue, specifically." She moves the magnifying lens away. "Good news is your cuts look clean." She pours water over my hands one last time.

Whilst trying not to sound accusatory, I pose another question. "But, I thought you said you were a toxicologist?" As the energy returns to my brain, so does my sense of caution.

"I am. Took college courses while I was in the service. I have a bachelor's in biochemistry, with a focus on plant science, and a master's in toxicology." She tightly wraps my hands in gauze, then adds a layer of clingy material to help it stay in place. "My experience overlaps with many fields," she says with a slight smile. "How do your hands feel?"

I rest my bandaged hands in my lap. "Not bad." I pause, then add, "Thank you."

"No problem. Your sugar?" She peeks at my phone.

I still feel slightly woozy. "Alright. Getting there," I reply honestly.

"No rush," she says. "Sit back. Relax." She gathers all her instruments onto the tray and walks back to the sink.

"And that's why you have all this poison? To research?" I venture.

"Correct."

"And that research is…what, exactly?"

"Mostly, I study toxins extracted from plant-based sources with the goal of creating antidotes or new methods of detection. My favorite part of the job, however, is discovering how potentially dangerous compounds can be used as medicine." She finishes cleaning the tray and medical supplies and begins to put them away. "I'm subcontracted by the military for my research. I have permits and paperwork for everything I have; it's all legitimate."

"Why not let the cops search, then?" I ask, growing bolder. "If you really have nothing to hide…"

"The justice system is far from infallible," she says, approaching the safe. "I have a right to privacy; I might as well use it. Good intentioned as I may be, a 'vault full of poison,' as you put it, would not look good to a jury." She closes the thick metal door. Just before turning the handle, she looks to me. "Be honest. Did you take anything from here?"

"No, nothing," I sputter. *Only pictures* I think to myself. I remember my phone is beside me. When her back is turned, I slide it into my pocket.

She turns the handle, engaging the lock. "Admittedly, I am impressed you managed to open it." She picks up the field journal I used. "I may need to tighten my security."

I shift gears, hitting closer to what I'd really like to know. "The day Matthew went to the police, I saw you watching him. Only a few days later, he said you called him into your office and interrogated him about Dr. Morrell, then told him to watch his back. If you weren't trying to threaten him, what was that all about?"

Her eyes fall to the ground. "I didn't mean to scare him off. I was vague because I thought the less he knew, the safer he would be—clearly I made a mistake." She sets her field journal back on her desk. "I've long suspected Dr. Morrell's death was the result of foul play, and I had a growing belief that Matthew had some knowledge of what happened. That belief was confirmed when I saw him talking to the police."

My eyes follow her as she collects a spray bottle and some paper towels. "I wasn't trying to threaten him; I was trying to offer help. To warn him that he might be in danger because of his report." She wipes the table and tosses the paper towels in the trash. "And, admittedly, I tried to learn what piece of information he had, but he wouldn't tell me anything. Can't say I blame him."

Several questions come to mind, but I chose the most

pressing. "So what happened at that party the night he died?"

She sits back down on the stool beside me, this time placing her leather doctor's bag on the table. "Why don't we start with you telling me your version of the events?"

"Well…" I start, nervously eyeing the knife at her hip. The black handle, previously concealed beneath her shirt, is now plainly visible. "You were seen standing over Matthew, holding a syringe. Then, when people started to notice, you ran off into the woods, and you let him die." My bandaged hands curl into fists as I think of the evidence. "I don't know how you expect me to believe you're innocent when you have a supply of cyanide and you *admit* to knowing he was a witness—"

She spreads her hands. "Open mind?"

With a fair bit of effort, I temper my accusations. I lean back a little and nod. "I'm just having a hard time imagining what explanation you could possibly have," I manage through gritted teeth.

"I'll show you," she says calmly. She unfastens the clasp on her bag and tilts it towards me. Cautiously, I peer inside. At first, I see a small selection of medical equipment: bandages, alcohol wipes, needles, and the like. Upon closer examination, I notice the assortment of vials lining the side, all of varying sizes and shapes.

"Antidotes to various toxins," she explains. She slides the B12 back in a vacant slot and shuts the clasp. "I greatly suspected poison was used as the murder weapon, but I didn't know what kind. So I came prepared—hence the wide selection of medications. I was worried they would come after Matthew, so I tried to keep an eye on him. When I saw him go to that party, I lingered in the woods nearby.

"I saw him stagger out of the house, struggling to breathe, and I ran to help. Before I reached him, however, another young man heading the opposite direction bumped into me. His hood was pulled down so it covered most of his face, though I remember thinking he looked older than most college students. I didn't stop to dwell on it, though.

"Unfortunately, after reaching Matthew and confirming it was cyanide poisoning, guess which bottle I found to be missing from my bag." She bobs her head towards it. "He

124

pick-pocketed the B12 from me. Matthew didn't have long, and I knew he wouldn't be revived without it. So I took the only chance I had. I chased after the man in the direction I'd seen him go, hoping desperately to get that bottle back."

"And?" I ask.

She shakes her head. "I caught up to him, but he smashed it on a rock, then escaped into the woods."

My mind wrestles with the new story. Could she really be telling the truth? If I believe her, am I just falling for a clever deception?

"If you're wondering who killed Matthew, I can assure you it wasn't me. The one you want is whoever that man was, though I doubt he was acting alone. I brought proof to the police—a test strip positive for cyanide—yet they still claimed it was alcohol poisoning for quite a bit. Prior to that, I'd suspected the police might be involved somehow, but that confirmed it for me."

A million questions swim in my head as I search for potential holes in the story. "And what if I don't believe you?" I ask, my eyes still darting to the safe.

She shrugs. "Whether you believe it or not, it's the truth." She stares at the fallen shelf, then gets up, leaving her bag on the table. "But tell me, Addy, if I really murdered Dr. Morrell and then killed Matthew to cover it up, why are you still alive?"

That is one question I haven't been able to answer. My mind starts to jump through hoops, constructing an explanation. *I'm trapped down here, and no one knows where I am, so she has time to try and convince me she's innocent. It's a strategic move. If I go back and tell people she didn't do it, it'll take the heat off when she really is guilty...*I stop, realizing I'm starting to sound like a totally unbiased research study funded by a Fortune 500 company to make their brand look better.

Is it a possibility? Yes. But is it the most *likely* explanation? I watch as she begins sweeping up the glass shards scattered all over the floor. A pinprick of guilt forms in my chest. If this was all a ploy to convince me of her tale, wouldn't she be more concerned about my doubts? They don't seem to bother her in the slightest, however. I suppose she may just be playing mind games with me. But then again...

What if...what if she really is telling the truth?

I feel my face turn red. Well, the first thing it means is that I broke into a professor's house for no reason. The full weight of what I've done finally comes crashing down on me. I—I committed a *crime*. I broke into a house and caused property damage. I could go to jail! What was I thinking?!

"I...I'm sorry about the shelves," I say timidly. I train my eyes on my shoes, trying to grapple with my fate. "Are— are you going to press charges?"

She stands the empty shelf back up and tosses the last dustpan of glass into the trash. The fragile pieces clink against each other as they fall. She turns towards me. "No, I'm not." Slowly, I lift my eyes. "You don't need to worry, Addy. You have nothing to fear from me. Beakers can be replaced. All's forgiven." She smiles warmly.

Relief floods my body. "You—you're not mad at me?"

She shakes her head. "Nah. In a way, you did me a favor. These should definitely be bolted to the wall," she says cheerily, tugging on the shelf. She puts the broom and dustpan back, then pulls her coat tight around her. "It's a bit chilly down here. Can I invite you upstairs to talk some more?"

Eager to get out of the basement, I agree. I shove my scattered belongings into my backpack and follow her up the stairs.

Chapter 20

Soup

As I climb out of the basement, I notice the wooden door of the hatch has been fully removed and is now lying beside the hole in the floor. Leighton glances at it. "It's strange. Usually it swings open, but I think something happened to the hinges," she says facetiously, eyeing me.

"Sorry about that," I mutter, turning red again. "I—I have the screws here." Once my feet are back on the pantry floor, I dig them out of my backpack and hand them over.

She accepts the screws and places them on a shelf with the hammer. With a smile, she waves me forward, presenting the kitchen. "Intruder or not, you're my guest now. Make yourself at home."

Awkwardly, I step forward. I never quite feel at home in other people's spaces, least of all now, under such uncomfortable circumstances. Still, I'm struck by Professor Leighton's kindness. I broke in and trashed her property, and instead of throwing me out or calling the cops, she calls me her guest. It's as if nothing happened—which makes me skeptical.

I find myself waiting for the other shoe to drop. When is this facade going to be broken and give way to explosive anger or homicidal tendencies? She can't possibly have forgiven me so easily, can she?

She darts past me and turns the overhead light on, then heads into the living room. The kitchen looks different in the light. Friendlier. It's now apparent that the cabinets are made of dark, textured wood, and the countertops are an even darker butcher block style. The retro fridge and stove are both an olive green color.

Now that I'm not in such a panic, I notice some of the details I missed. Small fossils and colorful crystals sit on a shelf above the kitchen table. Other shelves are full of little glass jars containing various dried spices. Mint, basil, nutmeg, cinnamon, parsley, chives, oregano, rosemary…A few more potted plants sit on the windowsill behind the sink, and others serve as a centerpiece for the table.

Trailing behind Leighton, I wander towards the living room. On my way, I glance at the front door and notice it is not only locked, but barred with a heavy wooden beam. For a moment, I pause, contemplating…

A creaking sound comes from the living room, pulling me from my thoughts. I continue forward and cross the threshold. The room is now illuminated by several floor lamps arranged throughout. I pass by the corner bookshelves I saw earlier and skim some of the titles, then turn towards the open wood stove. Two chairs and a couch face the stove, forming a semicircle around it, and a coffee table sits in the middle.

I inch closer, watching as Leighton stacks some pieces of wood, throws some newspaper in the mix, and lights a match. My eyes shift down and land on something surprising. Sitting on the coffee table is a well-worn leather Bible, bookmarked somewhere in the middle. It throws me for a bit of a loop. I never considered that Leighton might be a Christian.

She closes the glass window of the stove and stands. "There we go. It should warm up in here soon." I stare at the flame engulfing the wood inside. With the wood stove ignited and the lamps giving off a soft glow, the cabin almost has a cozy feel to it. For a minute, we both stand in silence.

"Well, I'm starving," Leighton says. "Are you hungry?"

"Uh—" Before I can answer, she charges towards the kitchen. I follow behind, awkwardly standing in the corner. She ducks into the pantry and emerges with a large jar of light-brown liquid—broth, maybe—a head of cabbage, and some carrots, which dangle from her fingers by the green tops. She sets everything down on a section of the countertop, then looks back at me.

"Have a seat, put your stuff down, make yourself comfortable," she says, gesturing towards the kitchen table. I pick a chair facing her and set my backpack on the floor beside me. Suddenly thirsty, I pull out my water bottle and take a drink.

She pulls open the fridge door and brings out a container of cooked chicken breast. I watch as she puts a large pot on the stove and turns on a burner. She dumps the contents of the jar into the pot, along with some water, and turns on the fan. I feel myself relax a little, grateful for the white noise. She retrieves a large wooden cutting board and runs the head of cabbage under the spigot. Setting it down, she pulls a chef's knife from a wooden block on the counter. It rings as it slides out of place.

"So," she says, putting the blade to the cabbage. "If you don't mind, I have a few questions for you." She easily slices through the green leaves.

"Like what?" I ask, my leg bouncing under the table. *Chop, chop, chop.* The knife makes a consistent clack on the cutting board as she moves through the head.

"You're not in any trouble," she reassures, waving her free hand. "I'm just trying to understand what happened. You must have switched out my key in the college lab after I left the room..." When I don't contradict her, she continues, "Were you planning to do so ahead of time?"

I know it's only fair of me to answer. "No. I just went in to do the assignment; I didn't know you'd be there. It was kind of an impulse decision when I realized your key was similar to mine."

She sweeps the first half of chopped cabbage into the pot with the knife. "So what key do I have on my ring?"

"It's, uh, it's my house key. Well, not anymore. My parents just changed their locks, so it doesn't really go to anything."

She slides the rest of the cabbage into the pot, then reaches for some of the vials of spices. Salt, pepper, and a few shakes of some other things. "So, acting alone, you got in the front door, found the cellar, unscrewed the hinges on the hatch, discovered the combination to the safe, and showed me where I need to patch some holes in my security—" She stops to glance at me.

I swallow, then nod.

Having received confirmation, she turns back to the counter. "Still, I'm left with one big question." She scrubs the carrots clean in the sink, then slices into them. In an instant, the green tops are separated from the orange bodies. "How did you know where I live?"

I hesitate, thinking of how I trekked to the cabin with Anthony. It's one thing to take a risk trusting Leighton with my own life—it's another to implicate other people.

"I—I found the cabin while I was on a walk, and I saw you outside," I say carefully, telling a half truth. I mean, it's not really a lie, right? "That's how I knew it was your house."

"On a walk?" she repeats while chopping carrots. She adds them to the pot. "You'd have to wander pretty far off the beaten path to find this place by accident."

"Well, I was looking for it," I admit, then quickly add, "I mean, I had a map. An old map, from the library archives. This cabin is like a historical site in Flickerwood."

She begins shredding pieces of chicken for the soup. "How long ago was this?"

"Uh...maybe a week ago or so?" I estimate. It's hard to remember.

Leighton swings around and sets a tin of crackers on the table. She pauses to look at me. "And what would make you want to visit this historic site in particular?" She returns to the stove and puts a lid on the soup, which is starting to simmer.

I consider how to answer this question. "I heard that it's part of an urban legend at Wynhurst, and that maybe those legends had something to do with the more recent murders, not that I'm sure I even believe in them, it just made me curious," I ramble.

Thinking of the history of the cabin reminds me of Anthony and his experience. I glance around, again seeing the herbs and crystals and plants everywhere, along with the bubbling pot on the stove. A new theory enters my head, likely born from adrenaline and exhaustion.

"You don't like, practice magic, do you?" I blurt out.

130

She turns to look at me. "What?"

"Like, are you into the occult and stuff?"

"Are you asking if I'm a witch?"

I realize this may have been a mistake. Well, there's no turning back now. "Are you?" I ask tentatively.

"Why—" she stops and gazes around at the glass vials and green plants adorning her house. In a moment of self-awareness, she purses her lips and raises a wooden spoon. "I can see how you might get that impression," she admits, "but no. I'm a scientist...And maybe a little crunchy, if I'm honest. But I don't practice witchcraft." She stirs the soup. "It's against my religion."

My mind returns to the Bible on the coffee table. "And... what religion is that, if you don't mind me asking?"

"Christian," she answers. "Jesus saved me when I was a teenager."

Something in me cringes at her use of the name "Jesus"— I'm used to hearing it in children's lessons and kiddie Sunday school songs. Adults tend to use more abstract words, like "God" or "Christ" or "Messiah." But I immediately feel guilty for the thought. *For whoever is ashamed...*

I hurry to respond, almost to make up for my initial feeling. "Me too. Christian, I mean. I don't remember a time before I was saved."

She smiles. "Well, then we have something in common." She disposes of the food scraps and puts the knife and cutting board in the sink.

My attention shifts to the plants on the table. The largest among them is sporting bright red berries, which stand out against dark green and almost purple leaves. "Wintergreen?" I ask.

"Good eye," she replies.

"Isn't wintergreen kind of...toxic?" I continue. "I'm sure it's for research, but doesn't it make you nervous to have on the kitchen table?"

She approaches the plant and plucks a berry from its branches. For a moment, she examines the red fruit, pinching it between her thumb and forefinger. "Eh," she says with a shrug, then pops the berry in her mouth. "I'm not really worried about it."

Horrified, I stare at her with wide eyes. She smiles, amused by my expression.

"Concentrated wintergreen oil can be poisonous, but the leaves and berries are perfectly edible. Minty." She nods towards plants in the other room. "Can't say the same for holly or winter cherry, however."

I peer into the living room at the others. I would have expected plants that could be toxic to look...well, less normal. "Are any of those dangerous?" I ask, motioning to the plants behind the sink and next to the cabinets.

She eyes the shelves. "Not to be too philosophical, but toxicity is more like a sliding scale. Nothing in the kitchen will kill you immediately upon ingestion, which is what I'm assuming you want to know." She points to a small, familiar-looking succulent, "But take aloe vera, for example. It's not poisonous, per se, but if taken in excess it can cause cancer or kidney failure." Turning to a tower of growing herbs, she continues, "Most herbs and foods, for that matter, become toxic at a certain dose, even if that dose is impossible to consume."

For a minute, I forget that I'm sitting in the kitchen of an old cabin and not back in the botany classroom. It's kind of nice.

"I saw you had a Norfolk pine in the living room," I share. "When I was in elementary school, they had one in the lobby. As a kid, I thought the branches had a nice feel — I've liked them ever since."

"I like them too," she says with a smile. "That one is purely for decoration."

Leighton turns back to the soup and ladles some into a bowl. My phone buzzes in my pocket. I see that Marissa texted me, wondering where I'm at.

Hey, just wondering if you're good. Recent events have me on edge, ya know

I look towards Leighton, whose back is still turned. If I really wanted to, I could ask someone to pick me up and get out of this situation. I look back at the phone. But I don't feel unsafe here. I text back.

All good :) Meeting with a professor

"Soup's done," Leighton announces, carrying a large bowl

132

to the table. "Would you like some?" I check my blood sugar. "There's not many carbs in it," she adds.

Maybe the smart thing to do would be to refuse. If I don't take any chances, I might actually make it out of here alive. Why give Leighton a *second* opportunity to poison me? I wasn't paying attention closely enough to see everything she added to the soup. However...I do still feel kind of crappy from the drop and then the spike in glucose. I could use some real food.

I stare at the pot on the stove. It's soup, but it's also more than that. It's a test of trust. Do I believe everything Leighton has told me?

"I...sure," I hear myself say. "Thank you."

"Do you like cabbage soup?" she asks, setting the bowl in front of me.

"Never had it," I admit. "I'm curious to try it."

She places two glasses and a pitcher of water on the table before taking a seat beside me. I eagerly pour some water, having since drained my bottle. I look over to see that she has her head bowed. I do the same, quickly saying a silent prayer. Usually I ask God to bless food and make it good for the body out of habit, but this time I really mean it.

I finish praying and find a text from Marissa.

Kind of late, isn't it?

I snicker. This certainly is a strange time to be meeting a professor. Strange place, too. Strange everything.

Chapter 21

Answers

"Alright, Addy," Leighton says, sliding the wintergreen plant out of the way. "Albeit you came here thinking I was guilty, it sounds like what you really want is information about the murders, and I do happen to have some of that. If you're interested, that is." She props her feet up on the chair opposite her own, opens the tin of crackers, and crushes some over her soup. "I've been trying to piece things together myself."

I sit up straighter and nod eagerly. "Please."

She takes a drink from her glass, then slowly lowers it back down. It makes a dull thud as the bottom connects with the wooden table. "I first met Dr. Morrell when he and Dr. Gaines interviewed me back in October. He was found dead just a few days before I started teaching classes. I thought the circumstances were suspicious, and with my background, I couldn't help but wonder if there was some substance involved. So I did a little digging.

"I talked to the janitor who'd been working that night, and he said he remembered seeing Dr. Morrell go to the break room and microwave some ramen around 6 pm, right when his shift was ending. I logged on to the school drive and saw that the last edit he made in the document he was working on was at 6:12, and he'd stopped in the middle of a sentence. Based on the security footage, the coroner estimated his time of death as 6:30. Meaning he died very suddenly, right after eating dinner.

"I thought I might have been a bit paranoid, but I went to the police with my concerns anyway. I explained my credentials and asked that they at least run a tox screen for common poisons. I'm not sure how seriously they took me, but they were already investigating whether foul play was involved. I mean, you remember, they had police tape up and everything.

"But then, in a very short span of time, the news started attributing it to a medical condition and ceased any discussion about the potential of murder. His family had the funeral and buried him before the investigation was even over, well before they could have done a proper autopsy. And then the police disappeared from campus."

"I remember those news stories," I chime in. "The first one I saw said it could have been foul play. But all of the stories after that said he died of natural causes. I started to think I was going crazy."

Leighton shakes her head. "No, you're not crazy. I called in to the police station, probably overstepping a bit, and asked if they had run any tests. They said they couldn't tell me anything."

I reach for the tin of crackers, and Leighton slides it towards me. "You're a good cook," I say, trying the soup. It's simple but surprisingly flavorful. "I never knew you could do something with cabbage besides make coleslaw and sauerkraut."

"I'm glad you like it," she says, smiling. She gets up and refills her bowl. "You're welcome to have more. There's plenty."

"Thank you."

She returns to the table. "Anyway. I poked around the break room a bit, swabbed the microwave and tested it for poison, but didn't find anything."

I freeze, my spoon halfway to my mouth. I realize I know something Leighton doesn't. The poison that killed Dr. Morrell wasn't in the ramen; it was in his water bottle. He must have taken a drink while eating dinner...

"I did, however, find a receipt from the college cafe left in his office trash can. I was around enough to know Matthew worked there most days, so..." she shrugs. "I wondered if he might know something. And you already know what happened after that."

I sip on my soup, trying to digest everything she just said. "So, if I'm following, you're suggesting that Matthew wasn't killed because someone saw him go to the police, but because the police *themselves* are working with the killer?" I ask.

She nods. "At the very least, I believe Chief Eric Boyer is involved somehow. After I gave up my chase and returned to Matthew's body, I tried again to tell the cops to check for poison. That time it wasn't just a hunch; I had the proof in my hands. Boyer is the one I gave the cyanide test strip to. He took it and assured me they would investigate, but then went on to blame Matthew's death on something else. To blatantly avoid any type of laboratory testing and claim the cause of death was alcohol poisoning—that's no mistake. That's corruption.

"This became even more apparent when they took me in for questioning. His partner was trying to get relevant information, but Boyer kept interrupting him. So I brought up the fact that I'd given them a test strip at the scene of the crime, and the younger guy had no idea what I was talking about. Evidently Boyer never even told him. He *really* wasn't a fan of me after that."

I sit back in my seat. "So...any witness that goes to the police could be a target? Is that what you're saying?"

She nods. "If they have information Chief Boyer and his co-conspirators would find threatening, absolutely. The person who reported me, for example, is only helping their case. But you, on the other hand...Well, if they know you were friends with Matthew, they might be worried you're too close to the truth."

Goosebumps erupt over my arms. How many people are involved in this? There's Dr. Morrell's killer, the man Leighton saw running away from Matthew, Chief Boyer, and potentially others. Until now, I had forgotten about something Matthew said the last time I saw him. That he had given my name to the police. At the time, I didn't think anything of it. But now...

Something else in Leighton's statement also bothers me,

like a stone in my shoe. My friendship with Matthew? I feel ashamed of the truth. I'd like to believe I'm here because something tragic happened to a friend. Not because I was already interested in the case and befriended Matthew for information, which is what really happened.

I stare at my empty soup bowl, unsure of what to say. Fear grips me as I comprehend that there could be multiple people who want me dead. It's balanced, however, by the late-night depression which has me questioning if I'm even a good enough person to deserve to live. *No one does good, not even one*...The verse echoes in my head but provides little comfort.

"Aren't you worried about your own safety?" I ask Leighton.

"I try to stay alert. Why do you think I have this?" she asks, gesturing to the knife on her hip. "But currently, I think my function as a scapegoat is preserving my life."

"Well...What am I supposed to do?" I ask, my voice shaking slightly. "If you're telling me the police can't be trusted, and there are people who want to kill me for what I know...there has to be someone who can help, right?!"

Leighton plants both feet on the floor. We lock eyes. "Deep breath," she says, inhaling with me. "You're not alone in this. The police aren't all bad. And now that it's confirmed Matthew was murdered, they'll involve the county and state police—there are still real law enforcement officers working on it. It's a little trickier, but justice isn't out of reach.

"We can help by doing what we've been doing—keeping our eyes open, asking around, gaining information. The more evidence they have, the better. Plus, you have me." She walks over to the counter and opens a drawer, pulls out a pad of paper and a pen, and scribbles something down. She tears off the paper and hands it to me. "I'm here to help; please take it. I don't give out my cell number freely. Call any time, night or day. I'll pick up."

Inhale. Exhale. I take the paper from her hands, noting the ten digit number scrawled on it. My stomach flutters upon seeing her knife again. What kind of help is she offering? I fold the paper in half and tuck it inside my backpack, then glance at the time on my phone. It's almost 10 pm.

Leighton must see me. "Getting kind of late. I can either drive you back to campus, or you can spend the night here, but regardless I have to teach at eight tomorrow morning."

"Uh, right," I say, gathering my stuff together. "You wouldn't mind giving me a ride back?"

"Not at all. I'm certainly not letting you walk back in the dark." She lays her keys in front of me on the table. "But I will need you to give me my house key back."

"Right, no problem," I reply quickly, embarrassed. I completely forgot. As she cleans up the kitchen, I work the key off my ring and return it to her, reclaiming my old house key.

"Ready?" she asks, pulling on her coat.

"Yeah." I stand up, put my coat and bag back on, and walk towards the front door. I hand her keys back, and she examines them to make sure they're in order.

"It's a pain to have to pick this lock, ya know," she says, but the statement is followed by a smile.

Just before her hand touches the knob, I stop.

"Uh, Professor—"

She turns.

"It was the water bottle," I blurt out.

She tilts her head to the side. "Water bottle?"

"The poison was in Dr. Morrell's staff water bottle. Matthew saw him having lunch with someone in the cafe the day he died. He wasn't sure who. He just said the man had gray hair and a short beard, and that he was tall and thin," I describe, trying to remember everything Matthew said. "Whoever he was, he switched their water bottles."

Her eyes grow wide as she takes in the information. "Ah, I see. So there *is* a third person involved." She taps a finger on her lip, considering. "Are there cameras in the cafe?"

"No," I reply, shaking my head. "At least not where they were sitting. I have a friend who works security. He said those cameras haven't worked in a long time."

"Well then," she says, setting her jaw. "I guess we'll just have to find out what gray-haired male staff members were around that week." She nods as she turns back towards the door. "Thanks for sharing, Addy. It's a good lead."

That simple? Try to find the guy based on process of elimination? I exhale. It feels nice to finally get that information

138

off my chest. Unlike me, Leighton seems like she might actually have the power to do something about it. "Thank *you*," I say quietly.

Leighton leads me out to her car, and I slide into the passenger seat. I shiver; the faux leather material is cold against my back. When she turns the key, the engine starts to rumble. Save for my grandparents' truck, I don't think I've ever been in a car this old. The dashboard contains a strip of wood paneling running across it, and the radio is a classic analog style with dials on either side.

I put my backpack on the floor beside my legs and buckle myself in. Leighton sets her hands on the wide steering wheel, and we pull out of the driveway. As we start towards Wynhurst, I suddenly remember that classes and homework and all of that are a real thing. "So…" I start, "about that lab assignment due tomorrow…Do you think I could get an extension on that?"

She side-eyes me from the driver's seat. "Let me get this straight. You want me to give you an extension on an assignment because you were too busy breaking into my house to finish it?"

I duck my head. "…half credit?"

Leighton cracks a smile. "How about this. Get it to me by the end of the day tomorrow and I won't take any points off."

I raise my head and relax back against the seat. "You got it."

As we approach campus, she slows the car down, stopping on the street just across from the freshman dorms.

"I'm not gonna get any closer. I don't know how much they're onto you already, but if we let them think you still suspect me, you might be a bit safer."

I nod. "Understood." I reach for the door handle. A wave of gratitude washes over me. This night could have ended very differently. "Thank you for everything, Professor—"

She waves a hand. "Don't mention it. And hey, call me Bryn."

I mirror her smile. Wordlessly, I exit the car. The chill of the night hits me like a wall, and at once I feel on edge. Save for the friendly glow from dormitory windows and the lights lining the sidewalk, darkness stretches out on all sides. I don't wait for her to drive away before starting to power walk towards the building. I resist the urge to full-on sprint, and I breathe a sigh of relief when I'm finally inside the lobby. Whoever is after me—if anyone is—at least I should be safe here.

Chapter 22

Beyond Belief

As I draw closer to my room, a different kind of anxiety fills me. I have no idea how I can even begin to explain to Marissa where I've been. I don't want to lie, but I'm not sure I have the strength to tell the truth. I pray the whole way up the stairs. *God, please don't let her ask a lot of questions...*

Bracing myself, I slowly open the door to our shared room. I'm relieved to find my prayers have been answered. The lights are off, and Marissa is already fast asleep. Thankfully, I won't have to answer any questions tonight.

As my head hits the pillow, the events of the evening come flooding back. I can't *believe* I stole Leighton's key and broke into her house, then openly and forcefully accused her of being a murderer. Two of my main goals in life are to avoid social embarrassment and ensure people have no reason to think negatively about me. Normally, I care so much how I'm perceived—far too much—yet all of that seemed to take a back seat.

I roll on my side, feeling my eyelids grow heavy. Should I feel guilty or accomplished? Maybe a bit of both. Either way, I did learn more about...Leighton? Bryn? Her first name bounces around inside my head, but it's foreign to me, so I resist using it. Gradually, I feel myself sink into the mattress as I fall asleep.

On Wednesday morning, I wake up to rays of sunlight

streaming in the window. Memories of what must have been a dream gradually resurface. It's only when I see my gauze-wrapped hands that I remember it wasn't a dream at all. I really was in Professor Leighton's house last night.

I sit up, startled by this fact. Another wave of embarrassment crashes over me. All that really happened? And now — I still have to go to class with her.

I reach for my phone to check the time and find that it's out of battery. A small feeling of panic sets in. Did I oversleep? It could be seven in the morning or one in the afternoon for all I know, not to mention my blood sugar. I scramble out of bed and dig my laptop out of my bag. I notice in passing that Marissa is already gone. Whew. It's 7:25 am. I still have time to get to class.

I hurry to get dressed. This time, I'm sure to load up my backpack with snacks, along with a phone charger. Not wanting to draw attention, I unwrap the bandages from my hands. The cuts are still visible but have long since stopped bleeding. I wash off the few marks of dried blood in the bathroom sink before bolting towards the dining hall. I still have time for breakfast, right?

Still nibbling on a french toast stick, I make it to class a few minutes late. Based on the number of people attending, however, you'd think I was early. Only a handful of students occupy the desks, and most of them are clustered in the back few rows. If Leighton is at all discouraged by these numbers, she doesn't let on.

"Ah, Addy, good to see you here," she says while marking her attendance sheet at the front of the room. I wave, though I'm not sure she sees, and take a seat next to Sid.

"I was starting to wonder if you were coming," she whispers.

"I forgot to charge my phone last night," I whisper back, plugging my cord into the outlet behind us. "My alarm didn't go off."

My eyes wander back to the front of the room. As usual, Professor Leighton's leather doctor's bag sits on the front table, only now I know what it contains. Syringes, vials of antidotes, plus the keys leading to her house, her basement, and her car, all of which I have also been privy to. She rounds the table and stands before the class. It's strange to know that, perfectly concealed beneath the fabric of her shirt and blazer, hanging on her left-hand side, is a knife. Somehow, all this knowledge is simultaneously comforting and unnerving. At least I know she doesn't have Matthew or Dr. Morrell's blood on her hands. That she's not a threat to me or my friends.

I believe so, anyway.

As we get up to leave at the end of class, Sid shoots me a look. "What happened to your hands?"

I look down at the scratches as I put my phone charger away. Half a dozen explanations come to mind: a cat scratched me, I got caught in a thorny bush, I grabbed a tree branch, I fell on gravel—but then I remember those would all be lies. Besides, I don't really want to hide the truth from Sid. We're good friends. We've been in this together from the start. I think she might understand. As long as we're careful to avoid being overheard, we should be safe.

"Uh...are you free later today? Do you think Micah would mind if we met in his room again?"

"Yeah, I'm sure he'd like the company. It's hard for him, still being in that room alone. I think he tries to get out as much as possible. Why? What's up?"

I shake my head. "There's something I really have to share with you guys. I'll tell you later. How about just after lunch?"

I text Anthony, and we all meet at Micah's dorm around 2:30. A pit forms in my stomach as I cross the threshold. It seems cruel, in a way, to still have Micah living alone in this room. Matthew's things have since been cleaned out. His pictures and posters are absent from the wall, and his bed is devoid of sheets, only housing the bare blue mattress supplied by the school. I wonder if it was harder to sleep beside all of his belongings, or if it's worse now that all trace of him is gone. I swallow the lump in my throat.

Micah shuts the door behind us, and for a moment there is silence. He pulls out the two desk chairs, and we all have a seat.

"So," Sid says, breaking the silence, "what was it you

wanted to share, Addy?"

I feel my mouth grow dry, so I uncap my water bottle and take a drink. *They're my friends,* I tell myself. *There's no need to be nervous.* "I..." I realize there's no way to tell this story without admitting what I did, so I might as well get it over with. "Do you guys remember how we talked about someone potentially breaking into Professor Leighton's house and finding evidence?" I scan their faces. They nod and mumble affirmations.

"Well...I did something stupid. Last night, I went to work on a lab for ecology, and Professor Leighton came in. She left me alone with her keys, and...I remembered how the police couldn't get a search warrant," I scramble to recall what drove me to do something so bold. "And I just wanted to help, so...basically, I took Leighton's key and went to search her house."

They all stare at me with wide eyes. I feel my face turn red with shame. No one condemns me, however.

"Wait, really?" Sid asks in disbelief.

I nod. "Really. See, that's what happened to my hands," I say, stretching my palms out for them to see. "Leighton came home from class early, and I broke some glass and fell while I was running—"

"She saw you?!" Micah asks, leaning in.

"But that's the thing!" I lower my hands. "We were wrong about her. She's not the killer."

"Wait, not the killer?" Sid asks, looking confused. "What do you mean? Micah literally saw her." She gestures towards him.

"That's just it!" I continue. "It was all a misunderstanding. She wasn't trying to kill Matthew; she was trying to save him. She had the antidote to cyanide poisoning, and she even showed me the vial. That night, someone stole it from her before she could administer it, so she had to run after them into the woods to try and get it back—"

"Hang on, if the vial was stolen, how did she show it to you?" Sid asks.

I pause. "I...I guess she had a second vial..."

"You *guess*?" Micah asks, his eyes narrowing.

"Are you sure it was the antidote? How do you know she

144

didn't just show you a random bottle and lie about the contents?" Sid continues.

"It was on the label, vitamin B12," I answer, trying to remember. I know I must have read it.

"Plus, I thought cyanide poisoning had to be treated with an infusion, not a syringe," she says, furrowing her brow.

Before I can begin to process that question, Micah jumps in. "Did she explain why she would even have that stuff on hand? I mean, most normal people don't just happen to be prepared to treat cyanide poisoning. Maybe she has the antidote in case one of her murders goes wrong." His voice has more of an edge than Sidney's.

"She did explain, actually," I say quickly. "She has a degree in toxicology, and she uses supplies like that to conduct research."

"Toxicology?" Sid repeats.

"So she literally admitted to doing research with poisons?" Micah says in disbelief.

"Well, yes, but—" I falter, trying to remember what convinced me she was telling the truth.

"So you're saying it was just a *coincidence* that she saw Matthew talk to the police and then was standing over him at the party a few days later? When he died. From poison. The thing she has an expertise in," he presses.

I wince. "I know it sounds bad when you put it like that— I was suspicious too—but it wasn't her," I protest. "She thinks it was actually the police who gave Matthew away. She's been telling the cops to look for poison since Dr. Morrell died, but they didn't listen to her. Chief Boyer is corrupt."

"Oh, so she told you not to trust the police, too? Convenient," he mutters. Sid squeezes his forearm, but it's clear his frustration is growing.

Sid looks from me to Micah, biting her lip. "I dunno, Addy. It does seem a bit fishy."

"What did she do when she found you?" The question comes from Anthony, who has been uncharacteristically silent thus far. "I mean, she caught you trespassing, right?"

"Right," I say, pointing a finger in his direction. "At first, I was convinced she was going to kill me. I was hiding behind a table when my CGM went off and gave me away. I had to run. That's how I broke the glass and everything." They all listen intently. "But she caught me. I thought I was a goner, but she didn't hurt me. She actually bandaged my hands and gave me some juice for the low—"

"You drank something she gave you!?" Micah exclaims, incredulous. He grips a fistful of hair.

"I didn't want to, but my sugar was getting really low. I didn't have a choice," I stress. "But I didn't die. Later, I even ate some soup with her, and I'm fine," I say, patting myself down. As I turn the events over in my head, the truth of it strikes me. "Actually, she kinda saved my life."

"Still," Micah says, lowering his voice. "That doesn't prove she's not the murderer. You could've just gotten lucky. Maybe she has some reason to keep you alive for the time being."

I pause, stifling the urge to be overly defensive. Of course they have questions; so did I. "I'll admit it's a possibility, but—coupled with the antidotes she showed me—I think it makes more sense if her story is true. After all, if she *did* already kill twice, why would she hesitate a third time? I'm just as big of a liability as Matthew, if not more so. It just...I'm asking for an open mind, here."

There's a break in the questions as they all seem to consider what I said. I start to have hope they're finally beginning to come around.

Sid frowns. "I dunno, Addy...are you just messing with us? Like, did this actually happen?"

My mouth opens, but I can't seem to find the words to reply. Did—did it actually happen? I turn from Sidney to see Micah and Anthony, but they also seem a bit skeptical.

"No, I'm not messing with you," I answer. "It really happened. I was there last night!"

"You really found that place in the dark?" Micah asks.

A new kind of fear wells inside of me. I've never had anyone just not believe me when I was telling the truth. Growing desperate, I reach for something to back up my claims. "Look, I can prove it!" I say as a lightbulb goes off. "I took pictures." I quickly pull my phone out and click on the album I made. Before fully considering the ramifications, I turn the screen towards them.

146

"Oh my gosh!" Sid recoils and puts her hand over her mouth.

I cringe, only now remembering what said pictures contain. My photos of the safe and the vials within probably won't help in convincing them of her innocence. "So, when I took them, I thought they would be good evidence against her, but it's really just supplies for her research," I sputter, trying to undo the damage.

Micah's eyes widen, and he pinches the bottom of my phone between his thumb and forefinger. Calmly, he lifts his gaze and looks me in the eye. "Addy, listen, I don't know what she told you, but you *have* to give those pictures to the police. I mean, they could be what puts Matthew's killer behind bars."

My grip on my phone tightens. "But she's not the killer, Micah. I want justice for Matthew, too, but putting the blame on someone innocent isn't right. What if the real murderer walks free?"

"You're not putting blame on anyone. You'd only be turning in pictures of the truth. It's not like you're framing her." He shifts closer. "If you're worried about getting in trouble, you can turn them in anonymously. Or you can send them to me. I'll go to the police for you if you want."

I try to gently pull my phone back, but he doesn't let go. Suddenly, I find myself in a tense, subtle game of tug-of-war. Sid and Anthony sit as silent observers. For a moment, we're locked in a stalemate. Then Micah moves.

"Here, I'll send them to my phone now, and you won't have to worry about it." His finger travels towards the screen, preparing to tap the share button. Something in me clicks. If those pictures leave my phone, I won't be able to take them back.

With both hands, I wrench the phone away from him and stand from my chair. "No," I grunt, turning away. In a flash, he lunges after me and grabs my arm. I feel myself yanked backwards.

"Micah!" Sid shrieks.

"Hey!" Anthony shouts, jumping out of his seat. He shoves Micah's shoulder, breaking his grip on my arm.

"Stop! Stop!" I hear Sid's voice.

With the time afforded to me by Anthony, I stumble out of Micah's reach and make a split-second decision. I jam my finger over the album and press the icon.

Permanently delete? This item will not be recoverable.
Yes, delete.

"There!" I yell, tossing my phone to the floor. "It's over. They're gone."

Micah pulls his shoulder away from Anthony and snatches the phone from the floor. With the desperation of a starving man searching for food, he pours over the screen. Finally, after finding the pictures absent, he turns to glare at me.

It's a look I've never seen him make. His face begins to turn a dark shade of scarlet, and his hands tremble with rage. I start to wonder if I should fear for my safety.

"Do you have any idea what you just did?" He takes a step towards me. "Are you an idiot!?"

Anthony swiftly and firmly plants himself between us. "Alright man, you need to calm down," he says, raising an open palm to Micah's chest. "We're all friends here."

All friends here. At least I thought so. Micah balls his hands into fists, and my heart starts pounding faster. Is there really about to be a fight? He clenches his jaw and—in an outburst of fury—forcefully swings his hands behind him, hitting only the air at his sides.

"Gah!" he shouts, kicking his bed frame. "Take your phone, Addy," he says bitterly, throwing it on my chair. He's not happy, but at least he's no longer on the edge of violence. Anthony lowers his hand.

I snatch it up alongside my bag and head straight for the door. I don't look back to see if anyone tries to come after me. I just keep walking as tears start to stream from my eyes.

I've never made anyone that angry. Much less someone I considered a friend, or at the very least a close acquaintance. I thought I would just share my experience with them, and it would be like any other time we talked about the case. I never imagined they wouldn't believe me, or that Micah would...would...I cover my mouth with my hand to muffle the sobs, trying not to draw attention from anyone passing by.

Traveling on autopilot, I head towards my dorm. Before

148

I climb the stairs, I realize Marissa will probably be in our room. Seeking privacy, I change course and duck into the bathroom in the lobby instead. It's rarely ever occupied.

While standing over the sink, I stare at my dark phone screen. Did I do the right thing in deleting those photos? They were irreplaceable, after all. The cops won't be able to get pictures like that. Should I have turned them in to the police, like Micah said? Evidence is evidence, and truth is truth; isn't it their job to sort out what it means?

Then again, this thinking is countered by Leighton's perspective. The justice system isn't perfect. It's a 50/50 shot if a jury of random people would take all that information and condemn her unrightfully. If that jury were anything like Micah, Sidney, and Anthony, the odds might be worse than that. I exhale, realizing just how much I'm banking on the fact that Leighton is innocent. Rightfully or not, I've taken up the role of judge. I just hope my verdict isn't wrong.

Was I even being wholly altruistic, just trying to protect Leighton? Or was something inside of me also afraid of facing the consequences of trespassing? Maybe of going to prison myself. What would people think of me? What would my parents say if they knew all of this was going on?

Gradually, my crying comes to a stop. I splash water on my face and dab it dry with a paper towel. Regardless, what's done is done. The pictures are gone, and I'm not getting them back.

Maybe it's for the best that Sidney, Micah, and Anthony stay suspicious of Leighton. It keeps them from becoming targets. Targets like me, right? I remember the slip of paper tucked in my backpack, and I pull it out.

Even amidst the madness, I have the presence of mind to put Leighton in my phone under a pseudonym, just in case someone were to see. I end up going with simply "Professor." I should remember that. I tear up the card and shove it deep in the trash can, burying the scraps beneath layers of paper towel.

Chapter 23

Foolish Wisdom

To escape the pain of thinking about my broken friendships, my mind turns towards homework assignments. I am still a college student with a full schedule of classes, after all. And if I stay in work mode, I can put off confronting my emotional baggage. I check the time. Wasn't there something I was supposed to do today? I snap my fingers when the answer hits me.

The lab assignment. Great. Well, I'd better just get it over with. I walk back to the natural sciences building. As I approach the door to the laboratory, another student is exiting. I've seen her around, but I don't know her personally. As she passes me in the hallway, I can see fear on her face. "I wouldn't go in there if I were you," she warns. I stop and watch for a moment as she continues down the hall, confused by the ominous statement.

Slowly, I crack the door open and peer into the lab. Her concern makes sense when I see who's inside. Leighton stands alone at a lab table, measuring and mixing samples in several test tubes.

"Addy," she greets as I enter.

I smile lightly. "Hey."

Now that I'm not afraid she'll turn around and murder me, I have an easier time focusing on the lab assignment. I block out the events of the day and bang out the questions.

150

When I'm done, I set my pencil down and take a breath. I look over at Leighton, who's now sitting on a stool reading a book. Her keys are in the analyzer machine, which is running. I might as well just hand in my work now.

I get up and cross the room. As I get closer, I recognize the book in her hands as the leather-bound Bible from her living room. I suddenly wonder if this Bible is also the book I've seen her reading at lunch. I stop a few feet away, waiting for her to notice my presence.

"I finished the lab," I say, raising the paper.

She bookmarks her page and looks up. "Great," she says, holding out a hand. "Do you have a minute? I can look over it now."

"I...okay," I say, unwilling to protest.

"Have a seat," she says, patting a spot at the table. I sit on the stool across from her. She pulls out a pen and starts to go over my answers. "Looks good...looks good," she mutters, turning to the second page.

My eyes dance over the Bible, trying to guess where she might be reading based on the location of the bookmark. Epistles maybe? Automatically, my mind starts to recite the few verses I try to avoid. *She's probably not in any of those chapters* I think, attempting to reassure myself.

I examine the variety of sticky notes and highlighter marks emerging out the sides, wondering what she's found in all those pages. I used to read my Bible every day, but I haven't done so in what feels like forever. Still, I was never really one to make notes.

"Interested?" Leighton asks, eyeing me over the top of the paper. She slides the Bible toward me. "You're welcome to read all you want."

I guess my observations weren't very subtle. My first instinct is to turn the offer down...but I *am* curious. I'm not sure exactly what I expect to find, but I'm suddenly gripped by the hope that something in it could fix me. Fix my faith. Answer my doubts and my questions—

I shut down this ridiculous line of thinking. It's just another Bible. It's not going to fix me. Still, reading is better than just sitting here, anxiously waiting for my paper to be graded and trying not to think about earlier events.

My finger slides under the cover, and I flip it open. A verse is scrawled in dark, bold letters.

For the foolishness of God is wiser than human wisdom, and the weakness of God is stronger than human strength (1 Corinthians 1:25 NIV).

I consider it for a moment, then move to the bookmarked page. My guess was close but not exactly right. The passage is not from an epistle but from Acts, chapter 22. A tangle of ink lines running beneath the words betrays where Leighton left off. I skim the passage, absorbing enough to recognize it as the apostle Paul sharing his testimony with an angry mob of Jewish people. I pause to read a section Leighton has underlined.

Verses 17-20: *When I returned to Jerusalem and was praying at the temple, I fell into a trance and saw the Lord speaking to me. "Quick!" he said. "Leave Jerusalem immediately, because the people here will not accept your testimony about me." "Lord," I replied, "these people know that I went from one synagogue to another to imprison and beat those who believe in you. And when the blood of your martyr Stephen was shed, I stood there giving my approval and guarding the clothes of those who were killing him"* (NIV).

At the words, something in my heart begins to ache. I look to the small note Leighton squeezed in the margin. *A shame when our testimony isn't enough…*

"Good work," Leighton says, slapping the packet down in front of me. "98%. You had one misidentification."

I quickly close the Bible and glance at the grade marked at the top. Mainly out of a feeling of social obligation, I flip to the one I missed and nod. My mind is not on the lab assignment, however. It's back in Micah's dorm, being interrogated about last night.

"Can I ask you a question?" I say to Leighton.

"Of course," she says, eyes trained on the packet. I realize she thinks I'm talking about botany.

"Uh, not about this."

Her eyes smoothly shift up from the paper to look at me. "Same answer."

Though we're alone, I lower my voice to a whisper. "If

the vitamin B12 was stolen and smashed, how do you still have the vial?"

She answers at her usual volume. "The one I showed you isn't the same one that was destroyed. I have a shelf full of them at home, and I've started carrying two on hand."

My shoulders relax. Of course the answer was that easy...but what about the other thing Sid said?

"How does the B12 work, anyway?" I say carefully. "How would you administer it?"

"Intravenous injection," she answers, speaking more slowly. "5 mL starting dose. Should produce immediate results."

"Direct injection? So not an infusion?" I ask, cutting to the chase.

In response, her posture subtly stiffens. She glances towards the door, then eyes me. For a moment, there is a tense silence, save for the sound of her fingers lightly tapping against the tabletop. My palms begin to sweat. Why would such a simple question put her on edge?

Suddenly, the tapping ceases. She sighs, and the hint of a smile shows on her face. "Alright, Addy. You've got me. Yes, you're right, lyophilized hydroxocobalamin—a form of B12—is usually administered through infusion to treat cyanide poisoning. But the formula I have is specially engineered to be more effective and safe for injection." She opens the clasp on the bag and again hands me the bottle to examine.

I trace the official-looking label with my finger. There's a long, scientific name printed on the paper, but it seems similar to whatever term Leighton just used. "Really? I don't think I've heard of that," I reply, remembering my brief, frantic Google search this afternoon.

"No, you wouldn't have," she says, then pauses. "I made it." She sets her bag to the side. "Technically, I'm not supposed to talk about it, as it's top secret property of the US military."

"Oh," I say, comprehending the gravity of her answer. I quickly hand the vial back, and she tucks it away. With a bit more thought, I ask a follow-up question. "Does the military have a lot of secret technology the public doesn't know about?"

She snickers. "It's kind of part and parcel."

"Right." Of course they do. My attention shifts back to

the bag. "You were ready to use that antidote on Matthew, though. Wouldn't that have been some sort of violation?"

"It would be," she says. "But lives take precedence over policies."

I nod, letting her words sink in. Hearing her easily answer my questions reassures me I did the right thing in deleting those photos...But why was it so hard for Micah, Sid, and Anthony to believe me? I suspected Leighton so much I broke into her house! It should mean *something* that my mind was changed, shouldn't it?

"You doing okay, Addy?" Leighton asks.

"Yeah, I'm alright," I reply, trying not to sound as broken up as I feel. I'm not *good,* but I'm holding it together.

"You sure?" she asks again. "Anything else you want to ask? Or share?"

I could just say no. It would be as easy as that. I could take my paper and keep to myself and go back to my dorm. But then again, who else do I have to talk to? Who else would even understand?

"To be honest, I had a bit of a rough afternoon." I size her up, still careful not to reveal anyone else's identity. "I tried to talk with a few close friends about what happened last night. How we were wrong to suspect you, and that the true killer is still out there." Only now does it occur to me that she may not be happy I shared all of that information, but her response is absent any reproof.

"How'd that go?"

My gaze drops to the ground with a sigh. "Not well. They were all skeptical, and they still believe you're guilty. But one friend in particular—well, he was really adamant and it got kind of tense."

"Tense?"

I choose not to elaborate. "Yeah."

She nods. "Well, I hate to be the cause of strife. Sorry about your friends."

"Thank you." I study her expression. "Doesn't it bother you that so many people think you're guilty when you're not?"

She shrugs. "It's a strange feeling. I'd prefer to avoid going to prison, so I'm a little afraid of that. But..." she nods towards the Bible. "The Lord vindicates. I know I'm

154

innocent. Why worry?"

A laugh escapes my throat. Lately, it feels like all I do is worry. "That easy? Just don't worry?"

Leighton grins. "Absolutely. I don't know why everyone doesn't do it." Her tone is brimming with light-hearted sarcasm.

I find myself smiling, too.

"Truthfully," she adds, "I have too many other problems to spend time stressing about what other people think. You can never please everyone."

Across from us, the analyzer machine comes to a stop. Leighton rises and crosses the room to retrieve the data and her samples. She returns with a tray of test tubes and the printout from the machine.

"Is that for a class?" I ask.

"Not exactly," she says while reading the report. "It's a project I've been working on for Dr. Gaines."

At the mention of Dr. Gaines, a pit forms in my stomach.

Leighton continues. "I don't know if he's mentioned anything to your class, but there are some abnormal levels of environmental contaminants in this area."

I shift on my stool. "Contaminants? Is it anything dangerous?"

She frowns, squinting at the data sheet. "It doesn't seem to be anything that would pose a massive public health crisis, at least for the time being, but he was concerned enough to have me look into it, which I think is wise. Mainly, we've found it to be water contamination. The town's drinking water is sourced upstream from where it originates, so it's not an immediate threat, but it's pervasive enough to be leaving deposits in the soil.

"His theory is that there's runoff from the old industrial buildings along the water, perhaps the sawmill and the quarry. These are samples of creek water from up north, near Stone Creek Park." She waves her hand over the test tubes, then lifts the printout. "They've come out clean, though. Which means that somewhere between there and campus, the water is picking up chemicals. I'm gradually working my way down."

"What kind of chemicals?"

She shakes her head. "A strange combination of industrial toxins. Ammonia, acetone, ether, formaldehyde, cyanide…"

"Cyanide?" I echo.

She nods.

"You don't...you don't think that could be related to the poisonings, do you?"

"I've been wondering that myself," she says, biting her lip. "I'm not sure how trace amounts of the toxin in the water could be connected to targeted murders, but it's certainly possible. Maybe the killer is sourcing poison from whichever abandoned plant is causing the pollution. Who knows? I'm hoping that pinpointing the source of the chemicals will shed some more light on the case."

As she fiddles with the samples, I decide to broach the topic of my suspicions. "Do you have any suspects in mind?"

"Save for Chief Boyer, not just yet," she answers. "You?"

I wring my hands together. "Do you...are you at all concerned about Dr. Gaines?" I ask, my voice a whisper. "It's just, I found something out about him by accident."

She raises an eyebrow. "What did you find?"

I hope she doesn't start to think all I do is go around invading people's privacy. "I didn't mean to read it, but I went to his office for a meeting, and this paper fell on the floor...apparently before he died, Dr. Morrell was on the verge of firing Dr. Gaines. And now...well, Gaines is the new dean." I await her reaction.

She nods, seemingly unsurprised. "Yes, that's all true. He told me himself. I can see how it looks bad, but no, I don't suspect Dr. Gaines."

"Why not?" I ask.

"Well, when he talked to me, he didn't seem all that upset by the prospect of losing his job here. He admitted he had another, higher-paying offer lined up at a different school, which he planned to take once they found his replacement here. After being promoted to dean, however, he decided to stay and help things bounce back in the absence of Dr. Morrell."

I let the information sink in, feeling a small smile emerge on my face. It's nice to hear one of my favorite professors is likely not a murderer after all. "Why was he being let go?"

Leighton shrugs. "Maybe you should ask him. My hunch is that Dr. Morrell wanted to get rid of the ecology program altogether. He told me as much in my interview."

156

I shake my head, frazzled. "Wait, what?" *My major?*

She nods. "My interview with both of them went well, but as I was leaving, Dr. Morrell caught me and warned me the school might not exist for much longer. Trying to save me the trouble, he said."

"And now?" I ask. "Are they still planning to get rid of it?"

"Not that I've heard," she says. "Especially with Dr. Gaines as dean, I don't think it's going anywhere anytime soon. Though I don't know how much the board knows about this or how far along they were in the process."

I exhale. Does this mean I'm glad Dr. Morrell died? If he hadn't, would I have been out of a major? I ignore the pang of guilt in my heart. No. It's okay to be happy my school still exists while also not rejoicing over the death of a professor.

"On top of that," Leighton continues, "Dr. Gaines wasn't even on campus the day Dr. Morrell died. He was off at a conference for college educators. Quite a number of professors went."

"A conference?"

"Yep." She reaches into her bag and pulls out a brochure, which she hands to me. "It was out west—Texas, I believe. Held the same weekend Dr. Morrell died."

I glance at the glossy trifold advertisement in my hands. The dates on the front show it spanned from Thursday—the same day Dr. Morrell died—through Saturday.

"Do you know who else went?" I ask, lifting my eyes.

To my surprise, Leighton already has her hand extended towards me, holding out a sheet of printed names.

"Great minds think alike," she says with a smile. "I spent most of my time compiling the list, but I intended to cross-reference it with the staff directory and Matthew's description of the man he saw in the cafe."

Gingerly, I take the list from her hands. "I could help with that," I volunteer.

"By all means. You probably know the professors and staff better than I do. You're welcome to take that with you. I have the file on my computer."

"You sure?" I ask. This goes against everything I know about the treatment of amateur sleuths."You're not gonna tell me I should just stay out of it? That it's too risky?"

She blinks. "Would that stop you?"

I consider the question. The rule-following perfectionist in me would answer yes, absolutely it would. But the part of me that's been stuck on Dr. Morrell's death all semester, the part that broke into Leighton's house, well..."No. Probably not."

"You're smart. You know there's risk involved. If you're determined to investigate, we might as well work together. Just be careful."

I fold the paper into the brochure and slide it into my backpack along with my lab assignment. I check my phone for the time. I've been here longer than I thought. "Well, I've gotta get to dinner. Thank you," I say as I gather my things.

She waves as I head out the door. "See you around."

Chapter 24

Surprised by Kindness

In a way, I'm relieved not to see any of my friends at dinner. I recognize some acquaintances at a long, crowded table and squeeze myself on the end, but hardly anyone says a word to me. I eat quickly and head back to my room.

Upon opening the door, I find Marissa sitting on her bed playing with her phone. All day, I've been trying to formulate answers to any follow-up questions she might have about what I was doing last night, but I'm still not sure what to say. I brace myself.

"Hey," she says absentmindedly.

"Hey," I return. I wait for something to follow the greeting.

"Oh, Addy—" Marissa continues. *Here it comes.* "Could you hand me my phone charger?"Her arm lazily points towards the white cord on her desk.

"Uh, sure," I answer, grabbing it for her. Is that it? I watch as she plugs it into the wall, then quietly sigh in relief. A big part of me is glad I don't have to explain everything to yet another person who won't believe it. But then again, there's another part of me that's a little...sad. It's kind of nice to know people care, that they're interested in where you've been and what you've been up to.

I look at my own phone before chucking it onto my bed. I don't want to think about who will or won't be texting me tonight. After catching up on some more homework, I try to make conversation with Marissa.

"How was your day?" I ask.

She shrugs. "Pretty normal." There's a brief pause while she lowers her phone. "Have you seen this new show on Netflix?" She tilts the screen towards me. I lean in to see, but I don't recognize the title or the cover picture.

"No. Honestly, I haven't watched much TV."

"Oh," she says with a twinge of disappointment in her voice. "Well you should, if you get a chance. I've been binge watching it since yesterday. The episodes aren't that long."

"Maybe," I reply, though I really don't plan on seeking it out.

Marissa nods. "So…did you go to the volleyball game on Friday?"

"Uh, no, I didn't." I didn't even know there was a game. I tend not to follow the sports schedule. "How'd we do?" I ask, trying to take an interest.

"Great!" she says. "We won three to nothing. It's a good team this year."

"Cool," I say, unsure of how to respond.

"What have you been up to?" she asks in return. "Anything fun?"

I try to think of the most fun thing that's happened recently. It's hard to look past all the dark and dreariness of the murders. There have been things I've enjoyed, like meeting Leighton, believe it or not, but that's not exactly what Marissa is asking.

"Um, I've been going to the historical society meetings. I read this book about the history of Flickerwood—it was pretty interesting. Did you know that people used to believe a witch lived in the woods just beyond campus?"

Her eyes flit towards her blank phone screen. "Huh. I haven't heard that one. I'm glad you found a club to join."

"Yeah. Thanks."

The conversation lulls, and Marissa returns to watching her show. Not wanting to seem desperate, I turn back around in my desk chair and try to look busy. Sometimes I wonder why I'm not better friends with my roommate. It's not like I have anything against her. But our conversations

160

are always just—like that.

I settle in to do a reading assignment that takes me the rest of the evening. Outside our room, I hear the click of the hallway door swinging open and shut as girls sporadically enter and exit. Keys jingle, other dorm rooms open, and there's laughter and chatter as people pass by. Just before bed, I finally check my text messages. A part of me was expecting to hear from someone—maybe an angry text from Micah, or a long opinion from Sid, or something from Anthony—but there is nothing. I set my alarm and lock my screen, trying to ignore the feeling of disappointment pricking my chest. I thought I'd outgrown the friend drama; isn't that kind of stuff more for high schoolers? I fall asleep with a few salty tears staining my cheeks and a lonely ache in my bones.

Before leaving in the morning, I decide to take a cue from Leighton and put my Bible in my backpack. At first, it feels strange to leave my room knowing it's in there. It's as if there's a red-hot coal glowing in my bag: a dangerous, explosive thing that will invite the ire of my peers.

I feel out of place when I set it on the table at breakfast. I look around, waiting for someone to judge me. To ask a question I don't have the answer to, or get offended by my religious material. But, of course, no one even notices me. A college student reading a book is not exactly a monumental occurrence.

Once I relax, I decide to go back to the basics. Christianity is about Jesus; all those other issues are only secondary compared to the Savior. I open to the Gospel of Matthew, acknowledging the bitter irony of the name with a short, involuntary laugh. Chapter one starts with a genealogy. All Scripture is God-breathed and useful, right? I resist the urge to skip ahead. However, after a few lines, the words "son" and "father" grind like nails on a chalkboard in my head. I can't help but wonder about all the women these lists leave out. The nameless, faceless characters who seem to have existed only to produce the next generation...

Anger starts to bubble in my heart, and I shut the Bible.

161

Does God only care about these sons and fathers? Well, then why should I care enough to read?

In a matter of seconds, the anger fades, and all I'm left with is existential fear and guilt. I set my elbows on the table and put my head in my hands. This is why I avoid reading altogether. If I stay away from prayer and the Bible, at least I can't say or think anything sacrilegious. Better to be a shallow Christian who makes it to heaven by the skin of their teeth than risk losing my salvation in a surge of frustration, if salvation is even something you can lose. *God, please, forgive me. I want to understand…*

I want to understand, but I fear I'll be crushed. Afraid God's answer is just black and white, stern and unchanging. Afraid He's already mad at me for the things I think out of anger. He just wants me to learn my place. To accept His authority and be happy about it. I am a puny human, a creature, and I have no right to complain. Just like the verse inside the cover of Leighton's Bible said, God is infinitely wiser and stronger than mere people. His ways are higher than mine…

With a burst of courage, I flip forward in Matthew and happen to land on chapter twelve. I read the first two stories, about harvesting grain on the Sabbath and the man with a withered hand. So far so good. But it's a line in the third section of the passage that stands out to me. A quote from Isaiah, according to the footnote. Of Jesus, it says,

A bruised reed he will not break, and a smoldering wick he will not quench… (Matthew 12:20a ESV).

Immediately, tears spring to my eyes. The gentle weight of the words hits me like a wave. *I'm* the bruised reed, and *I'm* the smoldering wick, and maybe I'm not such an enemy of God after all.

At lunch, I see Micah and Sid sitting together, but they avoid making eye contact with me. I sit alone at a table and, once again, start reading the Gospel of Matthew. I can't help but glance at the staff table. Leighton also sits alone, engrossed in the book I now recognize as her Bible and casually munching on an apple. All the other professors huddle together at the adjacent table, like birds trying to flee a cat. I suppress a smile; the sight is kind of amusing.

162

The idea to go and join her crosses my mind, but I know that publicly displaying any alliance with her would put me at greater risk. As I'm watching, there is one professor who approaches her: Dr. Gaines. Their interaction is brief, and they only exchange a few words before he turns to leave. I puzzle over what they might be discussing. Perhaps the research project Leighton told me about? My eyes follow him as he walks out the door.

I'm thankful Leighton gave me reason to trust his innocence, but I still don't have the full story. Maybe, like she said, I'll just have to work up the courage to talk with him myself.

Another familiar face catches my eye. Anthony walks into the dining hall with a full tray. He sees me and smiles slightly, but quickly averts his eyes, walking instead towards Sid and Micah. My shoulders slump as I sigh, turning my attention back to the Bible.

"Hey Addy."

I flinch, startled by the voice.

Anthony stands over me, seemingly having teleported across the room. "Sorry I scared you."

"Oh, you're good," I assure him. I close my Bible, wondering where this conversation is going.

"Mind if I sit with you?" he asks.

"Uh, you're welcome to," I say slowly, fearing another argument, "but if this is just about the pictures—"

He shakes his head, taking a seat. "Don't worry. I—I know you had your reasons."

I relax a little. "Well, then, what's up?"

"Listen, I'm not one to beat around the bush. What happened yesterday—that was crazy." He shakes his head. "I can't speak for Micah. I don't know him that well, and I know he's going through a lot, but he had me a little worried. For a minute there, I was afraid I'd have to throw hands." He exhales, clearly relieved things didn't go further. "I was gonna text you, but I wasn't sure what to say. Are you okay?"

I smile, grateful for Anthony's straightforward way of communicating. "Yeah, I'm doing okay. Not great, of course. But okay. Thanks for asking." I'd rather not share that it brought me to tears more than once.

"Of course, of course."

I hesitate. I'm happy I haven't lost Anthony's friendship, and I don't want to push it, but I need to know. "So…what do you think about everything I said yesterday?"

He spoons peas into his mouth, then stares into the distance, considering. "To be perfectly honest, I'm still thinking about it." He takes another bite. "I mean, you were suspicious of Professor Leighton before I was, and after hearing Micah's story, we were all pretty convinced she had something to do with the murders. So it's surprising that you've suddenly changed your mind." He shrugs. "But also, maybe that's a sign it's the truth."

He points his empty spoon towards me. "For the record, I do believe your story, that you broke into the cabin and everything. And like you, I'm stuck on the fact that she helped you instead of hurting you. Seems unlikely you'd be alive if she really were guilty." He takes a sip of soda. "Basically, I don't know what I believe about her. I'm not sure I would have deleted the photos myself, but I also don't blame you."

I nod along to his explanation. I can respect his uncertainty. "You don't?"

He shakes his head, and a strand of curly black hair falls onto his face. He brushes it away. "No. I know you were just following your convictions, and I can support that. Anyone would have panicked if someone grabbed their phone like Micah did. Besides, the idealist in me wants to believe justice can be done without evidence obtained by committing another crime."

I feel my face turn red. I smile sheepishly. "Yeah…"

"I didn't mean that as a judgement," he says, spreading his hands. "Like I told you, I did practically the same thing."

I snicker. "But no one was living in the cabin when you went."

"Trespassing is still trespassing." He smiles and shrugs. "Cool?"

I give him a thumbs up. "Thanks for not hating me."

He follows my gaze to Sid and Micah. I don't mean to stare for as long as I do. "They don't hate you," he says.

"Hope not."

"They'll come around," he assures, but his voice lacks its usual easy confidence. "The truth will come out at some point."

"You think so?"

"I do." He continues to eat his lunch, and I enjoy the warm feeling of friendship. "So, I have a confession," he says suddenly. There's a twinkle in his eye, which tips me off to the joking nature of his statement. "I actually only came over here to give another shameless plug for the Wynhurst Historical Society. Are you coming tonight?"

I laugh. "Well, now that I know we're on speaking terms, I might consider it."

"You should. It's gonna be at the Morrell house. Do you know where it is?"

"No, I've never been." Admittedly, I'm always curious to see where professors live, and this curiosity is only strengthened by the idea of seeing where the late Dr. Morrell used to call home, along with his wife, who still lives there. I contain my curiosity, however. I would also love to come just because I enjoy the historical society. And Anthony's company.

"I can show you," he says.

"Okay. Yeah, I'll plan to come tonight."

Chapter 25

Muffin

As I walk towards Dr. Edith Morrell's house, I keep checking my blood sugar. Anthony went early to help set up, but he told me where to go. What he failed to mention is whether or not this event would involve food.

Absent this information, my brain starts doing logical loops as I get closer. *Okay, I'm at 90. If there are snacks, which there probably will be, I'll be at a good place to have some. But then again, there might not be, or they could be low-carb, or I could be left waiting.*

I shake my hands out, frustrated that I'm spending so much brain power on this. Just before I reach the house, I decide I'd rather be safe than sorry. I grab a juice out of my backpack and stick a straw in it. Taking a sip, I put my foot on the first step leading up to the porch.

To me, the house looks massive. Much bigger than any of the other townhomes on the street. It's Victorian in style, with a large cylindrical section to the left, topped with a cone-shaped roof. The color also stands out; it's painted a pale shade of yellow, but it looks impossibly bright next to the browns and reds of the brick houses around it.

Just as I'm about to knock on the door, Dr. Edith swings it open.

"Addy!" she says with a smile. "So glad you could make it! Come in, come in."

Juice in hand, I walk in on a bustling scene. The inside is well-lit with lamps, giving it a soft yellow glow. The wooden boards creak beneath my feet. Dr. Edith leads me down a hallway and into a dining room full of students milling about. The table is set with refreshments—cookies, cheese and crackers, fruit, nuts—I should have just waited. Ah well.

"Please, have a muffin," she says, waving a hand towards the table. "Or a cookie or whatever you want—we have so much food."

"Oh, I'm good, but thank you," I say, raising my juice.

She frowns. "Are you sure? You really shouldn't leave me with any leftovers. Heaven knows I don't need them," she says, patting her stomach. With a smile, she floats off to talk to some other students.

I spot a corner where a bunch of backpacks are sitting, and I add mine to the bunch. I finish my juice, chuck it in the trash, and grab a handful of cashews. It's not long before I spot Anthony. He's crouched beside one of the bookshelves, thumbing through an old book with a faded green cover. Upon seeing me, he quickly re-shelves it and approaches.

"Hey! Have any trouble getting here?" he asks.

"Nope. You were right; I couldn't miss it."

"Cool house, isn't it? You know, it actually used to be a public library. Its construction was funded by some family that got rich in the furniture industry."

"Do you know everything about this town?" I ask with a smile.

"Not everything," he says with a serious expression. "But almost everything." He breaks into a grin. "It's kind of my job. But hey, I'm not speaking tonight. We get to hear from Jillian—she knows much more about architecture than I do."

As the presentation starts, we all scramble to find seats. In the process, someone knocks my bag over. I must not have zipped it up all the way, because pens, pencils, granola bars, and juice boxes come tumbling out. Anthony helps me gather everything up, and we sit together on two wooden dining room chairs.

After the presentation, as people start to leave, Anthony offers to help clean up. "If you don't mind sticking around, I can drive you back to campus, if you want," he offers.

"Sure. I don't mind helping," I reply. Walking through an unfamiliar part of town alone in the dark seems like a bad idea. Plus, I want to be polite. I help carry dishes to the kitchen, pack away the leftovers, and rearrange the furniture in the dining room. Before I know it, we're the only two students left.

We end up in the kitchen, where Dr. Edith stands near the sink, folding a tea towel. Anthony leans against the counter, and I stand awkwardly in the corner. I assume we should be heading out soon.

Anthony, however, seems to have other plans. He turns to Dr. Edith and suddenly asks, "Dr. Morrell, what are your thoughts on Professor Leighton?"

I jolt, my eyes flying wide open. Did he really just say that?! I rein my reaction back in, trying to seem relaxed. *It's okay. He's just asking a question. Besides, there's no one else here.*

At first, she seems as surprised as me. Slowly, she turns around to face us both. "Leighton? The ecology professor, you mean?"

He nods.

She wrinkles her forehead. "My thoughts? Why do you ask?"

"Well," Anthony says, "I'm sure you've heard about the police taking her in for questioning in the middle of class. A lot of people suspect she was responsible for—for the cyanide poisoning at that party."

She glances between me and Anthony. "Truth be told, I've never officially met Professor Leighton, though if the police suspect her, I'm sure they have a good reason." She studies him. "I know you, in particular, are prone to go adventuring, but until they have someone behind bars for that atrocity, you can't be too cautious. Both of you should be careful."

Her words remind me of my relatives' continual warning. My mom, my aunt, my grandmother: be careful at college. We love you. Be careful, be careful. My feet turn towards the door, ready to leave, but Anthony presses further.

"Have you considered that Matthew's death might have something to do with your husband's passing?"

Flabbergasted, I shoot him a look.

Dr. Edith purses her lips. "Listen. I know there are whispers about them being connected, but no one murdered Greg." Her bottom lip twitches almost imperceptibly. "They did a medical exam—like I said, he had a heart condition."

"But...what if?" Anthony stresses. His voice is compassionate and pleading. "I'm sure you don't want to think about it, but don't you want to know if something really did happen? What if—what if it was one murder to cover up another?"

"Anthony, please!" she barks.

He falls silent.

She sighs and shakes her head. This time, her reply is gentler, "I know you like looking for scary stories, but there are none to be found here. People die; it's a part of life. And some murders don't have any motive at all." She looks to me for support. "Addy, you don't believe any of this stuff, do you? It's all an absurd conspiracy theory. Just because something terrible happened on campus doesn't mean Gregory's death was also a murder. You know that, right?" Her eyes bore into me.

My hesitation is her answer.

Her head swivels between me and Anthony in disbelief. "Alright, listen," she says. "You want my thoughts on Professor Leighton?" She nods towards Anthony. "I'm sure he's told you all the legends about that cabin she's living in. But did he mention the true history of what happened there?"

Anthony wrinkles his brow in confusion. "What history?"

"I'm surprised you haven't heard," she replies. "In the scheme of things, it wasn't all that long ago. Anyone who's lived here long enough will remember.

"Around 20 odd years ago, the cabin was home to a single mother and her only daughter. At first, the two seemed like a fairly happy family, despite the circumstances. As the daughter grew older, however, it became clear that there was something...well, a little different about her.

"She didn't play well with the other kids at school and often chose to go off by herself. People started to say she was more like a beast than a child. She used to run through the forest like a wild animal, and some even saw her torturing little rabbits and stray kittens." Dr. Edith shivers. "As she got older, she got even more violent. Parents didn't want their children to be near her.

"Her mother began to have trouble controlling her. When the poor woman came into town, she would have bruises on her face or scratches all over her arms. Sometimes chunks of hair would be missing from her head. She always said she had such a wonderful child, and that everything was fine, but the ladies of the town—oh, we knew what was going on." Dr. Edith pauses with a pained expression on her face. "If only we had done something before it was too late. I often wonder if we could have saved her." She shakes her head sadly.

"You see what happened, don't you? This woman, she had a psychopath for a daughter. Cold, unfeeling, remorseless psychopath. And one night, when the girl was about nine years old, things took a turn for the worst. No one knows exactly what possessed her to do it, but something in her flipped, and she murdered her mother in cold blood. The police only found out by chance, when an off-duty officer saw the little girl standing at the end of the driveway covered in blood." She averts her eyes for a moment. "They took the girl away to the looney bin, and they buried her mother. Rest her soul, that woman."

She pauses, a stormy look settling over her eyes. "Any guesses what that little girl's name was?"

I stand frozen in place, my eyes trained on Dr. Edith. As much as I try to scramble for some other answer, I know what name she's going to say.

Almost silently, I breathe the word as she says it.

"Bryn."

"Wait, you're saying that the girl from 20 years ago is actually Professor Leighton?" Anthony asks.

"Of course, her last name is different, but it does seem too eerie to simply be a coincidence, doesn't it? I've been wondering myself if she only changed it to hide the truth." Her attention turns to me. "You said you were an ecology major, didn't you?" she asks.

All I can do is nod.

"Well, then I would advise you to be especially careful. Insanity, mental illness—they're not always apparent. Some people seem perfectly normal until one day..." she snaps her fingers. "Things can turn violent." The last word hangs in the air. She shrugs. "I don't know anything for sure, but, to answer your question, Anthony, *that* is my opinion."

"Um, we should probably be heading out," I say, hoping to stop Anthony before he asks any more questions.

He looks to me, then back to Dr. Edith. "Right, right. Thank you, Dr. Morrell. I appreciate you talking to us."

"Of course, Anthony," she says. Her posture relaxes. She picks up a plate of leftover muffins and holds them out to us. "Muffins for the road? Please, take some."

"Thank you," he says, grabbing two before I can protest. He hands one to me. I don't argue. I put on my coat and backpack and follow him out the door.

Anthony devours his muffin before we even reach his car. He pulls out his keys and unlocks it, then gets in the driver's seat. I sit in the passenger seat and observe, a small part of me expecting him to keel over.

"What?" he asks. "Do I have something on my face?"

I shake my head. "No, sorry. I just—" I change the topic. "I can't believe you came out and asked her all of that."

He shrugs, starting the engine. "I know information is dangerous and all—it's always a risk to share anything—but it's just Dr. Morrell. I've known her and her husband for over three years. They loved each other; she wouldn't have killed him. It's just sad to see her in denial." We pull away from the curb. "Why? Do you suspect her?"

I stare at the muffin in my hand. My sugar's come back down, and it does look good. I can't resist. I take a bite before answering. "To be honest, I was a little suspicious at first. But I guess there's no real reason to think she's guilty."

"Well, I'm still sorry to rope you into the conversation. I guess I should've thought it through a bit more."

"All good," I say automatically. As tense as it was, I guess I'd rather be included than not.

I gaze out the window as I eat, vaguely watching the houses whizz by. An uncomfortable, disturbed feeling settles over me like dark clouds. Though Anthony and I weren't exactly on the same page about Leighton to begin with, a mounting dread pushes my concerns to the surface. I can't face it alone. "So...what did you think about the story of the cabin?" I ask him. "And the suggestion that Leighton might be insane?"

He thinks for a moment. "I'm not sure yet. That was a lot, and it just came out of nowhere. But if it's true...well, you have to admit it's a strange coincidence, to have the same name as the girl who...you know, killed her mom."

"Yeah..." I say, feeling dazed.

"...maybe she really is crazy," Anthony ventures. "Like Morrell said, sometimes you can't really tell. Maybe it's like a Jekyll and Hyde kinda thing. She might not even remember doing it."

My stomach feels sick as Anthony's theory is fleshed out in my mind. Does Leighton really have a secret dark side? I mean, what are the odds that she would just happen to be in the same house, with the same name, at the same age as that girl would be...

Then again, there are reasons to believe this isn't the whole truth. Leighton didn't just black out at the party; she told me exactly why she was there and what she was doing. Plus, she was in the Navy. They don't let mentally unstable people join the military—my friend got denied for having taken an anti-anxiety med for a few months in high school. She can't possibly have been hospitalized in a psych ward. I mean, if a little girl really did kill her mother and become institutionalized, she's probably still in treatment.

"Are we even sure all that stuff happened?" I ask Anthony. "I mean, you said you've never heard the story before, right?"

"No, I haven't," he admits, "but there's an easy way to find out."

Chapter 26

Process of Elimination

We soon sit together in a deserted corner of the library, poring over newspaper archives.

"Bingo," Anthony says as he clicks on one. "Just like Dr. Edith said, dated 20 years ago."

I follow his gaze, mildly impressed by his research abilities. The column reads as follows:

> *Last evening, police responded to an incident at 6046 Hickory Drive after Officer Jack Ritner spotted a young girl walking near the road whose "hands and clothing appeared to be covered in blood." Shortly after, the girl's mother was rushed to the hospital in critical condition. Authorities say the residence contained evidence of a violent struggle, and a full investigation is underway.*

Anthony scrolls down further and flips a few pages. "Wait, is that it?"

I scan the page with him. "Looks like it."

He checks on some later editions of the paper to see if they ever reported more on it, but finds nothing.

"Huh," he says. "There's not much here, but it seems like the story is true."

"Part of it, at least," I say slowly. "Though Dr. Edith could be mistaken about some of the details. I mean, we have no

173

way of knowing what really went on in that house. Maybe a third person broke in, attacked her mom, and then fled, or maybe she acted in self-defense against abuse or something." My voice falters. The possible explanations rearrange guilt, but they do nothing to make the situation more palatable.

"Could be," Anthony says quietly, still staring at the computer. I can tell he's not fully convinced of my explanation, but then again, neither am I.

"And we can't forget that Edith Morrell still doesn't believe her husband was murdered," I continue. "She was trying to suggest Matthew was killed by a psychopath at random—she has no idea he was targeted because he witnessed someone switching Dr. Morrell's drink mere hours before he died. The things she says about the case should be taken with a grain of salt."

He bobs his head from side to side. "All true. Though I would give her a bit more credit than that. Her judgement about her husband is clouded by grief; that doesn't mean everything she says is unreliable."

"Okay. Fair point," I concede, unwilling to argue.

He sighs as he closes the tabs on the computer. "I wish we could figure out who it was Matthew saw."

My hand flies to my bag. "Maybe we can."

He looks at me with a confused expression.

I rifle through my notebooks and produce the brochure for the educators' conference and the list of names of those who went. Suddenly self-conscious, I hesitate before telling the truth. "Professor Leighton gave these to me. Apparently, a lot of professors were at this conference the week Dr. Morrell died, including Dr. Gaines. If we rule out all the faculty who were away when Matthew saw the man, we might be able to narrow it down to a few suspects."

He rubs his chin. "We could do that. Best lead we have." With a few clicks on the university website, he prints out a staff directory. It's longer than I expected.

When we finish crossing out the names of everyone who went to the conference, I write the physical description Matthew gave at the top of the paper—tall, thin, gray hair, and, at the time, a short beard. Anthony begins searching for faculty profile pictures on the computer.

174

It's tiring, going line by line. I catch myself yawning on multiple occasions, then laugh when it spreads to Anthony.

"Stop that," he says, mouth agape. "It's contagious."

"Not like I can help it," I say, smiling. As I begin to count the remaining names, something stands out. "You know, there is one group of people who didn't go to the conference: the board of trustees."

"Hmm," Anthony replies, then types something in the search bar. "It looks like there was a board meeting the same Thursday Dr. Morrell died.

"Really?" I ask, scanning the names.

"Here," he says, angling his laptop screen so I can see. A collection of professional portraits stare back at me. "These are all of the board members."

I look over the pictures. Out of about fifteen people, only two are women. Quite a few have gray hair, but I notice a comparatively young face occupying the position of chairman. He looks familiar, for some reason. My leg bounces beneath the table as a bad feeling creeps over me.

Where have I seen those glasses before? They're distinctive, with thick black frames. Those, with his dark brown hair and beard…A lightbulb goes off in my head. It's the man from church, the one I saw slap his baby.

I glance at the name below the picture. *Michael Sayer.*

Anthony's voice draws my attention elsewhere. "Didn't you say you thought one of the police officers was in on it?" he asks.

Though a bit confused by his question, I nod. "Yeah. He kept the poison under wraps. Chief of police, Eric Boyer."

"You remember that guy we met outside Dr. Conley's office? The board member?" His finger falls on another familiar face. "Didn't he say his son was the chief of police?"

That strange interaction comes flooding back as I take in the picture of a thin, gray-haired board member beneath Anthony's index finger.

At the time, he had seemed like an ally for supporting our suspicion of Leighton. But now…

"Dr. Robert Boyer," Anthony reads.

"Father of Chief Eric Boyer," I add, putting the pieces together.

For a few moments, we both stare at the screen in silence, unable to look away from the man.

"I can't deny that it checks out," Anthony says finally, scratching the back of his head. "Matthew probably wouldn't have recognized him, but he also wouldn't have seemed out of place meeting with a professor on campus. It's clear he was here on the day Dr. Morrell died—one of the few people who wasn't home or at the conference. And if his son is as corrupt as Professor Leighton says he is, it's not a stretch to believe it was him."

"Do you think there's any way to know for sure?" I ask.

Anthony thinks for a moment, then lunges for the keyboard. "Hang on a second." After a brief search, he pulls up a recorded livestream of the board meeting. He scrubs through to the very end, where everyone is rising from their seats. The man we now know to be Robert Boyer stands at the edge of the table. A staff water bottle hangs at his side, dangling from his fingers. He smiles and greets another man who approaches. As the second man turns towards the camera, I recognize him as Dr. Morrell.

Together, they walk offscreen just before the video cuts out.

My heart flutters in my chest.

In a faint whisper, the unmistakable conclusion leaves my lips. "It's him. It's really him. Dr. Morrell's murderer."

Chapter 27

Cold Invitation

When my Friday morning chemistry class lets out, I quickly rise from my seat and gather my things. I try not to dwell on the fact that this is the first time Sid has chosen to sit apart from me. Instead, I head straight for the door, fully expecting her to continue ignoring me.

Before I can exit the classroom, however, Sid stops me.

"Hey, Addy. How are you doing?" She forces a smile.

Confused, I study her face, suddenly missing Anthony's forthrightness. "I dunno," I say. "Wednesday was weird. How are you?"

Her eyes grow sad, almost pleading. "Listen, it was just a misunderstanding. Micah didn't mean to do anything crazy. He's just been through a lot...he's really struggling, you know."

I straighten my shoulders and try to keep a calm, even tone. I shouldn't be angry at Sid. It's Micah who flipped out on me. But something about her trying to justify his reaction makes me sick to my stomach. "I know Micah's hurting, but he's still responsible for his actions. You shouldn't be making excuses for him, Sid."

She glances at the floor and wrings her hands together. "I know, I know. You're right. He should really apologize, and that's on him."

For a second, I'm pleasantly surprised by her words. The

feeling is quickly quashed, however, by her follow-up statement.

"But Addy, you have to take partial credit for this." Everyone else has long since left the classroom, but she still glances over her shoulder before whispering, "I mean, you deleted what could have been a key piece of evidence in solving this case! And especially after all the trouble you went through to get it—I just can't wrap my mind around why you would destroy it so recklessly." Her tone is sharp and accusatory.

I shake my head, starting to check out of the conversation. "Sid, I tried to tell you. It's not her. Eric Boyer, the police chief, is corrupt, and Anthony and I were just looking into it last night. His father is that board member we met, Dr. Boyer, and he—" I cut myself off mid-sentence upon hearing footsteps outside the door.

We both freeze. Slowly, the footsteps grow faint as the person disappears down the hallway. I didn't see who it was, but I hope they didn't overhear our conversation.

When the coast seems clear, Sid speaks. "Addy, what if you're wrong about Professor Leighton?"

For a moment, I stand silent. I feel helpless to convey all the reasons why I feel so confident backing Leighton. "What if *you're* wrong?" I ask quietly. "It's like you haven't listened to anything I've been saying. It feels like you just want to argue with me."

"I don't want to argue with you!" she snaps, growing flustered. "I just think you should apologize for destroying that evidence."

A knife point reopens the wound in my chest when I comprehend that Sid really isn't here to mend bridges. "I'm sorry if I hurt you, but I don't regret deleting the pictures. And even if I did, it's not going to bring them back." I start walking towards the door. I'm not sure how long I can keep my composure.

"Wait, wait," she says with a sudden change in tone. She grabs my shoulder. "Forget the pictures for a minute. There's something else I wanted to tell you."

I stop and turn back around, curious. "Oh?"

"Micah got the news yesterday. Matthew's funeral is going

to be on Sunday at three o'clock. It's a few towns over, so his parents offered to pick us up around two-thirty. I figured you'd want to know, in case you wanted to come."

I swallow. The only funerals I've attended were for distant relatives: my great uncle and great grandmother, neither of whom I remember very much. "I...I would like to come, if there's room. Thanks for telling me," I say softly.

"Okay," she says. "No problem. See you Sunday."

In the hallway, Sid and I part ways. She exits the building through the side door, walking purposefully towards some other destination. I swivel away from the door and head towards the staff offices. I should still have time to catch Professor Leighton during her open office hours like I planned, though the focus I had this morning has been broken.

My thoughts bounce from one dark topic to another: my broken friendship, Matthew's funeral, and then Dr. Edith Morrell's story about the violent history of Leighton's cabin. Sid's question pokes at a small part of me. What if I *am* wrong? I shake the thought away.

I'm still trying to find something positive amidst the dreariness when I reach her office. Though it's closed, I can see light shining through the rectangular window in the door. I pace for a few steps before knocking.

"Come in!" I hear a voice say.

Chapter 28

The Side Unseen

I try the handle, which turns freely. Upon entering, the first thing I notice is that her office is set up differently than most. Standard practice tends to be to divide the room by placing the desk straight ahead, with a chair or two for students in front and the professor sitting behind, facing back towards the door.

Leighton, however, sits just to the right of the doorway. Her desk is parallel with the wall behind me, and she has a full view of the window along the far wall. I smile when I notice a small potted cactus in the sill.

"Good to see you, Addy," she says, looking up from her paperwork. "Feel free to have a seat. What can I do for you?"

I shut the door behind me, then sit down in one of the chairs opposite her. My fingers rapidly tap against the back of my palm as I try to contain myself. "I—I know who killed Dr. Morrell," I burst.

Her head rocks back in surprise. "Please, do tell."

"His name is Dr. Robert Boyer. He's on the board of trustees, and his son is the police chief you were telling me about."

She listens carefully, then nods. "I thought it might be someone on the board. I heard they held a meeting while everyone was away at the educators' conference." Her hand moves to rest on her chin. "Well, that would explain why Chief Eric Boyer is so keen to protect the killer; it's his father.

What led you to this conclusion?"

I recount how Anthony and I worked our way through the staff directory, then tell her about the video of Boyer and Morrell leaving the meeting together.

"A video? Do you think you could find it?" she asks, turning her computer over to me. In a few minutes, I manage to pull it up. She watches the footage intently.

"We...we weren't sure what to do. I didn't want to go to the Flickerwood police, especially after what happened to Matthew, so I figured I'd come to you."

"You made a good call," she says. "Don't worry about it. I can find the number for the state police and report it. Plus, that way it'll be my name on the line instead of yours. Can't guarantee they'll spring into action right away, but I can promise to try."

I let out a pent-up breath. "Really? Thank you." We rewatch the video one more time. "So now we know who did it and how, but...for what reason?" I ask. "Do you have any idea why Dr. Boyer might have wanted Morrell dead?"

"Great question," she replies. "Absent any evidence of a personal vendetta, my first thought is to look for monetary gain...I have been wondering if Dr. Morrell had a large portion of money to will away. Something along those lines."

Now there's something I hadn't thought about. "How would we find that information?" I ask.

"Well..." Leighton stops and glances at the clock. "Right now, I have a prior arrangement to meet with Dr. Gaines and discuss the contaminant research I've been doing. You're welcome to come along—could be a good learning opportunity. Though it's probably safer to leave this particular conversation in the confines of this room."

I blink, adjusting to the sudden change. "Sure," I say. "I'll walk with you."

She gives a thumbs-up as she slings the strap of her bag over her shoulder. "Great."

I follow her into the hallway, and she stops to lock the door behind her. "So how are things going with your friends?" she asks. "Any better?"

I'm caught off guard by the question; I guess I did tell her things weren't going well the last time we spoke. I bob my head from side to side. "Kind of. I seem to be on good terms with one of them, but the other two…I dunno. We'll see what happens."

She nods, turning away from the door. Her expression is one of sincere interest. It strikes me that, even amidst the chaos of unsolved murder, she actually cares how I'm doing.

We start down the hall. "I could give you some cliche about how friends will come and go in your life or assure you that things will get better—which are both true—but honestly, relating to people is always hard, no matter what age you are."

Her response is strangely comforting. It *is* hard, isn't it? I thought friendship was supposed to be easy, especially compared to romance, and I've always wondered why I find it so difficult. People say college friends are supposed to last a lifetime, but right now I'm not so sure.

"How are you doing?" I ask, returning the question.

She seems surprised by this. "How am I? Not too bad, though I must admit my self-confidence as a professor has certainly taken a hit. I expected there to be a learning curve for the new job, but I don't think it's normal to have over half your students either drop the course or cease coming to class, even for a first-time professor."

"Well, if it makes you feel better, it has nothing to do with your teaching ability. I think your class is great," I assure her, trying to be optimistic.

She laughs. "Thank you."

"What made you want to be a professor in the first place?" I ask, curious.

"Ah." She tilts her head. "That's a good question. There was an opening, it fit my credentials, figured I might enjoy imparting knowledge to younger people, a chance to share what I know." Her boots softly clack on the floor as we approach Dr. Gaines' office.

"Why Wynhurst? And Flickerwood?" In a moment of bravery, I ask the real question I want to know. "…Did you grow up here?"

She comes to a stop just outside the office door. Her head snaps in my direction. Of all the questions I've asked her, nothing has seemed to startle her so much. She considers me for a moment. "I did, actually. At least for part of my childhood. Right in the same cabin. Thought it would be nice to come back to my roots, sort some stuff out." She raises her hand to knock but hesitates once more. "Addy, what makes you ask that?"

My stomach drops as my brain scrambles for an answer to her question. Before I can find one, I'm saved by the door swinging open.

"Bryn, Addy, please, come in." Dr. Gaines greets us and waves us inside. "Can I get you anything? Coffee? Tea?"

"No, thank you, though," Leighton says, having a seat and rummaging in her bag. I similarly reject the offer and sit beside her.

He closes the door and sits back in his chair. His expression darkens. "So, I hear the contaminants are worse than we thought."

"Yes and no," Leighton says, setting data sheets in front of him. Among them is a map of Flickerwood. "The levels are even higher than we suspected, but the good news is it's not as widespread as we thought." She circles a spot on the map. "Based on my samples, the source lies somewhere between the sawmill and the woods along the southern part of campus. It shouldn't take terribly long to search it and find some answers."

Dr. Gaines holds his head as Leighton walks him through the plan to locate the source of the chemicals.

"What would I do without you? That sounds perfect. I want you on this as soon as possible. I'll call the health department again and make them aware."

"Thank you, sir," Leighton says.

"No, no, thank *you*."

As the meeting ends, we go our separate ways. Leighton has something else to get to, and I start to walk away, but suddenly turn back. I duck my head into Dr. Gaines' office.

My hands grow sweaty, but I force myself to continue. "Uh, Dr. Gaines…" I start.

He looks up from his desk.

"I…I just wanted to tell you that, when Sidney and I met with you last week, a paper flew off your desk and landed on the floor. We didn't mean to pry, but…well, I saw that Dr.

Morrell wanted to fire you a few months ago." I close the door behind me. It latches with a click.

He removes his reading glasses and sets them on the desk, then leans back in his chair. "Ah," he sighs. "That is, rather unfortunately, true." He gestures to the large dean's office around us. "And now I have his office. I know that doesn't look great." He grimaces.

"Listen, Addy. Professors have disagreements just like anyone else. To be perfectly truthful, Dr. Morrell and I butted heads quite often. I disagreed with his plan to clear trees for building projects in the southern part of campus, and he didn't like my push to expand the nature trails further north. I'm sure he wasn't a fan of me spending resources on environmental research, either. He didn't care for the ecology program, and I think his goal was to shut it down. But," he waves a hand, "it's just drama. We all have friends and enemies. Although we try to only speak well of the dead, everyone has some rough edges." Dr. Gaines chuckles. "Myself included.

"In case you need to hear it, I would never escalate to any kind of bodily harm for all that petty stuff. Past is past. Besides. Not to brag, but with my credentials and level of experience, there's an ample amount of opportunities elsewhere." Dr. Gaines furrows his eyebrows. "Truth be told, the *nicest* Dr. Morrell ever was to me was in the week or two before he died."

I swallow. "So you *do* believe Dr. Morrell was murdered?"

He pauses. "I can't say anything definitively, but after what came out about Matthew…it doesn't seem like such a crazy idea." Just as I'm preparing to leave, he adds, "Are you still concerned about Professor Leighton? It seems to me like you've changed your mind about her."

"I—no, I'm not concerned. I think my suspicions were misplaced."

He nods. "Good. I'm glad to hear it."

Chapter 29

Unity and Peace

Sunday morning, I stand in front of my closet, leafing through my dressier clothes. Anthony agreed to take me to church with him, but I neglected to ask him about the dress code. From what I know of baptist churches, some expect formal attire, and I don't want to show up in something too casual. Some places don't even let women wear pants.

I pinch the fabric of one of my dresses. But is this *too* formal? If my skin color is already going to make me stick out, I don't want my outfit to draw any additional attention. My hand skips to the one long skirt I have. A glance at the clock gets me to pull the trigger. Skirt it is.

As I tug it on, a new consideration strikes me. What if it's one of those churches that makes all the women wear a head covering? Ah. I wave the thought away. Anthony would have told me if that were the case, right? Besides, it's not like I have a proper head covering anyway.

Clad in my long skirt, frilly blouse, and winter coat, I head out to breakfast. When I'm done, I wait outside the dining hall. Before long, Anthony pulls up to the curb. In the daylight, I can see his car more clearly. It's the typical picture of a beater: a four-door sedan with faded green paint, save for one gray door that was clearly replaced. Assorted window decals litter the rear windshield, including one for Wynhurst University, and there are some scattered dents and

185

dings in the body. I smile. There's a sort of charm to it.

"Morning," he greets through the window. I can see he's wearing a dress shirt and tie. I'm glad I went with the skirt.

"Hey," I say. "Thanks for taking me."

"No problem! Happy to."

I tug the door open and climb into the passenger seat, holding my Bible in my lap. I've never been one to take my Bible with me to church, but something about the strange translation of the pew Bible at the other church and seeing Professor Leighton's attachment to her own copy inspired me to bring it along.

We ride off campus and cruise through town, eventually arriving at a fairly average-looking church building. The outside is painted white, with a faded marquee sign by the door reading: *All are welcome / todos son bienvenidos.*

A tall black man in a t-shirt greets us at the door. He hands me a program, and we continue into the sanctuary. I must visibly do a double-take, because Anthony looks at me and stops.

"What?" he asks innocently.

I hesitate, a little embarrassed by the truth. "Uh...well, it's just not what I was expecting."

"What were you expecting?"

I struggle for a moment before noticing the mischievous grin slowly appearing on his face. He knows exactly what he's doing.

"Ohhhh," he says, lightly smacking himself on the forehead. "You thought it'd be a black church. Nah."

My cheeks flush red as I smile back. "You didn't correct me."

I follow him to a row of seats, taking in the scene before me. Anthony wasn't lying when he implied I would be a racial minority, but I now understand what he meant. Rather than a majority of black or white people, the church members around us are from a wide range of ethnicities. Among them are families who appear to be Indian and East Asian, as well as African American and Caucasian. To my left, I catch a few conversations going on in Spanish. Thankfully, there are no head coverings. And—I check to be sure—I do see women wearing pants.

186

As the worship band assembles at the front, the congregation grows quiet. I stand up with everyone else, and the music begins. Though the songs and the instruments used to play them are different than what I'm used to back home, as I gaze around the room, a sense of peace begins to settle in my heart.

I didn't realize how homesick I felt for a church until I tried going with Micah. But that experience only sharpened the longing, like drinking salt water to quench your thirst. I was afraid this would be the same thing, but...for some reason, things already feel different here. Better. Warmer.

Some people sway to the music, raising their hands up high. Others stand still, maybe with a hand over their heart. Many are smiling, and some have their eyes closed, contemplating the words. I'm struck, I suppose, by the sincerity. Reading the words on the screen, I start to sing, too. Reading the words on the screen, I join in. It's been a long time since I've let myself sing this loud. It feels good.

Tears start to flood my eyes. I close them and let myself be covered in the chorus of voices—all singing to praise Jesus. That's what it means to be part of the Church, isn't it? To love despite the differences. Unity in diversity. I may not know any of these people, save for Anthony, but I can already tell we love the same Savior. And that Savior loves me, too. I feel safe. I feel at home.

By the end of the sermon, I know I'll be back next week.

Later that afternoon, I awkwardly get in the back seat of Matthew's parents' car. Micah sits on the left, I sit on the right, and Sid sits between us.

"Hey," Sid greets.

Micah nods in my direction, but doesn't say anything.

"Hey," I answer. "Thanks for giving us a ride," I say, acknowledging Mr. and Mrs. Bruner in the front. Sid and Micah also chime in with thanks.

"Of course, of course," Mrs. Bruner replies absentmindedly. She stares out the window as we go along.

"It's nice to know Matthew had friends, a community here," Mr. Bruner says. "So thank you all for that."

After what feels like a long time, we pull into a graveyard. It's vast and full of headstones. I look around, expecting to see a church building nearby, but I find none. There are crosses on many of the graves, vaguely religious symbols, but no concrete evidence of Christian faith is apparent. An uncomfortable, dreadful feeling stirs inside of me.

We pile out of the car and walk over to the gravesite. The casket is suspended over a dark, open hole. A cloth skirt lining the base tries to disguise this fact, but glimpses of the dirt can be seen through the gaps in the fabric. I get a shiver down my spine when the truth hits me. Matthew is inside that box. Or, at least his body is.

I stare at that casket the entire service as I listen to the speaker talk about life and death but never God. My imagination concocts scenarios in which the lid suddenly raises, and it turns out Matthew isn't really dead. He was just asleep, or in a coma, or he was raised up, and there was some mistake…but, of course, the lid remains shut.

The tears only start to flow after Mrs. Bruner takes the microphone and shares a heartfelt speech about her son and all the memories she has of him. Beside me, Micah sobs quietly as he stares at the ground. The wet streaks on his face gleam when they catch the sunlight.

As the speakers finish and people start to mill about, I'm left standing off to the side with Micah and Sid.

Micah sighs, wiping his nose with a tissue. "Addy…" his eyes are trained on the casket, "I…I just want you to know I'm not a violent person. I'm sorry things got a little tense the other day. I didn't mean to scare you."

I nod, processing the apology. "It's alright," I tell him, trying to force my heart to forgive and forget. Truthfully, I've been going over the interaction in my head for the past few days, wondering if I could have done something better.

Micah clearly cares a lot about Matthew. And, whether or not it's true, he really believes Leighton is the killer. To have that evidence snatched away…my heart softens. I do feel bad for him. It's like Dr. Edith Morrell convincing herself that her husband simply had a heart problem. Putting stock in one answer, despite evidence to the contrary, is more comforting than no answer.

As we climb back into the car, a verse from Ecclesiastes comes to mind. I look it up on my phone as we drive.

It is better to go to a funeral than a feast. For death is the destiny of every person, and the living should take this to heart (Ecclesiastes 7:2 NET).

It's been a long time since I really considered the concept of Hell. It's more of a vague, scary idea that lives somewhere in the back of my mind, keeping me from straying too far from the fold of God. The fear of Hell is not the only thing that keeps me coming back to Jesus, of course, but it's a contributing factor. To truly contemplate the reality of fiery, eternal judgement...an icy terror begins in my chest and radiates to the rest of my body. I feel hollow.

Lord, please forgive me. Don't let me fall away. And I know prayers for the dead can't really do anything, if it's already too late, but please... Somehow, let Matthew have known you before he died.

I don't know how to stomach the knowledge that anyone I knew is in Hell. Until now, everyone I knew who died was a Christian. So...I guess I'll just hold on to hope.

I don't understand how eternal punishment is a fitting or just consequence for the sins a normal person commits. I know the "right" answer. An offense against an eternal and worthy God is deserving of eternal judgement. But it brings me little comfort. I pray again as fear creeps into my mind that I'm questioning too much or getting dangerously close to denying God's goodness or supporting universal salvation—how much are you allowed to get wrong before you're not really a Christian anymore? Is feeling like there are things in God's word that are hard to accept, or even impossible—is that a sign I'm lost already?

I squirm in my seat on the ride home, trying to push the thoughts away. *Lord, forgive me. Lord, forgive me.*

Chapter 30

Behind Closed Doors

The car slows to a stop beside the sidewalk, and Micah, Sid, and I all pile out. With a final thanks and a wave, we watch Mr. and Mrs. Bruner drive away.

"It was nice of them to give us a ride," Sid says.

"It was," I agree. In the midst of mourning the loss of their son, they didn't have to think of us, but they did. "I hope they're okay."

"Well, as okay as they can be," Micah adds.

With no clear direction, we start walking down the path. "Uh, you guys going to dinner?" I ask after checking the time on my phone.

They look at each other, shrug, and then nod. "Yeah. Might as well," Sid says.

It feels almost normal, walking to the dining hall together. We fill our plates and sit at the same booth. There's still a lasting tension with Micah, but at least we're politely conversing now. Sid invites me to come watch the volleyball game on Tuesday—some of her friends are on the team. I'm not usually one for sports, but it might be nice just to hang out with her for a bit. I tell her I'll think about it.

Night has fallen by the time we start walking back to our dorms. As we near the point of parting ways, someone suddenly grabs my shoulder. I jump, letting out a small scream, and turn to see who touched me. "Anthony," I gasp.

"You scared me."

"Sorry," he says, breathing heavily. "But I thought you might want to see." He nods towards the president's house, which is situated on the very edge of campus. "I just saw Robert Boyer pull in at Dr. Conley's."

"Really?" I ask. "At his house?"

He nods.

"What for?"

"I don't know yet." He starts heading up the path towards the north side of campus, waving us along. "Are you guys coming?"

Micah and Sid share a glance before following behind.

"Robert Boyer?" Micah asks. "The board member who talked to us? Why are we interested in him?"

"Well, like I was trying to tell Sid earlier, we think he killed Dr. Morrell," I say in a hushed voice.

"What!?" she hisses. "Why do you think that?"

As we approach the house, Anthony holds out his hand, motioning for us all to stop. Trying to seem somewhat normal, we take shelter behind some trees and watch from a distance.

"We narrowed it down based on Matthew's description," Anthony answers quietly, briefly relaying our process.

A light is on in the bottom floor of the house, but all the curtains are drawn. Sitting in the driveway is an extra car.

"He must be inside," Anthony says. "I saw him park the car and get out, then happened to notice you all walking by, so I came to get you."

"Why would Robert Boyer kill Dr. Morrell?" Micah asks, crossing his arms. "I mean, they've probably worked together for years. Why now?"

"That...we're still working on," I admit. "One theory is that Dr. Morrell had some money Dr. Boyer hoped to get."

We quietly watch the house for a moment, then Micah says something unexpected. "Dr. Morrell did donate a rather large sum to the school in his will. Apparently he owned several of the businesses in town, and I guess they brought in a decent profit. He must've had more resources than he let on."

I shake my head in surprise. "He did? How large was the donation?"

Micah shrugs. "I don't know the exact number, but it was in the millions."

"How do you know that?!"

"You hear stuff working security. Our office is near the administration and fundraising departments. I mean, it's not exactly a secret."

"It didn't all go to his wife?" Sid asks.

"Guess not," Micah answers. "I would assume she was in agreement, but who knows."

"Yeah..." I mumble to myself.

"I wonder if Dr. Boyer was in the will, or if he thought he was," Anthony muses.

"Or maybe they just wanted access to that money," I propose. "Could have been a political reason. Maybe Dr. Morrell's vision for Wynhurst didn't align with his."

"Get the resources, get rid of a dissenter," Anthony mutters. "Could be."

"Murder, though?" Sid asks. "What about Wynhurst could be worth killing over?"

Before anyone can answer, the side door of the house swings open. I lean forward, straining to see in the dark. Robert Boyer exits onto the driveway, then promptly gets in his car. As he backs out onto the road, I feel both relieved and disappointed. I'm happy to have Dr. Boyer as far away from me as possible, but we also didn't learn anything.

"That's weird," Anthony says.

We all look at him. "What is?" I ask.

"Well, when I saw him the first time, I thought he had a backpack on. When he came out, it was gone."

"Maybe he just forgot it?" Micah says. "Or it was a trick of the light. It is dark out."

"Or maybe he dropped something off," I counter, visions of cyanide, bombs, or bags full of money flashing in my head.

"Like what?" Micah asks.

Anthony shakes his head. "I don't know."

At lunch on Monday, I don't see Sid, Micah, or Anthony, so I slide into an empty booth and unzip my backpack, reaching for my Bible. As I'm about to pull it out, I realize I forgot to

192

get a drink, so I get up and head over to the soda fountain.

As I cross the room, Anthony appears from the line. I show him where I'm sitting and continue on my quest for a drink. I pull a plastic cup off the stack and hold it under the ice dispenser. Some cubes clack into the bottom of the cup. Shifting to the right, I don't have to spend much time deciding what I want. I have a total of three options that won't spike my sugar: water, seltzer, or diet.

Deciding on some diet soda, I turn around to see Dr. Edith Morrell standing by our booth, talking with Anthony. I walk back to my seat, coming in on the tail end of the conversation.

"No, I think that would be a great topic to cover..." Dr. Edith says before turning to me. "Oh, hi Addy. Good to see you."

"Hi," I return with a nod. Suddenly, something behind her catches my attention. The door to the president's dining room opens, and Dr. Conley walks out carrying a tray, followed shortly by none other than Robert Boyer.

"Well," Dr. Edith says after a moment. "I'd better get going. Thanks, Anthony."

I wait a few seconds for her to pass out of earshot before nudging Anthony. "Look who's behind you."

He casually twists in his seat, then turns back to face me. "Looks like they just had a meeting with the board members."

"Most likely," I say, watching a few more professionally dressed men trickle out of the room. It's surreal to see someone I know to be a murderer walking free like anyone else.

Dr. Conley stops to interact with several students, giving fist-bumps and making small talk. At one point, he mimes dunking a basketball, and the students around him laugh. Though he's wearing a fairly inconspicuous blue suit, when he jumps, his bright yellow socks can be seen across the room.

Dr. Boyer, on the other hand, charges straight towards the tray return, rids himself of his dishes, then lingers by the door, clad in plain gray attire.

After quite a few minutes have passed, Dr. Conley returns his tray and joins Boyer in the corner. His expression grows serious, and the two men begin discussing something quietly.

I lean closer to Anthony and lower my voice. "What do you think that's about?" I ask, nodding in their direction.

He shakes his head. "Probably nothing. I mean, they do have to work together to run the school." He shrugs. "Then again, at this point, anything is possible."

Chapter 31

Bad Apple

Unsure of what to expect, I follow Sid closely as we enter the gym to watch the volleyball game. The bleachers are full of spectators, and the roar of conversation fills the room. The noise, combined with the bright lights and scoreboard, is a little overwhelming.

Sid waves to a girl I don't recognize, and we make our way to the empty spots next to her and her friends. The girl has dark, curly hair and a smooth complexion. On her backpack, I notice a large enamel pin of a UFO against a starry sky. Above and below are the words *The truth is out there*.

"This is Lisa," Sid says, introducing us. "She's on the cross-country team, and we play lacrosse together." Lisa smiles and responds with a friendly wave. She leans forward and tries to make small talk with me, but with Sid sitting between us and the background clamor, I only catch a few disjointed words. On the third try, I just nod and smile as if I understand.

As the game starts, Sid points out which players she knows. Even with the numbers on their backs, I find it hard to keep track of who's who. Despite my limited knowledge, I can see that Marissa was right; we do have a good team this year. The giant red digits on the home side of the scoreboard climb higher and higher.

After a while, I start to feel hot and slightly claustrophobic from being packed together with all these people. I take a drink from my water bottle, and Sid eyes me.

"Man, I should've brought some water. It's getting warm in here." She fans herself with a program. Slowly, I screw the lid back on. I'd like to help, but I'm not the type to share my water bottle with people. As I return it to the pocket on the side of my bag, I remember I do have something I could offer. My hand closes around a juice box, and I hold it out to her. "Do you want one of these?"

She looks surprised. "Don't you need them for your blood sugar?"

"I have plenty," I assure her. "Take it."

"Thanks!"

Her eyes are trained on the court as she absentmindedly unwraps the straw, pokes a hole in the top, and takes a drink. I follow her gaze, trying to understand her investment in the game.

"Ya know," Sid says after a minute or two, "I don't feel too well." Though it's hard to hear, it sounds as though her speech is slurred.

"You alright?" I ask, training my eyes on her face. Despite the heat, she looks white as a sheet.

"I—I think I'm gonna head out—" She goes to stand, but her legs wobble beneath her. Almost immediately, she collapses back onto the bleachers, barely avoiding hitting her head on the seat behind us. The juice slips out of her hand and falls to the ground.

I spring to my feet, eyes wide. "Sid, are you okay!?" I help her to an upright position on the seat. She leans forward and rests her hands on her knees, struggling to take in air. Worry starts to build in my mind. She's fine, right?

She nods. "Yeah, I'll be okay. I just—" she suddenly changes her mind mid-sentence. She shakes her head. "No. Not okay," she croaks.

"What? What's wrong?!" She tries to respond but can no longer produce any words. She can't breathe. "Help!" I shout. It's all I can think to do. "We need help!"

I look up to find the people around us watching in concern. Someone helps flag down one of the student worker security guards. He takes one look at Sid and radios the nurse at the bottom of the stands. I watch her grab a first aid kit and start rushing towards us.

"Is she choking on something?" the security guard asks.

I shake my head. "No, I don't think so. There wasn't anything in her mouth."

Nurse Bradshaw flies to our side. She kneels so she's eye-level with Sid. "Are you having trouble breathing?" she asks.

Sid nods.

"Do you have asthma?"

She shakes her head in response.

"Any pain?"

Sid gestures to her chest.

Nurse Bradshaw leans back to the security guard and calmly says, "Call an ambulance."

My stomach drops. In a matter of seconds, a volleyball game has escalated to a dire medical emergency.

The nurse turns her attention to me. "Does she have any food allergies or medical conditions? What was she doing a few minutes prior?"

"I...I don't know. I don't think so." My eye catches the juice box on the ground. "She was drinking apple juice. But I've never known her to have any type of food allergy."

Sid shakes her head.

"How about drug usage?" Nurse Bradshaw asks while checking Sid's pulse. "No one's gonna get in trouble. I just need you to tell me if you've used any substances."

I shake my head. "No, no I don't think so," I answer, my eyes still trained on the juice box.

*It couldn't be...*that juice was in my bag the whole time. There's no way...I look back at Sid, who's desperately trying to take in oxygen. Even if it seems impossible, what if? If it isn't from choking or an asthma attack or a food allergy...*Cyanide poisoning.*

I rip my cellphone out of my pocket, hands shaking.

"The ambulance is on its way," Nurse Bradshaw reassures. *But it might be too late.*

I search my contacts. Oh, what did I name her? *Professor.* I smash the call button. To my relief, she picks up after the first ring.

"Addy?"

I'm frozen for a moment, struggling to form words. "Professor—please, I need your help. It's…it's Sidney. She's struggling to breathe—I think it might be poison. Please come. I don't know what to do." I start to sob, but pull myself together. "We're in the gym. At the volleyball game—"

"Okay. Stay calm, I'll be right there."

Click. The phone hangs up. I try to steady my own breathing, running my fingers through my hair. I watch as Nurse Bradshaw twists open some nasal spray and administers it to Sid. I recognize it as naloxone; she thinks this is an overdose. A surge of hope rises as I half expect it to work, but it doesn't. In a few more moments, Sid starts to slump to the side, unable to hold herself up.

I wring my hands together. I can't believe this is happening. I start praying. For Sid to get better, for Professor Leighton to be fast. I watch as she's lowered to the ground in the aisle. She can't even lift her head, and her limbs begin to twitch.

On the right side of the gym, one of the doors suddenly swings open with force. The metal handle smacks against the wood, and the sound echoes off the walls. I see a flash of dark cloth as Leighton charges into the room.

She stops to scan the stands. I wave my hands over my head, desperately trying to get her attention. "Professor—" I start to shout, then realize she'll never hear it over the hundreds of other voices. "Bryn!"

Almost immediately, her head turns in my direction, and I can tell she sees us. She grabs the railing and swings herself onto the bleachers, then walks briskly up the steps.

As she passes, however, someone sitting near the front row stands and looks back at us

"Hang on—Stop her!" he shouts.

My blood runs cold. It's Robert Boyer. "Don't let Leighton near that student!" he yells, starting after her. "She's a prime suspect for murder, for crying out loud. Get her out of here!" He shimmies past the people on his row, trying to make it to the aisle.

The security guard is busy on the phone, but Nurse Bradshaw hears Dr. Boyer. She stands and steps forward, firmly planting herself between Bryn and Sidney. Bryn grinds to a halt just inches away from the nurse.

For a moment, the two stand in a silent deadlock.

My insides twist into knot after knot. I see a flash in Bryn's eyes that makes me take a step back. I remember the knife...the Navy...she looks ready to run someone down. Nurse Bradshaw, however, remains undeterred. Meanwhile, Sid is still on the ground, unable to breathe. A clock ticks in my head as I wonder how long she can be like this. Every second counts.

"Please, let her help!" I plead, struggling to restrain my tears. I can feel my heart pounding against my chest, and my palms are slick with sweat.

"Listen," Bryn says to the nurse. Her tone is even but firm. "I'm trying to help. For Sidney's sake, set aside any opinions you may have about me and hear me out."

"Don't let her through!" Dr. Boyer growls again, having just made it to the stairs. "The paramedics are on their way; just let them do their job. You let her by, and I'll see to it you never work at this university again!"

Bryn doesn't drop her gaze. "Ma'am, I have the utmost respect for your medical training and experience, so I hope you can have the same for me. I spent ten years in the Navy, six as a medic and four as a medical researcher. I hold a masters in toxicology and I have witnessed, diagnosed, treated, sampled, tested, formulated, and examined lethal substances worldwide in every form imaginable. If I know one thing, I know poisons, and *that* is textbook cyanide poisoning." She points a finger towards Sid. "If we wait for the paramedics, it'll be too late."

Nurse Bradshaw's eyes flit between her and the fast-approaching Robert Boyer. Bryn takes a small step forward, tensing. As she opens her mouth to speak, the nurse suddenly turns to the side. She nods.

"Go ahead."

With a startled look on her face, Bryn nods in return, then rushes to Sid. She drops her bag and pulls on some gloves.

"Alright, Addy, what happened?" she calls to me.

"I...I don't know...I gave her some juice..."

"That one?" she asks, gesturing to the juice box on the floor. She tosses me a vial of test strips. "Test it for me. Be careful."

I nod. My hands shake as I pop open the plastic container, remove a strip, and dip it in the sticky liquid. As the color changes, my eyes are trained on Sid.

Bryn kneels beside her. "Hi, Sidney. I know this is scary, but I'm here to help. Just hang in there and try to stay calm, okay?" She removes a vial and a syringe as she's talking and carefully measures out a dose. "This is really just a glorified vitamin shot. The B12 will bind with the cyanide and help your cells use oxygen again." She takes Sid's wrist and twists it over, exposing her inner forearm, which she swipes with an alcohol wipe. "Addy, results?"

Her voice shakes me from my daze, and I look down at the test strip in my hand. It's bright red: the highest concentration. "R-red," I stutter.

"Small pinch," she says to Sid, then plunges the needle into her vein.

In an instant, the plunger is down, and the needle is out. Bryn caps it, barely taking her eyes off of Sid. For a few moments, we wait.

"I thought I told you—" Dr. Boyer starts, finally pushing past the nurse. Whatever statement he planned to make is abruptly interrupted when Sidney takes a deep breath. She springs to a sitting position, gulping down air.

"Easy," Bryn coaxes. "Slow breaths. Don't make yourself sick."

At the realization of what just happened, the students around us suddenly break into applause. In a few minutes, her tremors cease, and her breathing becomes more normal. As Sid returns to health, Bryn seems to become aware of her surroundings. She looks behind her, taking in the cheers. If I'm not imagining it, a small blush dots her cheeks.

Dr. Boyer also looks flushed, but for a different reason. Though he wears a tight-lipped smile, his lip subtly twitches. His eyes dart around, as if searching for a target on which to bestow his rage. However, doing so would net him the disapproval of any decent onlooker, so he remains quiet. I shiver, uncomfortable being so close.

As the paramedics arrive, I vaguely hear Bryn explain what happened. Someone collects the juice box and test strip in a bag as evidence. I catch some speculation about

200

factory contamination.

As they wheel Sid outside, Bryn makes her way beside me. "You okay?" she asks.

I blink, trying to comprehend the question. "Yeah, yeah, I'm fine." At least physically.

"C'mon. I'll drive you to the hospital. I'm sure Sidney would like someone to stay with her."

"Okay," I say. That hadn't even been a thought in my head. "Yeah, thanks."

She sets a hand on my shoulder and helps steer me through the crowds. I steal a glance back at Robert Boyer, who's standing in the middle of the commotion with a sour look on his face. At the sight of me, his eyes narrow, and I quickly turn my head away. If I weren't already so emotionally overwhelmed, I might feel afraid.

Chapter 32

Visitors

I expect to feel some relief once we're outside, but I forget that it's dark already. The lights of the ambulance against the blackness just add to the overload. I stay close to Bryn as we head to her car.

Only once the car doors close do my senses get a break. There's a dull ringing in my ears caused by the transition from clamoring noise to sudden quiet. I take a slow breath and try to exhale some of my stress.

Bryn glances at me, then puts the key in the ignition and starts the car. We pull out of the parking lot behind the ambulance. Lights but no siren.

I don't know what to say, so I keep my eyes trained on the night passing by outside my window. Save for some storefronts that are lit as a burglary deterrent, the lights are out in almost every house we drive by. Flickerwood is a town with a bedtime.

The buildings fade as we head out of town, replaced by trees and empty fields. I'm not sure how long the drive is, but it feels like forever. A little outside the bounds of town, the backlit hospital sign finally comes into view.

As we turn into the drive and follow signs for the emergency room, I realize this will be the first time I've been to the ER. I've been a lucky diabetic—most of the others I've met have been hospitalized at least once.

"Do you want me to drop you off at the door?" Bryn asks as we approach.

"Uh—" I hesitate, scared of both appearing childish and of going by myself. "I—I've never actually been in to visit a patient alone—"

"It's okay," she says gently, stopping my anxious rambling in its tracks. "I'll go in with you. Not a problem." She drives past the doors and begins the search for a parking spot.

I exhale, relieved. "Thank you." I'm grateful for her company. Alone, I would have no idea what to do. For any of this.

As we approach the doors, my brain starts to conjure images of the types of patients that could be in the waiting room of the ER. Severed limbs, gunshot wound victims, people screaming in agony...

We walk through the automatic sliding doors to a surprisingly tame scene. There's a quiet waiting room that looks like it could be in any doctor's office. A few scattered patients sit, quietly waiting for an evaluation, but I can't tell what's wrong with them by sight alone. There are no gaping wounds or visible injuries.

The most eye-catching patient is a teenager sitting in handcuffs next to a police officer. I recognize the officer as Eric Boyer's younger partner: Hopewell, I believe. The teenager frowns and continually asks why he can't just go home. I wonder what the story is there.

I follow Bryn to the window of the front desk, and we speak to the receptionist. She gives us visitor badges to stick on and a room number, then opens the double doors which lead to the main part of the hospital. We step through into a long, empty hallway. Behind us, the heavy doors creak and begin to close automatically, latching with a heavy click.

The hall we find ourselves in seems strangely dim. The smell of antiseptic hits my nose. For a hospital, it's eerily quiet. There's no sign of anyone—staff or patients. The rooms here appear vacant. We pass by some abandoned wheelchairs sitting along the wall, then stop in front of the discolored white doors of a decades-old elevator.

Bryn presses the button to summon the car, and we wait, listening to the whirring of the machine as it descends. With a ding, the doors slowly open. We step inside and watch them shut, securing us in a rectangular box. Bryn presses a floor number, and the elevator hesitates for a moment before slowly lifting us up towards the desired destination. The fluorescent tube lights above us flicker, and I try to ignore the pressing feeling that I'm in a horror movie.

"Did you spend a lot of time in hospitals? As a medic?" I ask, mostly to dispel the tense feeling in my chest.

"A fair amount," she says, bobbing her head. "Mostly floating ones. As a whole, they were never my favorite place to be. Kind of ominous, aren't they?"

I nod. The elevator dings as we reach our floor.

Bryn smiles, lightening the mood. "So we'll give Sidney some familiar faces."

I smile back and feel some of the tension release. We step onto a more lively and well-lit floor, and a friendly doctor directs us behind the correct curtained partition.

I'm relieved to find Sid sitting up in bed, awake and alert. An IV with a saline bag is attached to her arm, but not much more. Her worried expression softens into a smile when she sees me.

"Addy! You came with me."

"Of course," I say, then immediately feel guilty knowing it wasn't my idea. I shake the feeling away. I can't blame myself for that. It's not that I wouldn't have, I just didn't even know it was an option..."Well, Bryn brought me." I gesture behind me.

Bryn stands near the corner of the room, giving us space. She nods politely. "How are you feeling?"

Sid's gaze freezes on her for a moment. "Uh, better than I was. Still trying to wrap my head around what happened... but I'm no longer on the verge of death, thanks to you."

"Glad to hear you're alright," she replies, sidestepping the thanks.

Sid, however, continues. "Seriously. I mean...cyanide poisoning!?" Her eyes widen as she stares into space. "Crazy. You—you really saved my life." She puts her hands to her temples. "And to think I was really afraid you were the guilty one. After Addy showed us those photos..."

My eyes fly open and I feel my face grow hot. I never

told Bryn about those pictures.

Slowly, she turns to face me with a quizzical expression. "Photos?"

Sid's mouth falls shut. The attention has shifted to me.

I turn my eyes to the floor. "Uh...I took some pictures when I was in your cellar. Specifically, of the vault with all the glass vials. At the time, I thought you were guilty, so I was going to go to the police, but then I changed my mind. I only showed a few friends—and then only because I was trying to convince them of your innocence—before I deleted them." I study my shoelaces. "I—I'm sorry."

Gradually, I lift my eyes, fearing this is the part in the story where a rift is created between two characters after it's revealed one of them has been hiding something. Trust is broken, and the second act is spent trying to correct the misunderstanding...

To the contrary, Bryn cracks a smile. "Oh, don't worry about it. I'm not surprised you took pictures. If I were in your shoes, I probably would've done the same thing." She shakes her head. "Honestly, it surprises me more that you chose to defend me."

The weight of dread vanishes from my shoulders. Is it really that easy? She's not upset? At this point, I almost feel like she should be, for all the stupid things I've done. But her posture is relaxed, and her expression bright.

Is this what mercy feels like? Over and over again.

"Wait," I say, as an implication dawns on me. "You let me go knowing I probably had pictures I could use against you?"

She shrugs. "Only so much I could do. It's not like I was gonna hold you hostage."

"So..." Sid interjects from the hospital bed, "if it wasn't you, then who put cyanide in Addy's juice box?"

Before either of us can answer, the curtain flies open.

"Well, well, well. Look who it is." Chief Eric Boyer saunters into the room, his gaze trained on me and Bryn. "It's funny, ya know, how you two always seem to be involved when a poisoning happens. Kind of suspicious, if you ask me." His eyes narrow.

I swallow, instinctually leaning away from him.

Suddenly, he turns towards Sid and pulls out a pad of

paper and a pen. "Young lady, I'm here to get a statement from you on what happened so we can track down whatever lunatic—" he glances at Bryn on the word, "—is running around seasoning things with cyanide." He clicks his pen. "If you don't mind, could you tell me what happened?"

"Well, I went to the volleyball game with Addy, and I said I was thirsty, because I forgot my water bottle, so she gave me a juice box. The next thing I knew, I was on the ground. Then Professor Leighton saved my life." She gestures towards Bryn. "I have no idea how that poisoned juice got into her bag."

"Mmm," Chief Boyer says, scribbling on his pad. He turns from Sid to look at me. "Sure, sure, it's possible someone planted it there...but we also can't rule out the obvious." He shrugs a shoulder, then steps towards me. He gets uncomfortably close, and I'm compelled to take a step back. Bryn swiftly closes the distance between us.

"What are you implying?" she shoots, holding his gaze.

"Oh, I don't think it's that hard to figure out. She gave someone a juice box, and they collapsed on the floor," he says, gesturing towards me. Despite the fact that he's only a few inches taller than me, he bends his knees to come down to my eye level, as if talking to a child. "Now, what rivalries do you have with your friends that you're trying to pick them off one by one, hmm? Did she steal your boyfriend?"

I feel my skin crawl. I've never been one to get in trouble. Corrupt or not, having a police officer out to get me was never something I thought I'd have to worry about. It doesn't strike me until now how incriminating it looks for me to have given Sid the juice. I might be spending some years in prison after all.

"Back up," Bryn says to him. She tugs me backwards and wedges her foot between me and him. "Your level of speculation is very unprofessional."

He straightens, but talks past her to me. "Addy, how about you come down to the station, give your statement, and we can clear all this up?"

"I—" I start, scrambling to defend myself, but Bryn jabs a finger towards me.

"Not a word." I snap my mouth shut. She turns back to

206

Chief Boyer. "She won't be going anywhere with you. Especially not without counsel."

His lip twitches. She's clearly getting on his nerves. "You sure do seem overly defensive of this student, *Professor*." He puts his pad and pen away and sets his hand on a shiny pair of handcuffs. "My *counsel*, Addy, is to cooperate and come with me." Fear surges in my chest. I scurry backwards as he steps forward. Does this count as resisting arrest?

My eyes turn towards the break in the curtain, and I'm startled by the figure I see standing there.

"Alright, alright," the man says, stepping forward into the light. "Take it easy. You really think this girl's friend is to blame?"

"With all due respect, the only way to say for certain is to question her—" Boyer argues.

But the man shakes his head and waves the handcuffs away. "We're in a patient's room, for Pete's sake, Eric. Let's not add unnecessary stress. These two have been through enough."

To my surprise, Chief Boyer listens, begrudgingly hooking his handcuffs back on his belt. "Sorry, sir," he says, his jaw tight.

"Sincerely, I am so sorry about this. Please, let me make it up to you. It's late, I'm sure you two are tired," he says, gesturing towards Bryn and I, "and Wynhurst is a scary place to be these days. Let me show you some hospitality. My house is only a short ways from here. You're welcome to stay there until your friend is discharged."

I stand silent, staring at the man before me. *Mayor Sayer*.

Chapter 33

The Mayor's House

I look to Bryn, hoping she'll know how to respond, but she looks just as shocked as me. As grateful as I am to the mayor for stepping in and saving me from being hauled off to jail, I'd really rather not go home with him.

Thankfully, Bryn shares my sentiment. She quickly regains her composure and answers him. "Thank you for your concern, sir, and for the offer, but we'll have to decline. I hope you don't take offense. I do have a class to teach tomorrow."

"Are you sure? I'm sure your students won't mind if you take a well-deserved break," he says.

She nods. "Yes."

I fear he will press the matter, but he waves a hand. "Ah, well I understand." He walks closer to Sidney and asks how she's feeling. They exchange some niceties before he turns back to us. "Well, if there's nothing more I can do for you folks, I suppose I'll be on my way."

As he starts to leave, I notice Chief Boyer still standing in the corner. His eyes glint, reminding me of a predator about to pounce.

"The doctors plan to discharge me tomorrow morning," Sid says from the bed. "If it's not too much trouble, would you mind giving me a ride back to campus?"

"No trouble at all," Bryn answers. "Just say when."

Boyer's handcuffs flash on his belt. I realize, as I watch

him step over the threshold, that the presence of the mayor is currently our only protection. I hate to do it, but...

"On second thought," I say, calling after him. "If you don't mind, and if your house is close, like you said, maybe it would be nice to stay until Sid gets out." *I hate this. I hate this. I hate this.*

"Of course, of course," Mayor Sayer replies quickly. "You're both more than welcome."

Anxious, I glance towards Bryn. She gives a small nod. "Fair point, Addy. We'll go together."

I breathe a sigh of relief. I'm thankful to not be going alone. A politician spending the night with a lone girl decades younger than him—well, that's a news story I don't want to be a part of.

Still, I'd much rather be in my dorm room, safe and sound. Having a joint sleepover with the mayor *and* my professor sounds...awkward, to say the least. I immediately start to second-guess my decision. Maybe jail would have been better.

After a brief goodbye to Sid, we follow Mayor Sayer to the elevator and towards the exit. Just before walking out the doors, Bryn darts towards the receptionist.

"Hi," she says pleasantly. "We're on our way out, but I just wanted to make sure you have our information in case you need to reach us with any updates on Sidney. We'll come to pick her up once she's discharged." Bryn proceeds to give our names, her phone number, address, and repeatedly says we'll be staying with the mayor tonight. After ensuring the information is on file, we exit the hospital.

"That's my car, there," Sayer informs us, pointing to a black BMW. He gives us directions on how to get to his house, but I'm not familiar with the area, so they don't make much sense. "But you can just follow me if you want. You can't miss it," he assures.

Bryn nods, confirming her understanding. "Alright." She flips her keys in her hand as we walk across the dark parking lot towards the car. It's not until we're inside with the doors safely shut that she takes a deep breath. She looks to me.

"Well, this is weird." The engine roars to life, and her headlights flash on.

I nod eagerly. "Very weird. I'm sorry for telling him we'd spend the night after you'd already gotten us out of it. I just saw Chief Boyer and figured it was the only way out—" I sheepishly explain.

"Smart," she says. "Probably a good move. Don't bite the hand that feeds you, right? If Sayer wants to help us, I suppose we should try and stay on his good side." She follows him out of the hospital drive and onto the main road. "If," she mutters, "helping is actually what he wants to do." Her voice returns to its usual volume. "We'll just be cautious, okay?"

"Is that why you told the receptionist where we're going?" I ask.

She nods. "Yes. Just a precaution. If something were to happen...well, at least one person knows where to look for us."

Grim, but smart.

Just as he said, the drive to Mayor Sayer's house is short. While technically still within the town limits of Flickerwood, it's located near the northern boundary line. There are only a few other houses on this street, and they're spaced far apart. We turn into his driveway, and I find myself looking at a large three-story structure. Small floodlights in the grass illuminate the outer stone facade and tan siding, while yellow light streams from the first-floor windows. The light falls near the mailbox, drawing attention to a yard sign promoting Sayer and his running mate for governor.

Bryn pulls in beside the BMW and shuts the car off. She peers out the windshield at the mansion before us. "Welp. I guess this is it." With one last mutual glance, we pop the car doors open and let the mayor lead us inside.

The door opens into a small foyer. From where I'm standing, I can see a sitting room to the right, complete with patterned couches and a fancy piano. To the left is an extravagant dining room, and straight ahead is a grand staircase leading to the second floor. Past the staircase and behind the dining room is the kitchen. I can just make out a woman standing at the sink washing dishes.

"Hello, my dear, I've brought some guests with me," Sayer calls while ushering us into the kitchen. He introduces the woman at the sink as his wife, Colleen. She smiles and

210

brushes a lock of gray hair behind her ear. After a simple exchange of pleasantries, she returns to the dishes and Sayer takes us upstairs.

The second floor consists of a hallway lined with doors. He starts by gesturing to the right of the stairs. "The room at the far end is ours, and the one beside it is for the grandkids. As you can see, the bed is a bit small." He pushes the door open enough for us to see inside. I glimpse a child-sized bed with a plastic frame, along with a bassinet and a rocking chair.

"Then we have the bathroom," he says, drawing attention to the room near the center of the hallway. We pass over to the left side of the stairs. "...and the office." I peek inside as we walk by. In the center is a dark brown desk, and campaign signs litter the room. He casually pulls it shut.

"Finally," he says, stopping at the last two doors, "these are our guest bedrooms."

Both rooms have a full sized bed with perfectly tucked sheets and some type of floral comforter. It reminds me of my grandparents' house.

As we turn to head back, my eyes are drawn to family pictures hanging on the wall. Bryn also stops to look. In one of the photos, there's a familiar-looking man with dark-rimmed glasses. He's standing beside his wife, who's holding a baby, and their little girl. *Michael Sayer*. The memory of his outburst at church floods my mind, and the uneasy feeling in my stomach only heightens.

"Ah, those are my grandchildren," Sayer informs us. "Aren't they gorgeous? And that's my son and my daughter-in-law."

I stare at the photo, unsure how to respond other than with a nod.

"Did you have any other kids?" Bryn asks. "Or is it just your son?"

He glances at her. "No, no it's just Michael. He has such a lovely young family—they mean the world to me. I couldn't ask for anything better."

Once downstairs, we all take a seat around the coffee table in the living room. Bryn sits rigid in her chair, looking more uncomfortable than I've ever known her to be. Colleen

211

offers us drinks and sets a fruit tray down.

"No, thank you," Bryn says, politely declining any food. I would love to do the same, but my blood sugar could use a boost. Not only that, but I'm no longer certain about the safety of anything in my bag. Not after what happened to Sid. After watching Colleen eat some fruit, I reach for a few apple slices.

As I bite into them, I notice the Bible sitting next to the tray on the coffee table. It's a large black book with a layer of dust covering the top. Still, I smile, feeling somewhat comforted to know I'm in the company of Christians.

"So, Miss Leighton, you've been quite the talk at Wynhurst these days," Sayer says.

She grimaces. "Not for good reasons, unfortunately."

He waves a hand. "Dr. Gaines seems to think you're an excellent professor, and I tend to trust his judgement. I am sorry, to both of you, that Wynhurst has not been the best lately. I truly love the school and, once all of this craziness ends, I hope you'll both still be around to get the full experience it has to offer. It's near and dear to me personally, as well as to the community."

"You're close with a lot of the staff at Wynhurst, aren't you?" Bryn asks. "You were friends with Dr. Morrell?"

Sayer takes a drink from his glass, though he doesn't break eye contact. "Yes, I've known many of the professors a long time, but I knew Morrell for the longest. We grew up together, right here. We both graduated from Flickerwood High."

"...I'm sorry," Bryn says after a beat. "For your loss."

He nods. "Thank you. One of the downsides of growing old. Having to bury your friends." He smiles sadly, then quickly shifts the topic. "But what about you? What brings you to Flickerwood, Bryn?"

If I'm not mistaken, Bryn flinches when he says her name. "Well, I guess the short answer is that I was looking for a change of pace. I spent the last decade in the Navy, the majority of which I worked as an SMT. I loved the work, but I finally decided it was time to start a new chapter." She tilts both palms face-up. "Here I am."

"Military, eh?" he says with a nod. "My father was an Army man." He draws our attention to another picture in the corner of the room, almost hidden behind a shelf. It's a black and white photo of a man in uniform. "If that's the short version, what's the long answer?" he asks.

Bryn taps her fingers on her knee, but smiles, sidestepping the question with relative ease. "Oh, I don't think we have time for all that tonight. If you don't mind, it's been a long day, and I think we're gonna head up to bed."

Sayer looks as though he's about to say something, but decides against it. "Of course, of course. Be my guest. It was lovely chatting."

We head upstairs, and I claim one of the guest bedrooms. While waiting for my turn in the bathroom, I set my backpack down at the foot of the bed and begin untying my shoelaces. The room has an old bluish-green carpet with a dark stain next to the bedside table, likely from a cup of coffee or tea spilled years ago. I lay my shoes beside my backpack, then switch the light off before heading to the now vacant bathroom.

After washing my hands, I splash some water on my face and scrub some of the plaque off my teeth with my finger. Good enough. It's only one night. I can survive.

When I come out a few minutes later, I see the mayor and his wife step onto the second floor and head to their bedroom.

He waves. "Let me know if you need anything."

I nod and smile awkwardly, then quickly turn towards the guest rooms. With one hand on the wall, I navigate the unfamiliar hallway, feeling my way back to my designated room. As I pass Bryn's room, I notice that the door is shut, and no light seeps from the cracks. I don't hear any sound from within. Did she go to sleep that fast?

I turn to my own room and slip inside, shutting the door behind me. A small beam of moonlight streams through the window, just enough to illuminate the vague shapes of the otherwise dark furniture. I release a breath. Peace at last.

Then my eyes catch a flash of movement in the far corner of the room. I freeze. The light bounces off the silhouette of a person.

Jolting into action, I gasp and lunge for the doorknob, the worst case scenario flashing through my brain.

"Shhhhh!" the figure hisses, swiftly crossing the room and gripping the doorknob, preventing me from opening it.

213

"It's just me."

As my eyes adjust to the darkness, I can make out the outline of Bryn's face. I release the knob and sigh, clutching my chest.

"Sorry," she whispers, spreading her hands. "Didn't mean to scare you."

"I thought you were in the other room," I whisper back, confused.

"I was, but after giving it some more thought, I figured it'd be safer to stay together. Heard the Sayers coming upstairs and took the opportunity to duck in here unseen. I'll just camp out on the floor," she explains, pointing towards her doctor's bag and a blanket sitting near her feet, then adds, "if, of course, that's okay with you."

A considerable part of me would much rather just have a space to myself instead of this strange, uncomfortable arrangement. But I remember the mayor and his wife at the end of the hall and wonder again why he was so insistent on having us here in the first place.

"Yeah, you're probably right," I answer. "Safer to stay together."

She nods and begins scouting out the carpet.

"Are you sure you don't want the bed?" I offer, feeling bound by the rules of politeness. "I can sleep on the floor."

She waves away my offer. "No, no, I'm good. Thank you, though. I want to be near the door, and I don't think I'll sleep much, anyway."

Without even removing her shoes or jacket, she lays down in the space just behind the door, covers herself with the spare blanket, and rolls to the side.

I slide under the covers of the guest bed and stare up at the ceiling, vaguely lifting my thoughts in prayer. I'm thankful Sid is okay. If it weren't for Bryn...I shudder at the thought. I can't believe I handed her a poisoned juice. How did it even end up in my bag?! Why—

My thoughts grind to a halt as the glaring truth finally hits me. Whoever poisoned the apple juice wasn't going after Sid...*they intended to kill me*.

A chill runs down my spine, and I pull the blankets tight around me, my heart pounding in my chest. Watery gray

214

eyes flash in my mind, staring me down as I leave the gym. Shouting, a failed attempt at sabotage, rings in my ears. *Robert Boyer.* And at the hospital, his son, Eric, blaming me and trying to persuade me to go with him...I don't know how they planted it in my bag, but they almost killed me.

A surge of gratitude towards the mayor wells inside me. Had he not shown up and kept me from going with Chief Boyer...my fate might have been much worse than prison.

Another fear starts to pulse in my brain. If they're after me, what about my friends? I snatch my phone from the bedside table and send a text to Anthony and—after a slight hesitation—Micah. I can explain more later, but for now I keep it short and sweet. *The Boyers targeted me. Idk how much they know. Be careful what you drink.*

I set my phone down and face the door. Faintly, I can make out the silhouette of Bryn's blanketed form lying on the floor. The danger she tried to warn me of has suddenly become very, very real.

I fall asleep while praying, over and over again, for safety.

Chapter 34

Hold Your Peace

I awake to Bryn shaking my shoulder. I sit up, assessing the situation. Everything is still dark, but the time reads 6 am.

"I was thinking of cancelling class," she says, folding up the blanket, "but now, I think it gives us a good excuse to get out of here."

Quietly, we make our way down the stairs. Just as we approach the front door, a voice echoes from the kitchen.

"Well, you're up early."

We both turn to see Mrs. Colleen Sayer sitting alone at the island counter. Steam rises from the mug beside her as she reads the newspaper.

"It's just that we have a class to get to…" I say quickly, backing towards the front door, but Bryn stops. Calmly, she wanders back towards the kitchen. I reluctantly trail behind.

"Could say the same for you," Bryn replies.

Colleen flips a page of the paper. "Oh, honey, this is my alone time. I savor the morning hours."

Bryn furrows her brow. "Must be hard, being the mayor's wife." Her voice has an air of compassion.

She sets the paper down and takes a sip from her mug. "It has its pros and cons, that's for sure. Men are…well, you'll understand when you get yourself a husband."

I'm sure my face betrays my shock at such a presumptuous comment. Bryn, however, appears unfazed.

She leans in, curious.

"Men are what?"

"Well…" she says slowly, clearly not used to expanding upon this statement. "They're just pig-headed sometimes. We don't always see eye to eye, but you gotta learn to live with that."

Bryn tilts her head. "So what do you do when you disagree?"

After taking a sip from her mug, Colleen lifts the paper, disengaging from the conversation. "I don't see it as my place to meddle in his affairs, my dear. I learned a long time ago that it's better to keep the peace."

"But…what if it's something that affects you both? An issue of conscience? What if, say, he's in danger of hurting someone you love?"

With a defensive huff, Colleen yanks the paper down again. "Am I being interrogated here in my own kitchen, during my precious, peaceful morning hours?" She sizes Bryn up. "Look, my husband is a good man. His decisions have served our family well through the years, and I support them wholeheartedly."

Bryn hesitates. "Your family. Meaning you and your son?"

Colleen doesn't look up from the paper. "Yes, of course. Who else?"

Bryn nods once, backing away from the island. "Thank you for your hospitality. We'll be going."

"Anytime. Safe travels," she calls after us.

Almost immediately after stepping outside, I feel like a weight is lifted. Bryn seems to brighten, too. Once we're in the car, she looks over at me.

"Wanna go out to breakfast?" She glances at the clock. "We have time. My treat."

I check my phone. Blood sugar is a little high, but that's to be expected. Between stress, lack of sleep, and being up earlier than normal, I'm surprised it's not worse.

"Sure," I answer. "Breakfast sounds great."

As she pulls out of the driveway, I quickly view my text messages. Anthony responded with several paragraphs of text, mostly asking questions about what happened. I skim it and send a short reply letting him know we can meet up later. There's nothing from Micah.

I set my phone in my lap as Bryn sighs.

"So...let's never do that again," she says.

"Agreed." I watch the Sayers' house gradually disappear in the rearview mirror. "Was dealing with murder and cyanide the change of pace you had in mind when coming to Flickerwood?"

She laughs. "No, not exactly. But, at least for the time being, I think this is where God wants me to be."

There's a lull in the conversation as I work up the nerve to broach the topic on my mind.

"I think you were right," I say finally. "It must be hard to be the wife of the mayor."

My mind suddenly thunders down a rabbit hole: *Why would I think it's hard? Because she's always in the shadow of her husband? Because he makes decisions she doesn't always agree with? Because she has less power? Because she always has to be the trophy on his arm? The unwavering supporter?*

Bible verses flash in my head. Isn't that what God commands of all wives? Of all women? Maybe Colleen has it right. Doing the dishes, preparing the snack, cleaning the kitchen, with an ever-present smile.

I glimpse Bryn's Bible sticking out the front pouch of her bag. My eyes travel from the dye in her hair to the lack of ring on her finger. I've never really felt like there was anyone I could share my questions with.

But maybe...maybe Bryn would be different than everyone else.

"How do you feel about a theological discussion?" I ask carefully.

"Sounds fun," she says cheerily. "What's on your mind?"

I resist the urge to shrink away from the conversation. "...have you ever heard of the egalitarian vs. complementarian debate?" As I say it, my insides squirm. It's one thing to be vague about having questions about God, but it's another to admit exactly what those questions are. Being specific invites opinions and advice and judgement and critique.

"About whether the Bible supports gender equality or male

leadership?" she asks. "Oh, have I ever. What about it?"

"Well…it's something I've been trying to work through. I'm not really sure what I believe about it. I mean, on one hand, there are a lot of verses in Scripture which seem to command male headship and a female submission in marriage and ministry. And I want to follow God's word, even if I don't understand it. There are a lot of difficult commandments; maybe this one is no different.

"But then again…I find it hard to accept the idea that women are just born into some divinely-ordained hierarchy. But the arguments I've heard for egalitarianism don't seem as airtight exegetically—not that egalitarians aren't true Christians—but your conscience has to be fully convinced, doesn't it? And mine just isn't," I ramble. "So…like I said, I'm trying to work through it." I glance towards her. "What do you consider yourself to be?"

As I await the answer, I brace myself for another soul-crushing blow, or perhaps a glimmer of hope.

Unexpectedly, Bryn chooses a third option.

"Hmm," she mutters. "I have my opinions, but it doesn't seem like sharing them will help you much."

"No?" I ask, somewhat confused.

"Knowing which 'side' I'm on isn't going to make the questions you have go away. Honestly, the only view of yours it would change is your view of me."

I start to protest, but realize the wisdom in her answer. I'd like to say I wouldn't judge her either way—that's the Christian response, isn't it?—but I can't say that's really what would happen. Wouldn't I look at her differently after learning she believed in one side or the other?

I remember my social studies teacher from high school. We talked a lot about politics in his class, but he would never reveal which party he sympathized with. I always appreciated that about him. I might not have learned as much from him if I knew his beliefs didn't align with mine. Maybe holding some things back is the mark of a good teacher.

"But don't take that to mean I won't talk with you," Bryn continues. "The things you're asking—they're good questions."

The last sentence catches my attention. "*Good* questions? What makes you say that?"

"It's good that there are things in the Bible you're wrestling with. Shows you're engaged; you really care." She turns into the parking lot of a small family diner. "Generally, the people paying the most attention in class are the ones with their hands raised."

I know questions aren't a bad thing, but it seems some questions are more acceptable than others. Namely those which don't raise doubt about the character of God or the infallibility of Scripture, and most importantly, those which are resolved in a somewhat timely manner. The longer my questions have lingered and even grown in intensity, the more I've felt like I'm on the outskirts of God's good graces. A fake Christian. A wayward daughter.

Sometimes it feels like I'm on the brink of falling off the wagon. Like I'm holding on by a thread, white-knuckling the wooden boards near the open gate which leads to the speeding road of destruction trailing behind us...

But according to Bryn, maybe questions aren't just tolerated, but encouraged. A sign I care? A sign I'm paying attention?

I suddenly visualize myself shift from near the back of the wagon of true Christianity to slightly right of center. What if—what if I'm right where I'm supposed to be?

Bryn parks the car and turns her attention to the restaurant in front of us. "I was a little afraid this place might have gone out of business, but it looks like they're still going strong."

Despite the row of empty storefronts in the nearby shopping center, a glowing "open" sign sits in the window of the diner, and a steady trickle of people flow in and out the wooden door.

"Is this somewhere you went as a kid?" I ask quietly.

She smiles. "On occasion. When my mom had enough money, we'd sometimes go out for breakfast as a treat. I would always get the chocolate chip pancakes and a big glass of chocolate milk. Jim, the owner, I think he'd shave a few dollars off the price for her." She frowns. "I wonder if he still runs the place."

I hang on her words, surprised to hear her volunteer information about her childhood. I try to think of a way to formulate a question, to get her to say more, but I can't pull

220

the trigger on anything. Bryn pops open her car door, and the opportunity passes.

As we enter the building, an elderly man in a Navy veteran ball cap heads outside. Bryn holds the door for him, nodding as he passes.

"Thank you for your service, sir."

He stops and turns to her with a smile. It clearly made his day. "Thank you, young lady."

"If you don't mind me asking, where did you serve?"

"Oh, well, I went on three tours during my career. I've been all over the world…" he proceeds to briefly recount the names of the ships he was on, some of the cities he saw and things he did.

"I was stationed there for a time, too," Bryn says, commenting on one of the places he named.

Without pause, he asks, "Oh, was your husband in the military?"

"Oh, no, I'm a veteran myself. I just left the Navy a few months ago."

He stops, the smile fading from his face. "Oh, sweetheart," he says with a wave, "you're too pretty to be a sailor." With a pat on the shoulder, the man continues out the door. Bryn makes no attempt to defend herself, but lets him pass without a word.

"Two," she says, approaching the hostess stand. We follow her to a booth only a few steps from the door as I try to wrap my head around what just happened.

"I can't believe he said that to you!" I say once we sit down.

Hearing me, an older gentleman at the table beside us leans across the aisle.

"I can't believe it, either," he says, chuckling. He turns to Bryn. "Don't let him get to you. I know a squid when I see one."

She breaks into a grin. "Thank you, sir."

He holds out a hand and introduces himself, explaining that, as a younger man, he was an engineer in the Marines.

I try to pay attention to the conversation that ensues, but they lose me a bit with the military jargon. Regardless, it's nice to see Bryn light up. After the rude comment from the other man, I'm moved by this stranger's kindness.

It's not until the waitress brings our food to the table that the man pays his check and leaves. Save for those entering and exiting through the door, we're left to ourselves in a fairly private section of the diner. The smell of coffee fills the air, along with the clink of spoons and mugs, of forks scraping plates and ceramic being stacked.

Bryn says a prayer over breakfast, then begins spreading butter over her pancakes.

"It's pretty cool to hear you talk about the Navy," I say, genuinely meaning it.

"Yeah?" she snickers. "There's plenty more where that came from, believe me."

I shower my home fries with ketchup. "You seem like you enjoyed it—what made you leave?"

She sighs. "I guess you could say it was a lot of little reasons. Changes in leadership, in policy. Realized I needed time to take care of myself."

I nod. The bell rings as another group of diners enter. "Is it normal for people to say rude things like that?"

Bryn shrugs. "I wouldn't say it's uncommon. Funny how you were asking about gender." She takes a drink. "Those two interactions about sum up my time in the military. Some people were supportive, most didn't mind, but some *really* had a problem with me."

Once again, I find myself baffled by the way she appears unperturbed by the opinions of other people. "Doesn't that frustrate you?"

"Not much I can do about it. I know what I believe and what I've accomplished. Why should I answer a fool according to his folly?" she replies with a smile, referencing a Bible verse. "If you're respectable, respect will follow. Clamoring for it only hurts you."

A rare feeling builds in my chest. Admiration.

Swiftly, however, my brain tempers it with cynicism. I've lived enough to know no one is good all the way through. The story Dr. Edith told about the cabin starts to replay in my head...

I know it can't be true. Not fully. There's too much dissonance between the compassionate, well-reasoned woman before me and the image of a bloodthirsty, psychopathic child. But people can change, and they can have skeletons in

222

their closet, and there's a lot of gray area between innocent and guilty. But she has to have some type of explanation. Some answer. She always does.

Like ripping off a Band-Aid, I spit it out. "So, last time we talked, you told me you spent part of your childhood in the cabin you're living in now. You asked me why I wanted to know, and I didn't answer you." I grip my fork tightly. "The truth is, I heard some things, and I have a—a personal question to ask."

She eyes me, setting her fork down on her plate. "What do you want to know?"

The room fades to the background as my vision tunnels on the person sitting across from me. "What…what happened to your mother?"

Bryn sits stiff as a statue. She answers slowly, giving nothing away. "What are you thinking, when you ask that? What did you hear?"

I swallow. "Well, I've heard—it's a story, that—that…" I lower my voice. "I know people have lots of reasons for doing things, and I know I'm not in a place to judge or anything…" I descend into a mere whisper. "Did you kill your mom?"

She sits back against the booth. For a few agonizing moments, she is quiet. I fear I finally asked the wrong question. I brace myself when she moves to speak…

"Thank you, Addy."

I glance up, surprised. "Thank you? For what?"

"Trusting me enough to ask."

My eyes dart around as I try to understand the logic behind the statement.

"I hope," she continues, "that you don't mind me asking you to trust me just a little longer. I will give you an answer, but some things are better shown than told."

Chapter 35

A Change of Heart

I study her face, feeling my heart beating in my chest. I've grown accustomed to Bryn's willingness to answer questions. I must have struck something close to home. Is this like her reluctance to share her opinion on complementarianism—she knows the truth will change my view of her?

It...it must be true. Right? Why else would she be so solemn? A twinge of fear darts across my brain. How can she *show* me how her mom met her end? Gory images flash in my head. Is her body hidden somewhere near the cabin?!

I shake the thoughts away. Thus far, the trust I've placed in her has proven to be a sound investment. She's not asking a lot of me; only for the benefit of the doubt. After yesterday, especially, she deserves that much. I nod. "I can do that."

She offers a light smile. "Thank you."

When the check comes, I reach for my bag, but she refuses my offer to help cover the bill or even tip. Feeling sheepishly grateful, I follow her to the register. As we wait in line, I notice an assortment of flyers tacked to a bulletin board on the wall. Among them are two faded missing persons posters—one of a young boy riding a bike, and one of a teenage girl.

When it's our turn, the cashier takes the check and begins punching in numbers. Bryn's eyes drift to a jar on the counter. It's a charity collection for a local food bank. Swiftly, she slides some bills through the slot.

As we walk to the car, I make it a point to thank her for the meal.

"Sure thing," she replies cheerfully.

My phone screen suddenly lights up with a call from Sid. After a brief exchange, I relay the information to Bryn. "The doctors say she's ready to be discharged.

"Sounds good. You can tell her we'll be right over."

The only indications that Sid was just hospitalized are some bruises on her arm from the IV and the patient identification bracelet still on her wrist. Otherwise, she appears fairly normal. She takes a seat in the back of the Monaco.

"How did things go with the mayor?" she asks as we pull out of the parking lot.

I cringe. "It was…awkward. But he and his wife seemed nice enough."

She nods. "That's good, at least. I was a little worried something would happen to you guys."

"Could say the same for you," Bryn chimes in. "Did the police give you any more trouble?"

"Not really. Chief Boyer asked me a few more questions before leaving—" She stops. "Wait, is that the officer Addy was talking about?"

"Yep. That's him," I confirm.

"So, is he the one who planted the juice on you?"

"Either him or his dad, Dr. Robert Boyer."

"Or someone working with them," Bryn adds. "Whoever it was had to be watching you closely enough to know both the brand of juice you drink and when to slip a tampered one in your backpack without being seen.

"How much danger is Addy in, Professor?" Sid asks. "They were clearly after her."

"Not to scare you, but I think you're all in danger. If they targeted Addy, then you, Anthony, or even Micah could be next."

At first, it startles me to hear her name Anthony and Micah. I suppose it shouldn't really surprise me, though. She's probably seen us together on campus. And if she can figure out we're all friends, so can anyone else.

She parks the car on campus and turns to look at both of us. "Listen. The authorities will eventually catch up with the investigation, but things are slow moving at the moment. In the meantime, you'll just have to take some extra precautions. Don't walk at night if you can help it—especially not alone, and especially not in the woods. Addy, you should empty all the snacks in your bag and replace them. All of you should be careful accepting food and drink from others, and avoid talking about the case in public. If you feel unsafe at any point, or if you notice anything unusual, let me know. I'm here to help."

She reaches into her bag and holds the vial of cyanide test strips towards me. "Use these if necessary, and be sure to tell Anthony and Micah everything I just said. Okay?"

I blink, then shake myself from my daze. My hands tremble as I grasp the test strips. Through my fear, I manage to reply. "Okay."

Though I'm not sure I catch any part of the lesson, Sid and I sit through the full period of botany. For the most part, Bryn hides her exhaustion well, though her shoulders sag slightly, and there's a heaviness in her eyes.

"I'm sure you just want to get some rest, but I told Anthony I'd meet him in the library and explain everything," I say to Sid when the class ends. "You don't have to come, but you're welcome to."

"No, of course I'll come! Just let me stop and talk to Micah. Maybe he'll want to come, too?"

I hesitate, reluctant to trample her hopes. "I did text him, but he didn't send anything back."

"Well, maybe he'll listen if I'm the one to talk to him. I mean, if he hears what happened last night, he might have a change of heart. We should at least try."

I can't argue. Besides, I'm sure if I had a boyfriend and had just been in the hospital, I'd want to go see him, too. Together, we start off towards the dorms.

I send a quick text to Anthony so he doesn't think something terrible has befallen us when we're a little late.

226

We make it to Micah's dorm and knock on the door. For a few moments, there is silence, then the rattling of the knob. He opens it cautiously, and for a split second he stands with wide eyes. I hold my breath, not sure what to expect. At the sight of Sid, however, he rushes forward and embraces her in a hug.

"Oh, I'm so glad you're okay!" he says, lifting her off the floor. "A bunch of people called and told me what happened. I was so worried." He showers her with kisses before inviting us both inside. "Good to see you, Addy," he says with a nod, acknowledging me in a much more reserved fashion.

"It's hard to believe," Sid says excitedly, "but Addy was right about Leighton. She saved my life last night. Without her, that juice would have killed me."

Micah smiles. "I'm so, so thankful things worked out that way." Slowly, we watch the smile fade from his face, and he scratches the back of his head. "But…that's where we might disagree."

Sid's face falls. "W-what do you mean?"

"Well, I'm just afraid to jump to a conclusion too quickly. It might look like Leighton is a hero now, but…well, just consider for a moment. What if that was her plan all along? What if she set it up to make herself look better?" He shrugs. "It certainly worked to get the cops off her back."

Sid stares at him in silence.

"C'mon," he says casually. "Can you at least admit it's possible?"

She thinks for a few moments, staring hard at him and at the floor. Finally, she answers.

"No. No I can't."

He jerks his head back in surprise. "What? Why not?"

"You weren't there, Micah. *I was*. She calmed me down when I thought I was going to die, she pulled me back from the brink of suffocation, and she came to visit me at the hospital. No, I can't believe she was simply concerned for her reputation. No more than I can believe Addy intentionally gave me poison to drink."

Micah shoots me a look as if to say that last part might not be so unbelievable, either.

227

I take a step back. "Sorry about that," I say sheepishly.

But Sid isn't concerned about me. "Can you admit that what *I'm* saying might possibly be true? Can you take my word for it, Micah?" she presses. His only response is to lower his eyes. "Doesn't it mean *something* that Robert Boyer, the one we're pretty dang sure poisoned Dr. Morrell, tried to stop her? If they were working together, why would he have protested?"

"I don't know, Sidney," he says, growing more frustrated. "Maybe we were wrong about Dr. Boyer. Maybe he knows what he's talking about."

At his words, Sid reels backwards. "Do you even hear yourself?! If it were up to him, I'd be dead. *Dead*, Micah."

"I know, in that moment, he made the wrong call, but maybe without Leighton you wouldn't have been poisoned in the first place."

Sid shakes her head in disbelief. "I'm starting to think the only thing you know for certain is that Leighton is guilty. All evidence to the contrary be dismissed." She looks down and exhales sharply.

His eyes soften, and if I'm not mistaken, fear flashes across his face. He reaches towards Sid. "Please, listen to me. Believe me, I want you safe more than anyone. Don't trust her—she's dangerous."

"Micah," Sid says, shaking her head. "I...I'm going. We'll talk about this later."

I'm on edge, unsure if Micah will become as angry as he was when I deleted those pictures. However, he just slumps his shoulders, defeated. We exit the room, closing the door behind us.

"I can't believe him," Sid mutters to herself.

As we head to the library, I stop by my dorm to grab some new snacks. I start by emptying my bag of its contents, separating out anything edible and piling it on my desk. I even turn the pockets inside out, careful not to miss even a stray crumb of granola or little piece of candy. In the end, I'm left with a small mountain of flattened granola bars, melted hard candies, crushed pretzels, and unopened juice boxes.

For a moment, I stare at the pile. Is something in there

tainted with cyanide? And if so, how close did I come to ingesting it?

Swoosh. I swipe my arm across the desk and watch as everything tumbles into the waste basket. Better safe than sorry.

Chapter 36

2 AM Energy

Thankfully, the library is nearly empty when we arrive. We find Anthony and move to a quiet corner in the back. Sid plops down in a beanbag chair, looking exhausted.

"So, what the heck happened last night?" Anthony asks. "What's going on?"

Together, we fill him in on the events from the last 24 hours.

He turns to Sidney. "What did your parents say?"

I face her as well, curious to hear the answer. I'm surprised I didn't even think about that until now.

She draws her knees up to her chest, curling into a ball on the beanbag. "I...actually didn't tell them. I made sure the paramedics didn't contact them, either."

"You didn't tell them you were in the hospital?" I ask.

She shakes her head. "No. They have enough to worry about as it is. I mean, they already have a son in the Navy, stationed overseas and risking his life diffusing bombs on a daily basis. They don't need another kid whose life is in danger. And with my mom the way she is..." Her eyes drop to the ground. "I don't talk about it a lot, but she's been battling cancer for the last three years.'"

A silence falls over us.

"I...I'm sorry, Sid. I never knew."

She nods, acknowledging my sympathy. "Three years,"

she mutters. "Compared to what she's gone through, all this poison stuff seems like nothing."

Anthony swallows. "I haven't told my parents, either," he says. "My mom would probably storm on campus and break down Dr. Conley's door." Sid and I both smile.

"Me neither," I admit. "And I can't even give a reason why."

Though the necessary information has been conveyed, none of us seem eager to leave. The conversation shifts to lighter topics, and I start to relax. I collapse into a beanbag chair beside Sid, laying my backpack beside me. Anthony fidgets in his chair, then jumps up and begins to browse the nearby bookshelf.

"Addy," Sid says suddenly. "What do you think happens when we die?"

I flinch, wondering if I heard her right. Lately, I've been so focused on my own faith struggles that things like evangelism have taken a back seat. I've felt like there's been enough to work out between myself and God. Plus, if I'm honest, I have a bit of a cynical view of the potential of converting people to Christianity. In my experience, people don't really change their minds, especially about things like religion, and I feel like evangelism just isn't my gift.

But now, when faced with a question like that, I immediately feel bad for my doubts and lack of faith. What if I'm supposed to be the one to bring Sid to Christ? I need to stop slacking on my prayer life and Bible study. Otherwise, how will I ever be a good witness of Jesus?...I pause. I shouldn't get ahead of myself. It's God who changes hearts, not me. And whatever I'm supposed to say now, He's already given me the tools I need. I say a small prayer before replying.

I turn my eyes to the ceiling, too spent to formulate a perfect evangelical answer. "Well. Some days I'm not sure, to be honest. And that scares me. But I believe that God exists. And that we'll meet Him when we die." I muster the courage to add the more controversial part, "And if you know Jesus, I think you live with God in paradise. But if you don't...I think God punishes people for their sin."

I fold my hands together, nervously awaiting her response. How can I defend the justice of a concept like Hell? How

231

can I expect Sid to be okay with it when it bothers me, too? Thankfully, she doesn't ask.

"It must be nice," she says finally. "To have confidence in where you'll spend the afterlife. That there even is an afterlife."

For maybe the first time, it hits me that her struggles may not be my own. In fact, they probably aren't. I relax my shoulders. What if this isn't a debate? I voice an honest curiosity.

"What about you? What do you think happens?"

"To be honest, I'm really not sure. It's hard not to think about it, though. I want to know what will happen to my mom, or my brother, if things were to take a turn for the worse. It also—I know I shouldn't think of myself when she's the one suffering—but it makes me think about my own mortality, too. Like, what if my health turns south? Last night was... scary," she says, staring off.

"Last night *was* scary," I agree. I remember the surreal terror I felt in the gym. "It makes perfect sense why you're thinking of things like that. It's only human. Actually..." a Bible verse from earlier returns to mind, "there's a part of Ecclesiastes that says something like that. How it's almost better to spend time at funerals and with tragedy because it reminds you that life doesn't last forever. You value it more."

She nods. "That's true. I value the time I get with my family more than I ever did before." A shadow of sadness crosses her face. "Sometimes I feel guilty for being here, at college, instead of at home."

As I try to think of how to continue the conversation, Anthony returns with a book.

"And this," he says, "is why we need an art department." He thrusts a garish book cover towards us. The background is plain white, but the title is in block letters with vibrant rainbow gradient coloring and strongly defined drop shadows. Beneath it lies a bunch of photos edited together—I can tell because one woman's elbow is on backwards—giving the appearance of a diverse group of people. Black, white, disabled, etc.

Sid breaks into a laugh. "Oh my gosh. Hang on, I've seen a worse one." She hops up and leads us to another shelf,

232

and the conversation shifts to a new topic. My first instinct is to try and steer it back to spiritual things, but something tells me I should take it easy. Maybe I said exactly what the Lord wanted me to say. No more and no less.

Chapter 37

Company in Misery

At the end of a long day, I head back to my dorm. The high of my talk with Sid has long since started to fade, and I begin to remember the negatives. For one, my blood sugars have been running high today.

In the absence of outside distractions, I start to focus on this problem. I know it's because I've been stressed and I didn't get much sleep and eating out is always difficult to account for. Still, I start to wonder if I'm taking good care of my health. If I'm managing my condition correctly. Am I a responsible diabetic?

Marissa isn't back yet, so I'm alone in the quiet. I stare at myself in the mirror and feel my thoughts spiraling. I squint my eyes, trying to focus on things in the room. Is my vision more blurry than usual? If I concentrate, I can feel a vague tingling in my feet, like pins and needles. Is that a sign the nerve damage has already begun? Am I losing feeling?

I lie down, gripped both by the fear of getting old and of dying young. What kind of horrible health conditions await me as I age? The truth is I'm in optimal physical health now, which means there's nowhere to go but down. Was that small piece of cake after dinner worth my vision? My kidney function? My reproductive health? The feeling in my feet?

I wrap myself in my blanket, trying to calm down. Honestly, what's the big deal if someone is out to kill me? Even if I make it through this, if I do everything right and fight for my life and solve the mystery...I'm still going to die. Whether by some freak accident, old age, or something in between, my life is temporary.

Does that make it valuable, like I told Sidney? Or worthless?

I struggle to sit up, feeling frail. I glance at my CGM, imagining the internal turmoil my cells are facing. Some days I almost forget I have diabetes. Sometimes I'm even grateful for the awareness it gives me about my own body and my health. But sometimes it makes me feel like a liability. Like a feeble person with a handicap. My health is fragile, and I'll collapse at any moment...

I hear a key in the door, and Marissa comes in holding an ice pack. She throws her stuff down and falls on her bed.

"Hey," I greet, happy for a distraction. "How are you?"

"Ehh," she groans. "Had to go see my doctor today. My arthritis is flaring up, and my joints are hurting worse than usual." She shifts uncomfortably, icing her leg. "Gonna email my professor and let him know I'm not coming to class tomorrow."

Just like that, the self-pity is exorcized from my body. It's replaced by the strangely comforting realization that I am not the only 20-year-old with a chronic illness. Even if it feels like it at times, it's a lie that everyone but me has perfect health. *Everyone* struggles with something. No one lives forever.

"I hope you feel better," I say, nodding in sympathy.

"Thanks," she replies with a small smile.

As Marissa begins drafting an email, I surf movies on my phone for the first time in a while. Just as I'm about to pick one, Sid's name pops up on my screen. I swipe to answer, curious why she would be calling so late. Maybe she had a thought about the case?

To my surprise, when I put the phone to my ear, I hear her crying on the other end. "Hey Addy," she says, her voice shaking. "I just got off the phone with Micah. We... we broke up."

My mind spins. I have no idea what to say. "Sid...I...I'm so sorry."

Her voice grows a bit more steady. "It's okay. I mean, I

broke up with him. I tried to talk with him some more tonight, but...he's just not the same, not since Matthew died. Not that that's a reason to leave—I know he's grieving—but that's not the only thing. He's just kind of lost it, honestly. He won't listen to anything I have to say, he's fixated on Leighton being the killer—he's beyond reason." She sighs. "Sorry. I don't mean to dump all this on you. I hope I didn't interrupt anything. I just wanted to call someone, I guess."

From her bed, Marissa gives me a questioning look. "She okay?"

With split attention, I shake my head.

"What's wrong?"

Silently, I mouth the word, "Boyfriend."

"What?" she asks, leaning closer.

Slightly frustrated, I move the phone away from my mouth and whisper, "She broke up with her boyfriend."

"Ohhh," Marissa says, sitting up in bed. "Well tell her to come over. We can watch a movie or something, get her mind off it."

I hesitate. "But what about your—" I stop myself as I'm about to ask about her joint pain. It strikes me that listening to the voice of self-pity and depression that tells us to keep our troubles to ourselves isn't good for much, save fueling more depression. Why not?

"You wanna come over here?" I ask Sid.

Two bags of popcorn, a chick flick, and several hours later, I find myself sitting on the edge of my bed, watching as Marissa wets the ends of Sid's hair with a spray bottle.

"Yeah," she explains. "My high school was a tech school, and I was in the cosmetology program. After I graduated, I worked as a hairdresser for a year before starting college. How short do you want it?"

Sid gestures to a little above her shoulder. *Snip, snip.* The scissor blades slide together, and hair falls to the plastic bag on the floor.

"How did I not know this?" I ask.

"I've told you, haven't I?" When I shake my head, she shrugs. "Huh. Well now you know."

236

When she's finished, she hands Sid a mirror.

Upon looking, Sid immediately breaks into a grin. "Wow! It's so different." She checks from side to side, then looks to me. "I'll have to get used to it, but I like it. What do you think?"

I nod. "It looks cute on you."

"I agree," Marissa chimes in. "That boy doesn't know what he's missing."

Sid's smile turns sad. "Yeah. He doesn't have a clue."

Chapter 38

Lockdown

"Did you get a haircut?" Anthony asks as Sid approaches our table. "Looks good."

She smiles, sliding into the booth beside me. "Thanks."

"I mean, not that your hair wasn't nice before," Anthony continues. "And not to say I really noticed—" he stops himself and waves a hand. "You know what I mean."

She nods. "I do, thank you."

I steal a glance across the dining hall. No longer am I the one sitting isolated: now it's Micah. He looks our way, but quickly turns his head at the sight of Sid, who does the same, like two magnets repelling one another.

"So..." Anthony begins.

I've come to recognize the specific tone he adopts just before giving a sales pitch for the historical society.

"Are you coming to the meeting tonight?" he asks. "You're both more than welcome."

"I dunno," I say, squishing my mashed potatoes under my fork. "Like Bryn said, it's probably a good idea to stay in, especially at night."

He nods, acknowledging my point. "That's fair. However, I'm the president of the club—they expect me to be there. Besides, we're meeting a little earlier than usual today. It shouldn't be as dark. We're doing a tour of the Flickerwood Sawmill Museum off campus. Free admission." He turns his palms up, hopefully awaiting our response.

"So we'd have to walk back to campus at night?" Sid asks.

"You wouldn't have to walk," he says quickly. "I could drive you both. It would actually be less walking than if we were meeting on campus; I'll drop you off right outside your dorm. Campus, museum, back. Boom." He studies our faces. "Look, I know it's not foolproof, but the way I see it, it's really no worse than going to class. Still, up to you."

"So you're going either way?" I clarify.

"I am."

I sigh. He does have a point. If we leave a little earlier in the afternoon, we shouldn't be out too late. As long as I watch my bag carefully and eat only the snacks I bring, there shouldn't be a big risk of being poisoned. "Well, as long as we stay in your car—no walking anywhere but inside the museum—"

"Deal," Anthony replies.

"Then I'll come with you."

"Sounds like a plan," he says with a smile, then turns to Sid.

She looks from me to him. "Well, if both of you are going, I can't let you go alone. I'll come, too."

His smile widens. "Great! I'll tell Dr. Edith to add you to the headcount. This'll be fun."

When Anthony pulls up outside my dorm, Sid is already in the passenger seat. I open the door and claim the back seat for myself. With the sun still fairly bright overhead, we start off towards the museum.

Gradually, we come upon a large wooden building with a giant wheel attached to the side. It's painted mostly white, save for a set of large black letters across the front which say *Flickerwood Sawmill*. Train tracks run beside it, and an old-looking locomotive is parked nearby.

"Wow," Sid says, "this is beautiful." I have to agree. Even against the browns and grays of winter, the mill is a sight to behold.

Anthony smiles. "Just wait till you see inside."

He parks the car beside some others in an empty field, and we all get out. I zip up my jacket to protect against the

239

chill in the air. *Beep-beep.* The car locks behind us. Anthony leads the way in through an open door.

Admittedly, this is not what I pictured when Anthony used the word "museum." I was thinking more of an enclosed, public building with heat and electricity, maybe metal detectors. The Sawmill Museum, however, is as simple as the name suggests; it's a preserved mill from the 1800s, with plaques and information added to the various parts of machinery. Extension cords and a generator provide lighting, but the chill of the wind seeps in through the gaps between the wooden boards which make up the walls.

My eyes are drawn to the large circular saw in the middle of the room. No plastic guard or glass barrier stands between us and its dull gray teeth, which point straight up into the air. I peer down through the holes in the floor, glimpsing some of the gears on the level below. Along the wall are stairs leading to a loft above us, but they're barred by a chain with a sign that says *under construction.*

Aside from the cold, I don't mind the rustic nature of the mill. It's quite interesting, and at least I don't have to worry about any security guards rifling through my bag and giving me a hard time about bringing in needles and outside food. The downside to this is that I do feel a little more jumpy. A building like this has a lot of cracks and shadows where anything—or anyone—could be hiding.

I'm grateful when we join the rest of the tour group waiting just beyond the entryway. Dr. Edith notices us walk in and gives a small wave before resuming her side conversation with a man on her right, presumably a museum employee. After a few more people trickle in, the man stands on the second step of the wooden staircase, raising himself above the group.

"Alright. Everyone ready to begin?" he booms, smiling. He walks us through the steps of operating the mill; first, a log is dragged in on a pulley system and lined up with the saw, then water is released to turn the wheel and move the blades. While it hasn't been used commercially for over 50 years, the sawmill used to be a key part of Flickerwood's industry. Lumber processed here would be sent out by train all over the Eastern United States, which explains the steam engine outside. He shares how the museum is working to restore and repair the building. That's why the loft is roped off; the floor is being patched, and it's not yet safe to walk on.

Of course, once the tour is over, Anthony lingers to explore the ins and outs, eventually ending up in a conversation with Dr. Edith. As Sid and I wait, watching the last rays of sunlight sink below the horizon, my mind begins to wander back to the events of Tuesday night. How *did* someone sneak that juice into my bag?

"It's nice to see you here, dear," Dr. Edith's honey-like voice is suddenly directed towards Sid. "I'm pleasantly surprised. I heard you had a bit of a scare a couple nights ago."

Sid smiles awkwardly. "Yeah, you could say that."

"Tsk tsk." She clicks her tongue. "Insanity. If you ask me, they should've sent all the students home weeks ago. With all the technology your generation has, they could probably keep teaching classes from a distance."

Anthony snickers. "As if that would ever happen."

Dr. Edith shrugs, rolling her eyes. "In any case, what matters is that you're all okay, at least for the time being."

"Did you hear it was Professor Leighton who saved the day?" Anthony asks.

At the mention of Bryn, her lip twitches slightly. "So I've heard."

"Seems like everyone's suspicion of her was wrong," Sid adds, furthering the conversation.

Dr. Edith wears a tight-lipped smile. "So it appears. Lucky thing that she was there. Though I'd still advise you to be careful. Like I said, some people can turn on a dime. Not to sound paranoid—but good deeds don't prove the absence of guilt. Some hide their darker sides with outward kindness."

Something in her words makes my hair stand on end. I shudder, then rub my arms, pretending it was from the cold.

"One of the university board members was also at the volleyball game: Dr. Robert Boyer. He actually tried to stop Professor Leighton from helping Sidney," Anthony continues.

She purses her lips. "Well I can't say I was there Tuesday night, but I'm sure he had a good reason for reacting the way he did. Everyone responds differently in an emergency."

"Was Dr. Morrell close with Dr. Boyer?" Anthony asks. "Did you know they were seen together the day he died?"

It's clear that the question catches her off guard. She furrows her brow before responding. "It doesn't surprise me. Yes, they were good friends. They met up every now and then, especially to discuss school politics. Why?"

"Is there any reason he may have been upset with Dr. Morrell? Did they have a disagreement or something?" Anthony presses.

I bite my tongue. Anthony's forwardness in talking to Dr. Edith makes me more than a little uncomfortable. Still, I can't fault him for asking things I've wondered myself.

"Not that I'm aware of, no," she replies curtly.

He hesitates. "So far, two Wynhurst students have been dosed with cyanide because they asked questions about your husband's passing. We have reason to believe Dr. Morrell was poisoned by Dr. Boyer and his son, and Professor Leighton agrees."

Instantly, her expression darkens. "Anthony. I thought I told you not to continue with this nonsense. Yet now you and Bryn Leighton are making theories about my husband's death?!" Blood rushes to her face, and she starts to tremble. "Who else have you talked to?! Does the whole campus think Gregory was murdered by one of his best friends?!"

I'm taken aback by her sudden defensiveness. Sid and I both flinch.

"No!" Anthony sputters, shrinking back. "No, I only talked to a few close friends, a-and Professor Leighton knows, but she's really the one who started—"

"Good, good," she says, exhaling. "It's just—I don't want this type of gossip broadcast everywhere, which I'm sure you can respect. What seems harmless can quickly spiral out of control."

We all bob our heads.

As I try to process what just happened, the truth hits me.

Who would have seen me drinking a juice box? No one, save for when I arrived at the Morrell house for that historical society meeting. And when would someone have had the opportunity to plant a poisoned one in my bag? I recall Monday in the dining hall—I walked away from my

242

backpack and returned to find Anthony talking to Dr. Edith.

Sweat forms on my palms as the realization sinks in. While we've been standing here, everyone else has slipped out the door. I'm suddenly aware of how alone we are. We need to leave *now*. Oh, I knew this was a bad idea.

Before she can say anything else, I put on a polite smile and reach for Anthony's sleeve. "We, uh, we really should be going now," I say, sure that my fear is apparent. "You mind driving us home, Anthony? We have a lot of homework, and Sid has a thing to get back to…"

He glances towards me, a little out of it, but he soon pulls his car keys from his pocket and follows us outside. I pray until my hand touches the handle of the car door. I pop it open, which triggers the soft glow of the interior light. Once inside, I immediately lock it behind me, breathing a small sigh of relief. Anthony is the last to get in, and I tell him to lock the doors, which he does with little protest.

"Everything okay, Addy?" he asks, twisting to face me in the back seat.

"Just drive, please? I'll talk on the way," I tell him.

He puts the key in the ignition and turns. The sound, however, makes my heart skip a beat. The engine turns over, but it doesn't start. From her reflection in the windshield, I watch the blood drain from Sid's face. Anthony turns the key again and again, but the engine refuses to work. "C'mon," he mutters under his breath. I look to my left and stare into the inky night, half expecting Dr. Edith to have followed us.

I find only an empty field. Everyone else is long gone — there's no one around to even ask for a jump-start.

He sighs. "I'll get out and take a look, I guess." He pops his door open and sets foot outside.

"Wait!" I object, pulling out my phone. "Just sit tight. I'll call someone."

But it's too late. Before I can even dial a number, Anthony exits the car, and I suddenly hear him yelling. From the darkness come sounds of a scuffle, and he disappears from view.

Instinctively, Sid and I both lean forward, but a man dressed in black plunges his head into the car through the open driver's side door. Sid screams and rears back as he attempts to grab her, scrambling to escape out her door. As she dives outside, she collides with another man. He grabs her wrist, but she sprays pepper spray wildly, causing him to release her. I hear her footsteps in the grass, running away. The man on the driver's side withdraws his head from the car and joins the pursuit.

I press myself against the back seat, hoping no one can reach me, and try again to dial a number for help. For a moment, I wonder if they even know I'm here, but this hope is crushed by a chilling sound. *Beep-beep.* The doors to my right and left unlock simultaneously.

I frantically glance to either side. My eye catches movement outside the door to the right. In a split-second decision, I lunge towards that side, desperate to re-lock the door before an attacker can open it. Sheer panic bubbles in my throat. It feels like every nerve in my body is on fire. *This can't be happening. This can't be happening.*

I successfully jam the lock back into place, but from behind me, I hear the left-side door open. A pair of hands suddenly close around my ankles, and I'm dragged back across the seat. I throw my hands out and try to grasp anything to anchor myself with, but the force is too fast and too strong.

As they pull me from the car, I kick my feet and scream at the top of my lungs. "Help!! Please!! I'm being kidnapped!! Help!!" Someone yanks my hair, and my body falls to the ground. My teeth rattle upon impact with the dirt below. Despite my thrashing, my hands are zip-tied behind my back, stretching my shoulders and painfully cutting into my wrists.

Beside me, I see Anthony in a blur, also struggling against his captors. With pushing, pulling, dragging, shoving, rolling, and carrying, we're both taken back inside the mill. For a brief moment, I'm encouraged in thinking Sid escaped, but shortly after they drag her in, too. My heart sinks.

"Help!" Anthony pleads with Dr. Edith, who's still standing right where we left her. I already know the truth, however; Dr. Edith Morrell has no plans to help us.

She looks down her nose at him, then chuckles. "How many times have I warned you, Anthony, not to go looking in places you shouldn't?" She studies each of us in turn. "Did you really believe I was just a bumbling old woman living in ignorance of the fact that her husband was murdered?!" Her voice is laced with disgust. "How stupid do you think I am?"

Anthony's face falls as the truth registers. "So Dr. Boyer was just the middleman. You were in on it! Let me guess. You wanted your husband's money for yourself, and you're working with the board..."

She rolls her eyes. "You just don't know when to quit, do you? You *are* aware that it's because of all your questions and theories that I'm forced to do this, aren't you? I hope it was worth it. Unfortunately for you, I'm not going to stand here and explain everything. You don't even understand the half of it." She points her shoes towards the door.

"Just answer one question," I blurt out in a moment of courage. What do I have to lose? The longer we talk, the longer we live. "Why'd he have to die?"

She snaps her head towards me, her eyes narrow.

I continue. "You were married for a long time, and Robert Boyer was an old friend. What changed? Why kill your husband now?"

"Why'd he have to die?" She sighs with mild irritation, as if recalling an inconvenience rather than a reason for murder. "You make a good point, dear. For a long time, things were happy. But then...well, Greg started to change. He wasn't the same person I once knew. Really, he wasn't so different from the three of you—he knew too much, and he started to think he could be some kind of hero." She turns to leave, but pauses one last time. Her arm goes rigid, and she jerks her index finger at me. "Watch this one. Kill her first." Having sealed my fate, she crosses the threshold, locking the door behind her.

Chapter 39

Overwhelmed

"Good idea," one of the men holding me grunts. "That one talks more," he says, referring to Anthony, "but you do seem to be the root of the trouble." He shakes my shoulder. "We've been watching you, ya know."

In the light of the mill, I now see there are six men total, with two holding each of us. They're all dressed in black, but they haven't bothered to wear face masks. One of the men holding Sid has bloodshot, watering eyes from his encounter with her pepper spray. None of them are people I recognize, but they fit the typical goon profile—young, maybe late 20s or early 30s, and tough-looking, with muscular builds and neck tattoos. Several have a black nightstick hanging from their belt.

Two of them walk me towards the back wall. Every step feels like one closer to death, but they're far stronger than me. There's nothing I can do. They slide my tied hands over a wooden post and shove me to the ground, then zip-tie my ankles together, making it nearly impossible to get up. My heart feels like it's about to beat out of my chest, and a surreal, floating feeling fills my head, as if I'm about to pass out. Having sufficiently incapacitated me, one man produces a small black case.

Slowly, he opens the lid and pulls out a glass vial, tinted brown to protect the contents from light exposure. A modern-looking pharmacy label is stuck to the side, but I can still make out a small icon of a skull and crossbones printed in red.

He glances at me with stormy green eyes, then stares at the bottle in his hand. Shadows dance across his pale, angular features. "They say you can lead a horse to water, but you can't make it drink…" He reaches into the case again and raises his other hand, this one holding a gleaming needle and syringe. He smiles. "But this should expedite the process."

He punctures the top of the bottle and draws the deadly substance into the syringe. Armed with the means of my demise, he starts towards me.

Apparently I don't possess enough respect for stoicism to die with grace. I scream at the top of my lungs and desperately struggle against the restraints. It's no use. All I can do is wiggle around, harmless as a flopping fish. The man shoots out a hand and tugs my coat and shirt away from my shoulder, revealing my upper arm. He lowers the needle towards my skin.

I didn't think I would go from touring a museum to being a murder victim so quickly. I'm not sure which I dread more—death itself or the pain of asphyxiation. Tears spring from my eyes, and garbled prayers and pleas fly from my mouth. I squeeze my eyelids shut, bracing for the all-too-familiar prick of a needle…

Thunk.

My eyes fly open at the sound of a dull thud, like a chef's knife hitting a wooden cutting board. I blink rapidly, trying to comprehend the sight before me. The needle—and the hand holding it—are flush against the wall, stuck there by a knife blade embedded in the wood.

The man stares at his hand with a panicked look in his eyes. He twitches his fingers, and relief floods his face when he realizes the blade is not actually piercing his flesh, but only his sleeve.

My gaze follows the apparent trajectory of the knife. I swiftly identify the origin as the figure standing just outside the door, which is now swung open. A black boot lands on the wood floor of the mill, followed by dark pants and the bottom of a long jacket. She crosses the threshold, stepping fully into the light: *Bryn*.

For a moment, all eyes are on her.

Hope swells in my chest, but the feeling is mingled with sudden dread. I'm sure she has some fighting ability, but does she know what she's walking into? Six vs. one? The fear of watching her die a gory, horrific death seizes me.

"Here's your warning," she says firmly, dropping her doctor's bag to the floor beside her. "Let them go and leave now. You can walk away unscathed."

The man closest to her breaks into a smile. He has jet-black hair and a pockmarked face. "*This* is your rescuer?" he asks in disbelief, eyeing Bryn from head to toe. He releases his grip on Sid, leaving her with his partner, and steps forward.

Bryn doesn't respond, instead directing her attention to the task of pulling on a pair of medical gloves.

The man pinned to the wall beside me chuckles, wiggling his fingers some more. "Sorry to disappoint, but you missed me. Got anything else up your sleeve?" She remains quiet. "No?"

"I'm actually glad you showed up. Four for three," the black-haired man continues. "We were gonna have to hunt you down next anyhow."

"Yeah, I figured," she answers dryly, snapping the glove against her wrist.

In a flash, he lunges towards Bryn, reaching to grab her and raising a fist at the same time. Moving even faster, she steps forward to meet him. Before he has a chance to touch her, her palm connects with his chin. Instantly, his head rocks back, and his body goes stiff. He teeters for a second, then drops to the ground at her feet, out cold.

There is stunned silence, followed by shouting and a clamor of movement among the goons. The man next to me starts tugging on the knife with his free hand. It takes him a few pulls to get it unstuck from the wall. "Thanks for the weapon—" he grunts smugly, but his thought is cut short as Bryn closes the distance between them.

She catches his hand as it flies back from the wall and twists his wrist, reclaiming her knife. Without hesitation, she

248

lands a blow to his neck, causing him to wobble. He stabs wildly with the syringe, but she grabs his arm and forces him towards the ground, at the same time plucking the syringe from his fingers. With a kick to his side, she releases his arm and buys just enough time to wedge the needle between two wooden boards in the wall.

Two more attackers approach, both brandishing small clubs. I try to draw my legs in close, shrinking away from the fight. As one advances, she lands a swift kick to his chest. The club falls from his hand as he stumbles backwards, landing on his backside. His partner charges forward, raising his club to swing. As he brings it down, she turns to the side, removing herself from its path. Using his own momentum against him, she strikes his arm and follows up with several kicks to the back. He falls forward, hitting his head against the wooden floor.

Quickly, she snatches the baton from his loose grip and turns to face another oncoming assailant. She raises the weapon just in time to block an offensive swing. The sticks clack against each other as the two exchange a flurry of blows.

Just past her, I notice the final man lingering on the outskirts of the fight, halfway between Bryn and Anthony. Left open, Anthony suddenly yanks his hand out of the zip tie and beelines towards Sid, who is also tied to a beam. The man catches the movement, however, and turns towards him with a baton. Anthony jumps back, narrowly dodging the swing. He's soon chased into a corner, with no choice but to dart up the stairs. With the man on his heels, he hops the chain, and both of them disappear on the floor above.

Smack. The sound of the baton hitting something echoes all the way down. I grit my teeth so hard my jaw starts to hurt. Thankfully, I still hear the patter and creak of two sets of footsteps running around. Anthony is still okay—for now, anyway.

A nightstick sails across the room, hitting a wooden support beam before clattering to the floor. Having disarmed her opponent, Bryn delivers a whack to the side of his neck.

Beside me, one of the men groans and tries to sit up.

"Bryn!" I call nervously, but she's already on it. Before

he can fully regain his senses, she grabs him by the back of the neck and the arm and rotates him away from me, kicking him into the other guy. Like bowling pins, they both topple to the ground.

She looks behind her, checking the spot where the green-eyed man with the syringe had been lying. I'm startled to find that it's empty. He's gone.

Bryn tenses, sweeping her gaze around the room. Where did he go?

Our answer comes in the form of a wooden creak, followed by the sound of rattling metal chains and a mechanical *whirr*. Slowly at first, the giant saw blade in the center of the room begins to turn. As the speed builds, the razor-sharp teeth become a blur, and the sound grows louder, filling the room.

The missing man then appears in the doorway with a sly smile on his face. He shrugs, gesturing at the saw. "Figured I'd raise the stakes. Make things a bit more interesting."

As Bryn studies him, her eyes suddenly widen in realization. "You're very confident for someone who ran away the last time we met."

An expression crosses his face—Irritation? Fear? Doubt?—then quickly disappears. "You weren't my target that night," he replies. "But now...you'll find when I have a job, I get it done. My methods worked on that boy, and they'll work on all of you, too."

For a moment, all sound in the room fades away, and I am aware of only one fact ringing loudly through my head. This...this person in front of me...this is the man. The man who killed Matthew.

"I'd call that a confession," she replies. Not waiting for him to come to her, she darts in his direction. He takes a fighting stance. She thrusts the nightstick towards him, but he catches it and turns her towards the spinning saw blade.

I inhale sharply as my imagination conjures predictive images of what it will look like if Bryn touches that saw. In my mind, the metal teeth rip into her skin, splatter her blood, sever her nerves, break the spinal column and render her two halves of a body. I shudder uncontrollably as my senses rush to simulate what it would feel like. The pain of the cut, the

250

scrape of the bone...The high-pitched buzzing of the saw only sets me further on edge.

The man bends Bryn towards it, holding her off-balance so there's only about a foot of space between her and the high-speed metal. I look on in horror, every muscle tense.

With an elbow, she jabs him in the side of the head, then swings her weight away from the blade. Pulling him towards her, she knees him in the stomach, then the head, and brings him to the ground. With his face pressed against the floor, she plants a knee on the back of his neck and draws her knife.

I cringe, anticipating a rush of blood. Instead of his neck, however, she grabs a fistful of his hair and slices it off.

She rises, releasing him.

He growls, immediately pawing at the shaven space on his head. "What—what is wrong with you?" He rolls to a sitting position, revealing the fact that his nose is a bit crooked. "What kind of a sick psycho?!" he calls after her, demanding an answer.

But she's already walking away, heading for the stairs. She hops the bannister and climbs up to the loft.

Around me, the goons start to stir, and I begin to worry about the syringe still in the wall. Fortunately, my fears are unfounded, as killing us is far from their minds. They struggle to stand, wincing and nursing wounds.

I look up. From where I'm sitting, I can see the edge of the loft. Anthony and the man are grappling in the area under construction. There's a metallic crash, and something drips on my forehead. Another drop falls on my arm—it's thick and black, like oil. A small stream leaks down to the floor below; they must have spilled it.

Bryn suddenly comes into view. I feel relieved, until there's a shout. In an instant, a pair of shoes appears over the ledge, and I find myself staring up at white soles attached to dark legs. My stomach drops.

Anthony kicks his feet as he desperately tries to pull himself back up, but the oil makes the wooden surface slippery. He begins to lose his grip, sliding off the edge and towards the whirring saw blade below. Its steel teeth whine, eagerly awaiting a victim to devour. As his fingertips fall from the boards, he reaches wildly, narrowly managing to catch himself on a small beam protruding just below the floor. He flings his free arm up, trying to get a good hold on something, but it slides right back down to his side.

The man who'd chased him up to the loft suddenly comes running down the stairs holding a hand to his head.

"Let's get out of here! C'mon!" he shouts, gathering the rest of his crew. Together, they flee, dragging out the unconscious man.

Above me, I watch Anthony continue scrambling for a second handhold. His palm slides through the oil, nearly falling for the third time. At the last instant, a hand shoots over the edge and grips his arm.

"Gotcha." Bryn stands over him.

He clings both to her and the wooden beam for dear life. As his head tilts down to look at the spinning blade below, I see his face. It's taut and full of panic.

"Look up here!" Bryn says, shouting over the noise of the saw. "You need to let go of that board so I can pull you up!"

His grip seems to grow tighter. "N-no offense, Professor, b-but are you sure you can lift me?" he wheezes. Something inside me wonders the same thing. "I—I'm almost 200 pounds..."

"Yes, I can lift you. I promise," she assures. "I won't let you fall."

His eyes turn downward again. "O-okay. I'm gonna let go now."

I hold my breath as he tentatively releases his grip on the beam. For a few moments, as he raises his other hand to grab hers, he freely dangles over the edge, supported by nothing but Bryn's grasp.

Holding both arms, she takes a step backwards and easily tugs him to safety. Soon, they both come down the staircase.

With the immediate threats gone, I become aware of the fact that I'm trembling from adrenaline. My hands are starting to go numb from the zip ties. Still, I'm mostly just grateful to be alive. For a moment, I thought for sure I was a goner...my eyes return to the syringe stuck in the wall. *Thank you, Lord. Thank you, Lord.*

I'm shaken from my thoughts when I realize Bryn is

252

crouching over me with her knife.

"You okay? Addy?"

I blink, coming back to the present. "Yeah, yeah, I think so."

She holds the zip tie around my ankles and slices through it. As she does so, I study the knife up close.

It has a black handle wrapped in brown leather for a grip. The edge of the blade is smooth, save for a small serrated section near the base, and it comes to a tip that is menacingly sharp. The steel gleams in the light.

She moves behind me to cut the tie around my wrists. The plastic snaps, and I'm suddenly free. Anthony drops my backpack on the ground beside me, and Sid stands next to me, having already been cut loose. I notice that the saw blade has been shut off. As I massage my wrists and move to stand up, Bryn collects her bag and shoves her sample of hair into a paper envelope. She takes the syringe from the wall, carefully holding it by the plunger, and places a cap over the needle.

"Addy," she says, tossing me a pair of gloves. "Up for a job?"

I pull them on obediently. "What do you need?"

She extends the syringe towards me. "Hold it just like that—don't touch anything else."

I take it from her hand, accepting the task.

"Leave everything else where it is," she says, then motions for us to follow.

Like a set of traumatized ducklings, we trail behind her. Once outside, she scans the area before leading us to her car. She holds the passenger door open for me, and Sid and Anthony take the back seat.

"I—I'm sorry we went out at night. It was all my fault," Anthony rambles, breaking the silence. "I should've listened to you, Addy. But I was stupid, and I trusted Dr. Edith, and she almost killed us all. If you hadn't been there, Professor— thanks for bailing us out, but I'm sorry you had to stick your neck out for us in the first place…"

Bryn glances in the rearview mirror. "Don't guilt yourself, Anthony," she says quietly. "It's not your fault you were attacked. Any of you."

"But still—" he protests. "If we would have just stayed in…"

She shakes her head. "You can't live in fear of everyone you know and every place you visit. All of life is a calculated risk."

He stops. "You're not upset?"

"Not at you, no."

There's a slight break in the conversation. Just as I'm about to ask how Bryn found us and got there in time, Sid pipes up.

"Why'd you let them go?" I turn to look at her. "All those guys...they were gonna murder us. You were outnumbered, but you were the better fighter. You had the opportunity to kill every one of them. Why'd you just let them run away? They're gonna come after us again."

Anthony and I exchange a look. I can tell he feels the same as I do; I'm glad she didn't kill anyone. What did happen was scary enough.

"A fair question," Bryn says. "As a general rule, I try to preserve life whenever possible. While the use of deadly force may at times be justified, in this particular case I believe it wouldn't have done much good. Those were hired men brought on to do the dirty work of violence and intimidation. If something happens to them, they'll simply be replaced."

Outside, we rocket down unfamiliar back roads lacking even a double yellow line. Dark trees race by. Bryn continues, "Killing them wouldn't have put us any closer to finding the root of these crimes. But you should know I don't intend to let justice go unserved, and I'm asking for your help with that part."

Bryn makes a few odd turns, and I realize we're not heading back to campus. In the woods on the outskirts of town, she turns into a dark driveway.

"How can we help?" Sid asks.

"Where are we?" Anthony adds.

I consider the syringe in my hand, and a vague idea comes to mind.

Chapter 40

Brought to Light

We pull up in front of someone's garage door, and a motion light flashes on, illuminating the house we're now parked beside. It's a one-story rancher with red brick lining the bottom.

Without answering any of our questions, Bryn simply gets out of the car and instructs us to follow. Cautiously, we all trod along the dark, concrete path to the front porch.

Bryn steps forward and knocks on the door. Not a polite knock, either, but a loud pounding, as if a SWAT team were about to break the thing down. I startle. She repeats this until a light turns on. We hear footsteps rushing around, then a voice calls from inside.

"Who is it!?"

"We need some help!" Bryn replies.

Slowly, the doorknob turns. The door opens only slightly, leaving a chain lock in place. Just barely, I can locate the eyes of a man standing in the gap, but his face is obscured in shadows.

"Ms. Leighton?" he asks, surprised. His eyes scan the rest of us. "What's going on here?"

"Forgive me for disturbing you at home, but these three were just the victims of a crime. Kidnapping and attempted homicide." She gestures towards us.

The man sounds even more confused. "What? Are the suspects nearby?" He looks past us, peering into the darkness around the house.

255

She shakes her head. "Probably hiding somewhere in Flickerwood, but not an immediate threat."

"Then I can give you the number for the police station so you can report it—" he says, but Bryn stops him.

"You're an officer, aren't you?" she asks.

"Well yes ma'am, but I'm off duty—"

"I know," she interjects. "I came to you for a reason."

Behind us, a car passes by on the road. The headlights bounce off the house and, for a moment, the man's face becomes visible. I recognize him as the younger policeman I've seen working with Eric Boyer. Officer Hopewell.

"Listen," he says, shaking his head. "I'm sorry, but I can't help you. The most I can do is call the station for you."

In my peripheral vision, I see movement in the blinds. They shake, as if someone was observing us from the window only moments ago. More footsteps can be heard, along with the whines of a fussing child.

"Ben," a female voice whispers, "who's at the door?"

He looks over his shoulder, then back to us.

"Please," Bryn says gently. "I don't mean to bring any trouble to your family. But we can't go to Chief Boyer— there is ample reason to believe he's involved in the crime ring responsible for the murders at Wynhurst."

"Mur*ders*?" he asks, with emphasis on the "s." "What crime ring? What do you mean?"

"Yes, murd*ers*. Dr. Morrell didn't die of natural causes. He was poisoned by a Wynhurst board member, Dr. Robert Boyer. And his son, Chief Eric Boyer, has gone through great lengths to conceal his father's guilt. Lengths which include treating me as a suspect."

Officer Hopewell blinks like a deer caught in headlights.

Bryn continues. "Why do you think Matthew Bruner was killed?"

He's quiet.

"He had information they couldn't risk getting out. He knew Morrell was murdered, and he saw the culprit. He was found dead only a few days after he shared this information with Chief Boyer. Did you know that?"

The young man swallows. "No," he says softly. "I didn't know that about Matthew."

256

"And now they're trying to kill *us*," Anthony says. "Because we believe the same thing as Matthew. Sidney almost died just the other night from cyanide, and tonight they came to finish the job for all of us."

Sid and I nod in agreement.

Officer Hopewell cracks the door open a little wider and flips on the porch light, bringing his face into view. "Who's 'they'?" he asks. "Can you give a description?"

"Six men, several armed with clubs, one of whom I recognized as Matthew's killer," Bryn relays.

"Plus Dr. Morrell's wife, Professor Edith," I add. "She essentially confessed to having a hand in her husband's death."

"Do you have any evidence?"

"Plenty," Bryn replies. "I have a DNA sample from the man guilty of poisoning Matthew in the form of some strands of hair, as well as possession of the main weapon in tonight's attack..." She nods to me. I raise the capped syringe for him to see. "Cyanide."

At the sight of the syringe, his jaw drops. His eyes dart from the needle to Bryn. "I—You're sure that's what it is?"

"Certain. But please, feel free to send it for analysis. I implore you to dust for fingerprints. Come investigate the crime scene. Make your own judgement."

"I—give me a moment," he stammers, his eyes glued to the syringe. He holds up a finger before ducking back into the house and closing the door behind him.

Through the door, we can hear muffled voices. Though I'm sure it's only a few minutes, it feels as though we wait for hours on the porch. When the door finally opens, I'm surprised to see a woman.

"Hi," she says, "Ben will be out shortly. He's just getting some coffee."

"No problem," Bryn says with a smile. "We appreciate his help."

"Mind if I ask who you are?"

"Not at all," Bryn says, extending a hand. "I'm Bryn Leighton, a professor at Wynhurst. And these three are students there." We say our names in turn.

"Sally," she replies, accepting the handshake. "Ben's wife."

In a few moments, the officer—Ben—reappears. He's dressed

in his usual uniform, with a coffee cup in hand. My eyes fall on the shiny handcuffs clipped to his belt, as well as the black handgun strapped to his hip.

"Alright," he says, "where did all this occur?"

We follow him into the garage where we find a police cruiser. After getting some supplies from the car, he takes the syringe from me. As Bryn suggested, he uses a kit to extract fingerprints from the glass. I'm relieved to no longer be responsible for the death injector and eagerly discard my gloves.

Hopewell also collects the hair sample, albeit with a concerned look on his face. We then pile back into Bryn's car, and he follows us to the sawmill.

When we pull up, he gets out of the car with a large flashlight. He shines the beam around the outside of the building and the field beside it.

"Do we know whose car that is?" he asks us, hovering over Anthony's sedan with the light.

"Y-yes, sir, that's my car," Anthony answers. "We drove it here for a group tour, but when we tried to leave, the engine wouldn't start."

With intention, Hopewell charges across the grass towards the vehicle. He circles it, looking above, below, and inside. The doors are still hanging open from when we were dragged out of it. Once he pops the hood open, it doesn't take him long to examine the engine and locate the problem.

"Yep," he says, "your spark plugs were definitely tampered with." He takes some pictures, then sweeps the ground with his flashlight as we head towards the building. Before entering through the door, he draws his gun and motions for us to wait outside. Carefully, he rounds the corner and switches the light on. With his weapon out in front of him, he walks through all three floors, ensuring the place is empty. Satisfied, he waves us all inside.

Upon returning to the place where I was kidnapped and nearly killed an hour ago, a sense of dread creeps into my bones. Officer Ben examines the scene, taking pictures, collecting evidence, and asking questions, then taking notes based on our answers.

"So, if these guys were really bent on killing you, how

did you escape? What happened?" he asks.

Sid, Anthony, and I all turn to look at Bryn.

"Well, she fought them off," Anthony says quietly.

With his eyes still trained on his notepad, he furrows his brow. "Who did?"

After a beat, Bryn answers. "I did."

Hopewell stops writing and raises his head. As he faces her, the truth seems to register in his expression. "Wait, you're telling me you fought off all six men?"

She nods. "Scared them off, at least."

"Ha," Anthony snickers. "That's an understatement. One guy was out cold from the start. They won't be coming back tonight—"

I elbow him on the arm, trying to subtly shoot him a look. "She was just defending us," I tell Officer Hopewell. "She didn't do anything wrong."

He glances between us. "Did you have a weapon?"

Bryn hesitates, then points to a black baton near the door. "I used one of their clubs. That's the one I moved." She pauses, then opens her jacket, revealing the handle of her knife. "And I carry this for self-defense...I've had a fair amount of combat training, and I was in the military."

He looks at the knife, then scribbles some things down on his notepad. "Welp," he says when he's finished surveying the area. "I would normally do this down at the station, but since you're not comfortable with Chief Boyer, I'm going to take fingerprints and statements here."

When it's my turn, he rolls my fingers onto an ink pad, then on a piece of paper. He explains this is to help differentiate my prints from others found on-site. With a recording device on, he listens to me recount the events again, then asks a few additional questions about Robert Boyer and Dr. Morrell's murder. When we're all through, he ropes off the area with police tape, then goes to his car to make a few calls.

"You don't think he'll call Chief Boyer, do you?" Sid asks as we head back to the Monaco. Bryn starts the engine and lets us warm up as we wait.

She shrugs. "Boyer is bound to find out eventually. In fact, I wouldn't be surprised if he already received a report from your attackers. What matters is getting Officer Hopewell to take us seriously without his influence, and I think we've done the best we can at that."

Just when I start to wonder if he's ever coming back, there's a knock on the window. I almost jump out of my skin when I see Hopewell standing there. Bryn rolls it down.

"The county police are going to come in and help with the investigation. Based on what I've seen and what you all have said, we're going to search the area for any suspects matching your description and work on bringing in Edith Morrell and Robert Boyer. We'll also open an internal investigation on Chief Eric Boyer to evaluate if there's any reason for concern."

"Thank you, sir," Bryn replies. "I appreciate everything you've done tonight."

"Any time, ma'am. I'd suggest you all go home and try and get some rest. Lock your doors. And don't hesitate to call if you need anything."

Chapter 41

Somewhere to Turn

I check my phone. The time is 1:32 am, and my blood sugar is 85. With the adrenaline starting to wear off, I'm hit with a wave of exhaustion. Feeling like a zombie, I pull out a granola bar and unwrap it.

"Are you all feeling okay?" Bryn asks. "Is there any reason to go to the hospital?"

There is tired silence before we realize no one actually answered her. "No, we're okay," Sid says.

"Then I plan to take you back to campus. Being behind locked doors and surrounded by people will probably be safest." We all nod weakly.

Bryn pulls up near my dorm first, and I drag myself out of the car. I shuffle over to the door and fumble for my student ID so I can scan into the building. Once inside, I climb up the stairs, unlock my hallway, and find my room. With each successive threshold I cross, I feel a little bit safer.

Half-asleep, it takes me a few extra seconds to unlock the door. Immediately upon opening it, however, I'm met with a distinct smell. Before college, my less sheltered friends had attempted to describe it as akin to skunk spray. Personally, having now been exposed to the odor myself, I wouldn't liken the pungent smell of skunk to the burnt, earthy stench that is marijuana. A wall of swirling smoke hits me as I enter.

Sitting in the glow of string lights, I can see Marissa and her boyfriend lounging on her bed and blowing puffs of smoke. Lo-fi music plays in the background. I also happen to notice a few glass bottles on the bedside table.

In an instant, I decide this is not something I want to walk in on, much less try and fall asleep beside. I turn on my heel and quietly shut the door behind me, hoping they didn't notice my presence.

In the hallway, I lean against the wall. Marissa must have thought I went out somewhere for the night and invited her boyfriend to stay. Where can I go? I could try and sleep in the lounge, I guess. But I'm sure an RA would come around and kick me out. Maybe Sid and her roommate would let me stay with them?

With only a loose plan in mind, I make my way back down the stairs. To my surprise, I run into Bryn in the lobby.

"What are you doing here?" I ask.

She holds up a familiar-looking black rectangle. "You left your phone in my car. I didn't want you to go without your CGM readings."

I look at the phone in her hand, then pat my pockets. Sure enough, my device is missing. "Thank you," I say, grateful. I take the phone from her.

"Glad I ran into you. Wasn't sure how I'd find you if you were in your room." She rocks back on her heels, putting her hands in the pockets of her jacket. "Were you coming to look for it?"

"Honestly, I didn't know it was missing until now," I admit. "No, I went up to my room, but my roommate...well, she's with her boyfriend, and they're, uh, using some substances. I was gonna see if I could stay with Sid, but—" I falter as something Sid mentioned earlier comes to mind. "I just remembered she's hosting some prospective students tonight, which means they'll already be crowded..." I bite my lip, the stress and chaos of the day finally washing over me. "So..." I say, a lump forming in my throat. "I'm not really sure where I'm gonna go."

I'm suddenly hyperaware of my existence. The sensation in my hands, the beating in my chest, the fragility of my life. The image of that needle, mere centimeters from my skin, flashes in my mind, and I can't shake it. I really almost died. That was *real*. I'm really trapped in this living nightmare where a villain I don't even fully know is out to kill me. If only I could just wake up.

A feeling like that of claustrophobia grips me. It's as if my consciousness is straining against my skin, desperate to escape the situation my body is in. My brain glitches between a crushing sense of reality and a state of dissociation.

Am I really going to die out here at college, alone and away from my family? When did I see my parents last? Was that the last time I would ever see them? I'm not ready to die. *Lord, I'm sorry, but I'm not ready to die. Please.*

Overwhelmingly, I just want to go hide. Or go home. Go crawl in bed under the covers and feel safe. Pretend none of this ever happened. But I can't. Because I don't have a car, and my roommate has taken over my space with her drug habits, and there are still murderers on the loose…I've been through so much today, but I don't even have a bed to sleep in.

A mixture of self-pity and dread soon causes tears to spring from my eyes, and it seems that no amount of social embarrassment can hold them back. All I can do is hide my face in my hands as I start to sob. I'm used to crying because of sadness, but it's been a long time since I cried out of fear.

My mind returns to childhood, back when I was very small and everything seemed so very big and confusing and scary. I remember the feeling of waking up to pitch blackness after the power had gone out. Of opening my eyes yet being unable to see anything but darkness. Or when I used to spend hours of the night staring at my closet door, terrified the monster inside was going to come alive and eat me.

My hands shake, and I feel sick to my stomach. I feel so physically ill all of a sudden, a part of me wonders if I was poisoned after all.

"Addy?" Bryn asks softly. "Are you okay?"

"S-sorry," I sputter, feeling self-conscious. Her voice rips me from my spiraling thoughts, and I return to the present moment. I reach for a nearby box of tissues and try to clean myself up a bit.

"No, no need to apologize," she assures. "It's okay if you need a minute."

She guides me to an empty chair and takes the seat beside me. She doesn't try to talk, but sits with me in silence as the tears flow. Only once my breathing becomes more steady does she speak.

"You don't have to worry. I won't leave you without a place to go. You're more than welcome to come home with me."

Do I want to stay at a professor's house and deal with the awkwardness of eating another person's food as a diabetic, or using their bathroom, or sleeping under their roof? No. What I *want* is for Marissa to not be smoking pot with her boyfriend in my room. But, under the circumstances...

I nod, starting to pull myself together. "You wouldn't mind?"

"Not at all."

I stare at the lobby door, suddenly realizing how Bryn must have gained access to the dorms. Staff IDs don't open the residence halls, but students hold the door for people all the time. Though it seems secure, truthfully anyone could walk in.

And after all I've seen tonight, it seems like staying with Bryn might be the safest place to be.

"Come on," she says gently, beckoning me to follow. I wipe my cheeks and walk out to her car.

Feeling drowsy, I stumble back into the front seat. She restarts the engine and shifts into drive. We head off campus and turn down some winding back roads, traveling into the woods. The gentle vibrations of the car almost lull me to sleep.

Out of nowhere, a sudden slam on the brakes jars me awake. I sit up straight, eyes wide.

"Sorry," Bryn says. "Deer." I catch the tail end of a skinny brown creature bounding into the woods on the opposite side of the road. She cracks a smile. "Brake check."

I clutch my chest as my breathing returns to normal. Thankfully, we soon reach a weathered wooden mailbox that marks the entrance to Bryn's dirt driveway. Slowly, she pulls in and drives up to the house. Before I can reach for the door handle, she motions for me to stay put. With her hand on her knife, she gets out and inspects the area. I hold my breath, praying for safety.

In a few minutes, she returns to the car and ushers me out. We waste no time getting inside the cabin and barring

264

the door behind us. It's chilly, but not as bad as outside. She turns on a few lamps, then does a walkthrough of the house, checking every door and window.

I stand awkwardly in the living room, wondering if I should follow her upstairs. Just as I set my bag down and decide to go up, Bryn reappears on the staircase, descending with her arms full of blankets, sheets, and a pillow.

"Can I help at all?" I call.

She reaches the base of the stairs and thrusts the bedding into my arms. "Sure. Feel free to make up your bed. Hope you don't mind the couch."

I feel myself smile. "No, the couch is fine with me." I'm relieved to avoid the weirdness of sleeping in another guest bedroom or stranger's bed. As I head over with the blankets, Bryn kneels beside the wood stove and starts kindling a fire.

"The good thing about sleeping down here is you'll be nice and warm," she says, her back to me. "For food, you're welcome to anything in the kitchen. Nothing in there is toxic. Just don't eat any plants from the rest of the house."

I snicker to myself whilst shaking out a sheet for the bottom layer. As if I would even think of doing so.

"The bathroom is that room there," she says, pointing at a nearby door, "and if you need anything else, just let me know. I'll be upstairs. Even if you're just worried you heard a noise or something, come and get me. I'm a light sleeper."

"Thank you," I reply, careful not to make any promises. Unless I hear someone actively breaking in, there's no way I'm waking her up. Still, the offer is nice. It's all nice.

As the fire crackles to life, the room starts to warm up. I take my coat off and lay it beside my bag.

"Can I do anything for you before I head to bed?" she asks with a yawn.

Realizing it's my last chance, I do ask for some water.

"Sure thing," she replies, starting towards the fridge. After handing me my drink, she makes her way up the stairs. Suddenly, I find myself alone.

I turn out most of the lights in the living room but find too much darkness unsettling. I leave one small lamp on. Along with the glow of the fire, it's pretty cozy. I check my blood sugar, use the bathroom, rinse my mouth with a little water, and run my hand over the branches of the Norfolk pine.

As I crawl under the covers, an ache of homesickness strikes my chest. I miss my old room at my parents' house. My childhood bedroom, where I always felt safe and everything was familiar. I curl up under the blankets. How did I end up here? How did I go from being a normal college student to a target for murderers? Because I heard the wrong story? Asked the wrong questions? Befriended the wrong people?

When I close my eyes, I can still see the glint of the needle and syringe. I always struggle to sleep in unfamiliar places, but the trauma of this night is an added obstacle. If I weren't so tired, it would probably keep me up. Thankfully, it doesn't take me long to drift off.

Chapter 42

Skin Deep

I do wake up several times during the night, however. Masked monsters, sharp needles, and violent encounters fill my dreams. Still, some rest is better than none, and I do feel better by the time morning comes.

When I first open my eyes, I'm a bit disoriented. For a brief moment, I forget where I am, and it takes me a minute to remember. Thin rays of sunlight stream in from the skylight overhead. Beside me, I can see that the fire in the wood stove has been reduced to a few glowing embers. It's still rather early in the morning, but I can tell I won't be able to fall back asleep.

I spring from the couch and head towards the bathroom. On the way, the sound of clanking metal causes me to glance to the left. I find that Bryn is already awake, lying on the bench press in a room filled with exercise equipment. Steadily, she lifts the barbell up and down. I scamper past the open doorway and arrive at my intended destination.

As I'm washing my hands, one of the dreams I had last night comes flooding back. Not of the darkly-dressed criminals, but of Bryn, standing in the dimly-lit sawmill. At first, her head was shrouded in shadows, though as I looked closer, it began to come into the light…What I saw was not her face, but something grotesque and monstrous. Like a TV tuned to white noise, with a mouth full of bright fangs. In her hand was her knife, but as I watched it grew longer, almost to the length of a sword, and it was dripping with blood.

I blink away the memory. I'm not afraid of Bryn. Not in the way I was at first, anyhow. But watching her single-handedly take down six grown men was, admittedly, startling.

And perhaps more than that, I think something in my subconscious is deeply unsettled by the question hanging open: What really happened here, in this cabin, all those years ago? Whatever it was, did it really drive a child to…to kill?

As I exit the bathroom, I nearly collide with Bryn. We both grind to a halt. She's in workout clothes—a t-shirt and some sweatpants. I quickly realize it's the first time I've seen her in short-sleeves. The muscles in her arms are far more toned than I would have expected.

Mainly, however, my focus falls to something else.

"Y—you have tattoos!" I blurt out in surprise. Apparently my lack of sleep is impacting my filter, as I immediately hear how tactless my statement sounded. "Sorry," I bumble, trying not to stare. "I just—I didn't know. They look cool," I add, internally kicking myself.

I don't have anything against tattoos. They're not even an unusual thing to see. I know some Christians don't like them, but even if I felt that way I wouldn't judge someone else for their conviction…I was just surprised. For some reason, I didn't expect to see them on Bryn.

I restrain the urge to further justify my reaction by sharing this runaway train of thought, instead choosing to remain quiet.

Bryn smiles, glancing at her own arms. "Yeah. Hard to escape the Navy unscathed." She extends her arms forward, palms facing up. "You're free to look. I'm not offended."

Mostly, the art is done in thin black lines, though there are splashes of color here and there. On her left forearm, a few inches above the wrist, there's a lighthouse with a compass rose in the middle. A faint yellow glow surrounds where the light would be. On her right, a green stem stretches between her wrist and elbow, with a few inches of space on either end. A dozen or so bell-shaped flowers hang from the stem, drooping towards her open palm.

"Recognize that?" she asks, pointing.

"Foxglove?" I answer.

She nods, then flips her arm over, revealing another flower on the opposite side, closer to her elbow. It has some more color to it, with pops of pink in the blossoms and green in the leaves.

"I don't think I know that one," I tell her.

"Rose periwinkle—also known as the graveyard plant." With a jokingly ominous smile, she turns to the side and tugs her sleeve up a bit. Pointy, star-shaped flowers cover her shoulder and bicep. Dark berries accompany the blooms.

"Nightshade," I say immediately.

She nods, pulling her sleeve back down.

Something in my brain clicks. "Aren't those the same three flowers in the journal—the ones that make up the combination to the safe?"

"*Were*," she corrects. "Had to change the code after *someone* cracked it." She side-eyes me, but is clearly amused. "But yes."

"What's so special about them?"

"Well, they all have two very important things in common. The first being they're all poisons with the potential to kill." She nods her head to the side, "And the second is their shared ability to heal. These three plants have helped diagnose eye disease, fight cancer, and treat heart failure." She drops her hands to her sides. "I like them because they remind me why I do what I do."

I take a moment to absorb her words. "So all your work with poisons—it's about saving lives. Not taking them." Suddenly, I can see my past self standing in front of the safe, ignorant of the fact that Bryn's true intentions—her vindication—rested in the very numbers I entered. Something she believes in enough to have tattooed it on her skin.

She nods. "That's always the hope, anyway."

She starts to move towards the stairs, and as she passes I catch a glimpse of more ink on her left arm. From what I can see, it looks like a seal of some sort, with an anchor and a life preserver—definitely a military tattoo. Briefly, I wonder about the meaning in the others, but decide that's a question for another day.

"I'm gonna rinse off quick, then start some breakfast.

That work for you?"

I check my blood sugar and wince. I'm certainly not in immediate need of food. "Yeah, that's fine." As she begins the climb, I gaze into the workout room. My mind wanders back to the sawmill.

Before, I liked to think if I were ever in a fight, my internal grit would somehow make up for my lack of athletic skill. Well, that vague, arrogant hope was stomped into the ground last night. There was nothing I could do. I couldn't prevent being taken captive any more than I could prevent that deer from running into the road on the drive over here. Anger burns in my chest when I remember the feeling of helplessness. How they dragged me from the car and tied me up. It's not like I didn't struggle—but it wasn't enough. My best efforts were as easy to thwart as a little girl's.

I might turn it into another gender crisis and convince myself God just designed women to be weaker and more fragile, always in need of protection from men, were my defender not standing right in front of me.

"Bryn—" I call after her, causing her to stop. "How— how did you fight off all those guys?" I shake my head, realizing the question is too broad. Obviously, it was through years of discipline, study, and training. I rephrase. "How can I defend myself? To keep that from happening again?" I pause. "Would you show me?"

"Of course," she says instantly, descending back down the stairs. "I can teach you a few basics now, if you're up for it."

I falter, taken a little off guard. "Sure. Yeah, now's fine."

She waves me into the exercise room and onto a wrestling mat lying in the corner. I hesitate before stepping onto the rubber, suddenly feeling nervous. The anger fades and I have second thoughts.

Bryn, noticing the change, pats her sides, showing her lack of weapon. "I won't hurt you, don't worry."

Right. Why am I nervous? I cross the mat and stand beside her.

"First thing, most of the fight is up here," she says, pointing to her temple. "There's always some type of reasoning behind a person's actions. You understand the why, you can predict what they'll do, and you're safer for it." Her voice is commanding.

270

I nod along, wide awake and trying to follow.

"There's a place for intimidation, but there's also an advantage to being unassuming. Gives you the opportunity for surprise. That initial surprise only works once, though, so you gotta commit. To that end, I'll show you a few simple strikes you can use."

She moves towards a punching bag and demonstrates how to use my hands, elbows, and knees against an attacker. For a final example of the techniques at full speed, she hammers the bag with a mix of strikes. It rocks back and forth, appearing to almost fall over. She waves me over. "Your turn."

At first, it feels awkward, but it doesn't take me long to warm up to hitting the bag. It's quite cathartic, actually.

Once satisfied with my strikes, she continues. "Equally important are your blocks. The most straightforward method is to block with the forearm." She positions herself in front of me. "Go ahead and swing at me a few times."

Tentatively, I do as she says. Slowly, with an open palm, I aim for her shoulder. Swiftly and easily, she redirects my hand with her forearm. I go a little faster as I gain confidence I won't hit her.

"Now you."

I swallow. Right. No reason to be nervous. I raise my forearm.

"I'll go slow."

She feints some strikes so I can get used to the motion, then speeds up slightly. Though I know she's still moving much slower than usual, it's a rush, blocking what's coming at me. Makes me feel a bit more in control.

"Good." She steps back, rolling her shoulders. "Alright. Last thing we'll do for today. If someone *does* grab you, you want to make it as difficult as possible for them to take you anywhere. Shift your weight closer to the ground, strike however you can. You might face people who are much stronger than you, but no one is stronger than gravity. If you can disrupt their balance and use leverage to your advantage, you have a good chance at winning.

"For now, I'll teach you a few basic escapes." She approaches me. "I'll demonstrate on you first, then you can practice on me."

"Okay," I agree.

"We'll start with the arm. Put your hand here, like you're trying to grab me."

She taps a place on her right arm, just above the elbow. I lay my hand where she tells me to.

"If someone is holding you like this, you want to bring your elbow over their arm in a circular motion. This breaks their grip and allows you to get a few strikes in before escaping."

Slowly, she mimics the movement before swiftly following through, forcing me to release my hold. Before I even know what's happening, her arm is free and I find my head being forced towards the ground.

She releases me. As I straighten, I realize I'm smiling. "Hey, that was pretty cool."

She has to walk me through the motion several more times before I get the hang of it, but once I do…it feels like a door has been unlocked. If I can pull off a move like that, what else am I capable of?

Thankfully, our session comes to a close just as my sugar is starting to drop.

"Thanks," I say earnestly, feeling a little more prepared.

"Any time." She eyes me as I check my phone. "Ready for some breakfast?"

272

Chapter 43

Poison and Medicine

The pan sizzles as Bryn cracks an egg into a pool of melted butter.

"How do you like your eggs?"

"Uh—it doesn't matter to me," I answer, mostly desiring not to be an inconvenience. "Whatever's easiest."

She cracks a second egg, and the yolk breaks, leaking golden yellow into the whites. Assessing the situation, she looks back to me. "Scrambled okay?"

I smile. "Sounds good, thanks."

I stir the pot of oatmeal I've been put in charge of, happy to have a way to help. I never knew oatmeal was so easy to make, and I now find myself questioning the purpose of the microwavable packets I've used all my life. In a few minutes, the food finishes cooking and we migrate to the table. I toss some frozen berries in my bowl to sweeten the oats and measure a dose of insulin. After Bryn prays over the meal, I start on my eggs.

"Did you sleep okay?" she asks.

I tilt my head to the side, considering. "Alright, I guess. As much as can be expected."

She nods. "Yeah. I didn't sleep well, either."

I hesitate. "Did last night get to you, too? The fighting and all?"

"You would think," she says, gazing around the kitchen.

"But honestly, I've had trouble sleeping ever since I moved. It's—well, it's hard to live in this house."

I perk up, realizing the shift in tone. "Why's that?"

She shakes her head. "I know what people say about this place. Witches, curses, the like. None of that is true, of course, but stories like that—well, there's often some truth behind them. I do feel like I'm haunted here. Haunted by memories."

I follow her gaze, taking in the room. It strikes me that I'm not the only person with problems. Everyone has their own burden to carry. And Bryn—from some traumatic event in childhood, to the things she must have seen in war—oh, the memories that must haunt her.

"Why choose to come back here, then?" I ask carefully.

She exhales, answering slowly. "Addy, have you ever loved something, yet been repulsed by it at the same time?"

She pauses for a moment, waiting for my reply. I search my emotions, and my thoughts fall upon something I do, in fact, feel that way about. All I can do is nod.

"Well, that's how I feel about this house. About the whole town, really. I have so many good memories here...and so many very dark ones. I didn't want to run from my past. So I came back, to face the things that haunt me." She glances towards her right arm. "Sometimes poison and medicine are one and the same."

She takes a sip of water, then lowers the glass back to the table. "Thought teaching might be nice, too. Poetic, somehow. Getting to share what I've learned, influence young people. But," she sighs, shrugging a shoulder. "A lot of things aren't going how I'd hoped. I'm starting to think I won't stay here long."

"Oh," I say, suddenly finding myself with a sinking feeling of disappointment. I've been so caught up in the mystery and, more recently, the threat of death, I haven't given much thought to the next semester. Though she only started a couple months ago, the prospect of going the next two years at Wynhurst without Bryn seems empty and dismal.

She looks at me and flashes a smile. "You know, as strange as it may sound, I'm glad you broke in that night."

"You are?" I ask, a little confused.

"Yeah, I am. I mean, if you hadn't, you'd probably still

think I was the murderer. As a whole, my classes may be a remarkable failure, but I've enjoyed getting to know you. You're a bit shy, but very bright. Not only that, but it's clear you care very much about others. You ask good questions, and I can tell you're a deep thinker. You could do anything you want, and excel."

I lower my eyes, slightly embarrassed by the compliments, though I can't help but smile. I've always wanted a professor or teacher to take an interest in me, but I tend to slip under the radar, fading into the background. I'm sure it's partially my fault—I'm shy, as Bryn said. I don't exactly go out of my way to engage with potential mentors.

But now...A social weight suddenly falls from my shoulders. I don't have to guess how Bryn feels about me. I'm not an inconvenience or an annoyance or a liability. She's not secretly still mad about the lab instruments I broke or the photos I took. She *likes* having me around.

"It's been nice getting to know you, too," I manage, which may be the understatement of the year.

"Divine providence," she says. After eating the last few bites of oatmeal, she pushes her bowl forward. "Well. Next thing is to water the greenhouse."

"The one outside?" My curiosity surges at the thought of the heavy padlock on the door.

She nods. "Let me get dressed, then we'll go out."

In a few minutes, she returns, clad in her usual jacket, this time paired with dark jeans and a maroon top. The handle of her knife is visible on her hip. My eyes are drawn to it, but I look away when she notices me staring.

"Why a knife?" I ask. "What makes it your weapon of choice?"

She slows, her keys jingling in her hand. "Number of reasons. Namely, though, I like the utility. A knife is good for far more than just fighting."

"But..." I continue, "for self-defense, isn't it kind of... well, brutal?"

She pulls the blade from its sheath and peers at the gleaming metal. "It can be. But it also depends how you look at it. If your goal is to kill, you may be right." She tosses it lightly. It turns once in the air before she catches the handle.

"But that may be a good thing. Makes you think twice before taking a life. A knife can stop a person without it having to be lethal."

A detail from last night comes rushing back. "That was no accident, was it?" She eyes me as she slides the blade back into its sheath. "When you threw that knife at the man with the syringe and caught his sleeve. He thought he got lucky and you had just missed his arm, but...you didn't miss, did you?"

The corner of her mouth turns up slightly, and a glint flashes in her eyes. "No, I didn't." She pauses. "I don't often."

I pull on my coat and head out the door, contemplating her words. On the one hand, I'm comforted by her moral code. On the other...an uncomfortable question is raised for my conscience. What happens when the blade *is* intended to connect with flesh?

Which is better? A quick and easy death? Or a torturous experience that a person survives?

I shake the thought away as we approach the door to the greenhouse. Bryn inserts a key in the cast-iron lock, and it springs open.

I'm not sure what I expected to find, but it's simply another space filled with plants. "I keep it locked just in case any kids or animals wander back here," she explains. "Some of these toxins are very potent, so just be careful."

She grabs a garden hose and begins spraying down a cluster of potted shrubs. A sprinkler system hangs above wooden tables lined with propagating flowers, herbs, and other small plants. It's pleasantly warm inside, especially compared to the external chill.

With her direction, I grab a watering can and help with the chore. As I do so, she explains some of the species to me. When all the pots are sufficiently damp, she winds the hose back up, and I remember that I'm currently missing my Friday morning chemistry class.

"I guess I should head back to campus soon," I tell her.

Bryn nods, but she does so slowly. "You know, I was actually going to ask if you wouldn't mind doing something with me today."

"Like what?" I ask, intrigued.

276

She examines one of the plants in front of her, picking a stray weed from the pot before answering. "You asked about my mom, not too long ago. And I told you I would come back to it."

I stand up straight, my eyes trained on her. Every hair stands on end as I wait for her to continue.

She raises her head and meets my eyes. "The truth is, my mother is still alive. Would you like to meet her?"

Chapter 44

Elise

My mouth falls open in shock. At first, all I can manage to say is, "Really?" As my brain catches up, I find my voice again. "Your mom is really still alive? Or do you mean it in, like, a figurative sense?"

Bryn spreads her hands. "Nope. No tricks. No metaphors. My real, biological mother is 100% still physically alive. We can go and visit her today, if you would like."

I take a moment to breathe, stopping myself before I bombard her with a million questions. Clearly, this is a very sensitive topic. She doesn't have to share any information with me, but for whatever reason, she's choosing to show me this part of her life. The least I can do is wait for her to explain, in her time, the things she wants me to know.

"If you wouldn't mind," I reply, "I would like that."

She answers softly. "I wouldn't mind."

We stop by my dorm so I can rinse off and put on a change of clothes. Thankfully, Marissa and her boyfriend have cleared out. I take what might be the fastest shower I've ever had in my life and, with a brief deliberation over what I should wear for such an occasion, I pull on clothes as quickly as I can. I rush back outside to see Bryn waiting beside the Monaco, leaning against the driver's side door.

With my bag in hand, freshly stocked with snacks and insulin, I get in the passenger seat.

"Get comfortable," Bryn tells me. "It's kind of a long ride."

Taking her advice, I shift my things around on the floor and stretch my legs out. She offers no further information about where we're going, and I don't ask.

She turns the radio on, and we talk about nonsense. The type of music we like, our opinions on coffee, our favorite season.

"How do you like it, being a traditional college student?" Bryn asks.

"Whaddya mean?" I respond.

"Living on campus, going to a four-year school, you know. What's it like? Would you recommend it?" she says with a smile. "Did I miss out?"

"You know, I almost ended up commuting to a community college back home." I wrinkle my brow, suddenly in awe of how many intricate pieces of my life this one decision determined. Had I not come to Wynhurst, I wouldn't know Sid or Anthony or Micah—I would be around a whole different pool of people, in a different town, likely one without any murders. But God...God put me here. "Does it make sense to say I think the traditional college experience is overrated, but it feels worth it to have tried it and *know* it's overrated?"

"Perfect sense."

"It's...it's weird. College is like a paradox a lot of the time. On one hand, you have everyone telling you not to waste these years. To go out and travel the world, join activities, explore the local area, make friends...but you have so little time, money, and energy that it's a struggle just to keep up with your classes. And even though you're constantly surrounded by people, it feels like you're in an isolated bubble. We're all in the same space, but alone."

"It is lonely, isn't it?" she says, reflecting. "That isolation isn't exclusive to students. In my experience, it seems like the Wynhurst professors are a closed club."

I snicker. "It probably doesn't help that they all believe you murdered one of them."

She smiles. "Nah, that can't be it."

As we approach the edge of town, we come to a stop at the sight of two cop cars parked in the road. Bryn rolls down the window, and we're approached by none other than Officer Ben.

"Good morning," Bryn says.

"Morning Ms. Leighton," he replies after recognizing her. "Did you have any further trouble last night?"

"No, sir. Nothing out of the ordinary."

"Good to hear. We're just doing routine checks of vehicles leaving the area. Trying to locate the suspects you named last night."

"I take it they weren't found in their homes?" she asks.

He bites his lip. "No ma'am. At this time it does appear they're attempting to flee the area. But we have plenty of county and state officers helping with the search and containment process."

"And Chief Boyer?"

"For obvious reasons, the details of that case are confidential," he says, pausing. "I will tell you we have launched an investigation."

She nods. "Thank you for your diligence."

He bobs his head. "Just doing my job, ma'am." He gestures towards the road ahead. "You're free to go."

As the checkpoint disappears in the rearview mirror, I ask a question of my own. "Last night, how did you know where we were?"

"I pieced some things together," Bryn answers. "Earlier in the afternoon, I saw Anthony's car driving off campus. Didn't think much of it, but then I had a meeting with Dr. Gaines. He found some more books that belonged to Dr. Morrell, so I offered to walk them over to Edith's office in the social sciences building. Her door was unlocked, but no one was there. When I walked in to deposit the books, I briefly rounded her desk and saw something peeking out from under it. It seemed...out of place."

"What was it?"

"A pack of juice boxes, with one missing."

I stiffen.

She swallows. "I asked another professor where she was, and he told me about the historical society meeting. Suddenly, it all made sense. I figured, being the president, Anthony wouldn't miss the big event. So, naturally, I showed up."

"Just in time," I say quietly. "Thank you. You really

saved our lives."

She nods. "I'm glad I was able to help."

My brain once more turns over the events of the evening. "Ya know, the way you talked about those guys that attacked us, that they were hired men...and then you told Officer Hopewell there was a crime ring responsible for the murders... it sounds like you think there's a bigger criminal organization behind all of this."

"I don't doubt it," she replies. "And based on what Edith told you, it's become clear that Gregory Morrell was part of it, too. It seems he had a change of heart about his involvement in illegal activity, however, and his accomplices didn't take kindly to that. I'd wager the Boyers and Morrells are only the tip of the iceberg, though."

My eyes widen as the pieces start to fall into place. "What kind of criminal activity? Micah said Dr. Morrell left millions to the university when he died. He thought he made the money from some businesses he owned in town, but that seems like a lot, doesn't it?"

"Did he, now? Yes, that does seem like an oddly large sum, especially considering the types of businesses I've seen around here. Mattress stores, bars, car washes, laundromats... unless, of course, they're only being used to hide the true source of the funds."

I think back to my economics class, trying to remember how money laundering works. You get money illegally, then pretend it came from a legal business so you can spend it without consequence. Right. So, if Flickerwood is full of businesses that, on paper, are doing really well, but in reality do nothing for the community or the local economy, it's no wonder poverty is on the rise. The town is bleeding.

"As for what type of crime generated all that money in the first place, that I'm not sure about," Bryn continues.

"If it's really that pervasive, and that organized—who would be in charge?"

"Another great question I don't yet have an answer for," she says.

With some answers and more questions to think about, the conversation drifts elsewhere.

After an hour or so, I know we must be nearing the end of our journey when Bryn turns off the highway. As we meander through suburban streets, each approaching house has me wondering if it could be our destination.

Where does someone like Bryn's mom live? A small blue house on the corner? A towering colonial-era mansion made of stone, or a white bungalow with an overgrown yard that looks about two days away from being condemned? Maybe she's a hoarder, or maybe she's secretly rich. Heck, she could be married with more children. I realize I've been given absolutely nothing to go on.

My gaze rises towards the top stories of homes, and we pass an apartment complex. Maybe she's still a single woman renting an apartment somewhere. I imagine us all sitting in a well-lit kitchen, laughing about how this was all a big misunderstanding. Maybe there's nothing dark to uncover after all.

I know the thought is probably a bit too good to be true. But it's nice to be removed from Wynhurst and Flickerwood for a bit. It's as if all of those dark, pressing things aren't as important, or as real. I feel like I can breathe again. I can smile. Just for a little while, I can pretend.

We pass the quaint houses and shaded apartments and continue on through a short stretch of open field. A large sign with white and red letters appears on the side of the road, and Bryn flips her blinker on. As she slows to make the turn, it's easy to read the name: *Susquehannock Hospital and Medical Center*.

My mind races to construct a new narrative as we wind through the hospital drive. Is her mother sick? How long has she been in the hospital? Unless...maybe she's not a patient, but an employee. Maybe that's where Bryn gets her love of medicine from.

We follow arrows away from the emergency department and the main buildings. The number of locations listed on the signs decreases as we go along, until we pull into the parking lot of a building called *Susquehannock Inpatient Behavioral Health*.

Admittedly, behavioral health is not a term I'm familiar

with. Bryn pulls into a parking space near the front of the building and turns the car off. She exhales.

"Here we are." Slowly, taking a moment, she pulls the key from the ignition. She puts her hand to the knife on her side and pulls it off her belt, sheath and all. I lean back in my seat, confused, as she reaches over and opens the glove box. "Do you have any pepper spray or pocket knives—anything sharp or dangerous in that bag of yours?" She places the knife in the compartment.

I smile sheepishly. "Nothing except my needles."

"Right," she says, remembering. "That should be fine." She closes the glove box and locks it. We get out of the car, and she stuffs her own bag under the seat, taking only her keys, wallet, and phone.

"Why do you ask?"

"You're not allowed to bring any of that stuff in, for the safety of the patients and staff." She starts walking towards the door.

"Oh. Makes sense," I say to myself. It doesn't exactly answer my question. I follow her through a glass door into a small waiting room. Opposite the door is a window to the receptionist's office, though no one is at the desk. To the left of the window is a locked, frosted glass door. I try to glimpse what lies beyond it, but all I see is a blurry, carpeted hallway. Bryn approaches the counter and rings the bell.

As we wait, my eyes scan the walls. Calming impressionist landscapes are hung in golden frames. In the corner is a water cooler and a door marked *restroom*. With a glance towards Bryn, I duck into the single-stalled bathroom. It did feel like a long drive.

As I wash my hands, I notice some brochures hanging on the wall for a program called Spring Haven. The first inside flap lists some conditions they help treat, like depression, anxiety, bipolar disorder, DID, schizophrenia...It suddenly clicks for me what behavioral health means. This is a psychiatric facility. I place the brochure back as the truth dawns on me. Bryn's mom is a patient at a mental hospital.

Trying to have a neutral expression, I exit the bathroom just as someone comes to the desk.

"Sorry for the wait. We're short staffed," the man

explains apologetically.

"No problem," Bryn says with a smile.

"How can I help you?"

"We're here to visit my mother, Elise Sayer."

At the name, I involuntarily jolt. My head snaps to attention. Bryn exchanges some more information about her name and date of birth, then the man collects both our IDs. When he leaves to make copies, I seize the opportunity.

"Sayer?" I ask. Dr. Edith said Bryn had changed her name, but never did reveal what it had been changed *from*.

She glances towards me. "Yes."

"Like—like the mayor? Are you related?"

She gives a slight nod, holding a rigid expression. "The same. Yes."

My questions are cut short by the return of the receptionist. He slides our IDs back over the counter and unlocks the glass door that leads to the hallway.

"I let her know you're here. She's in the lounge area down the hall."

"Thank you," Bryn responds, then steps towards the door. She holds it open, and I tentatively step across the threshold. It closes behind us with a hefty metal click. I'm gripped by a sudden fear, feeling trapped in a facility full of mental patients. I take a deep breath and straighten my shoulders. People are people, right?

The cleaner used must be different than most doctor's offices; it has a pleasant, lemony scent. The blue carpet looks new, and plenty of natural light pours in from the skylights above. As I follow Bryn, I feel goosebumps forming on my arms. What will this woman be like?

We pass some people in the hall who wave to us politely. Contrary to my imaginings, I see no one in a hospital gown. Most people are in normal clothing, though some are clad in pajamas. In a short distance, we find a large sitting area, complete with couches, tables, and a couple of vending machines. Two women sit at a table in the center, casually playing a game of chess. They're both reclined in their chairs, chatting and laughing. The one on the right glances in our direction and freezes suddenly.

Somehow, she looks both older and younger than I expected.

284

Her skin is weathered, maybe from working outside or smoking too many cigarettes, and her brown hair is choppy. A flowing shaw is draped around her shoulders, partially covering the top of her flowered dress. She looks like a woman in her element.

"My baby girl!" she squeals, running towards us. She wraps her arms around Bryn and squeezes her tightly. "Ohhh," she says happily, shaking her daughter back and forth. She pulls back slightly, rubbing Bryn's arms and meeting her eyes. "I love when you visit me."

Bryn looks startled at first, but her expression soon shifts to a grin. "It's good to see you too, Mom," she says, hugging her back. "I hope you don't mind, but I brought one of my students along." She gestures towards me. "This is Addy."

Elise Sayer turns towards me. "Student?" she asks Bryn. "Oh, right, right. You did tell me you were teaching, didn't you?" She extends a hand towards me. "Nice to meet you. I'm Bryn's mother, Elise."

I shake her hand, feeling a smile on my own face. It's nice to see something so...normal. And heartwarming.

"So this must be the daughter I've heard so much about," a voice says from the table. It's the other woman who was seated across from Elise.

"It most certainly is," Elise replies. "Bryn, this is Helen. She and I have started a chess club."

"Hi," Helen says, shaking Bryn's hand from where she's seated. "She really does talk about you all the time. She's so proud of you."

Bryn's cheeks become flushed. "Oh no," she says, laughing nervously. "I'm not sure I wanna know all the things she's told you."

Elise waves a hand. "Oh, only good things. C'mon, we have a lot of catching up to do. You're welcome to come back to my room."

Taking Bryn by the hand, she leads us through the halls and scans a card to open one of the wooden doors. It almost reminds me of a dormitory. The room is well-lit, with a tile floor and a rug underneath the bed. There's a bathroom off to the side, and even a small kitchenette with a microwave, toaster oven, and Keurig.

"Do you want something to drink?" she asks.

"No—" Bryn starts to say, but changes course. "Sure. I'll have some tea, if you have it."

A few moments later, we're all seated around a small table, grasping mugs of steaming green tea.

"So, you're officially out of the military? Ah, I'm so glad," Elise sighs. "I was always so worried about you."

Bryn shakes her head. "Mom, you don't need to worry about me."

Elise lowers her eyes. "Bryn, I am your mother. I will always worry about you." She smiles. "How's life as a college professor?"

"It's…a change of pace. Though surprisingly, has proven to be almost as exciting."

Though I could easily be seen as a third wheel, Elise makes it a point to include me, and I find myself laughing along with their conversation. She has a good sense of humor which shines through her various anecdotes and side-stories. I never would have guessed that spending time in a psychiatric facility talking with two women many years my senior would be a fun way to spend an afternoon, but here we are.

After Bryn has sufficiently caught her up on recent events, Elise takes the opportunity to tell us what she's been up to, what the facility is like, how the staff are treating her, and what friends she's made. Though she speaks highly of the place, I start to wonder why she's in here at all. She seems perfectly fine to me. I take in the sights outside the window. Leafless trees still wrapped in Christmas lights stretch towards a sunny sky, though some clouds are starting to roll in. They cast a shadow into the otherwise cheery room.

Elise leans forward, suddenly speaking in a whisper. "It's just…it's just the birds." Her expression darkens, but the smile quickly returns to her face, and she leans back in her chair. I let out the breath I was holding. Okay, so maybe there's a lot of loud chirping in the courtyard. That could be annoying.

Bryn tenses, but they continue the conversation, almost as if nothing happened. Progressively, however, her speech

286

becomes more and more bizarre.

"Oh, I had dinner with the president last night," she says with a straight face. "The secret service came, and they told me they had a message for me. They put a helicopter on the roof—it was invisible, you know—because no one can know about the money they left me. But they took it. They—" She curses and sets her mug firmly on the table. We both flinch. "They took my money, and I'm having a baby." She clutches her stomach, her eyes wide.

Bryn reaches across the table and takes her mother's hand. "Mom. Can you tell me where you are?"

Elise taps her fingers vigorously on the table. After taking a deep breath, she answers. "Spring Haven." Her shoulders relax, and she repeats it. "I'm at Spring Haven. No, I'm not pregnant...No, I think you're wrong...they took the money...shut-up!" she mutters, talking to thin air. I swallow, suddenly wondering if demonic forces really do have a hand in mental illness. I start to pray for the Spirit of God to be with us.

"Mom, who am I?" Bryn asks calmly and clearly.

She stops. "You're my daughter. Bryn." She looks at me. "A—and you're one of her students." She nods, confirming the truth to herself. "I'm sorry. Please excuse me."

She takes another sip of tea, and I'm hopeful the episode has passed. She sets the mug down and sits quietly for a moment. Without any warning, an awful shriek pierces my ears and causes me to jump. She screams at the top of her lungs.

"THE BIRDS! THE BIRDS! GET THEM OFF! GET THEM OFF! THEY'RE ON ME! THEY'RE ON MY FACE!"

Bryn springs from her chair, sending it sliding backwards, and her arm flies in front of me protectively. I scramble to get up and step back. Meanwhile, Elise Sayer throws herself to the ground and starts to claw at her hair, mouth, arms, and legs. She coughs violently, as if something invisible is clogging her throat.

Bryn grips my arm and steers me towards the door. "Back up, give her space." She smashes a red panic button on the wall and shouts down the hall. "Help! We need some help in here!"

Within seconds, staff appear to handle the situation. Rather than attack Elise with a sedative, like in the movies, I watch as they clear furniture and allow her to have a fit on the floor. She scratches up her arms, starting to draw blood. I'm glued to the doorway until Bryn tugs on my arm. "They've got her," she says quietly. "C'mon. Let's go."

I pry my eyes away and follow her back down the hall. It's only once we get halfway to the exit that I notice her lip quivering. Her eyes shine as we pass under the skylight; they're wet. As we reach the waiting room, she exhales.

"Excuse me a moment," she says before disappearing into the bathroom. After a moment of consideration, I walk to the other side of the room and take a seat, as far away from the restroom door as possible.

It seems like the right thing to do, to give her privacy. I don't want to hear her cry.

Chapter 45

The Cabin's Curse

I take the first bite of a foil-wrapped hamburger, tasting the savory patty, the sharpness of the cheese, the crunch of the lettuce and pickle, and the sweetness of the bun. I follow the bite with a couple crisp, salty french fries and wash it down with a diet soda. Yeah...I don't think I bolused enough for this meal. Ah well. I stare out the windshield and take another bite.

Bryn sits beside me in the driver's seat, eating her own burger. Neither of us have said a word about what just happened at Spring Haven.

She pops some fries into her mouth. "Comfort food."

I nod. "It's a good burger."

She nods back in agreement.

Once she's finished the last bite of her hamburger, she crumples the foil up, shoves it back in the paper bag, and sighs. "Alright." She sucks on the straw of her drink, and I hear the ice rattling around inside. With the remainder of her fries in hand, she leans back in her seat. "Here's the truth. Yes, I am related to the mayor. His granddaughter, in fact."

I pause, comprehending her words. "So your mom is his daughter?"

She nods.

"But...I thought he only had a son?"

"And that's what he would like people to think." As she

says it, she squeezes the paper cup in her hand, its thin walls bowing beneath her fingers. "See, though he tried to hide it, I learned at a young age we were related. It was probably around kindergarten when I first started to understand the concept of grandparents and last names. I came home from school with some questions for my mom.

"She told me the truth, as best she could. That Warren and Colleen Sayer were her parents, but they didn't want to see us. They didn't love her anymore.

"When I was older, she explained that she got pregnant with me when she was only fifteen. My biological father was another teenager she dated for only a short time. When he found out, he got scared and moved away. I've never met him.

"When my mom broke the news of her pregnancy to her own family, Warren demanded she resolve the problem quietly with an abortion. After all, as a budding politician and the only son of the town's leading furniture tycoon, he had a reputation to uphold. She refused, however. So he did what he could to protect the Sayer family name—he gave her an ultimatum. Abort the baby or get out.

"So, when she was fifteen years old, he threw his pregnant daughter out of the house. She dropped out of school, found work where she could, and couch-surfed while scrounging up enough money to get a place of her own. No one wanted to live in that old cabin, so the man who owned it rented it for cheap. At the time, it was little more than a shack, but it was our home.

"Of course, for those who asked questions, Warren spun the story in his favor. He didn't disown Elise; she ran away. She went crazy with boys, maybe did drugs, and he wondered how she could do this to poor old dad. He was the victim... and people bought it. The Sayer family had good rapport, connections, and money. They were well-liked, and it wasn't hard for Warren to gain a position on the city council and, later, be elected mayor. I guess as the years passed and he became even more popular, people's memories faded. Some forgot he ever had a daughter.

"My mom and I, on the other hand, were social outcasts." She laughs bitterly. "It was like *The Scarlet Letter*. The adults around us whispered about the scandal of this young mother and her child, and the kids at school repeated the gossip they heard from their parents. I was never able to make many friends."

She dips her head to the side, "Though, admittedly, it probably didn't help that I got into a lot of fights with the kids who made fun of us." She smiles. "I was a bit of a wild child. Mom worked a lot, so I had free rein of the woods, more or less. I ran around in the dirt, picked berries, climbed trees, and nursed my fair share of stray cats, baby birds, and injured rabbits back to health."

I smile, picturing her house now brimming with plants.

Her expression grows sad. "I would like to say things were always happy in our little home, which was a refuge all its own. But...it would take many years for doctors to officially diagnose my mom with schizophrenia. For me, the hallucinations and delusions you saw today were a regular part of my childhood. I never knew anything different.

"As the years went on, her episodes only became more frequent and more severe. Given the somewhat violent temper I displayed at school, I suppose it wasn't a far leap for people to assume I was to blame for the cuts and bruises they saw on my mom. But I was the only one who knew the truth."

Bryn crosses her arms, hugging her midsection. "I never hurt my mom, and she never hurt me. Only herself. She would draw blood from scratching herself up like that..." She takes a shaky breath. "I tried to take care of her as best I could. One night, when I was nine years old, she had a really, really bad fit. She got ahold of a kitchen knife and slashed open her arms. She started losing *a lot* of blood. In the process of wrestling the knife away from her, I became drenched in it. I was afraid she was going to die, and we didn't have a phone. I—I just ran to the end of the driveway, and luckily someone stopped.

"Likely from a combination of imprecise news reporting, fanciful gossip, and the influence of a certain local politician, the details of what happened were twisted against me. But, as you can see, my mom didn't die that night. Once she recovered physically, they transferred her from the hospital to a facility for mental health treatment. I was carted away in a cop car and—once being cleared of wrongdoing—placed into foster care with strangers." After a beat, she concludes, "*That* is the true curse of the cabin—for me, at least."

Silence hangs in the air. "I—I'm sorry, Bryn," I manage to say. "Sorry that, for half a second, I believed the stories people told."

"Can't say I blame you." She shrugs a shoulder. "Now you know." She finishes her fries and drops the empty container in the bag. "Well, there's my trauma dump," she says, flashing a facetious smile. Her usual optimistic demeanor returns, and she starts the car.

Chapter 46

Goodness and Anger

As we begin our drive back to Flickerwood, my mind settles on the tragedy of Elise's insanity and the cruelty of Warren Sayer. The memory of watching his son, Michael, raise his hand against his baby at church flashes in my mind, and I begin to speculate about where he may have learned such parenting methods. I start to seethe.

To cope with the feeling of helplessness, I start to invent heroic power fantasies. I should march up to them and say something. Do something courageous, like Esther, or the prophets, and set them straight. It's a shame I can't go back in time and defend Elise from her selfish and tyrannical father. I remember the image of Colleen Sayer corralled in the kitchen, washing dishes. I'd stand up for her, too!

Then, as quickly as it appeared, the wave of delusional invincibility recedes, and I'm brought back to my true reality, where I can't do much. I think back to the morning conversation we had with Colleen Sayer. Suddenly, Bryn's probing questions make sense. What *did* Mrs. Sayer do when her husband disowned their daughter? Is she a victim, or is she also culpable? Can both be true?

Thinking of the night we spent in that house makes me shiver. The mayor is not just a strange but well-meaning man. He is a callous man. A burning feeling fills the cavity in my chest. A feeling I pride myself in avoiding: hate.

293

Though I know, as a Christian, I should have grace, I can't help but have my entire view of this man uprooted and smeared with black. In my mind, he is no longer capable of good. Who would demand his teenage daughter abort her baby and kick her out of the house when she didn't comply? Not only that, but then blame her for running away and pretend like she never existed at all? All for the sake of preserving a false, shallow image of the perfect family.

"Have you considered the mayor as a suspect?" I ask suddenly, expelling the thought like a shot of steam released from a boiling kettle. "Maybe he's behind the whole thing!"

Bryn replies carefully, "It's tempting for me to suspect him, in light of everything, but I know bias clouds judgement. Just because he has done bad things doesn't mean he's guilty of *this* bad thing. I have to remind myself of that."

The injustice twists behind my ribs. "But, aren't you—" I stop, feeling the pressure drain from my system as I remember the obvious; if I'm this upset, Bryn must be ten times so. "Are you angry at him?"

Her grip on the steering wheel tightens. "Yes," she answers. "Of course I am."

I think of the grace she's shown me, and the Bible she's constantly reading. "Do you hate him?"

Slowly, she exhales. "Sometimes. I try not to. But it's hard to escape the feeling entirely. See, that's part of why I moved back."

"What do you mean?"

"Well, Warren Sayer and the wrongs he's done have had power over me for long enough. He's one of the few people I still really hold bitterness towards. I came to find some closure and make peace. Maybe even start a connection, either with him or some of my other relatives. But—" She takes a deep breath. "Even if he's not sorry. Even if he hasn't changed. I need to figure out how to love and forgive."

I stare at her, trying to root through my own feelings on the matter. "...I know the Bible says we should love everyone, but...how can you forgive someone like that?" I ask. "After all he's done, how can you be expected to just treat him like it never happened?"

Bryn pauses, considering. "I know I don't have all the

answers, but I don't think forgiveness means you have to pretend you forget what a person did."

I furrow my brow and draw from the verses I know. "Isn't that what God does for us? Removes our sins, as far as the east is from the west? Forgets them? Aren't we supposed to forgive like Him?"

"We are, yes. But it's important to note that the grace God shows us didn't come cheap. It's not as if He simply looks past the pain, suffering, and evil of sin, like a horse with blinders on. He *felt* it, sacrificed to pay for it, *died* for it. He removes it because justice has been served.

"I find comfort in the words of Jesus, 'Blessed are the ones who hunger and thirst for justice.' Those who long to see oppressors be held accountable, who wait for evil to be put in its place, and who are angry about the suffering in this world—I believe that's in line with the heart of God."

Anger? A red flag shoots up in my brain. Human anger does not produce the righteousness of God, right? "I...I guess I've always been told that anger is a bad thing."

Bryn nods. "I used to think that. But my mom—my adoptive mom, that is—well, she taught me that demonizing any one emotion will only give it more control over your life. Anger is an emotion, just like sadness, happiness, fear, or any other feeling. It's not evil. There's a time and a season for everything. Just depends on the heart behind it. 'Be angry and do not sin.'"

Until now, I've always figured I just wasn't a very angry person. I don't really hold grudges, and I don't spend time thinking about revenge or past slights, so I must be okay, right? But slowly, a suspicion creeps over me: I'm fooling myself. Bryn may have a point. Maybe so-called "bad" emotions are like pools of quicksand—the more you panic and try to flee, the stronger their grip on you becomes.

"But...certain types of anger are bad, right? Like, you're never supposed to be angry at God."

Bryn is slow to answer. "Well, it's always wise to tread carefully when you think of God. Holiness is not something to be taken lightly. That being said, I think you'd be hard-pressed to find a Christian who's never felt angry with God—or, at the very least, had some questions for Him."

At first, I'm skeptical. "I don't think anyone in the Bible questions God. Or, at least, none of the 'good' characters."

Her eyes fly open in disbelief. "Well that, my friend, couldn't be further from the truth. You have David, Jonah, Habakkuk, just to name a few. Questions about God's goodness, justice, and the problem of evil aren't new. In fact, one of the books that explores them the most is also perhaps the oldest book in the Bible: Job."

"Job?" I ask. "Isn't that about how Job is honored for not being angry at God, even though all this bad stuff happens to him? And when he does have questions, God basically tells him it's not his place to ask."

"I think, in order to understand Job, you have to take into account his friends. Back then they believed, as people often do today, that God makes good things happen to good people and bad things happen to bad people. Logically, they thought Job must have done something bad for all of the tragedy he experienced to befall him.

"But...they were wrong. God's actions can't be pinned down into such a narrow formula, and Job's suffering wasn't a punishment for any wrong. The answer God gives at the end of the book isn't cold, but quite compassionate. Playful, even. Rather than give Job a direct reason for his plight, he invites him to see things from His perspective. He details the vast array of interworking parts in the universe, showing that the human mind cannot fathom the infinite amount of factors God takes into account when making a decision. See, God's plans are not hidden because He has something scandalous to hide, but because they are too great and too wonderful for us to even begin to comprehend.

"What is admirable about Job is this: he never accuses God of wrongdoing. Of being evil. Making a mistake, perhaps, but I think that's the key in questioning God. There are a lot of things that don't make sense from a human perspective, and we *should* care about suffering, injustice, and a myriad of other questions. But foundational to those questions must be a trust in God's ultimate goodness."

I stare at the ground, feeling the weight of condemnation fall on my head once more. "I know," I sigh. "We should just obey God even when it doesn't seem to make sense. Lean not on your own understanding. Trust that His commands are good."

Bryn slows to a stop at a red light and studies me for a few seconds. "What do you think it means, to believe that God is good?" she says finally.

As the light changes, the car coasts forward once more. "Well…" I start to formulate an answer. "His ways are higher than my ways, right? What God says and does in the Bible is good, even if I don't understand it, or if it doesn't seem good. God defines what is morally good."

"So, if I'm hearing you correctly, you're saying that if you read something in the Bible which seems morally wrong to you, your first instinct is to ignore that feeling and conclude it must actually be good because God says so?"

Hearing it stated back to me heightens my frustration. "Yes, when it comes to commandments! Isn't that the point of obedience?" I snap. Feeling embarrassed by my outburst, I tone my voice down, but continue, "If I'm honest, it seems like God just arbitrarily decides what is good. It's not like there's any checks or balances on his power. If He says it, then it's suddenly righteous.

"I have feelings about what's right and wrong, but apparently those don't mean anything. Whenever people in the Bible follow their own conscience and do 'what is right in their own eyes,' they're condemned. I can't argue with God. For all I know, everything I believe to be good is actually bad and vice versa."

Bryn lifts an index finger off the steering wheel. "Hang on a second. I know Protestant Christians are very careful to say there is no authority above God, which is true, but there's a difference between God *deciding* what is good and God *being* what is good.

"Good and evil are not arbitrary categories. Goodness has its roots in God's nature, which is eternal and unchanging. God *is* love, and life, and the source of every good thing. The one thing God cannot do is be something other than Himself. He cannot just declare evil to be good—that goes against His very nature.

"Addy, you don't have to question your entire moral compass. Though we all have a sin nature which can make discernment difficult, there are still things that are obviously good, like caring for others and avoiding selfishness. Besides, who do you think gave you your conscience?" She shakes her head. "Your sense of right and wrong is not separate from God's; it stems from Him."

I keep turning her words over in my head, and before long, we arrive back at the cabin. Bryn pulls up next to the house, puts the car in park, and removes the key. "I'm sure you have schoolwork and things to do," she says, "but there's one more chore I could use your help with—especially if you've got something to vent." With that, she pops the door open and exits the car.

My curiosity piqued, I follow without protest. No sooner do I set my things down inside than she disappears into a closet and returns with one axe flung over her shoulder and another in her hand.

"Ever cut down a tree before?"

I step back, putting ample space between us, and shake my head. "Can't say I have."

She smiles. "Well, there's a first for everything." She holds the handle out towards me. "I'm getting low on firewood, and there are some dead trees that need taken down."

Carefully, I take the handle of the axe. It feels very foreign in my hands. For a moment, I consider resting it on my shoulder like Bryn, but quickly decide against it. I'd rather not put the blade any closer to my head, so I simply carry it at my side. I try to push away the intrusive image of swinging this thing and accidentally whacking my skull open.

We walk through the trees, crunching piles of dead leaves beneath our feet, and come upon one that is dark and sagging. It's on the smaller side, and the bark is peeling away from the trunk; it's clearly dead, or at least on its way out. Bryn explains where to cut and how to choose the direction for it to fall. I watch her carve a wedge with a few swings before she turns to me.

She nods and gestures towards the tree. "Your turn."

Nervously, I grip the handle of the axe. Bryn shows me how to hold it and how to swing. On my first try, the axehead

298

doesn't even pierce the wood. It simply bounces off, and I shut my eyes as it hits the target. This was always my problem with sports; I flinch away from the ball.

"Little more confidence," she says. "You've got this."

I take a deep breath and size up the tree standing before me. After a brief prayer that I don't kill myself, I swing with more force.

Thwack.

Satisfyingly, the blade sticks in the trunk, chipping away at the lesion. The impact vibrates through my chest. I smile.

As I grow more confident, I swing harder. My mind starts to wander.

What do I have to vent? What is it that I'm angry about?

Thwack.

I'm angry at Mayor Warren Sayer for what he did to Bryn and her mom.

Thwack.

Angry at the men who attacked us at the sawmill and made me feel so powerless.

Thwack.

Angry at Chief Boyer and Matthew's killer. Angry that he died a tragic death. Angry at Robert Boyer for murdering Dr. Morrell.

Thwack. Thwack.

Angry at Edith Morrell for poisoning my juice, hurting my friend, robbing my sense of peace, and fleeing like a coward. Angry that no one has gotten justice.

Thwack!

Angry that there are men in the world who trap their wives, slap their sons, and disown their daughters.

Thwack!

Angry that women always seem to get the short end of the stick, even in the Bible. As if it's just part of God's design. I am cursed just because of the gender I was born as. Stuck by divine decree under the benevolent boot of male authority. And I'm supposed to be happy about it.

Thwack!

Suddenly, a dull creaking sound reverberates through the tree, shaking every branch.

"Timber!" Bryn shouts, pulling me to the side. We watch as

the towering tree falls. The trunk pulls away from the stump, snapping the bit of wood that's left, and comes crashing through the branches of nearby trees, landing with a great crunch on the dry leaves below.

Only now do I realize I'm breathing heavy.

Bryn smiles. "How's that feel?"

I grin. "Feels good."

Chapter 47

Blindsided

When I finally make it back to my dorm, there's only one person on my mind: my mom.

I take a seat at my desk and stare at my phone. We clashed a good bit when I was still in high school, but our relationship improved a lot after I moved out. Still, I don't talk to her as often as I should. I regrettably tend to brush her off as an afterthought in my busy schedule.

Now, my heart brims with thankfulness. My mom loves me. She's in good health and has her sanity. I really don't appreciate her enough. I press call.

She picks up almost immediately. "Addy!?" she exclaims. "Hi, honey. Is everything okay?"

"Hi mom! Yeah, everything's okay. I was just calling—"

"Thank goodness!" she interrupts. "I was just about to call you. I'm here watching the news, and this story came on about your school. Did you know there's a multi-state search going on for one of your professors?!"

It takes a moment for me to realize the professor in question is Dr. Edith Morrell. I'm encouraged to hear the police are taking the search so seriously. I guess word has gotten out.

"Apparently she was involved in an attack on three students last night. Now they're saying it's somehow related to that other professor's death? Did you know any of these people?"

I freeze. My first instinct is to lie, or tell a half-truth and dismiss the question. My mom is going to *flip out* if I tell her I was one of the students in the attack. Ahh. Why does it feel like every time I make a good choice, it's immediately followed by a tempting scenario that I screw up? Just to keep me humble, I guess.

I bite my lip. I know what the right thing to do is. And it's a sin to know the right thing and then not do it. I sigh. Personal growth, here we go.

"Actually, Mom...I was one of the students who got attacked last night."

For a moment, there is silence on the other end. I grit my teeth; the tension is killing me.

"Wait...what?" she says finally. "What happened?! Are you okay!? Why didn't you tell me?"

"Yes, I'm okay, Mom. Honest. And the police are on it—everything's okay. How I got there is...well, it's kind of a long story."

I take the next hour or so to explain to her and my dad what's been happening on campus, the mystery of Dr. Morrell, and how I got involved. The whole time, I keep bracing for the part where they get angry I didn't tell them sooner and demand I come back home.

"Are you getting on the next train?" Mom asks. "Don't let any concerns about classes or tuition keep you from coming home. Your safety is most important. We can figure all that out."

"I...No, I was actually planning to stay," I hear myself say. "Maybe it sounds crazy, but I feel like I should be here. I can't leave Sid and Anthony, and my one professor has been watching out for us. Plus, the cops are actually close to solving the case, and we might have information that can help them," I ramble. I'm as surprised as anyone at my own decisiveness. Shouldn't I be jumping at the chance to go home?

"Are you sure?" my mom asks. "There are ways for you to keep in touch from afar."

"I'm sure," I tell her.

After a pause, I hear my mom sigh into the phone. "You know I would feel better if you were safe under my roof." *Here it comes...*"But I can't force you. Addy, you're an adult now. You have to make that decision."

My thoughts grind to a halt. Of all the things I expected my mom to say, allowing me to make my own decision as an adult was not one of them. I can hardly believe it.

"Wait, really?" I ask.

"Yes," I hear my dad say. "Though, as your mom said, we would love to have you here, safe and sound. But I can hear how important this is to you."

"Just promise me you'll be careful, okay? And keep me in the loop. Let me know what's going on over there. What you're up to," my mom adds.

"I…I'll do my best."

"Love you, honey." I can picture her smile on the other end. "And don't get *too* caught up in this investigating stuff. When you were little, I know it was your dream to be a detective."

I stroll into the dining hall for dinner and sit with Sid and Anthony.

"Where have you been all day?" Sid asks.

"Uh…" I think back, trying to remember what happened. "When we got back last night, my roommate was smoking, so I stayed at Bryn's house."

"You slept in that cabin?" Anthony asks with a shiver.

"Bet that was weird," Sid comments.

"Yeah—" I trail off, still thinking of the conversation I just had on the phone. "You know what's even weirder, though? I just talked to my parents, and apparently they saw a news story about us being attacked at the sawmill. The search for Edith Morrell and Robert Boyer is now, at the very least, a regional story. When I told them what happened, I was expecting them to demand I come home. But…they just said I'm an adult who can decide for myself." I stare at the booth in front of me, still trying to comprehend it.

"Lucky you," Anthony pipes up. "My parents saw the story, too, and—"

As if on cue, a familiar face suddenly joins the conversation. "Anthony Holloway, right?" I look up to see Dr. Conley standing over our table. His tweed jacket has a few wrinkles in it, and the buttons on his dress shirt are mismatched by one, leaving an empty buttonhole and loose fabric hanging at the bottom. Though typically clean-shaven, a scruffy five o'clock shadow is developing on his face. I'm surprised he's in the dining hall this late.

He directs his focus to Anthony. "I got your mom's message. Just wanted to let you know that I hear her concerns—believe me, she's not the only parent who's reached out." For a moment, his eyes glaze over like he's having a war flashback, then he continues. "I'll send out an email, but you can let her know we'll be having an assembly on Monday to address everything that's been going on. She'll be able to watch the livestream on the website. If she still wants to meet privately after that, I'll be happy to set something up."

Anthony opens his mouth to respond but, for once, he's at a loss for words.

Having said all of that, Dr. Conley straightens and seems to become aware of Sid and I. "Wow! The three of you are okay after last night. That's...so good." He smiles awkwardly, tripping over his words. "I mean, I'm sorry. I mean...thank you." He offers a small wave before walking away from us and disappearing out the doors.

Anthony covers his face with his hands, clearly a bit embarrassed.

"Well that was the weirdest thing yet," Sid states.

"I'm glad you thought so, too," I reply.

"He's probably just stressed," Anthony suggests, slowly uncovering his face. "It doesn't exactly look good that Wynhurst now has a professor and a board member wanted for murder. It's his job to explain things for the sake of the school's reputation—and enrollment numbers."

"You're right, though," I say quietly. "It doesn't look good, does it? What if Robert Boyer and Edith Morrell were able to stick around for so long because Conley *is* in on their schemes?"

"Guess we'll just have to keep an eye on him," Anthony returns.

Chapter 48

A Proud Institution

As promised, President Conley sends out an email apologizing on behalf of the school, along with the date and time of the assembly. Sid, Anthony, and I find ourselves back in Meyer Hall on Monday morning. Admittedly, I am kind of curious to hear how he'll handle things. It's not every day that your university has to confront issues like murder, kidnapping, and police investigations.

Suddenly, I feel a tap on my shoulder. I jolt with surprise, even more when I see who it is. "Micah?"

"Hey!" he says amiably. "I just heard about what happened on, what was it, Thursday? Are you okay?" His expression is one of concern as he peers down the row to Sid and Anthony.

I give a thumbs up. "Yeah, we're good."

Anthony nods in agreement. "Alright, at least."

"Good, good," Micah says, growing shy. "I was worried about you guys. Just wanted to make sure all was well."

There's an earnest look in his eyes, and my heart softens. Despite our differences, it's nice to know he still cares.

Sid's eyes narrow suspiciously. "You're only now hearing about it? It's been all over the news, and everyone on campus has been talking."

Micah straightens. "Yeah, well I wasn't around this weekend." His hand nervously moves to the back of his neck, then drops to his side again. "I had to go home and pick something up."

It sounds reasonable enough. College students run home for the weekend all the time. Yet—something about what he said seems off. I try to dismiss the feeling. He's probably just nervous to be talking with Sid after their breakup.

"Plus I've been sleeping a lot," he adds quickly. "Been doing a lot of overnights for security." He lingers awkwardly for a few seconds, then seems to comprehend there are no empty seats. "Well. I guess I'll see you all later." With a wave, he heads off into the crowd to find a seat. I turn my head and watch as he goes.

The room quiets as President Conley climbs on stage. Seeing him now, it strikes me that he looks…different. Even worse. His face is flushed, and his hair is greasy and unkempt. I can't help but wonder if the stress eating at him is rooted in worry for the school or…something else.

He clears his throat and steps towards the microphone. "Good morning, students," he begins. "We are here to address the—ahem—"

His sentence is interrupted by some more attempts to clear his throat and a cough. He picks up the glass of water on his podium and chugs the entire thing. Setting it back down, he continues.

"Excuse me. As I was saying. Good morning, students. We are here to address the—um—recent events and happenings that have been occurring on this very campus. Wynhurst University. A proud institution. And in the surrounding area of Flickerwood. Involving students from Wynhurst. And others. Thank you."

I shoot a glance at Sid and Anthony. "Is this making any sense to you?" I whisper.

Sid looks back at me, her mouth agape. "Not a bit."

"Maybe he'll recover," Anthony suggests optimistically.

President Conley's eyes scan the audience. "Very well. I know it has been hard, to say the least, in light of it. No one wants to think about it. Or talk about it. Or feel it. But we *must* think about it, or we are just as bad. There are members of our faculty who have not lived up to the university mission. But the show must go on! Can I get an amen?!" He thrusts a fist into the air and stares somewhere in the direction of the ceiling for a good thirty seconds.

The room remains dead quiet.

Finally, he drops his arm, but there's a manic look in his eyes. "Young people. Today! This generation. Is at Wynhurst University. They—they will become scientists, and doctors. They'll walk on the moon!" He gestures emphatically, spittle flying from his mouth. "And—"

He stops, seemingly losing his train of thought. "Sorry, right, right. I'm sorry—no, I'm not sorry. No, no, no, no. I'm not sorry for being so very sorry." He smacks his lips together, picks up his empty drinking glass, and frowns before setting it back down. "Together, we can end it!"

With that, he turns from the podium and walks towards the curtain behind him. Two other professors have to rush up and help him find the stairs. His steps are wobbly and he totters as he walks.

"Is he drunk?!" Sid hisses.

"Has to be," Anthony says in disbelief. "Unless he's having a stroke or something."

"Hopefully the nurse will check him out," she says.

"Yeah," I agree. "*Something's* up with him."

Questions about President Conley prove difficult to answer, as he retires into his house following the speech and remains out of view. The following day, different faces appear on campus. Serious-looking men and women in suits. Upon consulting my email, I learn that the board has called an emergency meeting, and they will be conducting a Q&A for staff, students, parents, and community members.

Walking into the Q&A, I feel immediately underdressed. Adults—either parents or community members—fill the back section of chairs. Sitting in front of them are the professors and, on the opposite side of the room, is the section reserved for students. Local newscasters and even some regional ones sit in the front row. On stage, a table is set up with a myriad of branded microphones, ready for a panel of board members. I sit down next to Sid in my sweatpants and hoodie, just hoping I remembered to put on deodorant.

The fourth person to take their place on the stage is

someone I recognize—Michael Sayer, the mayor's son. No sooner have I managed to soothe the anger flaring in my veins at the sight of him than another man takes a seat beside him, at the end of the table: Warren Sayer himself.

I haven't seen him in person since learning the truth about his daughter. It feels like red-hot lasers could spring from my eyes and fry him to bits. I don't think I'll ever look at him the same. How could I? As my thoughts reach a fever pitch of rage, a wave of guilt crashes over them, and so the cycle goes. This time, however, I take a deep breath.

I remember chopping down the tree, and how good it felt to admit my feelings. *God*, I start to pray. *I...I am angry. I am angry at that powerful man sitting on stage. He has been cruel to his family.*

Scripture flies to my brain. Whoever is angry is in danger of judgment.

But how do you forgive someone who has shown no remorse? Forgive someone whose sin isn't even yours to forgive?

Or yours to punish a voice rings in my head. Do I believe that God is just? That ultimately, He will make things right? Better than I ever could?

I exhale, putting it in God's hands. Sitting here burning with hatred won't help anything.

Still, a small coal sits in my stomach, a reminder of what this man has done. But I no longer fear a fire of rage will burn out of my control. Forgiveness doesn't make his actions right, but it's up to God to judge. Okay.

This simple act of prayer has made me feel a little better. Lighter. I tune back into the discussion.

"Yes," one of the board members continues, "we will be working with the police to determine if any other faculty members were involved in these killings. Though as of now, we have no evidence to suggest anyone else is guilty."

"What about that one professor who was questioned by the police a few weeks ago?" a voice calls from the audience. "The one who was on scene at the time of Matthew's death? What was done about her? Bryn Leighton, the name was?"

A flurry of movement ripples through the staff section as heads turn to glance at a seat on the end of a row, near the back. Bryn sits with her usual rigid posture and straight face, betraying no emotion.

"She was actually cleared of any wrongdoing—" one of the board members starts, but Mayor Sayer interjects.

"At the time, insufficient evidence was found to justify taking her into custody," he corrects. "But we will revisit that as well."

I swallow. I thought we were past that. The police—the real ones, anyway—they know Bryn is innocent. I try not to stress over the possibility of her going to jail.

Above the clamor of reporters, a voice suddenly emerges from the student section. "What about the aliens?"

The panel members exchange confused expressions. Someone passes the student a microphone. I strain my head to see.

Surprisingly, I recognize her as Lisa, Sid's friend who I met at the volleyball game.

More calmly this time, she repeats herself. "Are you going to investigate the aliens in the woods?"

There's a small delay before the room erupts into laughter. Even some of the board members stifle a chuckle. Warren Sayer cracks a smile.

"Now, we only have time for serious questions—" Michael says, looking stony-faced.

"I am serious!" Lisa protests. "It was only last semester. I went for an evening jog in the woods one night, which I do often to practice for cross-country." Gradually, the audience quiets. "I was on the northern trail, out past the music building, and as it got dark my mind started to wander. Somehow or another, I got off the path. It took me a few minutes to realize my mistake, but when I tried to find my way back, I started to think I wasn't alone." She pauses, biting her lip. "I only saw it briefly, but I'll never forget it. In the moonlight—there was this towering creature. Lights flashed around me, and I saw these dark, soulless, almond eyes. Then I turned and ran."

"Miss, we really don't have time for hoaxes," Michael continues. "I'm sure you want your five minutes of fame, but this is not the way to do it."

"I'm not lying! You can ask campus security; I called them for help."

309

He sighs into the microphone. "Did they also see the... thing you described?"

"Well, no, it was gone by the time—"

"Clearly it was some kind of prank," Michael says, cutting her off.

"No, you should listen to her!" Anthony springs out of his chair. "What about Elijah Martin, three years ago? Got lost in the woods, came back and said he was abducted by aliens. It was a well-documented search, news stories everywhere. But we don't say anything about him."

Looking annoyed, he turns to his father for guidance.

"Alright," Mayor Sayer says in a reassuring voice. "We'll look into the woods, as well. If there is some sort of prank or hazing ritual going on, we'll put an end to it. Until then, I want everyone to stay away from the trails and wooded areas, especially at night. If you must go near them, stay on the path. Security is going to start writing you up if they find you trespassing off the marked trail—which is what both of these stories have in common, if you notice. Just do what you're supposed to be doing, and there's no reason to fear. Okay?" His tone is condescending, like a father scolding his children.

The insecure, people-pleasing part of me immediately caves to his logic. I guess he's right, after all; if everyone had just stayed on the trails, none of this would have happened...

Quickly, I push that line of thinking away. Victim-blaming students over small infractions is just an excuse to distract from the real problem at hand. *Someone* or *something* unexplained is hiding out in the woods and terrorizing students who come near it. Could it really be aliens? Or is it something else altogether?

Chapter 49

The Playground

While trying to kill some time before class, I find myself alone, strolling past the playground just outside the administration building. Technically, the campus is open to the community, so kids are free to come and play. It also serves professors, faculty, and students who bring their children to visit.

Today, a handful of kids are climbing around on the monkey bars and zooming down the slide. My guess is they belong to the board members, who have been shut away in a meeting for hours at this point. As I walk past, I catch a glimpse of a familiar coat.

Bryn heads towards a nearby bench, then sits down near two other women and turns her attention to a clipboard in her lap. Both women's eyes widen when they see who just sat beside them and, with a shared glance, they quickly spring to their feet.

As they brush past me, I recognize one as a professor. She takes a short look behind her, then whispers to her friend. "You know, I think we were in third grade together."

The other woman also steals a glance at Bryn, then answers. "Wait, I think you're right. Wasn't she the weird girl that went crazy?"

The professor nods. "I just remember the time she broke Kyle Smith's nose…"

They wander out of earshot and find another bench on

the opposite side of the playground. Bryn is left alone.

I hesitate, unsure of whether or not I should interrupt her. After deciding social interaction is better than what I would be doing otherwise—namely sitting alone in my room—I approach the bench.

"Hey," I say awkwardly.

She looks up. "Hey, Addy. How's your day going?" Her voice is light and good-humored.

"Pretty good," I answer. Can't think of anything particularly bad. "You?"

She shrugs. "Could be better, I guess. Just filling out some consent forms for the office," she says, nodding towards the administration building a few yards away. "Now they want to run a background check."

"Ah," is all I can think to say. "Only on you?"

"No, no," she says, waving the thought away. "They're gonna run all the staff as a blanket safety measure."

"Oh, okay," I say, relieved.

The conversation lulls, and I suffer an awkward debate in my head about whether or not to sit down. Mercifully, I'm brought out of my thoughts when another woman comes by.

"Do you mind if I sit here?" she asks, hovering over the opposite end of the bench Bryn is on. Her young daughter hugs her leg, a diaper bag hangs from her shoulder, and she's holding a baby carrier. She looks vaguely familiar, but I don't think she's a faculty member.

"No! Not at all," Bryn says with a smile, gesturing to the empty spot. "Please. I don't bite."

"Thanks," the woman says, returning the smile. She sets down the baby carrier and diaper bag, then crouches to talk to her daughter. "Okay. Go have fun," she says, pointing to the playground.

With a shy smile, the girl detaches from her leg and bolts towards the sliding board. Finally, the woman sits down, gently rocking the baby with her hand.

"Ah," she sighs. "You here for the board meeting, too?"

"No, actually I'm a professor here," Bryn says, lowering the clipboard and showing her faculty badge. "Bryn Leighton."

"Nice to meet you. I'm Jodi," she says, shaking Bryn's outstretched hand over the baby carrier. Her eyes return to the playground. Her daughter has since found a few boys her age to play with. Jodi shakes her head. "She plays shy, you know, but once she's warmed up..." she gestures towards them. "Social butterfly."

"Eww!" one of the boys says suddenly, pointing down at the mulch. The others rush to his side.

The girl gasps in delight and lunges towards the ground. Victoriously, she holds a snake skin above her head. The other kids take a step back. Her eyes flash mischievously, then she does what any kid would do; she starts chasing them around with it.

A smile dances on Bryn's lips.

Jodi wears a concerned expression and shakes her head. "Rachel!" she calls.

Hearing her mother, the girl—Rachel—wanders over to the bench. "Mom! Look what I found!" she says with a grin.

"Hey, that's pretty cool," Bryn says, leaning forward. "Do you know what kind of snake it's from?"

Upon receiving such a response from an adult, the girl lights up. She talks excitedly with Bryn about venomous and non-venomous snakes, then turns to her mother, proudly swinging the snake skin out in front of her.

"Okay," Jodi says, leaning away. "Just put it down, and make sure you wash your hands when we go inside."

Rachel throws it in the grass before returning to the playground.

Jodi shakes her head. "Sometimes I wonder how she hasn't caught a million rare diseases by now, as much stuff as she gets her hands into."

"Ah, I wouldn't worry about it," Bryn says. "Good for the immune system."

Jodi snickers. "I guess." There's a pause before she asks, "Do you have kids?"

"Uh, no, I don't."

"Smart," Jodi says, followed by a smile. "Don't get me wrong. I love my kids. They're just a handful sometimes."

With impeccable timing, the baby in the carrier starts to cry. "Oop. He's hungry." She calls to the playground, "Rachel!"

Her daughter is hidden away in a plastic tube tunnel, engrossed in a game of hide-and-seek tag. Jodi stands up and calls louder. "Rachel! We need to go in—" Her shoulders droop. "She can't hear me, can she?" She looks to her son, whose crying has only intensified, then to Bryn. "I hate to ask, but are you going to be here for a minute?"

"I can be," Bryn responds.

"Would you mind keeping an eye on her? I won't be long! Literally just a couple minutes."

"Yeah, no problem," Bryn says casually, waving her inside. "I'm not going anywhere."

"Thank you so much. You're a lifesaver. I'll be right back." Jodi slings the diaper bag over her shoulder, then picks up the carrier and takes the screaming baby inside the building.

Along with Bryn, I watch the little girl on the playground, now feeling like I'm also responsible. Before long, her playmates are called away, ending the game of hide-and-seek. This doesn't seem to dampen her mood in the slightest, however. Her attention shifts to the larger, taller climbing section of the playground, clearly designed for kids older than her. She gazes up at a set of iron rings made for swinging across.

"You think she'll do it?" Bryn asks me quietly. There's a small smile on her face.

"Climb up there?" I ask in disbelief. "It's too big, isn't it?"

To my surprise, Rachel approaches the metal ladder. You can almost see the gears turning in her head. Stretching, she wraps her hands around the bar above her and steps on the first rung.

Bryn slides forward, poised to get up.

Grab, step, pull. Grab, step, pull. Once she's about halfway off the ground, she freezes, clearly having second thoughts. Slowly, Bryn stands, ready to offer assistance. With a deep breath, Rachel recovers and continues upward.

It's strangely motivating to see someone so small encounter a scary situation, recollect themselves, and then push through. It occurs to me that children are full-fledged people, with their own inner thoughts and decision-making processes which are refined over time.

She grips a ring and swings away from the ladder, grabbing the next one in the sequence. Only a few rings in,

314

she reaches her limit and starts to panic.

"Help!" she calls. It's a bit too high for her to simply jump to the ground. Bryn rushes to her side.

"Hey," she says gently. "Can I help you down?"

"Where's my mom?" Rachel asks, understandably uneasy.

"She took your brother inside to feed him. She'll be back in a few minutes."

"Okay," she says, sniffling. Bryn grabs her around the middle. With a half-turn, she sets her back on the mulch. In an instant, Rachel's face brightens, and she starts giggling. She stretches her arms up. "Do it again!"

Bryn looks confused at first, then smiles. "Do what?" She snatches the girl up and swings her around some more. "This?" Rachel squeals with delight. Bryn dips her head towards the ground, then pulls her up and spins in a circle.

The laughter, however, is cut short by a voice calling from across the playground.

"Having fun?"

Bryn promptly sets Rachel down and turns to face the speaker. Mayor Sayer stands straight, his hands clasped behind his back. His expression is stern and unhappy.

Rachel smiles and suddenly runs towards him. "Grandpa!"

The blood drains from Bryn's face as the truth dawns on her. Rachel isn't just any little girl. She's the girl in the pictures hanging on the wall at Sayer's house. The beloved granddaughter he talks so much about. Her cousin: Rachel *Sayer*.

Warren scoops his grandchild up in his arms with a grin. "Hey, Rach. Where's your mom?"

"Inside," she says, pointing to the building. As if on cue, the doors open and Jodi and Michael come walking out.

"I still can't believe you left her with a complete stranger!" Michael says, annoyed.

"What do you want from me? I had to feed him! It's not like I was being stupid. She's a professor, and I was only gonna be gone a few minutes—" she replies.

"Well, if you're so smart, maybe you could figure out how to watch both of our kids at the same time," he says, pointing to his head in an exaggerated fashion.

She shrinks away from him. "Hey, I do my best, okay? I could really use your help sometimes…"

He scoffs. "You know I'm busy with all of this—"

Their conversation is interrupted when Rachel speeds towards them and throws her arms around their legs.

While they're still a decent ways off, Warren looks back at Bryn. His eyes narrow, and he steps closer.

"Don't think you can fool me. I did some digging, and I know who you really are, *Professor Bryn Leighton*. I know what you're trying to do."

"What do you mean?" Bryn asks tentatively.

"Did you really think a fake last name would hide your identity?" he spits.

"I—my name isn't fake—"

"Really? Well I don't see a Mr. Leighton anywhere. Come on. You stayed in my house, yet never thought to mention who you were?"

Bryn bites her tongue. With a deep breath, she responds humbly. "No, I wasn't forthright with you, and maybe I should've been, but the whole situation caught me off guard. In the moment, I just wasn't ready yet. I did intend to reach out eventually, however..." She spreads her hands. "I'm not trying to hide anything. You're right. I'm Elise's daughter: your granddaughter."

I hold my breath, focusing my attention on Warren Sayer and awaiting his reaction. Bryn nervously tugs on the buttons of her jacket.

He glances towards Rachel, then back to Bryn. After what feels like a long stretch of silence, he begins to answer.

"Let's get something straight, here. *She*," he says, pointing to Rachel, "is my granddaughter." He glowers at Bryn, his words dripping with malice. "You are a stranger to me, and you'd better stay far, far away from us."

Stunned, Bryn opens her mouth to speak, but no words come out.

"I've got my eye on you, Bryn," he raves. "If you think you can come back here and hurt me or my family, you've got another thing coming."

"W-what? Believe me, I'm not here to hurt anyone—"

By this point, Michael has made his way over. He looks at Warren and Bryn, confused. "Hang on, she's not the one people were freaking out over, is she? Who was at the scene

316

when that kid died?" he asks. "Do you know her?"

Before Warren can respond, Bryn turns towards Michael and extends a hand. "I hope the rumors about me don't deter you. I've waited a long time to meet my mother's brother."

Michael freezes. He stares at her outstretched arm, seemingly paralyzed. His eyes grow wide as the realization settles over him.

"...Bryn?"

She nods in return. "Uncle."

Chapter 50

Family Reunion

A few small pellets of ice fall from the clouds and bounce on the ground around me.

"Mr. Mayor!" Someone from the sea of board members now pouring out the door of the admin building calls to Warren.

He glances towards the sound with a sour look on his face. Before leaving, he jabs a finger in Bryn's direction. "Watch yourself," he mutters ominously, then turns to his son. "If you've got any sense at all, keep yourself and your family far away from her." With one last look of disgust aimed at Bryn, he continues on.

Michael watches him leave, then turns back to Bryn. "I... it's nice to meet you," he says, almost in a daze. He shakes her hand. "I was starting to think I never would."

She smiles warmly. "Pleasure to meet you, too."

As they talk, the sound of sleet raining down on plastic and metal playground equipment grows louder. I start to feel the cold, wet sensation of ice falling on my head. At once, the skies let loose, and we find ourselves in an icy downpour.

Automatically, I head for the nearest place to take shelter in, other than the admin building. Round bits of ice bounce off the sidewalk as I hurry towards the cafe. Some of the sleet melts as it falls, and the moisture seeps through my coat. I pull the door open and shuffle inside, finding a seat somewhere. As I dust the ice out of my hair, I watch other people crowd inside to escape the elements. Among them, I spot Michael, with Jodi and kids in tow, and Bryn.

They claim a large table next to mine and, after ordering drinks and removing coats, settle into chairs. I can't help but listen in.

"So, I'm a little lost here. How do you two know each other?" Jodi asks Michael.

"Long story," he says simply. "We're related."

"I'm his niece," Bryn chimes in.

"Niece?" Jodi asks, looking confused. "Michael, I didn't think you had any siblings."

"Well, I had a sister," he says. "I can explain later." He waves her questions away. Somewhat reluctantly, Jodi turns her attention towards the baby and chooses not to press the matter further.

My attention stays on Michael and Bryn, but from where I'm sitting, I can catch only parts of their conversation.

"Where have you been for so many years?" Michael asks. "Have...have you talked to Elise? Do you know how she's doing?"

"Well, I've been all over," Bryn answers, giving him a summary. "And yes, I have. She's doing alright. Could be better, but she's come a long way."

His face lights up. "So she's okay? Alive?"

Smack. The end of a paper straw wrapper hits Jodi in the face. Across from her, Rachel smiles victoriously. Jodi blinks, taking a moment to respond, but she smiles and accepts the challenge. She takes her own straw and blows the paper back towards her daughter. Rachel snatches the wrapper off the table and reloads. As she raises the straw once more, poised to return the projectile to her mom, her dad grabs her hand.

"Rachel, stop it," he says sternly. "We don't do that at the table." He returns to his conversation with Bryn. "I...I never liked the way Dad treated her, after he found out about the pregnancy."

I'm startled by the stark and rapid change in his voice, from stern and angry disciplinarian right back to concerned and compassionate. He stares off, as if haunted by a painful memory.

"Honestly, it's amazing, having the opportunity to meet you. If he'd had his way..." he shakes his head, pausing before putting the hard truth into words. "Well, you might've never been born."

The corner of Bryn's mouth turns up, and a twinkle flashes in her eyes. "God had other plans."

"He must have," Michael agrees, nodding in bewilderment. "I haven't heard a single thing since you guys left town. I've been curious for a long time..."

"There's a lot I've wanted to know, too," Bryn says. They share a smile.

Tap. A small plastic bottle cap skids to a halt near Jodi. She slides it back towards her daughter. As Rachel reaches for the plastic cap on the table, her dad smacks her hand. "That's enough," he snaps. "Now sit still."

I lower my eyes, feeling disturbed by the physical punishment. He looks to his wife, who is holding their son in her arms. "Really?" he asks accusingly. "Don't let her do that. I'm trying to talk."

"Mike, she's only playing—" Jodi starts, but Michael shoots her a look.

"Well, my family, my rules, right?" he replies sharply.

Jodi falls silent. She motions to Rachel to get rid of the cap, backing her husband's command.

Michael turns back to Bryn. "So where's your mom living?"

Bryn eyes him, her smile gone. Slowly, she answers. "Susquehannock Hospital."

"Oh! What for?"

"She...she's in the psych ward."

Suddenly, his expression changes. He frowns. "Psych ward? Why?"

"You...you don't know?" She sets her hand on her coffee cup. "Michael, the reason the police came and separated us was because Elise has a severe mental illness."

He freezes, looking like a robot receiving a software update. His eyes are wide as he processes the information. "So...you're saying my sister is crazy? Is that what you're trying to tell me?"

Bryn holds up a hand. "It's not like she's totally out of it. I wouldn't use the word crazy. But she does have episodes

320

where she loses touch with reality. That's why—"

Michael cuts her off. "So you just put her in some facility?" His eyes narrow. "What, you didn't want to take care of your ailing mother? Just pawn her off so you could go sail the world and do whatever?"

She blinks, staring back at him. "What exactly is that supposed to mean?"

"I—well, I just don't like the thought of my sister being locked away in some looney bin," he sputters. "Would you want to be put away like that?"

Bryn straightens, leaning away from him. "To be perfectly fair, *I* didn't put her in a facility. The State did, when I was *nine*. I didn't get much say in the matter at that age."

Rather than back down, he persists. "Okay, but she's been there for, what, twenty years? I mean, I'm sure she's got her issues, but don't you think it'd be better if she had someone to take care of her at home? I mean, it's not like you have kids or anything to worry about—" Seeing her expression, he turns his eyes down towards his coffee cup. "Sorry," he says.

I hold my breath, waiting for him to course correct. Unfortunately, he digs the pit further.

"It's just—forgive me, but it seems wrong to me. After all she went through to have you and raise you...Maybe it's just me, but don't you think you owe it to her to give back a little?"

For several moments, Bryn doesn't move a muscle. I notice a slight tremor in her hands, but she presses them flat against the table until they're still.

When she finally speaks, her voice is tense, like a spring held under pressure. "I see." Carefully, she returns her hands to her lap. "I don't owe you any sort of explanation for my decisions, and you have no right to criticize me for things you know nothing about. However, out of respect for your concern for my mother, I will tell you this.

"I had no choice in her initial psychiatric hospitalization, but it was for her own good. She could not be trusted to take care of herself, much less me. Over the past two decades she has tried, repeatedly, to live on her own again, but it never lasted long. She would eventually decompensate and lose the ability to care for herself.

"When I came of age and had the money to do so, I moved her to a better facility. She is not 'locked away,' as you put it. She is free to come and go, but she chooses to be there, because she knows it's for the best. I visit her regularly, and I am on good terms with the staff. I know she is happy, safe, and well cared for."

She eyes him, tapping her foot. "I love my mom, believe me, I do. Sometimes I question if I'm doing the right thing... but you have no *idea* what it was like to live with someone who could be so detached from reality, suffering from paranoia and delusions about threats that didn't even exist, and harming herself in the process—trust me, this is the best thing for her. For both of us."

She pulls out a pen and a piece of paper, scribbles something down, then slides it across the table. "Here's her number. Call her any time you'd like. I'm sure she'd appreciate it."

He takes the paper and stares at it. She gathers her things and prepares to leave.

"Wait, where are you going?" Michael asks.

She stops. "To be perfectly honest, I am removing myself from this situation before I say something I may regret. You just met me today. You don't even know half the story, and yet you're already judging me. Clearly you're not actually interested in getting to know me."

"Hey," he says, spreading his hands. "You can't fault me for being concerned. I deserve a say in what happens to my sister, especially if she can't take care of herself."

She takes a step towards the door, but stops and turns back to face him. "May I remind you, Michael, that you had your chance. Unlike me, you were an adult when the State took custody of us both. You chose to forfeit that right a long time ago. I know they contacted our family. I know no one did a thing." I can hear the frustration mounting in her voice.

He stands up, reaching after her. "I...I was only 18..." he says pitifully. "Barely an adult. I didn't know what to do! You can't blame me..."

Bryn shakes her head. "I don't blame you for not taking me in, or for letting the decision-making fall to others, but don't tell me you were too young to pick up the phone!" Her voice rises with passion, causing a few heads to turn. With a deep breath, she lowers her volume. "That's an excuse, and you know it. How can you accuse me of abandoning my responsibility when you *chose* to cut contact with us entirely?!"

Rather than protest or apologize, he passes the blame. "But...Dad..." he says, almost whimpering. "*He's* the one who didn't want us to talk to you. To pretend you didn't exist. And *you* have no idea what *I* had to live with."

She glances between Michael and Jodi. "Not fully, no. I don't." She nods towards the paper she gave him. "But you're all grown up now. You can make your own choices. My number is there too, if you decide you're done trying to blame me and want to keep in touch.

"You have a second chance, Michael. Call your sister." She pauses, considering something. "If I could give an unsolicited opinion of my own—take care in how you treat your wife and kids. Sounds like you see a lot wrong with your father; careful you don't become him."

Without waiting for a response, Bryn charges out the door.

Michael throws his hands up in frustration. As he turns back to his family, he spots me. For a moment, we make eye contact. Afraid he'll try to talk to me, I gather my things and slip out the door behind Bryn.

Thankfully, the sleet has slowed, making the outdoors more inhabitable. Bryn is a fair bit ahead of me, and I make no effort to close the distance. I'm sure she needs her space.

As I walk along, however, she appears to slow down. She glances back, recognizes me, and allows me to catch up. When we're side by side, she sighs. "I'm sure you heard all of that."

Sheepishly, I nod. "I—I'm sorry." It's all I can think to say.

She nods. "Thank you. I am, too."

Gradually, we enter the natural sciences building and wind down the halls towards her office. She shoves the key in the lock, yanks the door open, and heads for her chair. As she sits down, she deposits the clipboard and her bag on her desk.

I meander to the chair across from her. "Jodi seemed nice," I mutter, mostly to break the silence.

With a half-smile, Bryn replies. "Yeah." Her eyes flit

downwards, and the smile fades. "Kind of a shame."

Just when I think that's all she has to say, she sits up. "Alright, Addy." With a sudden movement, she reaches for her bag and produces her Bible. "You asked me what I think about God's view of women. I'll tell you my opinion."

She slides her finger between the pages and opens to a bookmarked passage. Finding the right place, she lays the Bible flat on the desk and turns it towards me, pointing to a verse.

I hesitate. My stomach suddenly twists into knots as I consider the possibilities.

What if Bryn turns out to be just another voice telling me to accept that women are lesser? That *I* am lesser? Maybe she just wants to highlight how Michael isn't leading his family in a Christ-like manner. That he needs to be more loving, but ultimately does have God-given authority over his wife.

I try to brace myself to confront more Bible passages about how a woman's role is to be submissive. Obedient to husbands, fathers, and pastors. In essence, perpetual children who have no real right to exercise agency or control over their lives. I try to prepare for another great, soul-crushing blow to my self-esteem...

But another part of me can't shake the hope that she might actually have the answer I've been searching for. Some magic solution or argument that makes everything make sense. As unrealistic as it may be, it is this hope—that maybe the answer is just behind the next page or the next Google search or the next conversation—that keeps my eyes glued to the desk, eager to devour whatever she wants to show me. Captivated, I lean forward and peer down at the underlined verse...

Galatians 3:28, *There is neither Jew nor Gentile, neither slave nor free, nor is there male and female, for you are all one in Christ Jesus* (NIV).

As suddenly as it appeared, the wind leaves my sails, and I'm left feeling like a deflated balloon. I forgot the third option: that Bryn may believe in gender equality, but not be able to convince *me* the Bible supports it.

The verse is...disappointing. Galatians 3:28 is a passage

324

I've heard used a million times as a silver bullet slogan for egalitarians, but—at least for me—it doesn't seem to trump the verses elsewhere in the Bible that talk about male authority. As much as I want it to, it doesn't fix it.

My defeat and disappointment must show on my face.

Bryn raises an eyebrow. "Not what you were expecting?"

"I just…" I don't want to be selfish or difficult, especially with all the family stuff she has going on—

I raise my head, and we make eye contact. She deserves to know my honest thoughts. I take a deep breath. "The truth is, I've seen a lot of people use this verse to argue that men and women can have the same roles, but with the context and all, I don't think this passage says as much as they want it to."

"Tell me more," she invites.

"Well, this verse is talking about salvation. It doesn't matter what place you hold in society—Jesus accepts anyone who believes in Him. But that doesn't mean all the social roles were destroyed in day-to-day life. Christians still held their various stations in the Roman Empire. Slaves and servants were still supposed to obey their masters, for example. Gender isn't any different."

Bryn nods, looking impressed. "You've done some research. A reasonable argument, no doubt. But," she holds up a hand, "let me venture this. What are we supposed to *do* with the knowledge that God has offered salvation to all people and all nations? What purpose does it serve to know that all Christians—regardless of such social distinctions—are equal inheritors of God's salvation and the gift of new life?

"I could show you more verses to support my conclusions, but it's hardly a stretch to say it should drive us to action. We're supposed to read this and respond by treating each other differently in the here and now. With love, respect, impartiality, and equality, regardless of differences."

"I…" It stumps me a little, but not for long. "Treat each other with love, yes, but that doesn't eliminate the roles which exist," I repeat.

"Roles," Bryn mutters to herself. "And by roles, I'm assuming you don't just mean the division of labor, but hierarchical roles, which restrict teaching and leading to men. A patriarchal authority structure. Right?"

I squirm at the word "patriarchal." Patriarchy is a bad thing. That's the thing that kept women from voting and reading and going to school. Our society has progressed past these things, rightly so. The Christians who argue for role distinctions between men and women nowadays use fancy terms to dress up their ideas, like "complementarian" or "traditionalist." But, if I think about it, I can't disagree with Bryn's use of the word; the meaning is the same. I nod.

She reclaims her Bible. "What do you think of the story of Deborah?" she asks.

"The judge of Israel?" I shift uncomfortably, not happy with the side I find myself arguing for. "Doesn't the exception prove the rule?"

"What about the other female prophets?" Bryn probes.

"Like who?"

"Miriam, Anna, the daughters of Philip..."

I shake my head. "They're not, like, major prophets, though. Prophesying itself isn't the same as holding office."

"Queens, then? Queen Esther? Queen of Sheba?"

"Esther was still under the rule of the king, and the queen of Sheba wasn't an Israelite..." My brain rattles off a reason to dismiss any female contribution to the biblical narrative. Instead of growing frustrated, Bryn seems interested by our banter.

"Well, Addy," she says finally, shutting her Bible. "It seems to me that you're not questioning as much as you think. Seems like you've already made up your mind." Her voice is matter-of-fact.

Rather than reveling in a victory, however, I feel my insides collapse in on themselves. That isn't what I wanted to hear.

A verse from Romans pounds in my head, about how you must be fully convinced of what is right. If you do something while doubting if it is good, you are sinning.

I hang my head. "I don't *want* to believe women are confined to a lower role, the bottom position in this power structure, but I don't know how to believe otherwise...I wish I could be convinced, but it's hard to think I could ever believe in gender equality without doubting it at least a little. I'm just...I'm afraid."

"Afraid of what?"

I feel my face grow hot. "Straying from the truth. I'm afraid if I give egalitarian arguments a fair look, that I'll just be wrong. That I'd be dismissing or ignoring the truth of Scripture like people are so prone to do today. Following my own desires and acting against God's will." The terror presses down on me.

She pauses before answering. "I know the feeling. It's a wise concern, evidence of a healthy fear of the Lord. But consider this: what if, by defaulting to the complementarian side, you're already doing the thing you're afraid of? Reading outside ideas into the Bible and not seeing the true meaning in the text. I'm sure many Pharisees in Jesus' day thought they were 'playing it safe' by not believing a man who claimed to be God—but they were wrong.

"Like I said before, what if you need to trust God a bit more?"

"What do you *mean* by that?" I say, trying to suppress the edge in my voice.

I feel like I *did* trust God, but then…well, it felt like He betrayed me. Am I just supposed to trust in complementarianism? In patriarchy? Trust that it is good even though it seems so destructive? Trust that I'm still somehow "ontologically equal" even though it's that same immaterial substance defining my inferior position? Just because God put a few verses in Scripture? Honestly, it feels like every time I read the Bible I feel worse.

Bryn's answer cuts through my thoughts. "Trust that God doesn't command anything bad. Not abuse, or oppression, or inequality, or selfishness, or tyranny, or injustice. Trust that God is not out to get you. Trust enough to approach the Bible without having your mind already made up. You may be surprised by what you find."

Your mind already made up. I'm reminded of the last night I thought Bryn was the one who murdered Dr. Morrell. Another face also comes to mind, that of Micah…am I really doing the same thing to God? Making the evidence fit my preconception? Do I just need to listen? Oh how I wish that were true.

I've been too afraid to listen. Too afraid of being crushed.

Trust. A bruised reed he will not break, and a smoldering wick he will not quench...

"If God really does want equality between the sexes, why include those verses in Corinthians and Timothy and Peter?" I ask. "How do I know God is trustworthy?"

Bryn rests her thumb on her lip. "Well, why do you trust me?"

The question throws me off. Why *do* I trust her so much? "Well...your stories check out. They've been proven true. And you've shown that you have good character. You've been nothing but kind to me, even risking your life to save mine."

"Now, if so much of that trust is based on my actions, why continue to believe me when things look incriminating? When I didn't answer you right away about my mom, for example? Why assume the best?"

"I...I dunno. I know you. I feel like I understand enough about you to know what you stand for and what motivates you. I don't need to doubt you every time I have a question. You're not a stranger anymore."

She leans forward. "Then why doubt the God who gifted you with life and who *died* to redeem it? The God you have a relationship with?"

I stare at the desk, wrapping my mind around everything she's saying. "Are you really an egalitarian?" I ask. Bryn is smart and reasoned and respectable—if she's really convinced, maybe I can be, too.

She nods. "I have mixed feelings about labels. You don't have to believe what I believe. But I can show you where I'm coming from." She flips to the very end of the Bible. "If there's a place to start, I think it may be at the end. It's helpful to know the narrative we're a part of."

With a renewed commitment to an open mind, I lean forward to read.

"Seeing how concerned you are about context, rightly so, tell me: Does this promise apply to only one gender?"

Revelation 2:7b, *To the one who is victorious, I will give the right to eat from the tree of life, which is in the paradise of God* (NIV).

I swallow and shake my head.

"Or this?"

Revelation 2:17b, *To the one who is victorious, I will give some of the hidden manna. I will also give that person a white stone with a new name written on it, known only to the one who receives it* (NIV).

Again, I shake my head.

"Likewise."

Revelation 2:26-28, *To the one who is victorious and does my will to the end, I will give authority over the nations—that one "will rule them with an iron scepter and will dash them to pieces like pottery"—just as I have received authority from my Father. I will also give that one the morning star* (NIV).

My eyes widen, and I read the verse again. Authority? Ruling?

"When the Bible talks about slave and free, Jew and Gentile, men and women having an equal share in the inheritance of Jesus, what do you think that means?"

I stay silent, waiting for her answer.

"It is not only salvation, new life, and a ticket to living in the presence of God for all eternity, but it is also reigning beside Christ, because we are one with Him. To deny that is to deny part of the promises of God."

She folds her hands together. "So, when I think about gender and roles and authority, I think of that. That God's ultimate plan and the inheritance given to His children makes no distinction." She pokes a finger against the desk, annoyed. "And don't let yourself think for a second that examples like Warren and Michael Sayer are demonstrating God's perfect plan."

An angry undertone creeps into her voice. "Controlling your wife, micro-managing her, demanding your way, and calling it your right. That is manipulative behavior, which, for the record, is *not* something God approves of. And the image of a complacent, ever-smiling housewife who puts up with all sorts of mistreatment and whose main calling is always to have children—that is not the biblical ideal for womanhood."

I'm surprised to find tears springing to my eyes. It's not? Husbands who manipulate and order their wives around are not God's perfect plan? *Of course not,* another voice in me says. *God is good.*

But I needed Professor Bryn Leighton to say it.

Chapter 51

Flour, Milk, Butter, and Salt

The first thing I do after leaving her office is check my phone. I find a text from Sid.

Hey! Lisa wanted to meet Anthony and discuss everything that happened this morning, so we're all going to meet in the dining hall for lunch. Can you make it?

By the time I arrive, Lisa and Anthony are already deeply engaged in a conversation about UFOs and extraterrestrials. Sid sits next to Lisa on the outer side of the booth, trying to follow but looking considerably lost. She breaks into a smile when she sees me.

"I never knew there were other people who saw what I saw in those woods," Lisa says while looking at Anthony. She shudders. "It really sounds like your friend was abducted. And all the disappearances you mentioned...makes me wonder how many kids were taken like him but never returned."

Sid looks concerned. "Do we really think aliens are behind this?"

Anthony shakes his head and stares off. "Honestly, I don't know what to believe at this point. Is there a better explanation for what Lisa saw? Maybe there really is something other-worldly behind it."

Sid wrinkles her brow. "But it just doesn't make sense. You thought the other disappearances might be related to Dr. Morrell, but we know who killed him, and we know who killed Matthew. Leighton said there's a crime ring of some sort operating throughout Flickerwood. If the missing kids are in any way connected to Morrell's death, it's likely—as awful as it is—normal criminal abduction. What do aliens have to do with anything?"

Vaguely, I notice Bryn sitting on the other side of the room. As usual, she has the whole table to herself. She stands up and collects her tray. Assuming she'll return it and exit out the doors, I turn my attention back to my food and, like Sid, try to understand how the whole alien thing fits in.

A flash of movement in my periphery causes me to look up. I flinch in surprise when I see Bryn heading towards us. Unless they're particularly social, professors tend to stay on their side of the dining hall. But she approaches our table, breaking the invisible wall.

"Afternoon," she says with a nod. "How are you all doing?"

Anthony, Sid, and Lisa all jerk their heads up. Collectively, we respond with some approximation of "pretty good."

"Good, glad to hear it. Any dinner plans?" she replies swiftly.

A bit confused, Anthony answers on behalf of the group. "I don't think so. Only a plan to come back here."

"Perfect. I know it's short notice, but I'd love to have you all over for a nice meal. How's five o'clock?"

We glance at each other.

Bryn dips her head to the side. "Plus, I have some information to share."

"Works for me," I say, nodding.

"Could we do a little later?" Sid asks tentatively. "Coach just changed the schedule; Lisa and I have practice until six tonight."

"My work shift also ends at six," Anthony says.

"How's six-thirty, then?"

"Should work," Sid says, then turns to Anthony. "Did your car ever get fixed?"

"Yep. Good to go," he answers. "We all riding together, then?"

"If you don't mind."

"Not at all."

"Any allergies or special dietary needs? Diabetes aside," Bryn asks. "Beef roast work for everyone?"

331

We all nod.

"Sounds great," Anthony answers.

"Alright then. Addy, if you're free earlier, would you mind coming over to help?"

"Happy to," I reply.

"Then I'll pick you up at five-thirty, and the rest of you I'll see at six-thirty."

Having received confirmation, she walks away and exits the dining hall.

Lisa looks bewildered. "Uh—do we know her?" She smiles sheepishly. "Wait, isn't she the professor who saved Sid at the volleyball game? The one everyone was afraid of?"

I leave my dorm at five-thirty on the dot and find Bryn already waiting outside. I hop in the passenger seat.

"First order of business," she says, "I remembered I need to pick up a few things from the store."

We head to the lone grocery store in Flickerwood. It's a family business with a loyal base of aging patrons. A faded blue sign reads *Joe's Grocery and Deli*. We pull beside one of the few other cars in the lot: a gray minivan with a bumper sticker bearing the name of the church where I first saw Michael Sayer.

Bryn takes her keys and grabs a shopping basket as we walk through the automatic doors. The store is lit with dim fluorescent tubes, and the formerly white floor has turned gray from years of use. Bins of fresh produce sit throughout the first section, and old refrigerators hum beside them. From the registers comes the distinctive "beep" of items being scanned.

"Okay, I just need some flour, milk, butter..."

I feign a surprised expression.

"What?" Bryn asks.

"You don't churn your own?"

For a second she looks confused, but then chuckles. "No, for your information, I don't churn my own butter," she says with a smile, then adds, "I'd have to get a cow, first."

I grin.

As we approach the dairy section, an unseen mom can be

heard talking to her child, "Okay, you can pick *one* thing." Suddenly, a boy comes charging towards us, screeching to a halt in front of the ice cream.

His mom follows shortly after, pushing a cart with a baby in the top. Another woman doing her own shopping comes alongside her, and they strike up a conversation. The mom seems preoccupied talking to her friend and looking for groceries...that is, until her eyes fall on Bryn.

They fly open, and she freezes like a deer caught in the headlights.

"Jacob, get back here," she snaps urgently.

"But Mom—" he protests, but she lunges forward and drags him back from the ice cream. As Bryn turns towards the commotion, the woman makes awkward eye contact with her.

With kids in tow, the two women turn their carts around and quickly disappear into the next aisle, though not without a few glances behind them. Even when out of view, we can hear them muttering to one another.

"Craziness, the people out these days...oh, you just never know anymore...I hate to say it, but if you ask me, she should just go back to where she came from..."

Bryn shrugs it off and continues with her shopping. As we go to check out, we find there is only one lane with a light on. Sure enough, we end up in line behind the same two women. The cashier methodically scans the mom's groceries while loudly chewing a piece of gum. After loading her last item on the belt, the mother of the kids turns and hisses at Bryn.

"Don't think you can try anything. I don't know who let you walk free, but it ain't a secret—all this trouble we been havin'—" she waves her arm in a wide circle, "it all started when you came to town." She pulls her shaw tight around her. "You'd better watch out. I probably shouldn't say this, but there's a few people 'bout ready to take justice into their own hands."

Though trying to whisper, her words draw the attention of the cashier, who stares at us, watching the entire exchange.

"Excuse me?" Bryn says, appalled but not impolite. "Did I do something to you?"

"Well, you tell me," the woman scoffs.

"...because we've never met, yet now you're threatening me."

She shakes her head and moves up to pay. "I ain't threatenin' nobody. Just tellin' you how people really feel."

It doesn't take long for the woman to pay and high-tail it out of the store. Bryn sets her basket on the belt, and the cashier greets us.

"Find everything okay, sweetie?"

I cringe inwardly at the word "sweetie." It grates like nails on a chalkboard.

"Yes, thank you," Bryn replies evenly.

The cashier eyes her selection. "Doing some baking?" she comments. "My husband is always asking me to make cookies and cakes and that sourdough bread starter thing—you know. Of course he can afford to eat all of that and never gain a pound. Men." She snickers and shakes her head. "Are you married?"

"Oh, no. I'm not with anyone."

"Oh," the woman says, cracking her gum. "Well don't sweat it, darling. You'll find the one." She points at the scanned items. "Especially if you keep that up."

Bryn shrugs. "Not really worried about it. Whatever happens, happens."

This seems to catch the woman off guard. She freezes for a moment. "Well, you might change your mind as you get older. Lotta women do. They don't think they want kids when they're younger, but eventually it gets to 'em."

"I'll take a paper bag, please," Bryn says, sidestepping her comment. As she counts out bills to pay, the cashier studies her.

"You know, you have such a pretty face. If you smiled a little more, people might like you." She nods towards the parking lot, clearly referencing the mom from earlier. She lowers her voice to a whisper. "You look so serious—it's a little intimidating."

With a straight face, Bryn reaches for her bag and the receipt. "That'll be all, thank you."

When we walk back to the car, I see that the minivan parked beside us is gone.

334

Chapter 52

Dinner

Once we're back at the cabin, I help bake some bread, roast some broccoli, and make mashed potatoes for side dishes. Together, Bryn and I pull the kitchen table away from the wall and add another chair, finishing only a few minutes before everyone arrives.

Sid is the first one through the door, followed by Lisa.

"Wow," Sid says, looking around. "Your home is very beautiful."

Bryn beams. "Thank you. I'm glad you like it." She starts to make small talk with Lisa and officially introduces herself.

Anthony tentatively peeks his head inside before slowly stepping over the threshold. Nervously, he closes the door behind him and gazes into the living room, straining his neck to try and see farther.

"Smells delicious," he says as he wanders into the kitchen, still searching the area. "So...uh, where's all the poison?"

Sid and I jerk our heads in his direction. The blood drains from Lisa's face.

Anthony cringes. "Right. Sorry. Is that a rude question?"

"No, no, you're good," Bryn answers, amused. She explains her role as a researcher to Lisa, then assures him they're safely locked away in the basement.

"I wasn't really worried or anything. It's not that I think you would...I mean, I know you wouldn't...I trust you and

335

all. It's just, I have a history with this place, and it weirds me out a little. Not because of you—you've really fixed it up nice. But the cabin itself. A few years ago it was a lot more run down, see, and some friends convinced me to spend the night with them..." he rambles.

Bryn manages to steer him to a seat and, as she dishes out portions of braised beef, gracefully pulls the full story out of him. Once she sits down and prays over the meal, I reach for my knife and fork. The beautifully cooked food in front of me looks and smells *amazing*—but I stop when I realize no one else is eating.

Sid picks up her fork slowly and stalls by stabbing at different items. Lisa watches her anxiously, and Anthony stares directly at Bryn.

Bryn observes the scene, but says nothing. She simply raises her own fork and begins to eat, sampling each item. I'm quick to follow, and gradually the others join in. They soon mumble compliments to the chef.

Working up the courage, Lisa poses a question. "Professor Leighton...do you believe us, about the aliens? Do you think we're crazy?"

Bryn takes a bite of food and considers. After a moment, she replies. "I don't think you're lying, and you seem to be in your right mind. I think you saw *something* out there, but I highly doubt it was a true extraterrestrial. I'm inclined to believe there's a more mundane explanation for what you witnessed."

"Like what?" Anthony asks. "Nothing seems to make sense."

"I'm not quite sure yet...but, if my theory is correct, I think these so-called 'aliens' might be part of a ploy to scare people away from the area. There's something out there they want to keep hidden. Which brings us to the thing I wanted to share with you all."

We listen intently, watching as she produces her flip phone and pulls up an image.

"Do any of you know what this is?"

She passes the phone around the table. As it goes from person to person, I watch as they each wrinkle their brow in turn, racking their brains to see if they have an answer to

336

her question.

When the phone finally makes it to me, I look down at the small screen. There's a picture of a nondescript cinder block building surrounded by trees. A tall, chain-link fence topped with barbed wire encloses the structure. It looks very official, almost like a military base or prison, though much smaller. I certainly don't recognize it.

"That's from the northern part of the campus woods, isn't it? Past the music building?" Anthony asks. "The same area the alien appeared."

"Yes, it is," Bryn answers him. "Have you seen it before?"

"Well, I wasn't really supposed to be there, but I noticed the building when we first went looking for Eli. I've asked around, and most people never make it out that far. The few who know it exists say it's just a storage shed for campus security. They keep extra vehicles in there or something."

Bryn nods. "So I've heard. See, I ventured out there because of the project I've been working on with Dr. Gaines. We've been investigating the origin of pollutants that have been found in the creek, and I narrowed down the search to this area. I'm now convinced that the chemicals we're finding are somehow leaking from this building.

"Naturally, as it's on school property, I asked Dr. Gaines about it. As you've said, he told me it belonged to security. When I talked to the head of security, however, he informed me that I should talk to the buildings and grounds department instead. But buildings and grounds said it wasn't theirs, either. They suspected it belonged to the ecology department, which, as we all know, isn't the case.

"Dr. Gaines emailed President Conley, who sent a vague response, stating simply that the building is used for 'storage.' When Gaines requested special permission to access it due to the concerning amount of pollution it appears to be excreting, he received no answer."

"Strange," Sid comments. "So there's just this building on campus no one seems to know about?"

"Not only that," Bryn continues, "but there's no access to it. No driveway or trail leading up to it. It's unclear how someone would even get machinery there to store it." She looks down at the picture and mutters to herself. "Such a bizarre concoction of chemicals. Formaldehyde, cyanide, ammonia…If I didn't know any better, I'd say—" Her eyes suddenly fly wide. I can tell something clicked in her brain, and I lean forward to hear what she's about to say.

Before she can speak, Anthony jumps in. "Professor, there's something I'd like to share, too." He unzips his backpack and pulls out his map of deaths and disappearances. "Those aren't the only unexplained things in Flickerwood."

As people finish eating, we clear the table and allow Anthony to roll out the map. He once more recounts the stories of the missing young people, then waits for Bryn's reaction.

She studies the map intently. "I used to do this a lot in the Navy, you know. Find lost people," she muses.

"Well, how do you go about it?" I ask.

She straightens. "Well, the first step is usually to construct as accurate a picture as possible of when they were last seen." She points to the map. "In cases like these, your best bet would be to find any surviving family members or witnesses."

"In that case," Anthony says, "there's at least one person whose family we already know." He pauses suspensefully. "I haven't told any of you about this one, yet, but—Addy, do you remember the night we went to Dr. Edith's house for the historical society meeting?"

How could I forget? I nod.

"While we were there, I looked through an old high school yearbook she had on the shelf. For fun, I decided to find Dr. Morrell's picture.

"As I flipped through the pages, however, I also happened to land on Mayor Sayer. At first, I thought I was seeing things, or that there had been some sort of mistake. But…" he takes out his phone and scrolls through his pictures, "after doing some more digging in the archives and finding old documents, which took a while, mind you—it was as if someone had gone to great lengths to hide the fact that he ever existed—I eventually confirmed my suspicion."

He sets the phone down. Two yearbook pictures lie side by side in a photograph.

"The first person to go missing in Flickerwood was a teenage boy. His name was Walter Sayer: the mayor's twin brother."

338

A chorus of gasps erupts around the table. Quietly, I study the picture.

Warren sits up straight, a perfect picture smile plastered on his face. He's wearing a suit with a tie, and not one hair on his head is out of place. Walter, on the other hand, has a messy mop of hair that looks unkempt. Dark circles line his eyes, and it's clear he removed the tie and jacket from his suit. His smile is more of a sarcastic smirk.

Bryn appears to be deep in thought. After a minute or two, she turns to Anthony. "What happened? How did he go missing?"

Anthony shakes his head. "There really wasn't much information. He has a birth certificate from the local hospital, along with the mayor's. In middle school and the first year of high school, you can see both Walter and Warren in the yearbook, right beside each other. But the very next year, when he would've been in the tenth grade..." Anthony pulls up another picture of a yearbook page. "It's only Warren." Sure enough, Walter is completely absent from the picture. "I don't know what to make of it, but that year—he was just gone. Vanished. With no real explanation given. The town never had any record of him after that."

"Was there ever a search? Any signs of kidnapping or foul play?"

"Not that I found. No news story, no police report, no emergency response, no statement from the mayor ever referencing his brother. Like I said, it's as if someone intentionally tried to—"

"Erase his existence," Bryn echoes.

Chapter 53

Burn the Witch

I shiver as I walk to class in the morning. Mist hangs thick in the air, dimming the sun's rays and imparting cold drops of water to my skin. I'm up earlier than usual. Last night, our dinner conversation never did circle back to Bryn's realization about the chemicals. Something tells me whatever she has to say is important, though, so I'm hoping to catch her before class.

I wind my way towards the back parking lot. Sure enough, I spot her car, and I soon find her walking nearby. Just as I'm about to announce my presence, someone else steps out from behind a large vehicle. Startled, Bryn grinds to a halt. Her hand flies to her side, prepared to draw a weapon.

"Sorry, sorry. Hope I didn't scare you," Mayor Sayer says to Bryn. He speaks slowly, almost to an exaggerated extent. He flashes a smile, though not too wide. His expression is calm and collected: the image of a perfect politician.

"What are you doing here?" she asks pointedly.

His reply is casual and evasive. "Why am I here? Oh, I have a long history with Wynhurst. I'm quite passionate about this university, and I'm happy to help in any way I can…"

She shakes her head and replies sharply, "You know what I mean."

He gives her a confused look, so she continues.

"Need I remind you that, the last time we talked, you told me to stay away from you and your family in a vaguely threatening way. So, call me crazy, but it's a little alarming to find you jumping out at me in the fog."

He reels back, feigning surprise. "Jumping out at you?!" He shakes his head. "Why would I do that? I really didn't mean to startle you. Only a chance encounter."

She eyes him, then suddenly changes the subject. "Why don't you ever talk about your brother, Warren?"

His cool, collected facade quickly fades. "What?" he squeaks, his face turning white as a sheet.

"Your brother. Walter," Bryn repeats.

"Now where did you hear—"

"I find it funny how, unlike some of the other kids who disappeared in this town, there's no monument for him. No record of any search parties formed or ceremonies held for Walter Sayer, which seems odd, considering his place as the son of one of the founding families..."

"You don't know what you're talking about," he growls while shooting Bryn a look fit to kill.

"Don't I? Then please, enlighten me." He is silent, so she pushes further. "Did you disown him, too? Another casualty to save you and your family's spotless reputation?"

"*I* didn't disown him," Warren snaps. More quietly, he follows with, "You have my father to thank for that."

"I see," Bryn says. "So this is a generational pattern? Like father, like son."

Sayer's hands curl into fists. His next statement is explosive. "I am nothing like my father!" His hands relax at his sides. "What happened with Elise has nothing to do with Walter. I was always close with my brother, and it wasn't right, what they did to him."

"Which was what, exactly?"

"What's done is done," he answers. "Besides. It seems Walter and I are the least of your worries."

She stares at him. "What's that supposed to mean?"

He shrugs. "Well, I met with the board, with staff, with the parents of students—seems like there's a lot of people who would rather you not be at this university anymore."

"Well," she replies evenly, "if someone has a problem

with me, they can come to me directly. Now if you'll excuse me, I have a class to teach."

"Be my guest," he says, spreading his hands and stepping to the side.

She walks past him, and I trail behind, cutting across the grass to avoid getting too close to Sayer.

As we approach the natural sciences building, I'm brought to a full stop by the sight just outside.

A great crowd of people is gathered around the doors, blocking anyone from entering or exiting. Students, staff, parents, and others from the community are huddled together, many holding signs in protest. Poster board squares contain phrases like *Justice for Matthew* and *Protect Our Students*.

Bryn hesitates, but lowers her head and tries to push through the wall of people. "Excuse me, I just need to get to my class..." She makes it about two steps before the crowd stops her.

"Well good *morning*, Professor Leighton," a man's voice rings out. It's dripping with cruel sarcasm. "Actually, I don't think you'll be going to class today." My eyes locate the speaker. He's a large man with a reddish beard and an American flag bandana wrapped around his head. He looks the part of a biker gang member. My hair stands on end when I see the sign he's holding: a picture of Bryn with the eyes X'd out.

"We just have some questions," a woman chimes in.

With sudden awareness, Bryn lifts her head and tries to backtrack. As she does so, however, people start to fill in behind her, blocking the path to freedom. I stand back, observing from a distance. My heart starts to race as she's funneled into the center of the disgruntled crowd. Should I do something? What can I do?

"It's funny, isn't it, how Dr. Morrell is found dead, followed by Matthew Bruner, and then other students are attacked...all starting around the time you came on staff. What do you say to that, professor?"

Bryn scans the sea of faces, looking for the woman who asked the question.

Another person starts to speak. "We've been informed that you didn't give your consent to a background check,

342

either. Why aren't you forthcoming about your history?"

"Now that is simply a clerical oversight," she says quickly. "I have the paper sitting in my office, all filled out. Just need to turn it in. I have nothing to hide; I'll answer any questions you have—"

"Why should we believe you?" another voice says. It's jarring to recognize this one as coming from a long-standing Wynhurst professor. "From staff reports, you haven't been the best to work with. None of your colleagues seem to know much about you, and they consistently report feeling like the work environment has been unsafe since you came on board..."

"W-wh—" Bryn stutters, but isn't given a chance to speak.

"Not to mention the students," another professor says. "Where are they? Never in my career have so many students dropped a class in one semester."

"I mean, really, Leighton. Just yesterday you were seen arguing with the chairman of the board of trustees in the campus cafe. How do you expect to keep your job here?" The statement comes from a balding man in a suit.

Bryn's head swivels back and forth. The suspicion is coming from all directions. She no longer even attempts to give answers.

"Frankly, it's only due to the incompetence of your supervisors that you've remained in your position this long!" the loud man with the bandana thunders. "Your class is empty, staff and students are scared of you, and the police came and arrested you for crying out loud! How'd you bribe and blackmail your way out of that one?!"

"It's obvious you're hiding *something*."

Out of vicarious feelings of fear, I reel back.

"Hey, Addy!" Sid calls from behind me. "What's going—" She stops short, suddenly comprehending the scene before us. "Protesters?"

I nod anxiously. "I don't know what to do. Should we call someone?"

"I'll call security..." she says, pulling out her phone.

Bryn spreads her hands. "I know some things look bad, but I was never under arrest—" Her voice shakes.

"Shut-up!" someone else screams. The voice sounds familiar,

and I strain to see who it might be. "You killed Matthew Bruner, and I saw it plain as day!"

Micah steps into the clearing at the center of the crowd, forcing Bryn to back up. Emboldened by the support of the people behind him, he creeps forward. "You injected him with something, and then you ran into the woods when you saw that I'd spotted you." He thrusts a finger towards her. "And I know something else. She has poisons in her basement! I've seen pictures! Vials upon vials of cyanide."

A gasp runs through the group, followed by a renewed clamor. "Justice for Matthew!" Micah shouts. His cry is echoed by the mob, and it soon turns into a chant. "*Justice for Matthew! Justice for Matthew! Justice for Matthew!*"

Bryn is trapped in the circle of mounting fury, with nowhere to turn.

"Security is heading over now," Sid reports back. At the sight of Micah, she clamps a hand over her mouth. "What is he doing?!" We watch anxiously, unable to look away.

Micah pumps his fist in the air. "Justice for Matthew!" He lowers his eyes and takes a firm stride towards Bryn.

"You killed Dr. Morrell!" he screams, then takes another step. Bryn backs away in equal measure. Step for step. "And you killed Matthew!" He pushes her back further. "And it's your fault we live in fear!" With no room left, she steps to the side, now being chased around the circle. "You're a murderer! Everyone knows it!" He spreads his arms, gesturing to the crowd. "Justice for Matthew!" he calls again.

This time, he stands in place. In an instant, his hand shoots towards his hip, reaching for something. "And we will not wait."

A memory flashes like lightning in my mind. In the auditorium, Micah said he went home for something. Something he didn't want to talk about. Now, he's suddenly brave enough to confront Bryn head-on...*he's got a gun*. The realization rings in my head and exits my mouth as a scream. "Bryn!"

Evidently, she has the same thought. As he reaches down, she lunges forward, swiftly grabbing his arm and knocking him to the ground. The object left in her hand, however, is not a gun, but a cellphone.

344

After watching this exchange, the crowd suddenly becomes a much larger danger. If they were circling her like hungry lions before, now they pounce for their prey.

"Hey!" the bandana man shouts, dropping his sign. "Are you really gonna attack a student right in front of us?"

A group of men swarm her. In a heartbeat, they take her to the ground. One has a length of rope.

"Citizen's arrest!" someone calls, like that makes it better. Beside myself, I rush forward.

"Addy, wait!" Sid says, charging after me.

They bind her hands behind her back.

"What do you have to say for yourself?" they demand. But her face is shoved too far in the dirt to reply.

"Hey!" I shout. "Get off of her!!" I try to push into the crowd, but even my loudest scream is swallowed up by the noise and the chaos.

Not one to go down without a fight, Bryn struggles against the ropes, kicking and toppling a few of the attackers. This, of course, only encourages them.

"Justice for Matthew!" the loud man shouts. The chant resumes. He takes a length of rope, and in a flash it's no longer only around her hands, but her neck.

"Bryn! Bryn!" I become frantic, struggling to break through. Her face starts to turn a shade of red, and she stops struggling so much. My eyes dart around and, for an instant, I catch a glimpse of the mayor standing at a distance, simply watching.

The man with the bandana pulls tighter, with help from those around him. I don't take account of their faces. I don't want to. As panic rises in my chest, a sudden shot cuts through.

Bang!

The entire audience ducks, covering their ears, and turns towards the noise.

An aging man stands outside the circle holding a smoking pistol pointed towards the sky. "What in the sam hill is going on here?!" He lowers the gun and marches towards them with authority.

Upon seeing him, the men holding the ropes seem to return to reality. They release their grip and back away. Bryn coughs, gasping for air. The color slowly returns to her face.

The man rattles on. "I thought this town was well past the days of lynching witches and heretics, but it appears I've been mistaken." He looks on with disbelief. "Look at y'all. On a college campus no less. So much for progress."

"But—" a few people in the crowd start to make excuses.

"Hush!" he orders, firing another round in the air. "Isn't there any respect for law and order, or common decency?" His eyes fall on Warren Sayer, and his expression darkens. "And you, of all people, Mr. Mayor."

For a moment, Warren averts his eyes.

As if a spell has been broken, the protestors start to disperse. I notice that the older, local people leave first, followed by the younger ones from out of town. Micah speeds off, disappearing across campus.

The man's gaze turns towards Sid and me, and I feel the need to defend myself. I raise my hands. "I..."

"They're with me," Bryn croaks from the ground.

He looks at us, then looks to his gun. "Oh, don't worry 'bout it. Only blanks." There's a slight southern drawl to his voice. He holsters his gun, then saunters over to Bryn. He spits some tobacco on the ground before kneeling beside her, his knees cracking.

"You alright? Any broken bones?"

"Don't think so."

He flips open a pocketknife and cuts through the ropes binding her hands together. Now free, Bryn sits up and rubs her wrists. She climbs to her feet along with the old man and faces him.

"I owe you a great deal of gratitude, sir. I...I think you just saved my life."

"Oh, just doin' my duty as a citizen—" He stops and squints at her, studying her face. "You really are Sayer's girl, aren't you?" He shakes his head, chuckling. "Well, I never expected to see you around here again."

Bryn jerks her head back in surprise. "Sorry, have we met before?"

"Name's Jack Ritner, if that rings a bell."

After a few seconds, Bryn's eyes widen as a sudden realization dawns on her. She steps back in shock. "Officer Ritner?"

"Technically it's Judge Ritner now. I ain't on the force

anymore. Retired 'bout ten years ago," he replies. "Though your case is one I'll never forget. I've wondered about you now and then, how things turned out. They don't tell us nothin' after someone's out of our hands, ya know...You end up somewhere good? Nice family?"

Bryn slowly closes her mouth, which has been hanging open, and answers the question. "...Yeah, yeah I did. The social worker and her husband actually took me in, the Leightons. They fostered and eventually adopted me. I couldn't ask for better parents," she says, breaking into a warm smile. "I'd be lost without them."

"Glad to hear it. Stories like yours...they don't always have happy endings."

"No," she agrees quietly. "Of course, it's in no small part thanks to you that I made it this far." She shakes her head. "At this rate, you're starting to seem like my guardian angel."

Ritner snorts, apparently amused by the thought. "I ain't no angel, I can tell you that." He spits more tobacco on the ground. "So, what're you doin' back in Flickerwood?"

Bryn sighs. "Good question. Honestly, I'm beginning to wonder that myself. I dunno...I thought that maybe, by coming back, I could make sense of some things. That it might help me put some pieces together. Try to build some bridges with family...but here I am. On the ground, getting choked by an angry mob."

He chuckles. "Not much has changed."

She lowers her eyes and sighs. "Yeah, I guess not. I don't know what I expected."

"Oh, don't get all down, now," he says with a wave. "I've heard all about the investigatin' you been doin', ever since Morrell croaked. It's about dang time someone exposed ol' Rob and Eric Boyer."

"Wait, you knew about the Boyers?"

"Pfft, of course I knew. You could smell it from a mile away. Everyone knew they were mixed up in some kind of shady business, but no one could prove it. And if ya ask me, the mayor's in cahoots with 'em, too." He clicks his tongue in disapproval, then smiles. "This town may not like you, Bryn—it never has—but didn't you ever consider that Flickerwood needs you more than you need it?" He taps two fingers on his head.

"It's no surprise you drive people crazy. You're pullin' at weeds, and weeds never wanna be pulled. Folks don't like it when someone different comes around, cause it forces them to see their own flaws. Don't let 'em get to ya. Not much changes around here. Not without somebody working to change it. You and your mom are good for this place. Always have been."

Too little too late, the campus security car finally pulls up beside us.

Ritner touches Bryn on the shoulder. "If it means anything to ya, *I'm* glad you're here."

The head of security steps out of the car. "Someone called about a protest? Any of you know what happened?"

"Welp, I better talk to Jerry over here," Ritner says, then starts walking towards the car with a wave.

"Mr. Ritner? What are you doing here, sir?" I hear the guard say.

I step towards Bryn. For a second, I think she's about to cry. Her eyes glisten, as if wet with tears. Then she blinks, and I wonder if I imagined it. "Who was he?" I ask.

She watches him talking with security. "I knew him as Officer Ritner. He...he was the one who stopped to help me that night. The night I was taken into foster care. When my mom almost died."

I follow her gaze.

After a pause, she abruptly shakes her head and turns in a different direction, staring intently down the path Warren Sayer took to leave.

"If you'll excuse me," she says quietly, "I have to make a phone call." Swiftly, she turns and starts towards the door to the natural sciences building.

"Do you two have any information about what happened here?"

My head snaps towards the voice of the security guard. Sid and I walk over to him and answer a few questions. By the time we're finished, Bryn is nowhere to be seen.

As the security car drives off, Sid clenches her fists.

"I just can't believe him," she growls angrily.

I shake myself from the daze I was in. "Who?"

348

"Micah!" she says emphatically. "Attacking Bryn like that. And then just running off…" She starts walking. "I think he went across this way."

I follow her as we trek through campus. As we near the edge of the finance building, Micah comes into view. He stands in the shadows talking to someone. It takes me a moment to identify the other person as Mayor Sayer. As Sid approaches, Sayer turns and disappears around the building. I run to catch up to her.

"Hey!" she shouts at Micah. "What the heck was that?"

"What?" he asks, startled.

"Back there!" she says, gesturing behind her. "I can't believe you were a part of that mob. What's gotten into you?"

"It wasn't a mob—" he says defensively.

"No? Micah, they tried to *kill* her."

"That wasn't my fault! I wasn't a part of that!"

"Well you didn't exactly do much to stop it, did you?"

"I was on the ground! *She* attacked *me*, remember?"

"Oh, don't pretend to be so innocent. She thought you had a weapon or something, the way you were accusing her and firing up the crowd. 'We will not wait'—what's that supposed to mean? Sure sounds like a threat to me."

"I was just gonna get her on film," he says, flashing his phone. "You might not like it, but everything I said is true."

"Did the mayor put you up to this?" I interject.

"What?" he says, shooting me a confused look. "I don't even know what you're talking about."

"You were just talking to him," I press.

"So? He came up to me."

"Listen, Micah," I plead. "Don't believe anything he says. He can't be trusted…"

"Well," he interrupts, "I trust him a whole lot more than *her*," he says, vehemently referring to Bryn. He turns to walk away.

"Micah, we're just trying to look out for you," Sid calls after him.

He turns back. "Well stop!" He shakes his head. "I'm sorry, Sid. But you're wrong about Leighton. And there's nothing you can do or say to change my mind."

Sid and I watch as he storms off. Her shoulders slump.

"I...I know relationships don't always last," she says, her voice quivering. "But...I can't help but wonder, if it weren't for this whole thing...if we could've made it. There was a time...ah." She sighs. "Well it doesn't matter now, I guess. He hasn't been the same since." She exhales.

I swallow, feeling for her. I wish I could help, but I'm doubtful I could say anything to make the situation better. I nod weakly. "Yeah."

Chapter 54

Crescendo

I'm not sure why I go to my classes. It's hard to focus when you almost watched someone be strangled to death in the morning. I'm grateful when Sid and Anthony text me and make plans to meet up in the evening.

Quietly, in a booth near the back of the cafeteria, Sid and I catch Anthony up on the events of the morning. Without thinking, I take my insulin like usual, then sit staring at the food before me. Do I even know who's back in the kitchen? Who might be willing to poison a whole batch of food just to get to the three of us? What's easiest to sneak cyanide into? The BBQ sauce? Salad dressing? The syrup for the diet Pepsi?

I blink, coming back to earth. I can't be this paranoid. I have to eat. Especially now—or that insulin will become a big problem. I raise my fork. On the bright side, it doesn't really matter if we're overheard anymore. They already know. They're already after us.

"Shoot," Sid says, glancing at her phone. "I told Lisa I'd come to the orchestral recital tonight. She plays the viola—it starts in fifteen minutes. Do you guys want to come?"

Anthony and I look at each other, shrug, then agree. "Sure," he says. "Could be fun."

I nod. Some live music would be nice. Plus, I've been meaning to support the art majors more.

I speedily finish my dinner, fill my water bottle at the fountain, and pull my coat back on. We head outside, walking along the path to the music building.

With our student IDs, we get free admission. A couple of student worker security guards nod to us as we enter the state-of-the-art auditorium. Specially engineered speakers and soundproofing panels create a carefully curated listening experience—or at least that's what they tell all the prospective students on the tours. The music building is one of the newest on campus, as it was completely rebuilt after the fire that destroyed the original ten years ago.

The three of us shuffle into a row of seats near the back. The chairs fold down, like those in a movie theater. Despite the distance, we still have a good view of the stage, which is illuminated by bright white overhead lights.

As the show starts, the lights in the theater dim, focusing all the attention to the front. Following some brief introductions and an explanation of the theme of the concert, the first song begins. I scan the rows of musicians until I find Lisa. As Sid said, she's playing the viola. Her fingers fly up and down the neck, and her arm draws the bow so smoothly and precisely she could be a clockwork toy.

The music hums throughout the room, and I can feel the vibrations down to my bones. A smile comes to my face, which grows as the song reaches its peak. I close my eyes and let myself be transported by the melody.

Smack. A door at the back opens forcefully, and light streams in from the hallway. I turn to see the silhouette of a man stumbling into the room. He walks up the aisle towards the stage and begins looking for a seat near the front. Evidently, the rows are full, so he's forced to walk almost all the way back to where we're sitting. He finally finds a spot just a few rows in front of us.

With a pronounced tremor in his hands, he turns to push his seat down. As he does so, his face becomes visible in the few rays of light leaking in from the door. I jolt when I recognize him as President Conley.

I grab Sid and Anthony's attention and confirm that they also noticed. Conley sits with one foot in the aisle. His leg bounces up and down vigorously, and he erratically swings

352

his head around, gazing from one side of the room to the other. It's hard *not* to notice him. Every few minutes, he suddenly leans forward and cranes his neck, as if he's trying to find someone. Seemingly unsuccessful, he falls back into his seat.

After about the fifth time, without warning, he hops up and staggers back out the door. I look to Sid and Anthony, who wear equally confused expressions. I try to shrug it off, but...

"I think we should follow him," I hear myself say.

"What?" Sid hisses.

"I think we should follow him," I repeat, already grabbing my bag.

"—okay," Sid says, standing with me. Anthony is close behind.

"That's not normal behavior. Something is up with him," I add.

"Can't argue with that," Anthony agrees.

We slip out the back door and gaze down the hallway. It's mostly empty, save for the two security guards. Fortunately, I glimpse the form of Dr. Conley just as he turns down a side corridor. Conscious not to walk too fast and appear suspicious, we head after him.

He leads us down a small, dimly-lit hallway running parallel to the backstage area. Though muffled, the music from inside the auditorium still spills through the walls. At the end of the hall, nestled to the side, is a set of double doors. Conley pulls one open and disappears behind it.

After waiting a few seconds, Anthony puts an ear to the door. Hearing nothing, he carefully turns the handle, silently unlatching it. We peer down at a set of dingy concrete steps. With only a brief hesitation, we all step over the threshold. Anthony eases the door shut behind us, and we start down.

Though I try to be quiet, my shoes smack the concrete, and the sound rings off the metal railing. My heart pounds faster as we descend into what can only be the basement of the building. The air grows colder and the stairwell grows darker. Finally, we come upon the end. In front of us is another metal door with a small window. I feel my hands growing sweaty. What if Dr. Conley knows we're down here? What if he's waiting on the other side of that door?

After trying to see what we can through the window, Anthony places a hand on the exit bar. Ever so softly, he presses it. The door creaks as it opens, and we all peer out.

Thankfully, the room before us is empty. Of people, that is. Fluorescent lights illuminate the concrete floor and cinder block walls, though some are flickering like they're about to go out. It has the familiar, musty smell of a basement, complete with bare metal support beams standing throughout the middle of the room. To one side is a bunch of janitorial supplies. Mops, cleaners, buckets, brooms—that sort of thing. To the other is a collection of what seems to be furniture. Chairs, mostly, along with awards and various plaques and instruments. Tarps cover a lot of it, but much of the wood that shows through is marked with black stains.

"Left over from the fire, it seems," Anthony says, nodding towards it. We continue further into the room. Past the cleaning supplies and charred artifacts, we find another hallway. Before venturing down it, we stop just to the right of the opening, pressing our backs against the cinder block wall. Slowly, Anthony pokes his head around the corner. His quick withdrawal tells me he saw something.

Sid and I look to him expectantly, leaning forward.

"Dr. Conley just went into the last room on the right," he whispers, then peeks again. We all hear the *ka-clink* of a door latching shut.

Anthony waves us forward. Fueled by adrenaline, I follow him into the hall. Blue metal doors line both sides, as if they were designed to be used as classrooms. Moving single-file, we stay close to the wall as we start towards the targeted room. I peer through the various windows as we pass.

Many of the rooms contain overturned desks, empty chalkboards, and aged projectors. Whatever the intention, they're certainly not in use now. We stop just outside the last door. After a few moments of tense silence, we realize the problem.

"Can you guys hear anything?" Anthony asks.

I shake my head. The door is too thick. All that can be discerned is muffled voices. "I think he's talking to someone."

354

Anthony's eyes dart around, looking for a solution—then his gaze settles on the door to our right. It's smaller than the others, likely a maintenance closet of some sort.

"There are grates on the wall in the other rooms. There might be a vent in there we can listen through," he says, lunging for the handle, but it doesn't budge. He slumps in disappointment. "Locked."

Sid steps forward and examines the door. "It's not as heavy as the other ones..." she mutters, jiggling the handle. "Let me try something."

She pulls her wallet from her bag and—after a moment of hesitation—removes her student ID. "I can always tell them I lost it." She then grabs the door handle and jams the card between the latch and the frame. I watch in disbelief. That trick doesn't actually work, does it?

Suddenly, a noise echoes down the hall, originating from the direction we just came. It sounds like the door to the stairwell: a sharp *clank* as it opens and then, after a delay, a softer *clink* when it swings closed. We all freeze. Footsteps tap against the concrete floor. There's no mistaking it; someone's coming our way.

I start praying. With shaking hands, Sid frantically works at the door. She wiggles the ID card around until—*click*. Hurriedly, she swings the door open and we all pile in, narrowly avoiding the eye of the approaching stranger.

It takes a moment to gain my bearings. The closet we're in is narrow, and a large cleaning cart takes up most of the space. As Anthony guessed, however, there is a grate leading into the neighboring room. The voices are much clearer. Anthony and Sid, who are deeper in the closet, crouch near the grate, while I stay close to the door. I try to peer out the slats into the hallway, hoping to identify the source of the footsteps.

Anthony taps me on the shoulder, and I turn to see him holding Sid's phone out to me. When I take it, I see she's written a message in the notes section. *Conley's in the room with Robert Boyer!*

While I'm still processing this information, the person in the hallway comes into view. Through the bottom set of slats, I see a pair of men's dress shoes. Moving to the top, I get a look at his face. I type what I see and pass the phone back. *Mayor is in the hall!!*

Inspired by Sid's use of technology, I pull out my own phone and start a sound recording. I don't know how much of this it'll be able to pick up, but it's a start. Dr. Conley's voice carries through the vent, though he sounds even worse than he did at the assembly.

"Y-you owe me, man!" he raves at Dr. Boyer. "Y-you gotta hook m-me up. Gotta give me s-s-something. Just a gram or two. It's been *days*. Just a little bit…"

"Get ahold of yourself, man," Dr. Boyer snaps. "I don't have anything for you."

My fingers fly to my temples as I realize the truth. Dr. Conley really *does* have a drug problem. And not only that, but Robert Boyer is his supplier. That backpack he left at Conley's house—it must have been a delivery.

With a firm knock to announce his presence, Warren lets himself into the room. His gait grinds to a halt.

"Conley?" he asks, clearly not expecting this second visitor.

The president begins to plead his case once more, this time to the mayor. "P-please, I need more…I'm dying, here." He moans in pain and smacks his lips. "I can do whatever you want. I'll pull it together…"

"You'll pull it together?!" Warren shoots back. "What the heck kind of stunt did you pull on Monday? You have *one job*, and you royally screwed me over. No. I'm not helping you anymore. Deal's off. We're done here."

"B-but, just give me another chance! P-please—" Conley begs. The sound of fabric wrinkling tells me he's grasped the mayor in desperation.

"Get off me!" Warren barks. Conley's footsteps come in a cluster as he's shoved backwards into the door. I hear the smack of his palm against the tile floor. Though I can barely see, I can tell he's fallen over the threshold and is now sitting in the doorway, half inside the room and half out.

"Get lost," Boyer calls after him. "It's over."

In a flash, Warren turns on Boyer. "Now what makes *you* think you're any better? You're the one who got burned and put everything in jeopardy!"

"You're mad at *me*?!" Boyer retorts. "You're not the one

running from the cops! It's not your neck on the line, Warren, yet it was *your* plan that got me here. *Sure*, 'Just leave Leighton alone. Let her be the scapegoat. It'll be fine, trust me' — it's her fault we're in this mess! Her and those three kids."

"Exactly," Warren returns. His tone is venomous. "You didn't follow my plan. You were the idiot who talked to said kids, then publicly tried to stop Leighton from saving a student's life. That's why I said it's best to go hands-off." Irritation mounts in his voice. "I'm sick and tired of you undermining me. News flash, Rob, I don't need you. You're absolutely right. It's not my name on the line here. Handing your head over on a silver platter would make this whole thing a lot easier for me...but I'm doing you a favor."

Faintly, I think I hear more footsteps in the distance. At first, I think I'm imagining it, but they gradually grow louder. They're coupled with the sound of jingling keys.

"If, however," Warren continues, "I find you've been disloyal to me, I might just change my mind. It is true, after all. You did kill Morrell. No one will be the wiser. And don't even *think* of trying to drag me down with you—"

"President Conley—" a small voice squeaks, but stops short. Micah stands like a deer in the headlights, his eyes wide and mouth hanging open. Dressed in full security gear, he shines a flashlight directly on the open door before him. I hope he heard the whole thing.

Warren's head jerks towards Micah. He steps out into the hallway and immediately puts on a false smile. "Micah," he says easily. "You making your rounds?"

"Y-yes, sir. If it's all clear down here, I'll just be going, then." Slowly, he starts to back away.

"Well don't let me interrupt you. Please, come see for yourself."

Micah glances from the mayor to the president, who slowly climbs to his feet. "I-I'll take your word for it. All good." He turns and starts walking away.

Click. "Micah. Stop." Warren's tone darkens. My heart seizes when I see the jet black gun in his hand, aimed and ready. Micah freezes and puts his hands above his head. "Turn this way." Slowly, he does as he's told and turns back

357

to face the mayor. Dread fills my stomach.

"You're not actually gonna kill him, are you?" President Conley stutters.

Sayer ignores him. Slowly, he begins to step forward, closing the distance between Micah and himself.

"P-please. I didn't hear anything. I won't tell anyone. I won't be any trouble—" Micah pleads.

"I'm sorry, son. But you know I can't let you leave."

From somewhere inside me, a calm resolve rises to the surface. My emotions fade to the background, and my brain starts to calculate a plan.

One...

The mayor takes a step, moving closer to the closet door.

Two...

I grip the handle, tensing. He lifts his foot and takes another step, preparing to shoot.

Three.

I yank the closet handle down and slam it open as hard as I can. The metal door smacks the gun from his hand and sends it skidding across the concrete. As much as I want to retreat back into the closet, I know being trapped is a death sentence. I spring out towards the gun on the floor.

Warren recovers quickly and lunges towards me. The next thing I know, my feet fly out from under me, and I'm heading towards the ground. Anthony jumps between me and the mayor, kicking the gun even further out of reach. Ignoring the sting of hitting the concrete, I scramble back to my feet. As I do so, I see Micah out of the corner of my eye.

To my surprise, he hasn't taken off, but runs towards the action while talking into his radio, "Send help! Lowest level of music building, three suspects, wielding loaded gun, intent to kill." The president has disappeared, but Robert Boyer emerges from the classroom and charges towards the gun on the floor. Micah races him.

Meanwhile, Sayer lands a blow to Anthony's head and kicks him in the leg. We both step backwards.

"C'mon, kids, we've been doing this since before you were born," he snarls.

Boyer reaches the gun first. He knocks Micah to the ground and yanks the radio away from him. The plastic cracks as he throws it to the floor. Terrified, Micah sits staring up the barrel of a gun.

"Hey!" Sid calls from behind us. "I'm calling the police, might wanna stop me." She stands with her phone on speaker, talking to a 9-1-1 dispatcher. "Yes, we're on Wynhurst University campus, bottom floor of the music building. I'm looking at Robert Boyer, he's threatening us with a gun..."

For an instant, Boyer takes his eyes off Micah, who lunges towards the gun again. Feeling brave—or maybe stupid—I rush forward to help. I mean, I can't really comprehend the danger of a gun. I have no idea what it would feel like to be shot. I've only ever seen them used on a gun range, only at wooden targets...

Micah stamps his boot down on Boyer's foot and elbows him in the face. He grunts and loosens his grip on the gun, and we wrench it from his hands. Once again, it goes flying across the room. Angrily, Boyer shoves me away from him and starts tearing towards Micah. He may not have a weapon anymore, but he's an experienced criminal, now with a bone to pick. He wipes the blood from his nose.

Micah scrambles backwards. He runs into the classroom and rounds the corner with Boyer on his heels. I run after them, but Boyer suddenly stops in the doorway, a small smile on his face.

"No one move!" the mayor orders, now back in the possession of his gun.

I spread my hands.

"Might not want to shoot us, Mr. Mayor," Sid says quickly, pointing to her phone, which is still on speaker. Cops will be here any minute. Four bodies won't look so good."

Out of sight, the basement door opens with a clang as it hits the cinder block wall. Jangling keys indicate the arrival of campus security.

With a twinkle in his eye, Warren lowers the weapon. "No. You may be right about that." He exchanges a glance with Robert Boyer and nods. Boyer disappears into the classroom, shutting the door behind him. Before security can round the corner, Sayer breaks out running towards the end of the hall, then through another set of doors. With only a few seconds hesitation, Anthony and Sid take off after him.

"He's over here!" one of them shouts, and two of the full-time, experienced security staff come into view. Seeing Sid and Anthony, they begin running, too. Before I can say anything, they're out the back door.

My head swivels back and forth. The mayor has a gun... but he's not going to shoot anyone where he can be seen. Security is on him now, and the cops are coming...but what about Micah? And Robert Boyer?

Slowly, I open the classroom door, expecting to see them grappling inside. But the room is dark. In the far corner, my eyes pick out some motion. A door, made to look like an instrument locker, slowly swinging shut. I stop, comprehending the sight. *A secret passage.*

I dive towards it. If that door shuts, I might not be able to open it again. My hand slides into the gap, catching it just before it latches. I find myself staring into a long brick tunnel that slants gradually down into the earth. I check the room one more time. No sign of Micah. They must both be down there.

He's been difficult lately, for sure, but I can't just let him go in alone. He has no idea what he's up against. Dr. Boyer could be on him already...there's no time to waste. I grab a chair, prop the door open, and start down the long corridor.

Chapter 55

Foiling an Alien Abduction

Only a few steps from the entrance, the tunnel becomes too dark for me to see. I pull out my phone, sound recording still running, and turn on the flashlight. I don't want to draw attention to myself, but I can't walk in pitch blackness.

As I journey further, I hear the faint sound of footsteps up ahead. I stop, straining my ears to hear. Is it Robert Boyer or Micah? Or maybe both? I'm not sure what I'll do when I catch up to them, but I have to at least try and help. I continue on, muttering prayers with every step.

As if things weren't already disorienting, I start to come upon forks in the road. Narrow, winding side tunnels branch off from the main path, forcing me to decide which way to go. I listen for the footsteps and hope I'm headed in the right direction. The tunnel seems to stretch on for ages, thousands and thousands of red bricks and miles of concrete floor. My phone flashlight illuminates a small circle before me, but everything beyond is shrouded in inky darkness. Like driving in the fog—only a bit revealed at a time.

If I think about it too hard, all the dirt above me, I start to get claustrophobic. And then there's the question of what's waiting on the other side. An ambush? I push that thought away, too.

Eventually, I notice that the floor begins to slant upwards. With any luck, it means I'm heading back to the surface.

That it ends soon. The thought would scare me more if I weren't so relieved to be getting out of here.

Preparing to face whatever lies ahead, I glance at my blood sugar. Unsurprisingly, it's high. Suddenly, my eyes return to the path as a light shines up ahead. As I get closer, I can see a figure standing in front of an open door, letting moonlight leak into the tunnel. When my brain registers that it's a person, I freeze, afraid it might be Dr. Boyer. As the figure steps outside, their face comes into view. I squint, trying to see who it is...*Micah!* I pick up the pace, trying to catch up to him. He disappears from the tunnel before noticing me, however.

I reach the door. It's made of rough-hewn wood and has a cast-iron handle, like a barn door, or an outhouse. I press my ear to it, trying to hear outside. I can just make out the...crunch of leaves? I turn my flashlight off and, slowly, swing it open. The hinges creak as I do. I take a step forward onto dirt.

I glance around, finding myself in the midst of a sea of dark trees. The forest? Behind me, the door I just came out of is camouflaged to seem like part of a tree trunk. Once closed, it's almost indistinguishable from the false tree. I turn back around to survey my surroundings. To my right is a chain-link fence, and a little beyond that—just like in Bryn's photo—is a plain-looking building. I swallow. Things are starting to make sense.

I spot Micah a few yards ahead of me. He's still running. As I start after him, I keep my eyes peeled, searching the shadows for anyone who might be lying in wait.

"Micah!" I hiss. He's too far away to hear me, but I'm afraid to be any louder. Robert Boyer, Edith Morrell, hired henchmen, aliens...anyone could be hiding in these woods. Boyer didn't look concerned when Micah ran into the tunnel, almost like he wanted him to find this place. It makes me suspicious—he's not going to let us off that easy. We have to get out of here.

Just as I start to believe Micah will outrun any threats on his own, I hear a scream. Ice grips my bones; it's the scream of a man scared for his life. So much for escaping notice. I switch my flashlight back on and run as fast as my legs can carry me.

362

The scene I come upon makes me stop in my tracks. Only now do I realize I didn't fully believe Lisa's story, but at the sight, all doubt immediately leaves my mind. In front of me, Micah is pinned against a tree by a towering being standing at least eight feet tall. Its skin is a sickly gray-green color, and two bright flashlights hang from the front of its coveralls, one of them strobing. The disorienting light catches on a thick layer of fog emerging from behind it.

"Hey!" I shout, shining my own light, which seems small and silly in comparison.

Without letting go of Micah, the creature slowly turns its hairless head to face me, like a praying mantis eyeing its next victim. Two giant, almond-shaped eyes of pure blackness drill into mine. I start to tremble. *It's just a costume. It's just a costume. It's just a costume.* I tell myself over and over. *It has to be. Like Bryn said—they're just trying to scare people away from that building.*

"L-let him go!" I shout. For fear of losing its attention—or my nerve—I start walking forward.

"Addy?" Micah says, squinting. "Run!" he screams at me. "It's too late for me!"

I don't know what to say to him right now. Where to begin. My brain is occupied with the monster before me. I start talking. "Y-you don't want him. He doesn't have any idea what's going on. Just let him go—he's been on your side this long. It's not like he'll do you any harm." The being stares back at me, expressionless. It's unsettling, seeing your words have no effect at all.

"Behind you!" Micah chokes out.

I glance back to see another alien reaching a long, leathery, three-pronged hand towards me. I duck away, narrowly evading its grasp, then reach for the first thing I can think of to use as a weapon: my metal water bottle. I charge towards Micah and swing the bottle, aiming for the head of the alien holding him.

My blow lands around the chest area, and the creature lets Micah drop to the ground. The second alien catches up and grabs me with cold, stiff hands. It snarls with an animalistic growl, and its open mouth reveals a horror-show of stick-thin, razor-sharp teeth. I shrink away. *It's just a*

363

costume. It's just a costume. A very convincing costume, but still just a costume.

I flail my arms around, trying to whack something with my water bottle, but the other alien knocks it from my hand. They flank me and begin dragging me backwards.

Micah coughs, clutching his neck. He tries to stand, but stumbles.

"A—" he clears his throat, reaching towards me. "Addy!"

They unlock a gate in the chain-link fence and drag me towards the building. I can see more aliens approaching.

"Run!" I screech at the top of my lungs. "Micah, run! Go get help!! Tell them where I am! They're coming, go now!"

He stands, staring as I'm dragged away.

"Run!" I scream again, desperate. No one else knows we're out here. No one else will know what happened to me.

Thankfully, the truth starts to register. He notices the approaching aliens and takes off into the woods.

I focus on breathing. *He's going to get help. Someone will come. Bryn, campus security, the cops—they're coming.* Still, I have to live that long.

Don't panic. I try to remember what Bryn taught me about self-defense. First thing, a fight starts in the mind. They've definitely got the intimidation thing down.

The strobe lights are starting to make me sick, and I feel a headache coming on. I try to get a good look at my captors, but it's not comforting. The arms, the height, the eyes, the feet—the theory of an alien hoax made sense when I was sitting in the kitchen at the cabin. Now, it's harder to keep believing.

I dig my heels into the ground, trying to slow them down, and I stretch my fingers wide, grasping for cloth and costumes. My nails finally catch on a section of fake skin, and I tug as hard as I can. It pulls away from the person's wrist, but it doesn't tear. When the other leans close enough, I sink my teeth into the rubber and bite a chunk out of the suit.

I stop, surprised it actually worked. With a section of human arm now exposed, the alien growls at me again with big fake teeth. Feeling less scared, and just a little satisfied, I spit the rubber skin at his feet. My small victory is short-lived, however, as they shift positions. One holds my arms

364

and the other holds my legs, lifting me fully off the ground. I wriggle and squirm, trying to kick my feet and be a general hindrance. They're heading towards an open door on the side of the building. Light streams from a hallway of some sort.

What else did Bryn say!?

"What do you want?!" I demand, trying not to sob. "Where are you taking me?"

Unsurprisingly, they don't respond.

What do they want? If I know what they're after, maybe I can do something about it. Or at least I'll know what to expect.

What do I know? Some type of criminal activity takes place here. Something related to an entire crime syndicate in Flickerwood. So...what, the aliens want to kill any witnesses? Why not just shoot me, then? Why go to the trouble of kidnapping people?

As they try and back me through the doorway, my arm shoots out and grips the frame.

"No!!" I scream, clinging to the metal for dear life. Whatever they want, and wherever they want to take me, I want no part of it. With enough twisting and pulling, they work my fingers loose, but I catch my foot on the same place. With a great shove, they get me in the door, and it closes behind me. Above it hangs a glowing red exit sign. I try to make a mental note of that.

A third person in a lab coat stands off to the side, looking down at me. Their face is obscured by a full gas mask, which makes me question what I'm breathing in. Or even what I'm *about* to breathe in. Images of gas chambers fill my head.

Refusing to be dragged any further, I pull my limbs in close and throw my body weight to the ground. I drop to the floor like a rock. To my surprise, they let go of me. All three form a circle around me, preventing me from leaving.

Then, the alien to my right grips one of the three-pronged hands and pulls it off like a glove. The other alien does the same, and I watch as they both reach up to their heads. They lift off the top section of their costumes in turn, revealing that their real, human heads are actually much lower than I thought. It was the false top that made them seem taller. Underneath, both of them are also wearing gas masks.

"Well, guess the jig is up, anyway," one says, touching a

knob near the collar of the suit. Only now do I notice a faint hissing sound that gradually stops, and the fog around them dissipates. I feel a stinging at the back of my throat and wonder how much gas I've inhaled already.

"This one knows too much," the other one says, gesturing to me. Even without the alien heads, their voices are deep and distorted. They must still have voice-altering devices on.

"That she does," the person in the lab coat agrees, also with a distorted voice. "This one is Addy, I believe?" He checks something on a tablet in his hands. "Where's the other one?"

One of the aliens nods towards the woods outside. "Being tracked by G and H."

"Well," the man in the coat says, "they'd better catch him fast. He walked right into our hands."

"Where do you want her?" the alien asks, gesturing towards me. "Usual protocol?"

"I...may have to consult with the boss. She may be too much of a liability to hold, though we are due for another test subject."

My headache continues to worsen, and I start to feel like I'm looking down a telescope. The edges of my vision darken. Still, I try to follow the conversation. One phrase cuts through my brain. *Test subject?!*

"What's going on here?" I ask from the floor. If the amount of information I know is already dangerous, what's a little more? Worth a shot. "What's usual protocol?"

"C'mon. Up you go." The two aliens try to lift me again, but I shove at their hands and plop back on the ground. "No!" I scream. "Tell me where you're taking me."

The man in the lab coat kneels to the floor in front of me while the other two hold my arms.

"Now don't throw a tantrum. You wanna know where you're going? Well, let me tell you. You're gonna get a little introduction to our boss. If I were you, I'd try to make a good first impression, because your life hangs in the balance."

Feeling woozy, I let myself be lifted from the floor. With the man in the lab coat leading the way, they walk me down the long, bright hallway, which eventually leads to a ramp. The next level down contains more hallways lined with doors.

From what I can see as we walk past, many of the rooms

resemble exam rooms in a doctor's office, complete with an exam table and various instruments. Near the center of the building is a large space spanning several doors. It appears to be a laboratory filled with beakers, test tubes, and colored liquids. Inside, more people in lab coats stand at various tables, hard at work. They're not wearing gas masks, but surgical ones.

As we round the corner, we pass a set of double doors. Through a pair of round windows, I glimpse people dressed in scrubs standing around a table. I squint, trying to understand what I'm looking at. When the answer hits me, I quickly look away. It's an operating room, and they're at work on a patient.

Thankfully, that room is not our destination. Instead, they lead me through a door at the end of the hall. It takes a moment for my eyes to adjust, as this room is much darker than the hallway. Several men in white lab coats sit around a conference table, their eyes all trained on a large rectangle along the far wall. At first glance, it appears to be a screen. Upon closer examination, however, I realize that it's a one-way mirror. A window into a bright white room with a single chair in the center, eerily similar to experimental rooms in dystopian movies.

The chair is a dull blue color, and a strip of tile on the wall sports the classic blue-green hue of hospital furniture, exam tables, and scrubs. These muted shades are the only splashes of color in the glaring white void. A young woman, maybe a few years older than me, sits in sweatpants and a hospital gown. Sweat pours down her face, and her breathing is labored. Her cheeks are flushed, and her eyes dart anxiously around the room, unable to see the faces watching hers.

The man in the lab coat leading our little party steps forward to announce our presence. "Sir—"

Without taking his eyes off of the woman, a figure seated at the far end of the table raises a hand and waves us inside.

"Please. Have a seat," he says, though I get the feeling it's not a mere suggestion. I'm pushed into a chair opposite him. The shadows in the room obscure his form, and he has yet to face us. It seems my arrival is not as important as whatever is going on with the girl behind the glass.

As time passes, her state worsens. Her pupils widen so much they nearly fill her eyes. All of a sudden, she flings herself out of the chair and to the ground, screaming at the top of her lungs. The men watching scribble down notes.

I watch, horrified, as she screeches and claws at her hair, her face, and the walls. Her behavior is so extreme and erratic that the fear of some abominable mad science experiment creeps into my mind. Are they breeding science fiction monsters? Infecting people with rabies? Creating Frankenstein?

As disturbing as it is to see the woman thrashing about behind the glass, even more sickening is the reaction of her spectators. Or, rather, their lack of reaction.

"Blood pressure increasing," one comments.

"BPM 220 and climbing," another says.

Their tone is even and dry, as if reporting the weather, not the vitals of a woman in obvious crisis. This is what they do. Day in and day out. They all nod and scribble more notes. She is not a person to them. Merely a subject.

In the midst of her screaming and writhing, the woman suddenly freezes. Her body goes rigid, and she falls limp to the ground.

"Flatline!" one calls out.

In response to this news, the man at the end of the table lets out a disappointed sigh.

In the white room behind the glass, the door flies open, and more people in lab coats rush in. They roll in a crash cart and begin CPR. The wheeze of the breathing bag whistles over the speakers, along with a sickening crunch sound. It takes me a moment to realize what the sound is, but the truth makes my stomach churn. Ribs cracking.

The reality begins to catch up to me. Did—did I just witness someone die? It's strange how not-different it is from watching a movie. I know, deep down, that this is real life, but it's hard to fully comprehend that. Someone fell over. Her heart stopped. How desensitized am I? I wonder who she was. Who she is. How long has she been here? Is her family still looking?

"Lethal dose: 1.5 milligrams," one of the other men reports.

The boss curses under his breath. "And what do we expect

it to be in the next version? Potent is good. Killing customers is bad for business."

"Yes, sir," someone answers. "We're aiming for 5 mg..."

"Good. Get it done."

With that, the overhead lights come on, and all the scientists who were watching get up and filter out of the room. I'm left in my chair with an alien on either side, the person in the lab coat, and the man at the head of the table. He turns towards us, and I can see his face for the first time.

Chapter 56

Mad Scientist

I reel back in surprise. The man sitting before me bears an uncanny resemblance to someone I've seen too much of lately, though this man's hair is longer and swept to the side. Rather than a clean-shaven look, he sports a bristly gray beard.

"Walter Sayer." The name escapes my lips.

His eyes flash like fire. "Where did you hear that name, girl?"

"Is it yours?" I shoot back, filled with a sudden boldness born of adrenaline and frustration.

The corner of his mouth turns up slightly. "It's Addy, isn't it?"

I'm quiet.

He nods. "We've been keeping tabs, ya know. On you and your friends. 'Bout time we met."

"Can't say it's a pleasure," I mutter.

"Ah," he laughs. "Since you know so very much, what did you think of our little show?"

My eyes float to the window. Someone raises a defibrillator over the woman's body and delivers a shock to her chest.

"We've run thousands of these trials over the years," he boasts. "Our formulas are some of the best-tested in the world—that's why they sell so well." He flashes a smile.

As he speaks, the full, horrifying truth finally comes into focus. The overdoses, the money laundering, the alien sightings, the chemicals leaching into the creek—they're all byproducts of an extensive illegal drug operation infecting Flickerwood and beyond.

Robert Boyer, Edith Morrell, Warren and Walter Sayer— they're drug lords, profiting off the misery of others, and this is their lab. What's going on here is not some obscure, incomprehensible, chaotic evil. It is cold, calculated, and purposeful. These are not mad scientists. They are greedy scientists. They produce a substance, they test its effects, they take notes, and they hone their formula.

"So, for years, you've been kidnapping kids from Flicker-wood? Experimenting on them? Like her?" I venture.

He glances back at the window. "Don't take us to be cruel. We take good care of our subjects. Some are from Flickerwood—she was a local girl. But we ship them in from all over. Philadelphia, Baltimore, Mexico, Haiti, Cuba— where we can. More diverse sampling, then."

I pause before I respond, suppressing the urge to argue with him. Everything he stands for is morally reprehensible to me...but that's nothing new. What's important is getting information. What do I want to know? What do I *need* to know? "How does this work, with you and the mayor? What's his part?"

"Isn't it obvious?" he replies. "He's the diplomat. He smiles for the camera, shakes hands, and pulls the right strings to ensure I get the supplies and space I need. Meanwhile, I do the real work down here." He wrinkles his nose. "I can't stand to be around all those people. I'm a chemist, really."

My distaste must show on my face.

"Don't look so appalled, Addy. I manufacture chemicals to make people feel better, then test them for safety and efficacy. What's so bad about that?" He nods towards the woman, who's now being loaded onto a cot. "Unfortunately, not all tests go as planned—but that's part of the process. We're really not so different from any legal pharmaceutical company."

"...If they kidnapped their test subjects and killed their consumers," I retort.

"And if my business were respected in the public sphere, maybe I could go through the hoops of ethics committees and recruitment. As it stands, I work with what I have."

Before I can respond, he rises from his chair.

"And what I have to deal with right now is, well, you."

He nods to the masked man in the lab coat standing beside me, who's now holding a syringe. Suddenly, the alien guards clamp down on my arms as the man tugs my sleeve out of the way and brings the needle towards my skin. He stops, hovering mere centimeters above my arm.

My heart thumps away in my chest, kick-started to a million miles an hour.

"You see, Addy, here is my predicament. Thanks to consistent exposure to our aerosol hallucinogen and various test formulas, most of our residents are in a continuous state of delirium, confusion, and—quite often—ecstasy. They wouldn't know up from down even if they did escape. You, however, are a much larger liability. That beside you is a dose of cyanide. You could suffer the same fate as your friend, Matthew."

I take shallow breaths, afraid even the slightest movement could bump the needle.

"But," he continues, "you do have one thing working in your favor. You see, it's been a bit of a dry spell as far as test subjects go. So—if you'd be on your best behavior—I may let you live, so long as you cooperate. What do you say?"

I glance at the syringe, then back at Walter. I guess this is the part when, on principle, I'm supposed to choose the instant death of cyanide over taking part in his sick experiments, right?

Yet, I can't bring myself to do it. I stare into the white room, remembering the woman who was wheeled out just moments ago. I don't want to end up like that. To lose everything in my mind and spend the rest of my life out of touch with reality, acting as a pawn in their drug trade. Still, if I say yes, it might give me time. Time to escape.

"D-does everyone die, like that?" I ask.

He answers in a cold, sterile tone. "Well, everyone dies eventually. But no. We don't kill all our test subjects. As I said, some of them are actually quite happy. Our substances can have very pleasant effects—that's the point. But there's always the risk of having a bad reaction. Could be the best hit of your life. Could be a ticket to a paranoia trip ending in multiple organ failure. We're still working out the kinks."

He walks around the table, growing closer to me. The guard's grip on my arm tightens. "So," Walter asks, "what'll it be?"

My eyes flit to the needle at my arm.

"What do you want?"

"I want a chance to live," I answer.

He smiles, satisfied with my response. "Good choice." Just before the syringe is taken away, he leans forward, close enough for me to smell the mix of coffee and spearmint on his breath. "Be sure to remember this. You don't get a second chance. You will cooperate, or you will be executed. And I will make sure every guard and staff member in this building knows it. Do you understand?"

I nod weakly.

"Good."

The man in the lab coat removes the needle. I exhale.

Survival, now, is a gamble. If I try to run again, I need to make it count. Bryn's advice returns to my head. Sometimes it's good to be underestimated. Sometimes being small and weak is a strength. I hang my head. I let the tears I've been holding back flow down my cheeks. I don't protest when they guide me from the chair and take me towards the door. I want them to feel safe. To feel like they've won.

Once we enter the hallway, the man in the lab coat touches my shoulder.

"It won't be so bad. You might like it."

I guess he feels bad about the crying. Good.

He turns and walks down the hall in the opposite direction, leaving me with only the aliens. My brain whirrs with action, trying to figure out the best time to try and make a run for it. I know the exit door we came in, and we passed a few more. There's one on this floor as well. I've got one shot—one opportunity for surprise, and then I'll have to have the courage to follow through.

We stop in front of an exam room door, and one alien releases me in order to unlock it. As he inserts the key, I realize something. The remaining alien is holding on to my arm like one of the holds Bryn had me practice getting out of.

God, please be with me.

In an instant, I turn away from the door and circle my elbow over his arm, yanking free of his grip. He lunges towards me, but I jam the heel of my hand into the space beneath his gas mask, hitting his throat. As the other alien whirls around, my forearm instinctively flies up to block his hand, and I launch my fist. I land a smack on the head, just enough to get away, then turn and run down the hall, my sneakers squeaking on the shiny tile.

Wow! I actually did that. I can't believe that worked!

I can hear them behind me, and shouts break out among the staff. Up ahead, I see the glowing, telltale exit sign. Thankfully, the hallway in front of me seems to be empty of people, and there's a clear shot to the door. The Lord has answered my prayer. I can do it. I can make it home.

I suck in air and force myself to go faster. If I can just make it outside, I'll be halfway there. I can climb the fence. I'll have to. I reach towards the door, and relief floods my body when I touch the cold metal of the handle. I press my hand against it, and it gives.

And then, seemingly out of nowhere, an arm shoots in front of my shoulders and bars my path. I'm suddenly yanked backwards and dragged away from the door. Relief is rapidly replaced by an all-consuming hopelessness as my fingers leave the handle. My back slams into the guard's chest as I'm pulled against the wall. I would give more of an effort to fight back were it not for the knife blade now pressed against my throat.

I can't see my attacker, but he calls to the others in the same garbled, voice-altered tone of those in gas masks. "It's alright! I've got her!"

Chapter 57

Faith

"Listen, kid," the garbled voice says in my ear. The cold metal blade grazes the skin on my neck. I scarcely breathe, trying not to envision the sharp edge slicing my fragile blood vessels. "If you hope to live, you have to cooperate. Do exactly as I say. Understood?"

The guard drags me, heels scraping the tile, into a nearby exam room. Once I'm over the threshold, he shoves me forward, further into the room. I catch myself on the padded exam chair. Behind me, I hear the heavy door latch shut. Pushing myself back to my feet, I scramble to face my attacker.

A black gas mask covers his face, and he's dressed in the standard, bulky coveralls of the guards. On his feet is a pair of heavy-duty work boots, and in his hand is the gleaming knife, raised and pointing straight towards me. Instinctively, I step back, running into the chair.

As I study the knife, it strikes me: it looks familiar. Black handle, brown leather grip—

"Like my knife?" the guard chuckles. The voice modifier cracks, creating an eerie sound. "Got it off your friend. The one with the cabin. That boy led us right to her."

I feel the blood drain from my face. If that's Bryn's knife... what happened to her? The guard reaches for a lab coat hanging near the door as I process my situation. If they trailed Micah...and did something to Bryn...no one knows

I'm here. No one is coming to save me.

A deep fear sets in. It's all I can do not to break down in tears, overcome with sudden, crushing despair. The guard lowers the knife, just for an instant, to pull on the white coat. My eyes lock onto the door handle, and I lunge towards it.

Swiftly, he blocks my path, brandishing the knife. A white-hot rage fills me, and I throw myself towards him. "What did you do to Bryn!?" I scream. He catches my wrist and kicks me off-balance. I throw my hands up to shield my face, grasping wildly.

The next thing I know, I'm on my back in the examination chair. Both of my hands are bracing his right arm, preventing the knife from being lowered. Or trying to, at least. The guard leans down, his face mere inches from mine.

"Don't fight with me, Addy."

My heart pounds in my chest, my thoughts clouded by the impending fear of death or experimentation. It takes a moment for my eyes to focus. A small section of the lab coat sleeve is pushed back, revealing a dark ink drawing of... flowers? *Digitalis purpurea*: foxglove.

I raise my eyes to meet those behind the mask. Dark brown, familiar eyes. Rather than a threatening stranger beneath those many layers, my brain fills in with Bryn's face and form. My eyes widen with the realization. This person standing in front of me...it's her.

A million questions come to mind, but I can't ask any of them right now. Right now, all I have is a choice.

After a moment of deliberation, I stop resisting. I release my grip on her arm and let my hands fall to my sides.

"Good," she says curtly. She withdraws the knife and tugs her sleeve down. "Give me your phone."

I hesitate, so she reaches towards my pocket.

"*Now.*"

I quickly dig it out and hand it over. She glances at it briefly before pocketing the device.

"And your bag."

I wriggle out of the straps and let her pull it away from me.

"Now sit still and follow my instructions. No more running, or you might not live to see tomorrow."

I lie flat against the chair. She turns towards the cabinets lining the side of the room with my belongings in hand. Without looking back, she chucks a hospital gown and a pair of sweatpants in my direction.

"Put these on."

I stare at the flimsy blue fabric in my hands. The *last* thing I want to do right now is exchange my own clothes for these. Bryn is already in possession of my CGM readings, my insulin, my low supplies…literally everything keeping me alive. If the drugs don't kill me, the diabetes will.

I exhale, trying to keep myself from panicking. She knows what she's doing. She's on my side…though…I look back at her, frustrated by the situation. Why would she stop me from escaping? I was so close! It's thanks to her that I'm still here. Trapped inside this stupid drug lab, walking a tightrope between life and death.

The silhouettes of more people appear outside, approaching the door. Bryn rifles through my bag and the cabinets above, seemingly paying no attention. I remove my jacket, then free my arms from my shirtsleeves and slide them into the hospital gown. Sufficiently covered, I pull my shirt over my head and snap the gown shut. I finish changing my pants just as the group of people burst through the door.

At the front are two burly guards. They barge in and aim two large guns at my head. Stiff with fear, I press myself further into the exam chair, hoping I can somehow melt through the floor and escape.

"We have orders to kill if she resists," one announces.

"And does it look like she's resisting?" Bryn says from her corner.

"She just tried to run!" the other guard argues.

"Well she's not running now, is she?" She rises and calmly walks over, placing herself between me and them. "Just because you couldn't control her doesn't mean she won't work for the purposes of our tests. As you can see, I have no problems with her."

The guards mutter, clearly flustered at the insult.

"How am I supposed to do my job if we keep killing all the subjects?" Bryn continues, her voice hardening.

Reluctantly, the guards lower their weapons and stand aside. From behind them, a crowd of people in lab coats and surgical masks filter into the room. Bryn returns to the cabinet as the lab coats swarm me. I glance back at her, wondering if she's paying attention. Hoping she knows what's happening to me.

Anxiously, I comply as they position me. They recline the exam chair until I'm staring up at the bright light in the ceiling, and they start to attach electrodes and other monitors to my skin. No wonder a person would think they were experimented on by aliens.

Someone sticks a needle in my right arm and draws blood. Another swabs my mouth.

"Is there any chance you could be pregnant?" one of them asks.

"Uh, no."

"Good," she says, swiping her pen across her clipboard. "A potential side effect of our formula is near-instant miscarriage." She shakes her head. "Trust me, it's not a pretty picture."

For an instant, Bryn glances in our direction. Quickly, however, she returns her attention to the cabinets.

My stomach churns.

Finally, after an excessive amount of invasive sampling, they remove the wires and medical instruments and back away.

"All set," one of the lab coats says. There's a flash of a smirk in his eyes. "The doctor will see you now." He turns to Bryn. "She's prepped for administration of Test Formula 200-3."

Out of my periphery, I see Bryn nod and set something on a tray. With that, the lab workers stream out the door, leaving us alone.

Bryn approaches me. She wheels over a small tray of shiny instruments. In the glaring light and the surreal setting, I start to second-guess myself. Did I really see that tattoo? Is she really who I think she is? Did I actually just give my stuff to one of the lab workers? Her face is obscured behind the gas mask, and my brain starts to substitute other details, faces, and images which could be beneath.

Anxiety rises in my chest, and I start to panic. Almost unconsciously, I go to sit up.

She catches my shoulder. "Easy," she says through the voice modifier, lightly pushing me back against the chair. "Just relax."

I try to hold myself still, watching as she lifts a pair of exam gloves and tugs them on. For another brief moment, she slides her sleeve down, revealing the same tattoo. With her identity confirmed, I try to follow her advice.

She tears open an alcohol wipe and holds out an open hand. "Give me your arm."

I swallow, then shakily stretch my arm out, palm side up. She grasps it and cleans a section with the alcohol. As it dries, she places a needle and syringe into a vial and tips it over, drawing in some type of liquid. Her hand masks the label. I stare at the clear substance filling the syringe, wondering what it could be. The lab coats said it was the drug. But Bryn wouldn't actually give me some dangerous, experimental, illegal substance...right?

As she lowers the needle, fear seizes my heart. Even if it is Bryn, what if I'm wrong about her? I remind myself of a single phrase. A belief I am quite literally betting my life on. *She wouldn't hurt me. She wouldn't hurt me. She wouldn't hurt me.*

The needle breaks my skin, and she presses the plunger down.

My eyes follow her hand as she lifts the syringe away. As she does so, she glances up at the ceiling, and only now do I notice the cameras lining all four corners of the room.

"Test Formula 200-3 administered successfully."

Chapter 58

The Ghost of Flickerwood

We sit in tense silence for a few moments before I work up the courage to ask, "W-what now?"

"Now," she replies, raising the exam chair so I can return to a sitting position, "we wait for the drug to take effect."

I can't help but become hyperaware of how I feel physically. I wonder what's coursing through my veins. Will I actually start to feel different? Is my heart beating abnormally? Is it getting harder to breathe? Or is it all in my head? Is that my cue to start acting like I'm drugged up? If so, I don't even know how to act. I lay my head against the chair and stare at the wall.

When I was a kid, my parents took me to the county fair to watch a hypnosis show. I remember being afraid to volunteer because I was scared the hypnosis wouldn't work on me. If it didn't, I'd be stuck on stage in front of a crowd, forced to either try and convincingly fake being hypnotized or reveal that the trick didn't work and ruin the show for everyone. Needless to say, I didn't volunteer that day, but this is what I imagine it would have felt like.

The door swings open again, and the workers in lab coats return.

"Prepped for transfer to the OR?" one asks.

"All set," Bryn replies.

At the word, I lift my head up and strain to see her. *OR*?!

I remember the bright surgical light and the doctors surrounding a metal table. They're gonna cut me open?!

Bryn grabs something from the counter, and I see a flash of dark cloth before it's over my head. She clamps a hand on my shoulder as my vision turns to black. I can't see a thing through the bag.

"You walk where I tell you. Step out of line and things will not end well," Bryn says through the mechanical voice.

She pushes me out of the chair, and I find my balance on my feet. Someone else grabs my hands and ties them behind my back. Bryn nudges me forward, but my feet feel like they're made of concrete.

I feel sick thinking of the OR, and of surgery. What are they going to do to me? Implant me with drugs or some other kind of experiment? Will they put me to sleep? Or will I be awake for some horrible trauma?

"*Walk*," she repeats with urgency.

I obey. Though I'm terrified, I let her steer me down the hall. At first, my steps are small, a natural reaction to a lack of vision.

"Faster," she says. "Don't worry. I won't let you fall."

I take bigger steps, forcing myself to walk normally. *I can trust her. I can trust her.*

I hear the sound of another door opening, and I can tell we've entered a room. Bryn suddenly turns me to the side and pushes me down. I collapse, for a brief moment feeling a surge of panic as I believe I'm free-falling, before landing safely in a chair. Bryn snatches the hood off my head, removes the tie from my hands, then swiftly marches to the door.

Confused, I find myself in a familiar-looking white room, facing a large mirror. This doesn't look like an operating room. It looks just like the room the woman was in, where all the scientists were watching her...At once, it clicks. OR stands for *observation* room. I exhale in relief. At least I'm safe from surgery for now.

My relief is short-lived, however, as reality settles in. This is where they expect to see a reaction. Am I having one? Is this fuzzy feeling in my head a result of mental dissociation, or is it from that syringe? Is the pounding of my heart from a substance, or from my own internal chemicals?

The fear and the adrenaline.

I look around, wondering if it's the same exact room I saw earlier. Did...did someone just die in here a short while ago?

As minutes go by, I start to sweat. What were the symptoms and effects? What can I go off of to try and fake it? As I'm thinking, several bright red lights suddenly begin flashing near the top of the room.

The door flies open, and Bryn charges inside. Her disguise is so thorough that it takes me a few seconds to be sure it's her.

"Up!" she says, motioning for me to get out of the chair. Startled, I rise. She practically drags me by the arm towards the door.

We don't get far before another guard fills the doorway. "Where are you going?!" he demands, stepping towards us. He motions at me. "Don't you remember? She's a protocol six. Knows too much. Shoot on sight."

Bryn stops short. Slowly, she releases my arm and steps away from me, which feels like I'm being abandoned to execution. Swiftly, the guard draws a gun from his hip and points it in my direction. I flinch back, bracing for the pain of a real bullet. Or maybe there won't be pain. Maybe I'll be gone before I know what hit me. My mind races as I stare down the pitch black barrel...

Quick as a blur, Bryn grabs the gun and forces it off course. Her foot connects with his midsection, and the air whooshes from his lungs as he folds over. His grip on the weapon loosens, and she wrenches it from his hands. Without hesitation, she reels back and whacks him in the head with the butt of the gun.

Multiple times.

He staggers before falling to the ground unconscious.

Bryn pops the clip out of the gun, empties the chamber, and slides it to the far corner of the room. She rips the gas mask off, then turns back towards me.

I desperately try to catch my breath as my heart pounds against my ribcage. My body is trembling from fear, yet I feel frozen in place, unable to will myself to move.

Bryn sets her hands on my arms. My eyes focus on hers,

anchoring me to reality.

"Hey. You're doing great, Addy," she says with a nod of encouragement. Reassurance washes over me as I finally see her full face and hear her real voice. My breathing starts to even out.

"I...wha..." I start to sputter.

She squeezes my arms, shaking me slightly. "I'll explain, but we need to move *now*. Stay close."

I stay on her heels as we rush into the hall, which is rapidly filling with people. We race ahead of them. I'm thankful Bryn seems to know where she's going, because all of the blinding hallways look the same to me. "Basically, there's good news and bad news. Good news, police have come to help us." Suddenly, Bryn nudges me to the left, and we go through a metal door into the large laboratory. "Bad news, these guys know they're surrounded, and it just triggered their evacuation protocol."

She darts between lab tables and equipment, heading for a door on the other side of the room. "Most of their prisoners will be taken through the tunnels, but you—" Bryn screeches to a halt and yanks us both backwards. A group of guards step through the doorway, and a broad-shouldered man finishes her sentence.

"—are too risky to be kept alive."

We turn and book it back the way we came. Unfortunately, another set of guards enters from that side, blocking our path. We're forced to retreat into the center of the room.

"I don't like being herded," Bryn remarks.

"Nowhere to run," the guard in front of us says.

She tenses. "Get down," she says to me through gritted teeth.

"What?" the guard asks, as if she were talking to him. Bryn's hand flies to the flashlight on her coveralls, and she shines the strobe directly in his eyes. I drop to the ground and crouch under a lab table.

He squints and looks away for a second, blinking. It gives her enough time to grab two chemical spray cans off a nearby counter. As the guards rush her, she presses the nozzles and aims for their eyes. They immediately double over, clutching at their faces.

From my hiding spot, an internal debate rages inside my

head. A part of me is happy to let Bryn take care of things ...but another part of me feels like a victim. Is this who I want to be? The one cowering under a table? Some of the guards who got sprayed are already squaring up to attack her again. Others lock onto me and start heading my way.

I look to my left and notice a fire extinguisher strapped to the table. Quickly, I yank it from its holder. A guard reaches towards me. I pull my feet in close and whack him in the head with the metal canister. He curses and flinches away, but two more guards zero in. I pull the pin, aim, and shoot.

White foam bubbles out of the nozzle and hits them in the face, repelling them. The white starts to fill the room. I jump up, not content to stay on the floor.

Just as we seem to be gaining ground, a figure emerges in the doorway.

"Alright, alright, that's enough!" Walter yells. He steps over the threshold, and I see a towering, muscular guard beside him. "We're on a schedule, here."

Bryn turns her head in his direction. He breaks into a smile and holds up a hand, signaling for the guards to stand down. "My, oh my. Bryn Sayer. Never thought I'd see you here."

"Leighton," she corrects swiftly. "Don't call me that."

"Ah," he nods. "I can respect that. I have mixed feelings about the Sayer family myself, as I'm sure you can relate."

"Because your father disowned you?" she probes.

"In no uncertain terms, yes," he replies bitterly.

"Why?" she asks.

I don't expect him to answer her, but he surprises me.

"Truth be told, my brother and I have always had a... complicated relationship. He was the perfect son—straight As, boy scout, class president, so on and so forth. And I was the embarrassment. The trouble-maker. The delinquent.

"I 'disappeared' because my parents sent me to some youth camp in New Mexico and tried very hard to make everyone forget they ever had a second son. Trust me, I know the feeling of being cut out of the family." His voice seethes with animosity as the white cloud of extinguisher foam swirls around him.

Quickly, his expression returns to normal. He shrugs.

"But I suppose things worked out in the end. What I saw as my greatest curse became my greatest strength. Thanks to my father's rejection, I gained anonymity. A non-existence. True freedom. I'm a ghost." He spreads his arms wide, and a smile forms on his face. "Warren and I work together in our own way. He talks smooth and puts on a good show, like always, and I make the gears turn. It's a well-oiled machine."

"Save for the fact that you're about to be arrested," Bryn adds.

He waves a hand, dismissing her comment. "You know, it's unfortunate we're meeting under such circumstances. I've always had a soft spot for you and your mother, considering your situation. If you ask me, Warren went too far with what he did..." he stops short, then clicks his tongue.

"In any case, you're here now. And I hear you're rather clever yourself. Degree in toxicology, experience with labora-tory work. I was always good at chemistry, too, as you may have guessed." He gestures to the room we're standing in. "Who knows? Maybe we could have gotten along." He tilts his head to the side. "Maybe we still could."

"No," Bryn says immediately. "Don't waste your breath. We are not the same." She glances at the various doorways, all blocked by guards. "Cut to the chase. If you really have such a soft spot for your grand niece, then tell me. Are you going to let us go?"

His expression darkens. "Barring a change of heart, then — regrettably — no."

He raises a hand from behind his back, revealing a small syringe. I don't need to ask to know what's in it. "A fitting end for someone who's spent so much time studying poisons, don't you think?"

With his other hand, he signals to the guards. As if someone just unpaused a video, they all come to life and descend upon Bryn. In a split second, her knife is drawn. Rapidly, she strikes the closest one in the face with the handle, then catches another in the ribs with her foot. She pulls her elbow back, hitting the chest of the man behind her, and throws a punch straight ahead.

The man in front of her blocks her first swing, but she follows up with the knife. Decisively, she slashes his arm and cuts a line on his cheek. Bright red oozes from the wounds. It's the first time I've seen her draw blood.

She kicks him back, momentarily clearing a circle around herself. "Here's your warning!" she shouts, bringing her boot down. "Attack me again and I'll have to hurt you."

He wipes the blood from his face, then starts to laugh. "You're cute, stomping around. I'll admit, you're quick, but you hit like a girl. Face it, this is the end of the line." He starts towards her, flanked by the other guards.

She takes a step back. "Look, we both have places to be. You've gotta get out of here before the police flood in. Be smart, and walk away."

"Or what?"

"Or I'll dislocate your shoulder and fracture your arm. You'll be out of commission for weeks, and it might never heal the same." Her face is stone serious.

He shakes his head. "You're bluffing. If you could do that, you would have already. You don't have it in you. By nature, you're too nice. Too merciful."

Bryn's eyes harden. "Don't bet on it. You clearly don't know me at all."

Stupidly, he springs towards her. As promised, she grabs his arm and forces him towards the ground. Using the edge of a lab table for added leverage, she kicks him down. There's a sickening pop as his shoulder rotates too freely, followed by a crack as his arm slams on the table. He moans in agony.

"Mercy is not the instinct that comes naturally."

Releasing his arm, she turns to face the others, who suddenly seem less eager to attack. The few that do receive the same ruthless treatment. I cringe.

"So you can toss them around," the large guard beside Walter says, stepping forward. My hair stands on end.

It's soon apparent that he has more training than the others. He easily blocks Bryn's strikes and lands a punch to her stomach. She's pushed backwards. He advances and hits her again. And a third time. He shoves her against the wall, and she winces in pain. Walter strides up beside them with the needle.

When I realize what's happening, I rush forward. Sayer rapidly closes the distance between himself and Bryn, faster than I could ever reach him. I can only watch as the shiny, silver tip of the needle—such a small thing, really—pokes through the surface of her skin. It's so fast, so quiet, so unceremonious, that I second-guess whether it really happened. I skid to a halt. Walter backs away with the empty syringe, its poison contents now transferred to their target.

Immediately, the large guard drops Bryn and snatches at me. I backpedal, but he catches me by the neck.

"I got 'em from here," he says confidently. Walter nods and tells the others they can leave. I claw at the hand around my throat, struggling to take in air as I watch Walter disappear out the door.

My eyes start to water, distorting the image of Bryn's crumpled form on the ground. I try to kick or scratch at his face, but my arms are too short. The fire extinguisher drops from my hand. I intentionally go limp, but he doesn't release me. The edges of my vision start to go black.

Chapter 59

One Shot

"Stop!" a voice calls from across the room.

The guard growls, still squeezing my throat. When he doesn't respond, a glass beaker flies through the air and nails him in the head. Glass shards scatter across the floor. He flinches and whips around, angry.

Bryn is on her feet, knife drawn. She crosses the room with the blade raised. Seeing the knife coming at him, the guard is forced to release me.

I fall to the ground, gasping for air. Standing over me, the two of them become locked in a rapid exchange of blows. For every punch thrown, the other blocks, deflects, or dodges. I try to think of how to help, but I don't think I can even get close. They're moving too fast. I grit my teeth, knowing that one slip up could make the difference.

Bryn suddenly breaks through his defenses and delivers a slash to his thigh, slicing right through the coverall uniform. He soon retaliates, once more pinning her against the wall. With a swift hit to her hand, her knife goes skidding across the floor.

My heart sinks. His eyes follow the knife, and a victorious smile creeps over his face.

"Now what?" he taunts. "You've got no weapon, no chance—"

When his gaze returns to her, however, his face falls.

Without missing a beat, she pulls a handgun from somewhere in her many layers of clothing.

Bang!

The guard collapses to the ground holding his knee. Through gritted teeth he curses at her. "Bitch!"

With shoulders back and smoking gun in hand, she walks away from him and mutters under her breath, "I've been called worse."

As she approaches me, I spring to my feet. The closer she gets, the more apparent it becomes that she is not well. Her face is taut and pale, and she starts to cough.

"Addy," she says, forcing shallow breaths from her lungs.

The joy of victory is quickly overshadowed by a sinking fear. She may have won the fight, but she's still been poisoned. If something isn't done soon...

She fumbles with her pockets and pulls out a small glass vial of vitamin B12. Gasping, she searches for a syringe, but finds only a package of broken glass; it's been shattered.

She tosses the useless pieces to the ground, the loose shards rattling as they hit the tile floor. Quickly, she grabs my arm and pulls me into the hall, though I'm supporting her more than she is me.

A place that was buzzing with people just a few minutes ago is now completely deserted. She opens the door to the nearest exam room and starts going through the drawers. Her hand stops on a packaged needle and syringe. With the instrument in hand, she sits down on the exam chair and tears open the plastic. She tries to draw the antidote from the glass vial, but her hands are shaking.

After a moment, it seems to dawn on her. She looks up at me.

"Addy," she says in a hoarse voice. "I can't do it. You have to."

My mouth drops open in disbelief. I panic. "What? No, no, I can't—"

She locks eyes with me. "Yes, you can. I'll tell you exactly what to do."

She holds out the vial and the syringe, which I take from her. She points to the syringe.

"Draw 5 mL of air, then puncture the bottle and press the stopper down."

I do as she says. Once, there was a week my health insurance was stupid and the pharmacy gave me vials of insulin instead of pens. I try to remember that week.

I push the air into the bottle and draw out a little over a 5 mL dose. I tap the glass and watch a small air bubble rise to the top, then shoot a little liquid out of the needle to get rid of it, evening out the measurement.

"Okay."

Bryn removes half her jacket and rolls up a sleeve, her complexion growing even more sickly. "You have to hit a vein," she chokes out.

I freeze. "B-but, I've never done that before, that's not—"

She cuts me off. "That's okay. You can do it. I believe in you."

"W-what if I can't?"

"You have to."

The question of what will happen if I don't catches on my tongue. I know the answer. If I don't, Bryn will die. And quickly.

She points at a band of rubber in the drawer with the syringes. "Tie it around my arm. It'll help," she croaks.

I grab the tourniquet and tie it tightly just above her elbow, like they do when I get blood drawn. She tightens her fist and points to a blue line in the crook of her arm.

Stalling, I grab an alcohol wipe and clean the spot. I feel my stomach lurch. Veins and blood vessels still make me queasy…but I have no choice. I have to try.

Bryn's shaking becomes worse, and her breathing all but stops. I force myself to stay calm as I hover over her skin with the needle. One shot.

I'm suddenly hit with a memory of the first time I brought a glucose meter home. I remember sitting at the kitchen table, hovering over my finger with the lancing device, unable to press the button. Like some invisible force wouldn't let me harm myself, even for only a drop of blood. And I remember screwing the needle on my insulin pen the first time, hesitating before putting the tip to my skin.

I look down at Bryn's arm. I did those things because I had to, or I would die. And I will do this thing because I have to, or she will die.

I tap the blue vein with my finger, then gently ease the needle under the skin. I inject the liquid, then remove the syringe. A spot of blood appears where I punctured her arm. I tell myself that's a good sign.

For a few long seconds, Bryn only seems to get worse. Her eyelids droop as she floats out of consciousness. Without thinking, I set the needle aside and grasp her hand, tears streaming down my face.

God, please. Don't let this be the end.

I try to reassure myself that everything will be okay. She got the antidote, it's just a matter of time. She's not dying.

But I still can't help but think like she is. Trying to prepare myself for the worst, I guess. How will I be able to walk out of here and go back to living my normal life if I watch her die after saving me? She's only here because she came to my rescue. *Oh.* I rest my forehead on my hand.

It's hard to believe it's only been two months since the semester started. I try not to run through a dying montage of memories in my head, but it's hard not to. My mind scrambles to answer how I got from day one of class with Professor Leighton to now, standing over Bryn's limp body...

Slowly, her eyes open. Breath returns to her lungs, and relief washes over me. I must have done something right. She sits straight up in the chair, sucking in air.

I grin from ear to ear. "You're alive!"

She blinks at me and gazes around the room. As her breathing returns to normal, she smiles.

The victory is short-lived, however, as the red lights that have been flashing continuously thus far now turn to a steady orange glow. A pre-recorded voice echoes through the nearly empty facility.

"Warning. Detonation in five minutes."

Chapter 60

Out With a Bang

Moving swiftly for someone who almost died, Bryn springs to her feet. She pulls her chunky flip phone from her pocket and dials a number, then talks while speed-walking down the hallway, occasionally gripping the wall for balance.

"Officer Hopewell, get everyone away from the building. They know you're here, they've already evacuated. The place is set to blow. Based on a rough prediction of the size of the blast, I'd say nothing in a 600 foot radius is safe."

"Are you still inside?!" comes the muffled reply.

"Not for long. Exiting east door. Expect an injured person."

"How long do we have?"

"Less than five minutes."

She shoulders open the door to the large central laboratory and hangs up. "Quickest way out is through there," she says, gesturing to a door on the opposite side.

A trail of blood is smeared across the floor, evidence of the guard dragging himself towards the exit. Afraid of what we'll find, I round the lab tables after her. He's at the base of the door, trying to pull it open.

Bryn snatches her knife off the ground and walks towards him. At the sight of her, he shrinks back. She readies the blade, but instead of attacking, she slashes a strip of cloth from her lab coat.

"You wanna make it out of this alive? Hold still."

Kneeling beside him, she slides the cloth under his leg, then ties the ends together. He groans as she tightens the knot.

"I don't need your help," he spits, but doesn't fight back.

"Addy, door," she orders. Quickly, I grab the handle and swing it open. Bryn crouches, grabs him under the arms, and drags him over the threshold. She nods down the hall to a door with a glowing exit sign.

"Third door on the left," she says while looking at me. "Go."

Having grown used to complying with her requests, I step towards the door without thinking. A few strides in, however, I realize how much slower Bryn is moving while dragging the guard. I look to the door, then back to her.

"You said 600 feet?" I ask nervously. "Five minutes?"

"Yes. Go."

I stop, stuck in indecision. I could admit that I have less survival instincts, fewer fighting skills, less strength, and less experience than Bryn. Admit that I'm only kidding myself if I think I could come close to her level of competence in an emergency. Admit that I'm a civilian, and the best thing for me to do is be humble and let her be the hero. Go and save myself.

Or. Another voice in my mind argues. I could have humility *and* bravery. Not sell myself short and not let someone die just because I was having self-esteem issues. Can I really, in good conscience, walk out of here and let them potentially perish? Bryn could leave if she wanted, but she's choosing to save a man who would not have hesitated to kill her just a few minutes ago. Am I not willing to risk my life for the person who *saved* mine?

I stand up straight and jog back towards her. "I'm not leaving you behind. How can I help?"

"That really what you want?" she asks through gritted teeth.

"Yes."

She pauses, then nods. "Alright, Warner, get over here!" she shouts. I hurry to her side. "Hand on shoulder, hand on wrist!" She shows me how to position myself, and together we sling the guard's arms over our shoulders, one on each side. "Now move! Move! Move!"

He's heavier than I expect, but I let the adrenaline fuel my muscles.

393

"Step, step, step, good!"

We cover ground faster and burst out the door. The sky is dark, but we're met with bright floodlights. A small group of men in tactical uniforms rush forward to help. They've cut a hole in the chain-link fence, and they load us onto a UTV.

Desperately, I grip the handles on the seat as we take off into the woods. I squeeze my eyes shut, bracing for the explosion or for us to crash into a tree.

Seconds go by, and the building remains unchanged. Just as I start to wonder if nothing will happen—

BOOM!

A great cloud of fire bursts forth from the lab, engulfing the whole thing in flames. I feel the heat on my face, and the brightness forces me to squint my eyes. As the tongues of flame recede, dark black smoke pours into the air, swirling above the trees.

Beside me, Bryn pulls a pen from her pocket and starts winding the cloth tourniquet around it. She then twists the pen to tighten the band.

"Are you crazy?!" the guard shouts. "You're gonna take my leg off!"

"Trust me, your leg will be fine!" she shouts back at him. "And believe me, if it isn't, it's not from the tourniquet. You're in far more danger of bleeding to death."

He lies back in defeat.

The trees grow thinner until we finally emerge out of the forest and drive onto the asphalt of a Wynhurst campus parking lot. The rectangular lot is dotted with haphazardly parked cop cars and other emergency vehicles. In the distance, the wail of fire engine sirens can be heard, gradually growing louder as they approach the scene. The UTV screeches to a halt next to an open ambulance. Paramedics rush to the guard, and Bryn hands him off.

"Close range gunshot wound just above the right knee, 9 mm Glock round, anterior entry wound, posterior exit wound," she spouts as they load him into the back. Before any questions can be raised about why she has so much information, she sets off towards a couple of officers in the center of the chaos. I follow close behind.

394

As we get closer, I recognize one as Officer Hopewell. The other wears something I've only seen in movies: a dark blue jacket with the letters FBI printed on the front. I gather from his demeanor that he is in some position of authority, which is further confirmed when he starts to speak. His badge reads *Special Agent Johnson.*

He steps forward and confronts Bryn. "Okay, Ms. Leighton, have you finally decided to explain what the heck is going on here?! You phone us out of the blue, tell us to show up at your house where we find two internationally wanted criminals tied up on the front lawn and some poor shell-shocked kid huddled inside. Meanwhile, you run off with no preparation, no plan, and no backup, against our wishes, to infiltrate a high-profile drug lab which—by the way—I'm only just now hearing about. You drag us all the way out here to be your escape chariot in a plan we never agreed to and then, not half an hour later, we receive another phone call telling us we're all in danger of being blown to bits!"

He points towards the UTV we were on. "Now you had better send a massive bouquet of flowers to every one of those guys who chose to stick their neck out for you and stay behind. Those are good men we could have lost because of you." He shakes his head. "It's starting to feel like you're the one calling the shots here, and I'm telling you that's not how this is going to work. You're going to have to answer some questions, starting with what on earth inspired the bout of insanity that made you go in there alone?!"

I feel my own face grow hot with embarrassment; I've never handled confrontation well.

Bryn's face remains steady. She is quiet for a moment. With a small movement she nods towards me. "I took a risk, sir. I believed Addy's life was in imminent danger, and it was the best course of action I could think of."

His eyes fall on me. I suddenly become self-conscious of my thin hospital gown top. I cross my arms in front of my chest, somehow hoping to hide myself behind them. Agent Johnson opens his mouth as if to say something, but stops himself.

Bryn continues. "Unfortunately, once they spotted your forces, they began evacuating staff and prisoners through underground tunnels, and my cover was blown. I didn't know about the bombs until later, when the warning alarm went off—I didn't intend to risk anyone's life purely for my sake."

For the first time, Officer Hopewell speaks up. "We would have stormed the building if it weren't for the hostages. When they saw us, they started sending threats, saying they would kill the prisoners."

Bryn nods.

"So they escaped through tunnels? Where are they now?" he goes on.

"That I don't have an answer to, sir. But I would love to assist you in any way I can. I do have military experience in recovering missing persons."

Agent Johnson sets his jaw and stares her down, clearly still annoyed, but the anger is gone from his eyes. He pulls out his radio and presses the button to speak.

"...suspects are on the move. Likely armed and dangerous, and are holding hostages. Witness says they escaped through a tunnel system. I want our perimeter widened and bolstered...bring in K-9 units to canvas the area...keep on the lookout for any tunnel entryways or egress points."

Bryn pats down her laboratory uniform and pulls off the gas mask hanging loose around her neck. Agent Johnson finishes his announcement and releases the button on his radio. She holds the mask out towards him, pointing to some wires. "Not sure if they've turned it off, but this headset is dialed into their communication system. Could be of use."

He nods and waves another FBI agent over. She takes the radio headset and goes off to study it.

"Now, Ms. Leighton," he says. "I need you to let me do my job. We'll do the investigating. We'll find them." He pauses, and I expect that to be the end of the story. Go home. Let the police be police. Lock your doors and stay out of the way. But he goes on. "However, I'm also not stupid enough to turn down help from someone who could provide useful information. Do you have any other tips that could lead us to their location?"

Though he's not talking directly to me, I feel like I have something to contribute. "There's an entrance to the tunnels in the basement of the music building. That's how I ended up

396

in the lab; I followed Micah and Robert Boyer through an underground passage. The path branched off in other directions, too. They could lead anywhere."

He speaks into his radio. "Have fire department clear it, then investigate tunnel beneath the music building. Witness states it branches off. Identity of one suspect is Robert Boyer."

Bryn nods towards me, looking slightly impressed. "Good detail."

Any nerves I had about speaking up melt away with assurance that I said something right.

She continues, "Based on what I saw in that laboratory, this has been a large, ongoing drug trafficking operation. They must have a network of importing and exporting routes, and the tunnels may very well be a large part of that. If we look at the history of disappearances and crime in Flickerwood, it may give us an idea of how they operate and where they are."

Agent Johnson nods in agreement.

"And I have good news," she adds, "I know someone who has done much of the research for us already."

"Oh?"

She turns to me and pulls my phone from her pocket. Stretching it towards me, she gives a simple command. "Call Anthony."

With Bryn, a police officer, and an FBI agent watching me, I find his number in my contacts and press call. It rings twice before Anthony picks up.

"Addy?!" he says.

"Hey...um, are you on campus?"

"Where did you go?! We turned around and you were gone. Now there are all these police and stuff outside. I can see them from my window—"

"Yeah, I'm fine, I can explain later. You're in your dorm, then?"

"Yeah," he answers. "Why?"

"Good! Uh..." My brain falters as I look at the two men standing over me. "Some people want to talk with you..."

Bryn holds out an open palm, offering me an out. I gladly hand her the phone. She points towards the senior residence halls. "We'll follow you." I start forward, leading the small group towards his room.

Bryn puts the phone to her ear as we walk. "Hi Anthony, this is Professor Leighton. You're not in any trouble, but Addy and I are heading over to your dorm now with some officers. We need to take a look at that map you have of the disappearances in Flickerwood, along with any other information you have about illegal drug activity or murders occurring locally. I think you can help us track down some suspects."

As we cross the parking lot, I notice that a rather large crowd of spectating college students has gathered on the edge of the action. They part to let us pass through.

By the time we reach the building, Anthony is already in the lobby ready to let us in. He takes us up to his room, anxiously chattering about how it's not usually so messy...

I remember what it looked like when he had it nicely decorated for the historical society meeting. This time, however, it looks completely different. The small living area has been overtaken by books, posters, and newspapers, dealing with everything from Area 51 to regional folklore and local history.

He spreads his hands. "I promise I'm not crazy," he says emphatically, squeezing his eyes shut for added emphasis. "I just got a bit...carried away."

If they make a judgement about it, neither of the men let on.

"One second, I'll just grab the map for you..."

He ducks into the bedroom and returns with the document. He rolls it out on a small table near the kitchenette, and we all stand around it.

"I'm in the historical society at Wynhurst—well, this year I'm the president—and I had a friend who disappeared in these woods for a few days. They found him, but he was never quite the same, and then I learned there were other disappearances in Flickerwood, and I thought they might be connected, so..." he nervously over-explains.

Officer Hopewell holds up a hand. "No need to be nervous, son. You've got good instincts."

Anthony exhales and falls silent.

Agent Johnson taps each location. "Train station, woods, park, apartments..." he turns to Officer Hopewell. "Any input about your town?"

Hopewell points to the southern part of the map, where many of the red dots marking untimely deaths are clustered. "This coincides with where a lot of our overdose and illegal substance calls come from. Looks like Leighton may be right about there being a concentrated area of operations."

Johnson nods. "Yes, but this thing is bigger than Flicker-wood. They haven't just been trading locally; they've been shipping stuff out. Now, they could be stuffing logs and floating 'em down the river, but based on the hot spots we have here, I'd say the two most likely transportation methods are either by truck or—"

"The train," Bryn finishes.

Agent Johnson reaches for his radio. "Rodriguez, get me an exhaustive train schedule for Flickerwood Station. I want to know every commuter train, freight engine, or hand car that rides these tracks within the next twenty-four hours, understood?" He releases the button and reaches for the map. "Mind if I borrow this?" he asks Anthony, already in the process of rolling it up.

"No, sir. Take it as long as you need!"

Agent Johnson turns to leave, along with Officer Hopewell. He stops before reaching the door.

"And you two," he says, pointing towards me and Bryn. "Go home. Get some rest. It's late. You've had a big day." He tugs the door open. "But do call if you see or hear anything."

Chapter 61

Pit Stop

Johnson and Hopewell leave the door ajar as they exit, but I don't follow them immediately.

"What happened to you guys?" I ask Anthony. "Did you catch the mayor? Where's Sid?"

Sadly, he shakes his head. "No, unfortunately, we didn't catch the mayor. I still don't know how he got away. We were right behind him in the stairwell, then he rounded a corner and...boom. He was gone. Security was right there, too. By all accounts we should've got him, but it was like he up and disappeared.

"We told the police everything we saw. They're still looking for him, as far as I know. Not too much later, Sid got a call from Micah. He's in the hospital, apparently. She went to go visit him."

"Hospital?! What happened?"

"He'll be alright," Bryn chimes in.

We both turn to look at her.

She elaborates. "He came to my door when he was running from the guards dressed as aliens. Told me where you were and what had happened. But he had some sort of reaction to the gas they release from the suits. I gave him some anti-convulsant medication and he seemed alright after that, but I called an ambulance to be safe. Then I went to get you."

"Wait," Anthony says, confused. "Micah came to *you* for

help?" He turns from Bryn and looks to me. "And what happened to you?"

I tell him about following Micah into the tunnels, being taken into the lab, and narrowly escaping. He looks at me with wide eyes.

"What!? That's crazy! You were there? And almost got blown up?!" He shakes his head in disbelief. "So you're telling me that, not only has there been a secret drug lab violating all forms of scientific ethics operating on campus this whole time, but... Walter Sayer is running it?"

I nod. "Was, anyway. It's a pile of ashes now."

Eventually, there's a lull in the conversation, and I start to feel like it's an appropriate time to leave. Although, I also get the feeling the night isn't quite over. I turn to Bryn. "So...what now?"

"Now...I think I'm going to pay a visit to my uncle." She shrugs. "If Warren is still out there, maybe Michael knows something of his whereabouts. And if he doesn't, I have plenty to tell him."

I hesitate before working up the courage to ask. "Would—would you like company?"

She looks at me, then smiles. "You wanna come along?"

"Only if you don't mind."

"Not a bit." Her gaze turns to Anthony. "Before we go, I do have a favor to ask, however."

"From me?" he asks, pointing to himself.

"If it's not too much trouble. See, my car is parked at home in my driveway. Would you mind giving us a lift?"

Anthony makes a pit stop at my dorm so I can change out of the hospital gown and into some real clothes. I do so quickly, then dig out a purse I keep for special occasions. I fill it with the few things Bryn salvaged and a couple more snacks for good measure. My bag, water bottle, and most of my belongings were destroyed in the explosion, but I'm choosing not to think too hard about that right now.

I run back outside to Anthony's car and hop in the passenger seat. Bryn sits in the back, waiting patiently. Anthony puts the car in gear, and before long, we pull into the driveway of the cabin.

"Thank you," she says, popping the car door open. "I'm

401

going to run inside quick. If you can hang tight, I'll only be a minute."

We watch as she climbs the wooden steps to the porch and fumbles with the key. The door opens as she twists the handle, then she disappears inside.

Anthony stares at the darkened cabin. After a moment, he shivers. "I know now that there's nothing behind it, but this place still gives me the creeps. Is that stupid?"

I shake my head. "No, I don't think it's stupid. I mean, you lost your friend here."

"Yeah...I guess I did. Even after being found, he was never the same guy he was before he went missing."

The beams of his headlights illuminate the stump of the tree I chopped down. I'm not afraid of the cabin like Anthony. It doesn't make me uneasy. I have good memories here.

And yet, I can still relate. Maybe it's just the weight of knowing what happened here. The pain and struggle of isolation, mental illness, and self-inflicted violence. There's a bittersweet feeling attached to the house, the good and the bad mixed together, like the taste of cough syrup.

The door swings open and shut again. Bryn quickly locks it, then trots down the steps. Her dark gray overcoat blows behind her, and her leather doctor's bag is slung over her shoulder. She stops at Anthony's window and knocks. In response, he rolls it down.

"I'll follow you back to campus, just to make sure you get home safe. Don't want to make you paranoid, but you can't be too careful. You and your friends' testimonies will be crucial in a court case—unless you want to come with us, that is."

Anthony swallows. "No, no I'm good." He rolls up his window and looks at me. "You sure you want to be out running around?"

"I mean, there are so many cops out looking for these guys, it's not like they're about to commit another murder. They're just focused on trying to escape..." I say, trying to reassure him and myself in the process. I stop when I see the graveness in his expression. "Yes," I say simply. "Yes, I know it's not the safest. But who knows if staying inside is any safer? I'm sure I want to go."

"Just be careful, okay?"

"You too. Thanks for the ride." I reach for the handle.

"Addy, wait—can I pray for you?"

He places a hand on my head, and we both sit with our heads bowed. He prays for my safety and protection, along with Bryn. He prays for the police to be successful, and for justice to be done. Amen.

Chapter 62

In the Neighborhood

I get in the passenger seat next to Bryn as she turns the key. The engine roars to life, slowly warming the interior. Once we watch Anthony safely enter his dorm building, Bryn turns the fan down on the heater. The background noise quiets, and I feel still for the first time tonight.

For a few moments, there is a silence between us. Peaceful, yet not empty.

Bryn glances towards me from the driver's seat. "I'm surprised you're not jumping at the chance to ask for explanations, now that we're out of the lab."

I shrug, realizing how unimportant that information seems now. "I'm in no hurry. Figure you'll tell me when you want to. You usually do."

She smiles, shaking her head. "You must trust me."

I answer sincerely. "I do."

"Good thing. If you hadn't recognized me, or decided to fight me more—well, it was a risk, but I'm thankful things turned out the way they did."

I exhale. "Me too."

"But really," she continues. "There's nothing you want to know?"

I gaze out the window, envisioning the needle as it sank into my arm. Whatever was in that vial is still coursing through my veins. I shiver at the thought. Are there any side effects I should be expecting?

"What did you inject me with?"

"Nothing," she answers.

Confused, I press on. "Nothing? But you drew something into that needle; I saw —"

"No, no," she clarifies. "Yes, I did actually give you an injection. But it was nothing. Diluent. The stuff they dissolve other medication into. Mostly water."

"Oh," I say, the tightness in my chest loosening. I wasn't aware how anxious I'd been to hear the answer.

"What else?"

"Why'd you stop me from running out of the building? Why not just let me escape on my own?" My voice has more of an edge than I mean it to.

"Why'd I grab you away from that exit, you mean?"

My hand moves to my throat, remembering the blade pressed against it. "Yeah."

"It wasn't an exit. I took one of the alien uniforms and snuck in dressed as one. I found a staff room and saw posters detailing their procedures and the layout of the building— that's how I knew what to expect. They plant false exit doors among the real ones in case someone does try to escape.

"Like they said, you triggered their shoot on sight protocol. If you had opened that door, you would have walked into a hallway full of armed guards prepared to kill you."

I swallow, gaining a whole new perspective of that incident. Suddenly, my hand being yanked from the handle isn't sabotage, but saving.

My eyes travel to her side, where her knife is usually stowed. "Did you also take one of their guns?"

"No, I didn't."

I remember her getting rid of the one gun she did claim. "Then where'd you get the one you shot that guard with?"

"It's mine."

I struggle to come to terms with the answer I'd been suspecting. "But...what about the knife? I thought you didn't have a gun."

"What made you think that?" she replies simply.

I pause, my mouth half-open. I try to recall the conversation we had about her choice of weapon. She preferred the knife because it forces you to think twice before deciding to kill someone. But...I guess she never said she wouldn't use a gun.

The more I think about it, the more I feel foolish for my absent-minded assumption. She *was* in the Navy, after all. Of course she doesn't have a vendetta against firearms. You don't fight a war with only a dagger. "Have you been carrying that the whole time?!"

"Well, I suppose that depends on what you mean by 'the whole time.'"

I think back to the first day of class, then of meeting her in the laboratory. Back before I knew the truth about her, I thought the knife was the only thing I had to fear. Now, come to find out, that gun might have been on her person even then...I could press for a definitive answer, but it's not truly important. The weapons don't matter as much as the character of the person carrying them.

It dawns on me, perhaps for the first time, what it must mean to have been in the Navy. To have been to the places Bryn has been, to have seen combat. It's taken me a long time to understand the potential implications. My question comes as a near-whisper. "...Bryn, have you killed people?"

She exhales slowly, her eyes glazing over as if looking somewhere in the past. After a long pause, she gives a very small nod. "Yes. I have."

I nod in response, processing the answer.

"I've seen and done a lot of things," she adds quietly. "War is an ugly place. You do what you need to in order to survive, protect others, and accomplish the mission. I...I know that God doesn't total up your good deeds and weigh them against your bad. Salvation isn't based on the equation of good contributed minus damage done, but...I'd still like to believe I've preserved more lives than I've taken." She taps the steering wheel with her fingers. "After all this is over, I'll tell you anything you want to know about that time in my life, but I just want you to keep in mind—there's a lot of trauma and darkness in my past, but those things are far from the whole of my story."

I'm not sure what to say. Looking for a tension-breaking out, I check my blood sugar. 82.

I snack on a small bag of pretzels as Bryn drives into the

406

wealthy part of town. She pulls into a large driveway and puts the car into park. A neighboring dog starts to bark at our arrival.

We get out and walk to the door. As we do so, a few drops of rain splash down on my head, and the wind starts to pick up. Bryn rings the doorbell. Despite the glow of light from the living room window, it takes a few minutes for someone to come to the door. When it finally opens, we're greeted not by Michael, but Jodi.

At the sight of us, she jolts in surprise. "Bryn! And Addy. What brings you here so late?"

Bryn smiles pleasantly. "Had some urgent family matters to discuss. Mind if we come in?"

She stands aside, holding the door open for us. "Of course not. Please. Is everything alright?" We step into the house just as Michael puts the footrest down on his recliner.

"Jodi, who—" he stops as he sees Bryn.

"She says there's a family emergency, Mike," Jodi relays.

"Is it Elise?" he asks quickly.

"No, no," Bryn replies. "It's about your father."

Michael sighs, looking almost disappointed. "It really can't wait? We were just about to go to bed..."

"No, I don't think it can," Bryn says firmly. "I won't keep you forever, but we need to at least have a conversation."

Begrudgingly, Michael joins me, Bryn, and Jodi at the kitchen table.

"Have you seen or heard anything from Warren recently?" Bryn asks.

Michael's eyes drill into hers. "No more than usual," he answers. "Why?" Though having just sat down, he jumps from his chair and turns away from the table, heading to the counter behind him.

"Well," Bryn says, looking from him to Jodi, "if you weren't already aware, he's wanted by the police. Earlier today, he was spotted in the basement of a building on Wynhurst's campus, where he held four college students at gunpoint, one of whom was Addy," she says, pointing a thumb towards me, "and fled the scene. Not to mention the fact that he's implicated in the murders of Matthew Bruner and Gregory Morrell, as well as an international drug trafficking operation."

The blood drains from Jodi's face, and she looks back at her husband. "Mike, did you know any of that?"

He grunts and brings four full coffee mugs to the table, then sets one in front of each of us. I stare at the unsolicited beverage before me, wondering if there's any chance it could be decaf. The last time I drank regular coffee, my sugar spiked and stayed high for hours afterwards. Something about the caffeine. I look to Bryn, who, thankfully, doesn't seem eager to drink it either. She pushes the mug away.

Michael brings out creamer and sugar. He makes his coffee to his liking and takes a sip, seemingly oblivious to the rest of us. Only once he sits down does he answer.

"You can't believe all that garbage on TV. He probably had a good reason. Are you sure it was a gun? Could have been anything," he says, directing the question to me.

His confidence causes me to immediately second-guess myself. I have to run back the memory in my head and double-check, but I stop as I realize how stupid this is, slightly disappointed that I cave so easily. "Yes, I'm sure it was a gun," I say, indignant. "I touched it!"

He pauses and looks to Bryn, then has the audacity to ask, "Are you sure it was him threatening college students and not the other way around?"

"I have far more reasons to doubt your word than hers," Bryn counters.

His eyes narrow. "What's that supposed to mean?"

"Well, for starters, you're the chairman of Wynhurst's Board of Trustees, and a lot has come to light about the school. As a board member, you worked directly with Dr. Boyer, and you were even on campus at the time he planted the poison for Dr. Morrell. Of course, there's also Dr. Conley, the puppet president controlled by drug dependency, as well as the unmarked laboratory allowed on school property...not to mention the fact that your dad is the criminal mastermind behind it all. It's hard to believe you didn't have any knowledge of what was going on. I wouldn't be at all surprised to learn you had a hand to play—"

Michael violently shakes his head. "I didn't know any of that stuff about Boyer and Morrell. What laboratory? My dad isn't a part of any of it, and neither am I. You've got

408

the wrong guy."

Bryn studies him, drawing her brows together. "Really? You really don't know anything?"

He takes a swig of coffee. "No," he says, annoyed. "I don't!"

"And I take it you didn't know that Warren has a twin brother named Walter?"

His face scrunches in a confused expression. "Now you're really making stuff up. If my dad had some long-lost brother, don't you think I would know?"

Bryn sits back against her chair, her eyes widening. "No, of course you don't know. Because if you did, you'd be running like everyone else." She taps a finger on the table. "Michael, has Warren tried to reach out to you? You may think you know him, but you don't. Not really. He's lying to you."

From somewhere in the living room, a baby monitor suddenly floods with the sound of a child crying. Jodi goes to get up, but Michael springs to his feet and grabs it before she has a chance. "I'll get him," he says, then charges down the hall.

"Is all of that—what you said about Mayor Sayer—is that true?" Jodi asks.

Bryn nods. "Do you know something that could help us?"

She bites her lip, hesitating. Just when it seems like she might say something, Michael comes thundering back into the living room whilst carrying a crying baby in his arms.

"Honey, what do I do? I tried the pacifier, checked his diaper..." he says, pleading for help.

"Did you rock him?" she asks.

"Yes, I did that," he insists.

The baby wails.

"Sometimes it takes him a while—"

"Can you just take him? I'm not good with this."

With a sigh, Jodi rises from her chair and scoops up the baby. "Yes, of course." She starts to gently bounce him in her arms. "Are you hungry?" she coos. "You just ate." She positions him against her shoulder and starts to pat his back. His ear-splitting cry still fills the house.

Michael, freed from his responsibility, returns to the table. "You know," he says, pointing to Bryn's coffee, "I thought you might like that mug. It used to be Elise's."

I examine the faded mug more closely. The words *Flickerwood, PA* are printed on the side in a black, script-like font, and there's a small chip out of the top. The background is decorated with numerous speckled woodpeckers. It takes a second for me to realize what they are: northern flicker birds.

Bryn frowns. "My mom hates birds."

Michael looks confused. "Really? Strange. She loved them as a kid." He picks up his own mug, which shares the same design, but it's covered with trees instead of woodpeckers. He peers down at his drink, then sighs. "I could use something a little stronger. Do you want anything?"

"I'm good," Bryn answers.

He opens a door off to the side of the kitchen and disappears into the basement. As he descends, the sound of another door opening carries from the hallway, followed by two little feet trotting in our direction. Rachel, clad in purple pajamas, soon stands at the edge of the hallway, presumably having been awakened by her brother's crying.

"Mommy..." she starts, then her eyes fall on Bryn. She breaks into a huge smile before running at full speed and wrapping her arms around Bryn's middle. "Mommy, what is she doing here?"

Bryn freezes, surprised, then pats her on the head and stands up from the chair.

"Your cousin just stopped by to talk to your daddy, sweetheart," Jodi calls from the living room. Rachel prances over to her mother and pokes the top of her brother's head.

"Mommy, why is he crying so much?" she asks, then whispers to the baby. "Shhh. It's okay."

"I don't know," Jodi answers. "But he sure seems upset about something." She looks down at her daughter. "What are you doing out of bed?"

"I couldn't sleep, Mom," she whines. "Can you read me a bedtime story?"

"I'm a little busy right now—"

Rachel looks over her shoulder, then turns back to her mother with a smile. "Mom, can Bryn read me a story? Pleeeease?"

Jodi turns to us. Bryn spreads her hands. "How can I be most helpful?"

She purses her lips, debating. "Would you mind?"

"Not at all."

She looks to her daughter. "Okay, okay. But listen to me, only one. You can go pick out a book. I'll be over in just a minute." Speaking to us, she says, "Bookshelf is in her room."

Not wanting to be left alone with Michael and Jodi, I follow as Rachel leads us down the hall. She takes Bryn by the hand and tows her over to a colorful bookshelf in her bedroom. I stand to the side as they scan the titles.

Rachel suddenly points towards the top. "I want that one!"

I place a finger on the spine of the book I think she's talking about, but she shakes her head. "No, the other one!"

Bryn grabs her under the arms and lifts her to her hip, allowing her to reach the shelf. "Which one?"

Behind me, I hear a creak in the floorboards, but think nothing of it. The creak, however, is followed by a menacing voice from just outside the room.

"You put her down, and walk away slowly."

We all turn to see the man standing in the doorway: *Warren Sayer.*

His arms are outstretched, and his hands are clasped around his gun. The barrel is pointing straight at Bryn.

Chapter 63

Flicker

At the sight of her grandfather holding a weapon, Rachel's eyes grow big as quarters.

Warren continues. "I told you before, I'm not gonna let you waltz in here and attack my granddaughter. And don't you dare think you can use her as some kind of shield to hide behind—"

Almost automatically, Bryn sets Rachel on the ground and plants herself between the girl and the path of the gun.

Subtly, his expression changes. It's clear this move surprised him. "Don't touch her!" he barks, doubling down.

"Are you insane?!" Bryn exclaims. "I'm not going to hurt her—*you're* the one pointing a *gun*!" She releases her grip on Rachel, who cowers behind her. "Are you really going to shoot someone in front of her? Like that won't scar her for life. She's scared of you! Look at her."

He falters slightly. "Don't pretend to be innocent. You came here for revenge! It's thanks to you that I've been reduced to this. For years, I've been a respected part of this community, yet here I am running around in the shadows, hiding from the law. Are you happy?" He waves the gun a little too freely.

I look to Rachel, and my priority becomes getting her out of danger. I extend a hand towards her, hoping she'll take it. Thankfully, she does. *It's not me he wants, it's not me he wants*

I tell myself as I lead her away from Bryn. She hides behind me until she reaches her bed and dives beneath it.

Bryn shakes her head, incredulous. "Do you even hear yourself?! You and your brother have been working in the shadows for decades, slowly but surely poisoning the town with your drug trafficking and financial exploitation. In your own selfish quest for power, you eliminated anyone who got in your way—friend, family, or otherwise. What have I ever done to you? Nothing! I had no idea you were even connected to the murder of Dr. Morrell; all I did was follow the threads.

"Face it, Warren, with every dirty dollar you've made, you've dug your grave a little deeper. Now you have to lie in it, and the only person you have to blame is yourself."

Bang!

Before I can think, Sayer's gun goes off. A loud ringing sounds in my ears, and Rachel starts to cry. Immediately, Bryn crumples over. She lets out a groan of pain and clutches at her midsection.

The mayor leaps away, retreating into the hallway.

"Bryn!"

I run to her side, absolutely convinced she's dead. This time she's really dead. This has gotta be the end of her luck: her third strike, her last life. He just shot her straight through! And there's no antidote for that.

"Oh, ouch," she hisses, her face parallel with the ground. Wincing, she suddenly straightens.

My mouth falls open as I search for the blood. "Bryn?"

Through the pain, she flashes a strained smile. "Bulletproof vest. I'll live...Still hurts, though." She exhales and takes a step forward. Down the hall, there's suddenly a scream. She speeds out after him.

Barely thinking, I follow her into the hall. Jodi stands near the edge of the living room with her cellphone in one hand and a baby in the other. Her face is pale—she looks sick with fear. "Where's Rachel!?" she demands.

"Who are you talking to?" Sayer growls, locking his eyes on the phone. He steps towards her.

She starts to back away, but continues talking to the person on the other end. "Yes, the address is 113 Levit Drive..."

413

Her voice shakes. "Please hurry. He has a gun."

He lunges towards her.

But Bryn is faster. Before he has a chance to raise his gun, she grabs his hand, forcing the barrel towards the ground.

He loses his grip on the weapon, but manages to strike Bryn in the abdomen, right where she was shot. She whimpers in pain, dropping to one knee.

"Are you still walking!?" he yells in frustration. "Maybe you *are* a witch." He reaches for his weapon, but Bryn slides it away from him.

"Addy, gun," she calls, climbing back to her feet. Swiftly, she passes it to me.

Though I don't want to, I take it from her. I hold it gingerly, keeping my fingers far away from the trigger. *I'm holding a loaded gun. I'm holding a loaded gun.*

"Fifteen minutes?" Jodi asks, speaking into the phone.

Sayer's eyes dart between me, Bryn, and Jodi, unsure of which problem to address first.

"It's over," Bryn says, placing herself squarely in front of him. "You've been found out. Give it up."

Behind Jodi, Michael comes running up from the basement. "What was that noise—" he stops when he sees Bryn and the mayor. "Jodi? Dad? What's going on?!"

"Warren shot Bryn!" I spout automatically. My eyes fall on Jodi's ghastly expression. "And Rachel's okay! She's in her bedroom." I nod towards the door, trying to hold a loaded gun in as non-threatening a way as possible.

Jodi rushes past me and into Rachel's room.

Michael's eyes fall on his father, and on Bryn clutching at her side. "Is...is that true?"

Warren ignores his son's question. Instead, his eyes settle on Bryn. His expression changes, further charging the air with tension—the uneasiness that comes from being in the presence of a man seething with rage. He's not running away anymore. He has something else in mind.

"Elise should've listened to me," he says, glaring at Bryn. "I knew from the moment I found out about you that you would destroy this family...and I was right." He springs at her, again going for her sore spot.

"How could I destroy something I was never a part of!?"

Bryn returns, evading the bulk of his swing. "You've been trying to kill me since the day I was conceived!"

Sayer steadies himself against the wall and backs Bryn into the living room. "If it weren't for you," he growls, "Elise would still be the daughter I knew!"

He lunges again, but this time Bryn gets a good hold on him. With the force of all his momentum, she throws him past her, and they tumble into the kitchen table. The impact shakes the coffee mugs, and the Flickerwood woodpeckers begin to wobble. Dark coffee splashes out the side, and Bryn reaches to steady it.

As she does so, she suddenly freezes. She stares at the mug, tracing the chipped edge with her finger, and a realization unfolds in her expression. She looks back at Warren.

"Birds," she whispers quietly. Her eyes sweep back and forth, as if she's running calculations in her head. "No, it can't be...but..." She looks back at the mug, then back at Warren. "The birds." She takes a step towards him. "In the lab, I heard it—Walter's formula can cause miscarriage in some people. And you knew that. Of course you did. I'm sure Walter was willing to give you a small sampling of his product, after all you've done for him. *That's* what he was talking about. That's the truth, isn't it? You didn't just kick her out. Your daughter wouldn't go to a clinic, so you took matters into your own hands." Her eyes bore into his. "You... you drugged my mother."

Warren stands very still. He doesn't drop eye contact, or try to argue. In fact, the hint of a smile creeps over his face.

Bryn's hands curl into fists. "You served her your brother's drugs in her favorite mug, and I...I spent my childhood listening to her brain replay the memory the only way it knew how!"

Michael's mouth falls agape as he looks on.

Warren tilts his chin up. "If only she had listened to me..." He shakes his head. "A shame it didn't even work on you." From the counter, he suddenly draws a large chef's knife and slashes at Bryn.

In an instant, her own knife is drawn and ready. She deflects his blade with hers and, in a furious tangle of limbs, sends his knife skidding across the kitchen floor. Holding him by the collar, she slams him into the cabinets, knife raised.

"My mother didn't just go insane. Her illness was *induced*. By you!" She grips him tighter, rage bubbling in her voice. "*You* stole her dreams, her potential, her future. She will never be the same, and I have spent my entire life trying to unpack the damage you did!"

Her hand trembles with fury, and I start to get afraid.

Despite his usual cool demeanor, fear flashes across Warren's face. For an instant, Bryn's knife hovers in the air, and my breath catches in my throat.

In a great motion, she brings her arm down and slashes the knife with a snap of the wrist.

Thwack!

The blade embeds itself in a cabinet, piercing through the wood mere inches away from his head.

Sayer clutches his chest, eyes wide and confused.

She releases his collar, and he slides towards the floor. "I didn't come to kill you, Warren. Revenge was never my goal." She shakes her head. "I'm not your judge."

Forcefully, she tugs the knife from the cabinet door and turns away from him. Angry tears well in her eyes. "Watch him," she orders Michael, who steps towards his father.

With a long, shaky exhale, she approaches me. Thankfully, she takes the gun back and unloads it. She eyes Jodi, who stands just inside the hallway, with Rachel hiding behind her. With a small groan of pain, she puts a hand on her side.

In only a few seconds, however, Michael suddenly calls out. "Uh, Bryn?!"

Chapter 64

A Woman's Place in the Kitchen

She turns. Sayer emits a strange gurgling sound, and foam starts to bubble from his mouth. His arms and legs are trembling.

Bryn's eyes narrow, and she swiftly marches towards him. "What's wrong with you?" she demands. "If you're trying to fake something, it won't work on me."

"I-I'm f-fine," he stutters, glaring. In a sudden burst of movement, his arm flails out to the side. The motion opens the flap of his suit jacket, revealing a spot of blood just above his right hip, showing through the fabric.

"What's that?" Bryn asks sharply. She grabs a pair of gloves from her bag, then tugs his shirt up. Broken glass spills out. Startled, she picks up one of the larger shards and examines it, then shakes it at Warren. "Why do you have this!?"

"What is it?" Michael asks nervously.

"One of Walter's newest drug formulas," she explains, rooting through the shattered pieces. She soon pulls out another label. "Two vials of it, which are now leaking into his bloodstream through the open wound."

Warren's twitching continues. "G-get away f-from me!" he stammers, swatting at her. Sweat begins to pour from his forehead.

As requested, Bryn stands and takes a few steps back. "You do know what this means, don't you?"

"So I'll be high for a while. Who cares?" he says, his speech garbled.

"No," she says, leaning down to his eye level. "Warren, this is *six times* the lethal dose."

He glares at her, but listens.

"You're—you're not coming back from this. Even if you somehow were to survive, judging by what happened to Elise, you'll have permanent brain damage. Do you understand?"

"Jodi, call an ambulance!" Michael shouts in a panic.

"They're already on the way!" she answers.

"It'll be too late," Bryn says quietly.

Michael frantically gazes around the room, but the truth is starting to sink in, even for him.

The room falls silent, broken only by the unsettling sound of Warren Sayer's jerking limbs slapping against the tile floor.

"He's going to die, isn't he?" Jodi asks from the hallway.

No one answers her. No one needs to.

She presses Rachel further behind her, nudging her into a bedroom.

Michael stares down at his father. "You...you were right," he breathes, talking to Bryn. "I...I can't believe he...he did that to Elise. I didn't know." Tears shimmer in his eyes. "Oh, Dad..."

We watch as Sayer helplessly thrashes about on the floor, undone by the very substance he profited from for so many years. The crown jewel of his underground empire having turned to a curse, he's now destined to die tasting the very poison he gave his daughter to drink.

"...No." Bryn states suddenly.

It's at this point I realize she's not looking at Warren, but at her mother's mug. Her eyes turn back to him. "No, that's not the end of the story." She exhales forcefully and straightens her shoulders. "Enough people have been hurt. I can't make any promises, but I'll try."

Michael and Jodi look to her, confused. She pulls her jacket off and tosses it over a chair. "I'm gonna need some help from you two. First, I need a thermometer."

418

"Uh, okay. Give me one second," Jodi says before running into the bathroom.

Bryn nods as she unbuttons the sleeves of her shirt and rolls them up past her elbows. "Alright," she says, once more crouching beside Warren. She presses two fingers to his neck, but he growls and tries to push her over. She easily evades his sloppy attack. "Pulse is high," she mutters, then quickly spreads each of his eyelids, peering into large black pupils.

Jodi returns with a thermometer and a first aid kit.

"Thank you," Bryn replies, taking the device. She swipes the forehead scanner over him, and it beeps. The display glows red. "Temperature is high," she says, glancing at the result. "Do you know anything about Walter's formulations? What's in them?" she asks Warren.

He shakes his head. "No," he answers gruffly.

"I figured," Bryn sighs. "Let's see. We know it's not an opioid or depressant. Based on the effects, it's likely some type of synthetic hallucinogen. Now, what would cause your symptoms? Muscle spasms, elevated pulse and body temp, dilated eyes..." She draws her brows together. "You know, they say things like schizophrenia and psychosis are often related to an imbalance in a certain neurotransmitter—" She suddenly draws back and raises both hands. "That's it!"

She grabs her knife and begins slicing his shirt off. "Addy, get me some ice packs. Michael, help me get some of these layers off." I run to the freezer and pull out all the ice I can carry. Bryn and Michael strip off his shoes and socks, cut his pants to shorts, and remove all but his undershirt. "The involuntary muscle movements are causing him to overheat," Bryn says, placing ice under his arms and between his legs. "We need to maintain a safe temperature."

"What's wrong with him?" Michael asks.

"Serotonin toxicity. A severe form. The good news is there's a medication that could treat it. The bad news, unfortunately, is that I don't have it." She pauses, biting her lip. "But—I may be able to synthesize it."

She hops to her feet and grabs a pen and a piece of paper from the counter, then begins scribbling numbers down. "Where are your pots and pans?" she asks Michael. "What cabinet?"

"Uh—" he freezes. "I...I'm not sure."

Bryn looks up and frowns at him. "You're not sure!?"

"Here," Jodi says, jumping in. She opens two large cabinet doors below the counter.

Frantically, Bryn pulls out cooking equipment: a pot, some plastic wrap, a kitchen scale, and a glass measuring cup marked with milliliters. "Carbon, hydrogen, nitrogen…" she mutters to herself. "Piperine." She lunges for the spice cabinet and pulls out a pepper mill. Furiously, she grinds flakes of black pepper onto the scale, then swipes them into the pot.

"Michael, I need the purest, strongest liquor you have."

He looks incredulous. "Now?"

She stops. "Not to drink! Yes, now. I'm serious."

She then rushes down the hall to the bathroom. In the vague hope of helping, I follow. She throws open the medicine cabinet and the doors beneath the sink, then starts reading the labels of cleaning products. She tosses most of them to the side. Finally, she grabs a drain cleaner and some rubbing alcohol, then speeds back towards the kitchen. On the way, she glances at Rachel, smiles sheepishly at the cleaner in her hand, and quickly says, "Don't try this."

She picks up the pen once more and continues her calculations. "I have to get the measurements just right, or it might cause more harm than good." After double-checking her math, she measures out the rubbing alcohol and pours it on top of the ground pepper.

Tick, tick, whoosh. She turns the knob on the stove, and the flames of the gas burner come alive.

Michael returns from the basement with a bottle in hand.

"Sorry in advance," she says before yanking the kitchen sink sprayer out and slicing through the tube with her knife. She adds some of the drain cleaner and Michael's vodka to the pot on the stove, then covers the top with plastic wrap. With a clean knife, she punches a hole in the plastic, shoves one end of the tubing through it, and places the other end in a pitcher filled with ice.

Having assembled her scientific-looking contraption, she grabs something from the pantry and dumps it into a mug — tea leaves, I think — then lights it on fire. "Partial combustion of organic material…" She pours water on top, extinguishing the flames, then chucks the mug in the microwave. Once it's bubbling, she strains the liquid through a coffee filter, lifts a small section of the plastic wrap, and adds it to the boiling pot.

She then returns to the lower cabinet and emerges with a copper pan, into which she dumps the stovetop concoction. After resetting the tube apparatus over the new pan, she turns the heat up.

I glance at the paper she's been using for calculations. It's full of numbers, messy scientific equations, and chemical symbols that make my brain spin.

Warren's face is flushed, and his pupils look like two giant black marbles. Thankfully, whatever Bryn has been doing seems to be finished. She kills the heat and removes the pan. Carefully, she pours some of the liquid into a fresh mug, adding a few cubes of ice for good measure.

"Drink up," she says, holding it out to Warren.

Rather than take it, however, he shoves her hand away. "I-I t-t-told you; g-get away from me!" he shouts. "I-I'm n-n-not gonna drink y-your crackpot potion. I-I don't w-w-want anything from you!"

Bryn's grip on the mug tightens, turning her knuckles white. She takes a deep breath, and her hand relaxes. "Your pulse is climbing, which is putting pressure on your heart and blood vessels. If you don't do something, you're bound to have some sort of massive cardiovascular failure." She raises the cup. "In case you didn't realize, I'm trying to save your life."

His lip curls in anger. "I know!" he yells. "Why?!"

The last question has a different tone to it. Desperation? Fear? Earnestness?

Bryn draws her head back, watching him intently.

"Y-y-you said it yourself!" he continues. I've been n-n-nothing but cruel to y-you. Why would you want to save me?" He raises a trembling finger. "And d-d-don't give me some bull crap about how we're f-f-family. What is it, really? Are you just so self-righteous—"

"No," she responds firmly. "We're not family. I already told you the reason; I'm not your judge."

"S-so y-you want me alive so I can r-rot in prison—"

"No, that's not what I'm talking about. You and I, we have the same Judge. And one day, we will all have to face

Him. Believe me, I have skeletons in my closet, too. I'm far from righteous. But someone knelt down and saved me with his own blood, so this is the least I can do for you."

His brow furrows. "Who?"

Bryn answers without skipping a beat. "Yeshua. Jesus Christ."

Warren's eyes narrow. He stares at her in utter disbelief. His mouth freezes in a half-smile, as if he's unsure whether or not to laugh. I can almost see the gears seizing in his brain as he struggles to comprehend what he's just been told.

Bryn interrupts. "Now, unless you feel ready to meet Him, I'd suggest you let me help."

He's quiet, but he drops his hand and allows Bryn to raise the mug to his lips. His tremors prevent him from holding it steady, so she reluctantly positions herself behind him, cradling his shoulder and tilting his head back until he's drained the cup.

Outside, sirens blare, and red and blue lights shine inside the windows. Michael rushes to the door, and police flood in, guns drawn, in search of Warren. They soon find him sitting on the kitchen floor, convulsing.

Slowly, his state begins to improve. At first, it's so small I wonder if I'm imagining it. Sure enough, however, his trembling begins to still. He regains control of his limbs, wipes his mouth, and sits up straight. The black centers of his eyes gradually shrink back down to size, and the redness fades from his face. Paramedics roll in and take him out on a stretcher, though the police handcuff him to the bed.

Bryn follows behind, now holding her side. Agent Johnson comes to greet her.

"What happened to go home and get some rest?" he asks sternly.

Bryn smiles. "Oh, just had to visit some family."

He shakes his head, but the shadow of a smile crosses his face. He's not really mad. "You'll be happy to hear that we apprehended the escaped suspects at the train station where they were trying to board some freight cars. We've successfully recovered five hostages, two of which have been identified as missing persons from Flickerwood."

"And now you've got the mayor, too."

He nods. "And now we've got the mayor, too. Thanks to you two and a call from a Mrs. Jodi Sayer." He gestures towards her.

We watch them load Warren into the ambulance and close the doors.

"I only hope we have enough evidence to convict him of all he's guilty of," Agent Johnson mutters. "High-profile guys like him can be hard to nail down."

I suddenly remember. In a rush of excitement, I pull my phone from my pocket. Sure enough, the audio recording is still going. I finally press stop.

"I don't know how good the sound quality is, but I've been recording the whole time, from the basement of the music building until now." I hold my phone out for him to see.

His face could not have looked more pleased if I'd handed him a gold bar. Bryn lights up.

"Addy, you're a genius."

I beam.

"Mind if we take a look at this?" he asks, reaching for my phone.

"Well," I say, pulling it back a little. "My CGM is on here, I'll need it back fairly soon—"

"No problem," he assures me. "We'll just download the audio quick." He takes my phone and hands it off to another agent.

"Well," Agent Johnson says, "you two have been instrumental in this case. I hope you know that. Is there anything I can do for you?"

Bryn continues clutching her abdomen and starts leaning to the side. "If you don't mind, sir, I could use a ride to the hospital."

Chapter 65

Happy Ending?

After sleeping for a good ten hours straight, only briefly interrupted by the need to give myself a dose of basal insulin, I finally get out of bed and start to feel human again. I check my phone to see seven missed calls from my mom. Though not without a sigh, I call her back and assure her I'm alive and doing okay. Upon hanging up, I feel guilty for my annoyance, and remember to be grateful to have parents that care.

I'm sure last night's events are all over the news, but I try not to look at the TV as I eat breakfast. Mainly, I'm anxious to know how Bryn is doing in the hospital. Not willing to wait until Anthony and Sid head over, I board the Flickerwood bus for the first time. It lets me off just outside the main entrance to the hospital, and I walk through the large glass doors. Once inside, I push past my social anxiety and approach the front desk, where the receptionist gives me her room number.

Just as I'm starting to wonder if I took a wrong turn and got lost in the hospital's maze of hallways, I spot Bryn through an open curtain. Quietly, I slip into the room as she converses with a nurse. She's sitting up in bed with gauze and ice packs lying on her chest. The nurse stands beside the bed, attending to her IV.

"Hey, what is that?" Bryn asks as the nurse goes to inject something into the line.

"Try to relax, ma'am. It's just some morphine—"

"No, no, I don't want any of that," she states firmly, waving it away.

"It's standard," the nurse replies. "You did break some bones..."

Bryn gently moves her hand away. "No. I don't consent. Please don't give me any controlled substances."

Looking surprised, the nurse lowers the syringe. "Do you have a history of—"

"No, I don't, but I'd rather not develop one. Just bring me some Tylenol."

"Are you sure?"

Bryn nods. "Yes, thank you...Listen, I just want you to know, I used to be a medic in the Navy. I've worked in healthcare, I know the drill, and I'm warning you—I'm going to be a horrible patient."

The nurse cocks her head.

"Don't worry," Bryn adds. "I won't throw any punches."

At that, the nurse snickers and shakes her head. "I'll be back with that Tylenol."

She walks past me and out of the room, leaving us alone.

"Doesn't feel so good to be poked and prodded with who-knows-what, does it?" I say from the edge of the room.

Bryn looks my way, then breaks into a smile. "Addy!"

I smile back and approach her bed. "How are you doing?"

"Little worse for the wear, but I'll heal up just fine. That bullet—and maybe being pushed into the wall in that lab—left me with a few broken ribs. I'm lucky it's not too bad, though. They'll send me home soon enough."

At the sound of the curtain rustling behind me, I turn to see a short, brown-skinned woman swiftly enter the room, followed by a tall man with skin several shades darker than hers. Though sporting a buzz cut, the curls in his jet black hair are still apparent. The woman takes one look at Bryn and quickly exclaims something in Spanish.

"Look at you!" she says, switching to English. "You survive ten years in the Navy, but you come back to Flickerwood for six months and boom!" She gestures with both hands at Bryn's condition. "This town is trying to kill you, Bryn."

Though she shrinks away from the woman's somewhat

aggressive volume, the shadow of a smile forms on Bryn's lips. "I'm okay. Honest." She looks over at me and gestures to the woman in front of her. "Addy, meet my mom, Yesenia." She then nods towards the tall man near the curtain, "And my dad, Kylin."

My brain takes a few minutes to catch up. The woman turns to me and nods politely, then returns to fussing over her daughter. This…this is Mr. and Mrs. Leighton. Her adoptive parents.

"What did the doctor say?" Yesenia demands.

"They said I'll be fine. I'll heal up in a few weeks…"

"How long?"

"I dunno, Mom, two months max."

She clicks her tongue. "And where is the snake?"

"Warren? He's in jail, currently."

"Good," she says with a nod. "He'd better be. Are they gonna keep him there?"

"All depends on the trial, but they should have enough evidence for a conviction…"

"Do you need anything? Have you eaten?"

"Mom, I'm okay—"

The tall man—Kylin—glides forward and gently sets a hand on the woman's shoulder. "Essie, I'm sure she just needs some rest."

At his touch, Yesenia exhales and rocks back on her heels. "I'm sorry," she says in a more relaxed tone. "I just worry about you. That's all."

"I know, Mom. It's okay."

Yesenia smiles warmly, then approaches the bed. "Oh, it's good to see you. It feels like it's been forever."

"Watch my ribs—" Bryn squeaks as her mom squeezes her in a hug.

Her dad approaches and touches her arm, planting a kiss on her forehead. "Missed you, Bri."

"It's good to see you, too," Bryn replies.

Yesenia steps back and takes in her daughter's condition for a second time. "*Mija*, you're getting too old for this."

Bryn's eyes fly wide, mildly offended by the comment. "I'm still in my twenties, thank you very much."

Her mother raises an eyebrow. "Twenty-*nine*."

426

Bryn waves a hand. "Age is just a number. I'm not decrepit quite yet. I've still got some good years left."

Her dad smiles and shakes his head. "We love you. Glad to see you're doing well."

"Is lying in a hospital bed doing well?" her mother mutters.

Her dad chuckles. "Same old Bri. Not much has changed."

"Is this the right room?"

I glance back to see Anthony, Sid, and Micah standing in the hallway. Sid's holding a small bouquet of flowers. They all peer behind the curtain.

"Yeah," I say, unfreezing and stepping aside. "Come in."

"Ah, you must be well-liked," Yesenia remarks as they enter. "Who are all these young people?"

"Students from Wynhurst. Addy and Sidney were in my class," Bryn answers, pointing to us. Her mom floats forward and introduces herself and her husband to each of them.

"In all the excitement, I completely forgot. How do you like the professor thing?"

"It…it's alright," Bryn says. "Not sure how many people I really got through to. Then again, it's been a weird semester."

She nods. "Well, at least you're giving it a try. If not this, I'm sure you'll find something you like."

Her dad agrees. "Whatever you want to do, wherever God leads—just know you have our support," he assures.

Her mom pats her on the hand. "We're very proud of you, Bryn." She smiles. "Now, are you sure there's nothing I can do for you?"

Bryn bites her lip. "Well…they were supposed to bring me breakfast about two hours ago…"

"On it!" Yesenia exclaims, then rushes off. Kylin nods, then follows his wife out of the room.

Bryn smiles and shakes her head.

"How are you?" Sid asks, tentatively stepping forward.

"Oh, I look worse off than I am," she says, explaining her injuries.

Sid glances back at Anthony and Micah while holding out the bouquet. "We got you some flowers."

"Thank you! Very kind," she says, happily accepting the gift. She sets them on her side table, arranging them in a pretty manner. "Nice to have a bit of green in here."

"So what happened after you guys left last night? We heard they caught pretty much everyone...the Boyers, Edith Morrell, the mayor..." Anthony asks.

Between me and Bryn, we relay much of the saga of yesterday. When we finish, Micah steps forward. He looks down at Bryn, and his face grows red.

"I...I just want to say I'm sorry I didn't believe you. And for participating in that mob—" he covers his face with his hands. "I'm sorry, Professor. I can't thank you enough for getting Addy out safely, for trying to help Matthew, and for saving my life. I was wrong about you. I was stupid, and I put your life in danger—"

"Micah," Bryn says, cutting him off. Slowly, he removes his hands from his face. "Can you do me a favor?" Her tone is gentle. "Don't hold any of that over your head. Okay? Don't even give it a second thought. All's forgiven." She extends a hand. "We're good."

He hesitates. "I...but the crowd...you could've..."

"I know," she says. "But I didn't. It's okay."

At last, he reaches towards her and shakes her outstretched hand.

With a nod, they part ways, and Micah turns back to us. "And you guys...I'm sorry about everything. I was just trying to do right by Matthew, but I got carried away, and I didn't take the time to listen."

"Hey, we're good, man," Anthony says quickly.

I nod. "Past is the past. And anyway, if you hadn't gotten help, I'd still be in that lab."

Beside him, Sid smiles sadly. "It's nice to be friends again."

Anthony gazes around the hospital room, inspecting the flashing machines and cords running everywhere. "So," he says, drawing closer. "Professor Leighton, after all this, do you think you'll stay in Flickerwood?" It's phrased as a casual question, but I hone in on her, listening for the answer.

"Honestly," Bryn says, "I don't think I can. I'm glad I came back, but I need to move on."

If my mind isn't sure how I feel about this, my heart certainly is. It sinks into my shoes. I swallow. "W-what about Wynhurst?"

"They'll find another professor. Probably a better one than me."

"But...don't you want to see what Flickerwood is like without Warren Sayer and all the drugs and dirty money? And your little cousins?"

She shakes her head. "I'm glad Walter and Warren are finally facing their crimes and aren't controlling the town anymore, but even without their presence, this place just holds a lot of bad memories for me. Flickerwood may be my beginning, but it's not my end. I can always come back and visit Rachel and her brother—if their father will let me, that is—but my home isn't here."

I grow quiet, knowing if I try to talk any more I won't be able to hold back the tears springing to my eyes. I guess that's it, then. She really is leaving.

Sid, Anthony, and Micah ask more questions about where she'll go and what she'll do, keeping up polite conversation. But their words fade to white noise for me, drowned out as I sink into the cavernous image of being in Flickerwood, going to school at Wynhurst, getting a degree in ecology, without Bryn.

Kylin and Yesenia return with food and a nurse in tow, who gives Bryn the Tylenol she requested. Quietly, I step towards the back and slip out of the room. I quickly find the bathroom and duck inside. I try to tell myself I'm in here to check my sugar and fiddle with my CGM, but I know that's not the whole truth.

I shouldn't be upset. Or at least not this upset. Professors come and go—school only lasts four years, anyway. And really, I've only known her for a couple of months. Yet, the tears start to stream down my cheeks. *Why am I crying?!* I look in the mirror, frustrated with myself. At 20, I should only be crying over failed romantic relationships, not some random professor's change of career.

The door to the restroom swings open, and a stranger walks in. She takes one look at my tear-stained face, then ducks into a stall. I roll my eyes at myself, my face turning red. I'm in a hospital bathroom. People probably think I'm in here crying over the death of a family member or something actually serious—but no.

Why do I care so much? I never missed any of the dozens of teachers and professors I've had over the years.

Why is she any different?

Of course, the answer is obvious. Nothing has been the same since I met Bryn. My entire life has been turned upside down, and my horizons expanded in ways I never imagined. This whole semester, I've been caught up in mayhem and peril and a murder investigation. Yet, in the midst of the chaos, I started to feel like I might be on the brink of something. Something I might be meant to do—well, it feels like the rug has been ripped out from under me. My life won't actually change after any of this. Bryn will leave, and things will go back to normal.

I wipe the tears from my face and try to close my heart off to the barrage of thoughts. I pretend she's just another professor, like the countless ones before. I can't expect her to stay for me.

I walk back to the hospital room and rejoin Sid, Anthony, and Micah. Bryn is laughing and joking with her family.

"So," she says, turning towards us. "Anyone think they wanna make a career out of detective work?" There's a twinkle in her eye.

There's a pause, and I look to the others for their answer. After a beat, they break into laughter.

"Heck no," Sid says. "I've had enough of that."

"I second that," Anthony says. "I prefer reading about cases that have already been solved."

Micah nods along. "I...I don't think I've fully recovered from this one yet."

Seeing their reactions, I smile and laugh along. Inwardly, however, I pose the question to myself. A career in detective work? It was never something I'd seriously considered. But...well, as my mom said, it was my dream job as a kid. When did that dream disappear?

430

Chapter 66

The End of a Matter

As the remaining weeks of the semester tick by, I try to forget about Bryn. She still teaches my botany class, but we don't talk all that much. On the off chance that we do, it's only about coursework, and then only briefly. She seems busy, so I try not to drag out our conversations.

I guess sometimes God puts people in your life for only a short time. But that doesn't mean they can't have a real, lifelong impact. Bryn changed my life for the better, and I will forever be grateful for that.

I still get sad, if I think about it too much, but it's probably for the best. After all, maybe it's time for me to do some things on my own. I don't need her to mediate or repair my relationship with God. People come and go, but He remains. And I don't need her in order to make decisions about who I am or where I'm going.

As I walk across campus, Philippians 4:13 comes to mind: *I can do all things through him who strengthens me* (ESV).

I've often heard it quoted, but it's started to take on a new meaning. It's not a guarantee of instant success, or victory, or earthly prosperity, but a promise that God will provide the strength to endure under any circumstance. Whether rich or poor, hungry or full, lonely or overwhelmed, happy or hurting, comfortable or in pain, healthy or sick, scared or confident, anxious or self-assured, full of faith or questioning, in safety or in peril, from the first breath to the last—He will be there.

I put my hand on the door to the admin building and pull it open, then walk down the hall towards the registrar's office. I talk to the student worker at the front desk, who confirms my appointment and then leads me to the assistant registrar.

"And what brings you in today?" she asks, peering at me from behind tortoise shell glasses.

"I was wondering—how much would it affect my projected graduation date if I were to change my major?"

Slowly, she pulls up my file and looks through my completed course sheet. "What were you thinking of changing to?"

"Uh, criminal justice."

She nods. "Mm-hmm. And what would you hope to do with that degree, honey?"

I clear my throat, trying to be a good self-advocate. "Well, I'm not exactly sure where I would end up, but it's a field that interests me, and I can see myself being happy in a variety of areas..."

"You realize a lot of what criminal justice prepares you for is police work or corrections," she says, staring intently at my CGM. "A lot of intense, physical work. You sure you'd want to take on something like that?"

I follow her gaze to my arm, then sit up straighter. "Yes. I'm sure," I say firmly. What's to stop me from joining the police? I could do it if I really wanted to. It would be hard, but hey, anything worth doing is hard. "I've talked to my parents and my advisor. This is what I want."

She looks down at my papers. "Well, hun, if you switch now, the good news is you've taken mostly general education classes at this point, so it really wouldn't push you back too far."

As she talks, I start to have second thoughts. I do want to study criminal justice, but...can I really just toss ecology so easily? There's a special place in my heart for the people, and the subject...

"What about a double major?" I blurt.

She stops and stares at me, lowering the glasses. "Are you willing to take summer courses?"

As I exit the office and head into the main hallway, I nearly

432

collide with someone.

"Bryn!" I say, surprised.

"Addy," she says with a nod. "How are you doing?"

"I'm pretty good. How are you?" I return politely.

She glances up at the sign hanging above my head, then back to me. "Yeah? I feel like we haven't really had a chance to catch up after everything that happened...well, I know it can take time to recover from an experience like that. How are you holding up?"

"Little tired, just trying to get through the semester," I answer, a little confused. I glance behind me and realize the registrar is in the same hallway as the counseling center. "Oh," I say, pointing behind me. "Actually...I just went in to change my major."

She looks surprised. "Really? To what?"

"Well, I'm technically doing a double major now. I added one. Should still be able to graduate on time..." I shift my weight from foot to foot. "Criminal justice."

Though she tries to hide it, she smiles. "Is that so?"

I nod, then ask again, "How have you been? Getting ready to move, I guess?"

"Ya know, I actually wanted to talk to you about something. Would you be available to meet up for a coffee or something sometime?"

We sit in the back corner of a small cafe in town. Rather than coffee, we both order tea. White peach tea for me, chamomile hibiscus for Bryn. The building used to be a bank, so across from us is the original heavy-duty door to the vault. I take a sip of tea, trying to contain my emotions. What could she possibly have to say?

"So," Bryn starts. "Do you remember the FBI agent we met? Johnson?"

I nod. How could I forget? "Yeah."

"Well, a few weeks after Warren and Walter were arrested, he approached me and asked if I would be interested in a job opportunity."

"Wait, really?"

She nods. "He explained that they've been looking for

someone to review a particular set of unsolved cases. Those which they can no longer afford to devote large-scale resources to, but which are worth a second look. Mainly involving missing persons. Based on my background, he thought I would be a good fit for the position.

"So…you're gonna take it, then? That's what you'll be doing?"

"Yeah, I'm gonna take it."

"Congratulations!" I say, taking a drink of tea, hoping to drown the part of me that still doesn't want her to leave. "I'll have to call you if anyone I know goes missing," I joke.

"But…that's not all," she says. Her tone is quiet, almost nervous. "In my negotiations with them, I made a request."

I tilt my head, curious.

"I asked if I could bring on a partner. A junior member; a paid intern, if you will. Eventually I talked them into it."

I sit still as a statue, unwilling to truly believe what I think I'm hearing, for fear of disappointment. I wait for her to say it.

"Addy…would you like to come with me?"

My mouth falls agape.

Bryn quickly adds more information. "It'll take a while to get things moving, with all the paperwork and clearances that are required. I was thinking you could finish college, then, if you so choose, you could start after graduation. There's no pressure to answer me right now. You can take your time, think about it."

I swallow, recognizing the wisdom in thinking it over. But I already know my answer. "Yes," I say immediately. "I… I would love to."

Bryn's eyes widen. "You're sure? There is a measure of risk involved…"

I clear my throat and give a more level-headed response. "Yes, I'm sure. I mean, of course I'm going to talk it over with my family and everything—that may be the hard part—and I'll read over all the paperwork, but…I know myself."

I remember the beginning of my college career, ambling out of high school just hoping to make a safe choice. "Bryn, if I don't say yes to this, I'll never say yes to any risk worth taking."

434

At last, she smiles. "So I made a good call, then?"

I nod, still in disbelief. Not only does she want me to go with her, but she was willing to negotiate a job at the FBI for me. "Yes! Thank you! I'd love to come with you."

"I was hoping you'd say that."

I decide to wait and tell my parents about Bryn's job offer when I see them in person for Easter break, which happens to be this weekend. As I pack my suitcase, I glance over at the calendar. It hits me that there's only about a month left until the end of the year—I'm almost a junior. I shake my head in disbelief. Feels like I was a freshman just yesterday.

I say goodbye to Marissa, then head off to the train station. It feels kind of poetic, standing here at the end of a journey, waiting for my ride home. I check the time. As expected, the train comes into view a few minutes behind schedule. Along with a handful of other people, I board the car and find an empty seat by the window.

As the wheels turn and the train pulls away from the station, I'm transported away from this world of murder, mystery, and detective work. I pass instead into the non-space of travel, knowing what awaits me on the other side is a place so familiar it's become foreign. Foreign because I am not the same person I was when I left it.

I check my blood sugar and smile at the piece of paper tucked into the pages of my Bible. An employment contract for the FBI. My key to the next strange world ahead.

Epilogue

1 Year Later

After a complete change in administration and some extensive involvement with both authorities and the media, Wynhurst was able to recover much of its former reputation as an academic institution. If anything, the added publicity actually served to draw in more students, many of whom came hoping to sneak into the hidden maze of underground tunnels or have an alien encounter of their own.

The new administration also managed to clean up the more literal mess of smoking rubble left behind in the northern forest. With containment efforts and decontamination crews, the chemical byproducts of drug production were eventually cleared from the water supply. And, much to the chagrin of said self-proclaimed urban explorers, construction workers were hired to block off the tunnels that remained.

I can't help but wonder how many years it will take for the memories to fade into myth, for the stories passed from seniors to freshmen to sound less like the nightly news and more like a tall tale. How long for people to forget that the hidden laboratory in the forest that snatched the children of Flickerwood was not simply another spooky legend, but the truth.

436

As for the culprits themselves, it turns out that insufficient evidence was not a problem we had to worry about. A few days after the arrests, Dr. Gaines discovered a book belonging to Dr. Morrell wedged behind a filing cabinet in his office. A thick layer of dust testified that it hadn't been moved in quite some time.

When he pulled it out, he found himself holding a Bible, and hidden inside one of the pages was a letter. In painstaking detail, Gregory Morrell had written a lengthy confession. He explained how he, Edith, Walter, Warren, and Robert had been friends since high school.

The drugs were Walter's idea, due to his proclivity for chemistry, but the rest quickly joined in on the scheme, which became a decades-long conspiracy. Gradually, the group embedded themselves at Wynhurst, using the school as a cover and space to set up shop.

They'd had a few close calls over the years, causing them to readjust their strategy and take measures to remain hidden. When staff at the university got too close to discovering their activities and tunnel entrances in the basement of the old music building, they burnt the whole thing to the ground, ensuring any evidence was unrecognizable. When others wandered too close and witnessed something they shouldn't have, they were given cyanide — a convenient chemical they had on hand, due to it being produced as a waste product in their drug-making process, as well as something no investigator would think to look for.

When a few of the subjects almost escaped the lab, they realized they needed a better cover, so they came up with the alien hoax. A perfect success, as seen in the case of Elijah Martin, who survived his encounter but whose mind was so broken by their testing and confused by the deception that he had no information to use against them.

But mostly, they were able to operate entirely unhindered. They made money hand-over-fist, and planned to retire somewhere extravagant.

The last few lines read like this:

This is a dangerous game, I know, but my conscience is convicted. It's time for it to end — I have to come clean.

If you find my body, you'll know what happened, and who's to blame...

Signed: *Dr. Gregory Morrell.*

When the trial was all said and done, the sentences were as follows:

Robert Boyer - For his decades-long involvement in drug trafficking and related crimes, the exploitation of Dr. Conley, and the murder of Dr. Morrell: *life in prison without parole*

Eric Boyer - For his part in covering up the murders and illegal drug operations, as well as his failure to fulfill his duty as a law enforcement officer: *40 years.*

Edith Morrell - For aiding Walter by importing much of his supplies, money laundering, attempted murder, and acting as the whistleblower who revealed her husband's plan to confess, ultimately causing his demise: *50 years*

Walter Sayer - For a laundry list of crimes related to his illegal enterprise, including kidnapping, human trafficking, child exploitation, wire fraud, racketeering, murder, and, of course, drug-related activity: *10 life sentences*

Colleen Sayer - For supporting Warren in his criminal endeavors, hiding evidence, and financial fraud: *15 years*

Warren Sayer - For multiple incidents of attempted murder, massive money laundering schemes, public corruption, exploitation, soliciting others to commit violent and illegal acts, and generally pulling the strings behind the scenes: *life in prison without parole*

Additional Scripture References

Listed below are instances in which a Bible verse is alluded
to, referenced, or paraphrased, though not cited in-text.

Page	Chapter	Bible Ref.
73	11	Mark 9:24
131	20	Luke 9:26
137	21	Romans 3:10-12
161	24	2 Timothy 3:16 (NIV)
162; 297	24; 46	Isaiah 55:9
222	34	Proverbs 26:4
232	36	Ecclesiastes 7:2
295	46	Psalm 103:12
295		Matthew 5:6
295		James 1:20
295		Ecclesiastes 3:1
295		Ephesians 4:26 (ESV)
296		Job 42:3; Psalm 139:6
296-297		Proverbs 3:5 (NIV)
297		Judges 17:6, 21:25
297		1 John 4:8, 16
297		James 1:17
302	47	James 4:17
308	48	Matthew 5:22
326	50	Romans 14:5, 23
328		Matthew 12:20a (ESV)
329		1 Peter 3:7
329		2 Timothy 2:12

About the Author

The Witch of Flickerwood is the debut novel of writer
E.C. Watts, who has loved storytelling for as long as she
can remember. Outside of writing, she has a degree in
social work and holds a day job trying to make the world a
better place. She lives in South Central PA with her
wonderful husband, Teague, who's responsible for the
beautiful cover art and flower illustration. You can find
them on their shared website, www.pumpkintea.com. You
can also follow her on Instagram @theoneminded.

If you enjoyed this book and found it meaningful, please
consider leaving a review to help others find it, too.
Thanks!

Flowers for the FBI

www.ingramcontent.com/pod-product-compliance
Lightning Source LLC
Chambersburg PA
CBHW020539120726
47903CB00001B/47

* 9 7 9 8 9 9 2 7 8 1 1 8 2 *